A Blackwater Press book

First published in the United States of America by Blackwater Press, LLC

Copyright © Kate Mueser, 2023

Printed and bound in Canada by Imprimerie Gauvin

Library of Congress Control Number: 2022944911

ISBN: 978-1-7357747-9-4 (paperback)

Cover design by Eilidh Muldoon
Interior illustrations by Giuseppe Monterisi

This book is a work of fiction. Names, characters, organisations, locations and events portrayed are either the product of the author's imagination or are used fictitiously.

Blackwater Press
120 Capitol Street
Charleston, WV 25301
United States

www.blackwaterpress.com

MIX
Paper
FSC® C100212
FSC
www.fsc.org

The Girl with Twenty Fingers

KATE MUESER

For Paul, Ben, and Ella

CONTENTS

I. ALLEGRO

THREE YEARS EARLIER
NEW YORK CITY

Mozart. Why did it have to be Mozart? Sarah loved the gut-punching melody of his D minor concerto, but if her fingers weren't flawless, she couldn't veil her lack of technical prowess with expressivity.

She didn't feel nervous, but the heaviness in her middle and moistness on her palms told a different story, and she wiped her hands on her lap for the umpteenth time. *Picture the audience in their underwear.* A ridiculous, amateur antidote to stage fright. The people in the seats weren't freaks disturbing her private rehearsal; they had changed into viscose or tweed, sacrificed an evening of Netflix and chill to have her take a fire iron to their feelings; she was armed.

This audience was particularly ruthless: a mix of seasoned music professors, graduate students with tight concert schedules of their own, and the freshmen who believed they'd been born as the next Midori, Yo-Yo Ma or Evgeny Kissin. A few local residents, knowing they would have to purchase pricey tickets to see the same fingers in a few years, also turned up for exam recitals, outing themselves by clapping between movements or overdressing.

With a bachelor's degree plus another two years of study under her belt, a solo performance with orchestra stood between her and her second degree. *Master of Music, Piano Performance.* Many of the other master's students were showing off with quadruple lutzes — virtuosic workouts by Rachmaninov or Liszt, but she and Professor Rosenstein had picked a different kind of challenge. One they both thought she could master with her more nuanced, less showy style.

Backstage, as the orchestra delivered a merry if uninspired rendition of Mozart's D major "Prague" Symphony, K. 504, Sarah checked her nylons for runs and assessed her short, bright turquoise shift dress in the full-length mirror leaning against the wall, flattening the fabric over her narrow hips. It had been a lucky find, an off-season markdown at the outlet, where it was rare to spot a size six in the stack. Many classical musicians donned black and white, as if they were serving champagne at a corporate function; she wasn't about to be boxed as boring.

The final cadence. The calm, polite applause swelled and dwindled. Coughs punctured the silence. The stage door was opened by an undergraduate oboe major who earned his beer money working at the music school concert hall. Sarah would have found his scraggly goatee unappealing if it weren't for its authenticity; he smelled of soap and tobacco as she stood next to him, vulnerably. Then the light. Her shoes clicked loudly on the wooden stage floor, covered with scratches invisible to the audience, caused by pointy heels or dragged instruments.

Reaching the imposing Bechstein grand with a Hollywood smile, she caught eyeballs in the dark rows as her vision adjusted. Grabbing the edge of the keyboard, she bowed, letting her hands slip down to just above her knees — a prelude she had repeated alone in front of the mirror in the practice cubicles a hundred times, a thousand times, a hundred thousand times.

The strings opened ominously, the cellos rolled their triplet sixteenth notes, the violins fixed an agitating off-beat rhythm as the woody tones of the string instruments enfolded her. Random images had a way of flashing in her head right before she touched the keys, like at the threshold to sleep: the yellow tulips near the practice building that meant the semester's end; the decades-old piece of bubble gum under the highest C on her favorite practice piano; the penny-loafered MBA student from two weekends ago, who'd said afterward, "I knew you'd be a good fuck" (she said nothing); the growl of her stomach that was both hunger and the nervous inability to digest for the moment. Performing was not only creation, but also suppression. What was the secret to clean concentration when there was no such thing as the absence of thought?

Then the yearning melody swelled out of her fingertips like a voice. Professor Rosenstein, who would sing her pieces with an old man's vibrato, too voluminously for his cupboard of a studio, always said, "I play on stage as if I were in my living room, and in my living room as if I were on stage." If only I had an orchestra in my living room, Sarah would tell him.

She echoed the ensemble on the piano, eyes on the conductor, a fellow graduate student with a penchant for energy drinks and Tevas. After nailing the opening, she navigated through the first movement. Being on stage was like sitting next to her own body on the piano bench, watching herself like a mother watches her child, crossing her fingers and hoping she would get through it, but also innately, biologically confident that she could.

Breathe. She tried to focus her wandering mind on every note (*Not too fast!*) and every phrase (*Don't stumble!*), squashing the voices in her head, beating them into oblivion, charging onward bar by bar because there was nowhere else to go.

Filling her lungs with air, she dove into the cadenza. Alone under the spotlight, the Bechstein was loud, jarringly intrusive, but not out of place. She tripped up briefly, her unintended chromaticism suddenly standing over her shoulder like a gargoyle, but plowed ahead, oblivious to the ugly moment. No performance is perfect; it's about how you cover up your mistakes, her teacher in high school had told her as she pulled on the edge of a torn fingernail, slipping it surreptitiously into her pocket when she got it off, so he wouldn't find it on the floor. Mozart didn't leave much room for makeup.

As the first movement drew to a close, she wiped her hands on her lap; how fortunate that the front row was sparsely populated, that people were always drawn to the middle of a room where they felt safer.

The silence was short, then she billowed her arms and danced elegantly through the second movement, carefully phrasing the lyrical melody, opening her mouth to sing along silently. She kept her eye on the conductor, his elbows bent and pinkies raised, to make sure she stayed in time until the Romanze faded like a starry lullaby.

She'd almost made it! The first movement had been nearly immaculate, the second a delicate excursion. In the silence before the final movement, Sarah's sigh of relief filled the space between her and the keyboard. *Da-da-da-da-da.* She visualized her opening D minor arpeggio, then set a swift tempo, launching the Rondo in an unaccompanied flurry.

Bang!
Bam!
Butchering!

The beginning lay there bleeding on the block, unrecognizable as she stumbled through a cacophony that shattered her concentration. The conductor's sideways glare blended embarrassment, sympathy and horror. *Just keep it together.*

As the quick Allegro assai progressed, the cleft in her fragile control widened, the arpeggios essential to the theme took on an atonal flair. This was Mozart, not Schoenberg, goddammit! Each wrong note rattled her even more as the keyboard grew foreign. Had this Bechstein been built with unusually wide keys, a prototype for a new model, a misunderstanding at the factory? She blinked down at her hands through the tears in her eyes, but saw double, as if she had twenty fingers.

Like a brakeless bus flying forward, abandoning any attempt at dynamic variation, she recalled her first ski trip to Lake Tahoe, age eight, when she had lurched off the beginners' slope, skidding on her hip a hundred yards down a steep icy incline, her skis pulling along sticks and pinecones. A stranger had yanked her to her feet, gripping her tightly under her arms like the child she was, and she wondered whether he might be one of the angels she knew were out there. Today, she could have used an army of angels.

The cadenza approached, and she encountered it with trepidation, wobbling the trills, wishing she could wrap herself in the cover of the strings, letting them absorb her. With the end in sight, she instinctively rushed toward it, slaughtering the final scales and crashing through the closing cadence.

She felt herself rise from the bench, avoiding the conductor's pained eyes; he grabbed her hand for the obligatory joint bow, the wiry hairs on the back of his hand poking her fingertips.

As the tears crept over the rims of her eyelids before free falling down her cheeks, she looked apologetically into the emotionless faces dotting the hall, haloed and detached from their bodies by the muted lighting. Hands met hands in a forced applause more full of pity than admiration. Professor Rosenstein's head was lowered, his eyes hidden from her, palms on his knees. The first impression left by her opening bow and turquoise shift had been overwritten by an indelible catastrophe that rendered all those hours alone in the cubicle futile. All she'd wanted was to share something — no, to be — remarkable.

January 21 - Munich

Sarah half expected it to disappear one of these days, gone missing without an afterthought or a 'Reward' sign, as if it had never left its footprints on her floor. But, of course, it was still there gloating when she opened the door to her quiet one-bedroom apartment, screaming at her over the racket her key made in the lock.

You should be practicing. *YOU SHOULD ALWAYS BE PRACTICING.* The voice that had sometimes coaxed, sometimes goaded her for so many years didn't go into hibernation when she stopped playing. The box of hammers and strings watched her aloofly, pointing its eighty-eight fingers.

Da-da. She cast a sideways glance at the pouting Schimmel, but what she heard was a Bechstein and the yawning octave that opened the solo in Mozart's Piano Concerto in D minor, K. 466, then nothing. It had been a mistake to put the instrument there, filling her new life in Germany with her past.

Clink-clank! She tossed her keys onto the desk and turned on the TV. Any noise would do to cover up the Schimmel's whining. The piano stood up straight adjacent to the front door, sleek and stately like a tuxedo. It looked beautiful yet lonely, casting a geometric shadow on the otherwise undressed wall, and she wanted to touch it again. Even more, she wanted touching it to be as magical as it used to be. Wilhelm Schimmel, who founded his piano manufacturer in the nineteenth century and earned international renown, had a name that meant 'mold' in German. How fitting, thought Sarah; gone to waste like her talent.

She turned away from the Schimmel and busied her fingers with her usual distraction: opening a bottle of Bordeaux. It had been on sale for €3.29 at Aldi, but the label looked fancy. French, at the very least. She grabbed a bag of frozen mixed vegetables from her gla-ciered freezer and poured them into a pot, turning the stove up to the hottest setting. Hunger was taking its pickaxe to her wine-stained stomach but filling it up too much would make her feel undisciplined. Self-control had always been her strength.

When the vegetables started dancing, Sarah drained the pot and threw in an egg, watching it coagulate. Scrape, scrape, scrape. A dollop of ketchup to cover the brown spots, and voilà. She'd picked up a soft pretzel on the way home, just before closing time, rescuing it past its prime from a basket full of crumbs. Dipping it into the mass on her plate was sacrilegious. What would her coworkers at the food magazine think if they knew that, for her, eating was always a tug-of-war between staying thin and rewarding herself? It was impossible to really enjoy making food, especially just for one plate.

"*Nein*! Much too heavy! You need a more delicate touch when you play Mozart. Caress the instrument. Don't forget that he did not have a modern piano." Even after three years, Professor Rosenstein's crickety voice still echoed in Sarah's ear. He had never returned to Munich after fleeing for New York in 1938, a time when music was the least of people's worries, but perhaps the best of their solutions, the only goodness left. The professor would have been pleased that Sarah was there, in his hometown, but would tsk tsk — like when her pedaling was too heavy or her runs sloppy — if he found out she had swapped Middle C for asdfghjkl and had hardly touched her instrument since her last lesson. For six years, Sarah would trek with gloved hands to his studio each Monday for her weekly lesson, chewing gum to distract from the knot in her belly, even though she knew his criticism would be kind, kinder at least than the other fac-ulty members.

Sarah wiped the ketchup off her plate with the last bit of pretzel and leaned back in the kitchen chair, its legs perpetually off-kilter on the decades-old wooden floor, warped from season after season of humidity changes. *Krick-krack!* Wood in any form hides music in its fibers.

She put the plate in the sink and turned on the TV. Some real-ity show with amateur chefs. It was lighter fare than the stuff she'd watched in high school to teach herself German (the classic crime series *Tatort* and Wim Wenders films), but not a bad way to expand her vernacular vocabulary. On an old tape recorder, dug up from the depths of her closet at her parents', she had recorded herself saying *Ich heiße Sarah, ich spiele gerne Klavier.* At first, she was mortified to detect the swallowed Ls and upfront Rs that outed her not just as a foreigner, but as an American; then her accent gradually improved. After spending half of her junior year and a couple of summers studying piano in Berlin, it had become nearly undetectable, a slight affectation.

Nevertheless, the stranger on the train had known right away, when their paths had crossed earlier that evening on her way home from the food magazine's downtown office. In fact, he had known before she'd uttered a word that she wasn't from around there. Resting a hand on Sarah's elbow after stepping off the train with her at Munich's central Stachus station, he had said, "I would regret it later if I didn't stop now to find out where you're from and where you're going." That wad of kitsch should have made her ears bleed if he hadn't sounded so sincere. It wasn't that she hadn't noticed him, standing at the door on the subway train with ear buds peeking out like plastic sideburns, his summery curls straying from beneath his woven winter hat. He didn't fit what Germans would call her *Beuteschema* — her type. He was taller, stockier and blonder, but his casual assertiveness was magnetic.

Sarah held the scrap of paper in her hand with eleven little numbers on it, written hastily in his tall and narrow script, the 1s with long trunks, the 7s with belts, German style. She glanced at the Schimmel with the desire of a former lover as it continued to serenade her with her failure. Her stomach rumbled while digesting her half-hearted meal. What did she have to lose?

Here's mine, Sarah typed. **Maybe next time above ground?"**

January 25

Sarah was sure she was about to get stood up in front of an audience. Shoppers, commuters, clumps of teenagers drifted by on Munich's Kaufingerstraße despite the January nip, even though the stores had just closed minutes earlier.

Theo, the stranger from the train, had texted back and she had agreed to meet him for drinks. He was probably the beer type. Sarah found beer unenjoyably bitter but had memorized the names of sundry local brews in case of an emergency. *Spaten, Löwenbräu, Hacker-Pschorr.*

Like a music box ballerina without a tutu, she slowly turned three-hundred-sixty degrees, feeling slight next to the massive Karlstor gate that opened into the city's main shopping boulevard, trying to glimpse faces nuzzled in winter gear. *Where was he?*

At quarter past eight, she felt a hand on her arm; the other one was in the front pocket of his hoodie. His blond locks spilled out from under his hat. The chill was already leaking through Sarah's socks; she was glad she'd chosen pants instead of a dress.

"I could eat a whale." Theo was looking around, past Sarah's head, as if their encounter were again happenstance. "Can we fill up someplace? I know a good *Imbiss* without a dress code."

She skipped to keep up as he trotted off the main drag, taking narrow side streets south toward Sendlinger Tor, the gate that frames the downtown area from the south. Then he dodged into a kebab shop with a faded sign that Sarah would have overlooked. Just drinks, not dinner, they'd said; forks and plates come with expectations on the side. She wasn't hungry — she'd had an early quasi-meal of cereal and yogurt — but ordered a spinach-stuffed *börek* anyway to be polite. He chose a platter with everything on it: several different meats on skewers, salad, rice, fries, and a beer.

"When there's paint on my hands, I don't bother washing them to eat until the whole idea has taken shape. No half-way shit, you know?" Theo picked up two fries at once with scrubbed fingers. They chewed quietly amidst a mashup of Turkish, German, Russian, English, and a Scandinavian language at the tables around them. In the right corners and crevices of the Bavarian capital, Munich was every city.

Sarah lifted her shoe to cross her legs and her sole stuck to the floor. Theo clearly wasn't pulling out any stops to impress by taking her to this place. His self-assuredness piqued her curiosity and his down-to-earth spontaneity pinched her like a masseuse's thumb in a knotted muscle; it must be good for her.

"So you're an artist?" she asked.

"I guess you could say that. I design posters that have catchy phrases on them, like the kind everyone wants to hang in their hallway or office. There's a huge market out there for affordable art that's still handmade. You know, from the heart." Theo pounded his chest and looked Sarah in the eye. "After I sell enough posters, I want to do merch like t-shirts and phone covers and stuff."

"What kind of phrases?" She put down her *börek* and took a sip of her *Apfelschorle*; the sparkling apple juice tickled her tongue and shoved a burp up her esophagus.

"Like, 'If God is watching us, the least we can do is be entertaining'." He swept his hand from left to right, as if reading the words on the wall. "Stuff like that."

Cheesy, but — melt it, slice it or string it — the goo sells, and so do good looks paired with his brand of boyish confidence. Looking at the way his sideburns crept down his jaw at just the right length, curling ever so slightly, she reckoned he could pull it off.

"Interesting." She was leaning forward in her chair like Larry King. "How many posters have you sold already?" Sarah had learned that asking questions was generally a safe strategy on a first date and she felt more like a journalist than she ever did at work.

"My cousin's girlfriend just ordered three!" He stopped chewing and was looking intensely at Sarah. "I've wanted to be an artist since fifth grade, when I had to give a speech on Picasso and paint a cubist cat. It was like that cat had been inside of me for all of my ten years, ready to jump out. So all my posters are infused with cubism. Not with fucking cats — you'd need a plunger to unclog the internet if I crapped any more cats into it. The letters are oversized, and they're like a window to an image inside of them, so there are a couple different levels going on. Even cheap art can be artistic as shit. See?"

Theo pulled his phone out of the front pocket on his hoodie, the screen split in three places. Swipe, swipe, swipe. He stopped at one that read 'All the world's a stage.'

Shakespeare. In high school she had had an English teacher who dressed up as the Bard and staged shorter versions of his most famous works in class. She had been so enthralled that she downloaded his lesser known plays on her own and read them late at night in bed when her parents thought she was sleeping. She memorized the antiquated innuendos, touching herself when Hamlet said to Ophelia, 'It would cost you a groaning to take off my edge' — the full extent of her teenage rebellion.

A puking infant, a whining schoolboy, a toothless septuagenarian. She found the seven abstractly rendered ages of a man's life, from *As You Like It,* inside the brightly colored lettering on Theo's phone. Not bad at all; she was genuinely awed by the way he embedded words and literature in images and colors, but would she pay €19.95 plus shipping for a glossy print, no frame? Would thousands of other people? Art only brought wealth to the Lang Langs and Jeff Koons of the world, she thought bitterly.

"Creating something gives me such a high," said Theo. They locked eyes; she rubbed her moist palms on her pants. The stubble on his chin had more apricot than his Labrador blond curls, the skin on each earlobe was sagging slightly around a ringless oval hole; she fingered the silver stud in her own ear.

"So how many posters have you sold already?" She didn't want to seem like she was letting him off the hook.

"I'm just getting started, but I've already hit like a thousand followers on Instagram!"

He took a bite, a bit of everything on the fork, changing the subject with his mouth full. "And you write about food?" He tossed his phone onto the table. "Isn't that like selling flies to an army of frogs? Everybody likes to eat. You must have a huge fan club." He winked.

"Ha! Not that I know of." She scanned the rack of promotional postcards by the WC in the back. *The grass may not be greener, but the palms are definitely taller.* (A travel agency.) *Small talk doesn't have to be a big deal.* (An English language school chain.) "Even if I did, my boss wouldn't be in it. She chewed me out in front of the whole team this morning! I had organized everything for the March cover feature, but the writer I'd commissioned bailed on me at the last minute. He had been my most reliable stringer. Is it so hard to keep your word?"

"He sounds like a flake!"

Sarah pulled at her fingernail until a piece came off. "Actually, I'm a pianist," she confessed. "I mean, I was."

"A pianist — that's not something I hear every day. The Mozart kind or the Elton John kind?" Theo smiled, an eyebrow raised, slouching with one arm over the back of his chair.

"Maybe I should have been the Elton John kind. Who knows — in another life? No, the Mozart kind." *But what if...* The thought of leggings and rhinestone bodysuits — not to mention needles, late nights, casual sex in hotel jacuzzis — was arousing. She wished she had ordered a beer, too; her cheeks were flushed, as if she had. "Performing classical music is also a mix of creating and recreating. You have to stay true to the score and the historical context, like you do with Picasso and Shakespeare. But you also want to put something personal…" She coughed and began again. "You want to make it new."

"'The object of art is to give life a shape.'" He put on his best British accent.

"You know Shakespeare pretty well. For a German." She tried out her playful voice, careful not to overdo it. She stared at Theo's hands, wondering whether they would feel rough on her skin, noticing the smudge on the outside of his left palm (ball point, not paint). They had left-handers' annoyances in common: incompetent scissors, the upside-down script on giveaway pens.

"It's my job." He was theatrically stoic, exaggerating a German accent. "But it's true about music, too. Where can I hear you play?"

"I don't anymore," she blurted too brusquely, looking around to see if anyone else had heard her. "I was going to become a concert pianist, but…" Blink, blink, blink; she couldn't let the excess moisture escape from under her eyelids. "But I just wasn't good enough." The words, a virgin announcement, spilled onto the table like a knocked-over beverage, a childish embarrassment.

"That can't be true." He ran his fingers through his curls, reordering them.

"I do have a very beautiful piano at home, but…" *It yells at me,* Sarah wanted to add.

"Dreams don't just die all by themselves, without a shot to the head. What happened?"

Sarah's earlobes throbbed. She had never talked about the piano in the first hour of a first date before; the personal question made him sexy. Other men had been more interested in how she could ever dump California (last she checked, they were in a long-distance relationship) and what Americans truly thought of *The President* (no comment).

"It was Mozart that did me in. Mozart is merciless." She turned her bottle of fizzy juice in circles, letting the base rest on the table as if it were glued to a tiny record player.

"That sounds like the title of some murder mystery, 'Mozart is merciless'." Theo chuckled and Sarah joined in. It felt good to laugh instead of cry over her dashed ambitions, but would she later regret bringing up such a painful memory?

"That murder mystery would be too scary for me. But it's true, Mozart just makes you feel… naked. His music leaves nothing to hide behind. It's all or nothing in the music world. You can't just be good; you have to be perfect. I'd thought I could make up for not being perfect by being unique."

It was, she had slowly been coming to realize, not a simple disappointment, but the breakdown of an entire American upbringing that promised, even guaranteed, individually tailored success for each one-of-a-kind child. *Work hard and you can become whatever you set your mind to*, the bread and butter of her childhood, was slowly cracking like the ceiling in *The Truman Show*.

"I tried art school for five semesters. They said I should sell fucking washing machines instead."

"They actually said that?" She was relieved to be talking about him again.

"Yeah, for real. I may have gotten into a few heated arguments with my professor, too, but he's the one who told me my work didn't have any depth. I was pretty down about it for a year or two before I came up with my posters. But my dad believed in me. He always wanted me to go into business and get some secure job like he did, but I was able to convince him that my posters would one day earn me enough. I don't need a lot, but he did give me a loan to jump start things."

Theo pushed his plate to the side and reached across the table to rest his hand on her forearm.

"Listen, can you play me some Mozart right now?"

Sarah looked around, confused, but was relieved not to find a piano anywhere. "Here? I can't see how…"

"I mean on the table with your fingers. I want to watch your hands and your face."

Half of her felt embarrassed, the other half angry, but when she looked at him she saw that it was a genuine request. Without letting herself think, she closed her eyes and let her fingers dance to Mozart's Piano Sonata in D major, K. 576. How much of it would she remember? Straight away she felt guilt at the stiffness in her wrists. The quick runs and trills became fumbled approximations, but at least the slightly sticky table edge bore it in silence. She stopped when her memory gave out in bar sixteen, then opened her eyes to wait for his criticism.

"You look like one in a million when you play, you know. Don't give up, Sarah," he urged. "You just need to make music in a new way. Nickname your piano Elmo, or draw a rainbow on it, or some silly shit like that."

How could he be so sure that she could find reconciliation? They'd only just met. Sarah smiled at his wacky suggestions. He had been dropped by the art world and was making a comeback on his own. Maybe she could, too.

As the evening wore on, the hole-in-the-wall bistro filled up with students lining their stomachs with saturated fats ahead of their Friday night binge, those coming or going from blue-collar shifts, regulars who turned up every week to drink liters of Turkish tea on the house.

"Want to go have a drink someplace else?" Sarah needed some air.

"A buddy of mine manages this place not too far from here. You should meet him. He's into music, too, just not the Mozart kind."

Theo pulled his hat down over his ears; she wrapped herself in her scarf and coat, covering her belly that was bloating uncomfortably from the *börek*. They stepped outside and she welcomed the cold air as it enveloped her, cooling her cheeks. It wasn't long until a poorly marked entrance led them down a flight of stairs to a small, dingy room with half a dozen round tables on one side, the other side open for either dancing or mingling when it got busier.

Things were just starting to pick up when they snagged the last two stools at the bar called *Nirgendwo*. Nowhere. Drum and bass rumbled in the background; rows of bottles glistened on the wall behind the bar, sufficing as decor. The bartender, a short guy with chin-length hair the color of pencil lead, finished pouring and grinned as he came over to Theo and Sarah. "Where did you find such a pretty girl?" Then he addressed her. "You watch out for this *Schlawiner*. He's full of wild ideas!"

"Rule number one, don't believe anything Andreas says," Theo joked. "Andreas, the electric guitarist; Sarah, the classical pianist."

"A fellow musician! Then on the house," Andreas thumped two *Paulaner* onto the counter and turned to the next customers. Theo and Sarah clinked bottles, looked each other purposefully in the eye, and took a sip.

"You know what they say here in Germany, don't you?" Theo asked.

"Seven years of bad sex if you don't make eye contact when you toast! I've heard that one before." Sarah held his gaze for a few seconds until he looked away. "But bad sex is better than no sex, they also say."

"I wouldn't know," countered Theo. Their stools were so close together that their knees were touching. "Actually, Andreas was at least half right."

Hearing his name from down at the other end of the bar, Andreas winked, raised his arms, and wiggled his fingers as if miming a virtuosic work for piano. Sarah remembered the sticky tabletop and her feeling of guilt returned. Not so long ago, she would have enjoyed playing for any audience, even an audience of one, and even on a tabletop; she would have remembered more than sixteen bars and gotten so absorbed in the sonata that Theo would have had to tap her on the shoulder to stop her.

"I should watch out for you?" She feigned concern, picking up the bottle.

"I don't know about that, but after I saw you play on the table back there at the restaurant, I had an idea. Let's call it The Theo and Sarah show. You play Mozart, or Elton John, or John Legend, or whatever, and I'll show my posters — it'll be like a pan-artistic evening. Did I just fucking invent that word?" He looked at his shoulder, as if expecting a pat.

"Like a *salon*. There were a lot of those here in the eighteenth century." A few years ago, she would have jumped at the proposal. Picasso was close with some French composers like Poulenc and Varèse, she remembered from one of her graduate music history courses; that would have been a place to start. Back then. Not now. "I told you, I don't play anymore."

"You did. But I'm not talking about a high-brow audience analyzing your every keystroke. I'm thinking of a room full of happy people listening for fun. No pressure, just music. And I've already seen what those hands of yours are capable of."

Fun. Could music be that again?

Theo put his palm on her thigh. He moved forward quickly until their lips met, pressing confidently against her, sweeping his tongue against hers, sliding his hand up to her rib cage, resting his thumb against the underwire of her bra. She felt a knot in her middle contract or unravel; she wasn't sure which. He tasted bitter, fermented, but his lips were soft. Even as they kissed, she considered his idea with a mix of longing and apprehension.

"Think about it, Sarah." Maybe it was that easy to become a pianist again.

Suddenly, Andreas was standing across the bar again. "What else can I get you two lovebirds?"

"Something good, Andreas. We're toasting to The Theo and Sarah show. Art meets music. We'll throw in a few snacks and nice people and it's going to be a blast."

"Well then, if you're going to toast, I'll open a bottle of champagne. As long as you invite me to your show." Andreas filled three flutes as they threatened to bubble over. "To The Sarah and Theo Show!" He was a good decade older than Theo, with skin like a peach the day after it should have been eaten, wilted by nicotine and night shifts.

"And what about you, Andreas?" Sarah asked. "Do you have a band?"

"Yep. I get my crew into *Nirgendwo* every few weeks for a live gig. In fact, we're supposed to play tomorrow, but the sound system is busted."

"Do you want me to take a look?" Theo asked, casting an apologetic glance at Sarah.

"Yeah, would you? I mean, I don't want to steal you away from Snow White here."

"I'll be right back." Theo squeezed Sarah's elbow as he stood up and disappeared with Andreas.

Sarah was alone, just like that, still sipping her champagne at the bar. She was tousled from behind as newcomers rolled in from the street, lurching toward the counter to collect their drinks, some cushioning their collisions with winter coats still on.

Swallowing the last sip, she checked her phone. It was well after midnight. What was taking so long? Theo's half-empty glass was still at the bar, but he was nowhere. Nowhere in *Nirgendwo*. Slowly, uncertainty crept in. Was she about to get stood up in front of an audience for real this time?

Fatigue scratched at her eyeballs, dried her contact lenses; she rubbed her eyelids, careful not to smear the shadow on them. Plum dream, shimmer not matte. Her alarm had gone off at 6:00 a.m. so that she could be the first one in the office, like yesterday and the day before, and the day before that, even though there was no one else there that early to notice.

As Sarah stood up to put on the coat she'd been sitting on for safe keeping, Theo resurfaced with a monkey. The sleeves of his hoodie were pushed up to his elbows, revealing the animal with a lion-like mane and fierce, but playful little eyes, crouched on an excerpted tree branch. The ink was black, but the shading had been done so expertly that she wanted to reach out and pet the tattoo. Would it bite?

"Hey, I'm really sorry. I didn't mean to bail on you. I thought it was just going to take a minute, but the mixer is gimped and he's missing a part we gotta borrow."

Sarah was annoyed but didn't want to nag. Not on the first date. Not after such a personal conversation and promising kiss. "No big deal. Tell Andreas thanks for the drinks." She tried to downplay it, but decided, "I'm going to go."

He kissed her briefly on the lips as if they were a couple just heading out for work in the morning. Have a good day, honey, see you later. "Don't forget about The Theo and Sarah Show." Thumb and pinkie to his face, he mimicked a phone call as the monkey gazed blankly at her from his forearm.

They drifted apart as she jostled her way to the door, wishing for a tugboat.

January 26

Thump, thump, thump. The first thing Sarah heard was the disturbingly irregular pounding of a basketball against the pavement outside her window. *Thump, thump, thump.* A lousy metronome. That neighbor boy didn't even have a hoop, just a ball.

She opened her eyes. The glow framing the shutters dated the sunrise at minus half an hour, maybe three quarters of an hour. She stretched out her left arm onto the empty half of the bed and rubbed her eyes with her right hand. That kiss, her first in a long while, was a timpani still rumbling through her. Then the anger came: like a sunburn, the warmth was healing in the moment, but it ached hours later.

She sighed as she stood up and went into the kitchen, rubbing her temples and listening to her own breathing. Inhale, exhale, in 6/8 time. Closing her eyes, she stuck her hand into the dish of espresso capsules, opening them to discover a yellow one in her palm. A lucky color, the color of sunshine, daffodils, and lemonade, none of which she had today.

She drank the cappuccino standing, watching the sleet through the kitchen window spit from a grumpy sky. *Schneeregen*, snow-rain, because it is both at the same time, annoyingly indecisive.

Sarah was annoyed with herself, not so much for having to jealously count the couples that left *Nirgendwo* early (the night was for better things when it had burned down to a stump), but because *he knew too much*.

She made another cappuccino, this time plucking a yellow capsule from the bowl with her eyes open, so as not to change paths mid-course. The last yogurt in her refrigerator was passion fruit fla-

19

vored. That sounded much more romantic and exotic in English than in German — *Maracuja* — and brought back memories of the complimentary juice at the hotel during a childhood trip to Maui. Nine-year-old Sarah had tasted heaven. The yogurt's expiration date was January 24; there was a two-day grace period, right? She poured corn flakes directly into the plastic container and ate quickly.

Her phone offered little consolation — no messages from Theo, no breaking news, not even a weather update — but maybe it could give her something else. Something she hadn't experienced in a very long time. It took a bit of scrolling until she found it: Argentine pianist Martha Argerich and Italian conductor Claudio Abbado performing Mozart's Piano Concerto No. 20 in D minor, from 2013, shortly before Abbado passed away. Sarah pressed play with a sigh and a heavy thumb but also a rush of anticipation, as if she were calling an ex at 2:00 a.m. The Bose speakers, a housewarming present from her parents, dutifully did their job.

She left Mozart on as she showered and grabbed her warmest sweater, hastily brushing on mascara and rouge. As the recording concluded with silence, she closed the door behind her, turning the apartment key until the lock slid into place with a clink. She knew where she needed to go, but would she find it again?

Bits of ice scratched her umbrella as she wandered through the *Altstadt*, the Old Town. A handful of tourists were looking lost, wiping off their Google maps with wet fingers, bulging like sausages with plastic garbage bags over their coats. She passed a Starbucks and St. Peter's, Munich's oldest church, meandered right, left, right again through a few side streets, and almost missed it. Then she double-backed and took a deep breath when she saw the aged sign: *Notenfachgeschäft Bauer*.

Ding dong ding! One of those booby trap bells was activated by the door. Inside, the walls were lined to the ceiling with disorderly shelves stuffed with spines reading Strauss, Brahms, Debussy, Schoenberg, Chopin. The scores were new, even if the music they held wasn't, but the shop reeked of time, of another time. Yellowed photos of tuxedoed men, most already reposing soundlessly underground, were signed *"für Franz"* by Vladimir Horowitz, Alfred Brendel, Glenn Gould. The names were familiar, like old neighbors, but she felt like an intruder in their space.

Make music in a new way, Theo had told her. He was right, she knew, even though she was still miffed at him. She still had no idea how, but one thing was clear: She and music didn't stand a chance if she didn't face up to Wolfgang Amadeus Mozart.

"How can I help you?" A spindly, bespectacled, elderly man, his face wrinkled like a wad of paper pressed flat again, peered down at her from behind the counter.

"I'm looking for Mozart's Piano Concerto No. 20, K. 466," her voice said. She was clenching her fists and made a conscious effort to loosen them, curving her fingers against her thighs.

"D minor? I believe I sold my last copy earlier this week. With piano accompaniment or the full orchestra version?" A fastidiously tied paisley silk scarf hid his neck.

"With piano accompaniment is fine. I would prefer the G. Henle edition, if you have it." The German publisher was known for remaining faithful to the first printed editions. Even if she could dig up an orchestra and fit it in her apartment, it would unearth her unbearable memory of the conductor's glare during the third movement. And it wouldn't give her another shot at finishing her master's degree, the coveted MMA, or, even more, becoming a professional performer.

"*Freilich.* One moment, please." He disappeared behind a tired tapestry dividing the small shop from a nook of an office.

"American?"

She hadn't even noticed the other, even older man, who'd buried his nose in a shelf with a faded, hand-written sign reading 'Romantic works for piano solo.'

He'd asked in English with a heavy German accent, but Sarah stuck with German. "*Ja.* But I live here in Munich."

"Good people, the Americans. They have elected some unfortunate presidents over the decades, sadly, and have an odd obsession with their own flag. But I will never forget what they did for us. I have never been to America, regrettably — some things are never meant to be — but I know its people have good hearts."

She responded with an obligatory smile and nod, letting her eyes drift around the shop for the third or fourth time, up and down the chaotic shelves, across the overlapping oriental rugs on the floor. Her phone beeped, alien in the preserved analogue haven. She glanced at the lock screen before burying it in her pocket again.

Theo Vogl: Hey I've got a venue for The Theo and Sarah Show. Hope you didn't...

"You are a pianist?" He unexpectedly seized her hand, turned it over and pressed his thumb onto the pads of her fingers, one by one. His thumbnail was brittle, yellowed and grayed by the years, like the paper they were surrounded by. "You have the fingers of a pianist. They are strong and resilient. And I can feel that you have diligently practiced your arpeggios. They always leave their mark." He dropped her hand and gripped the handle of his cane with fingers bent like branches.

Sarah was stunned. Who was this man and what did he know about her, let alone the arpeggios in the third movement? She looked down at her hands self-consciously; such a bad habit, tearing the edges of her nails, leaving them jagged and sore, although she had admired, even envied, the surgeon's skin on Professor Rosenstein's hands, untarnished like beach pebbles struck by a million waves.

The man before her was hunched with age but would not have been tall in his youth. His ankle-length camel wool coat was still buttoned to his neck in the stuffy shop; his crooked green beret could have capped a sergeant.

"I used to be a pianist."

"There is no such thing as a used-to-be pianist." He frowned, tapping his cane on the ornate rug.

The shop owner reappeared, shaking his head. "I don't have it in stock and the publisher says it can take six to eight weeks. Would you like to place an order anyway?"

"The Henle edition of Mozart's D minor concerto? I have a copy." The elderly customer butted in with a straight face. "It's from the mid-eighties, probably well before your parents even met, but Mozart hasn't made any changes since then, as far as I'm aware. You may purchase it from me for a small, but appropriate fee." He turned to the shop owner. "That is, if you don't mind, *lieber Franz*."

"As the lady likes."

Before Sarah could utter a word, the deal had been sealed.

"It will cost you one American dollar. I don't think that will be too much, will it?" He produced a calling card that also appeared to be from the mid-eighties and read 'Otto Steinmann,' followed by his address. "You can come tomorrow afternoon to pick it up. Three o'clock would be fine, if you don't mind, after my mid-day nap."

Sarah's first inclination was to politely decline and quickly find the door. But she had already set her mind on encountering the D minor concerto again and couldn't turn back now.

"Ok, then. I'll be there."

Slipping the card into her pocket, she stepped out of the shop, pulling her scarf over her lips and breathing into it. Then she remembered Theo's message.

Hey I've got a venue for The Theo and Sarah Show. Hope you didn't forget. Andreas promised me free drinks tonight for fixing that bitch of a mixer, and you too for being left at the bar so long. That wasn't supposed to happen! Wanna come see his band?

Was that an apology after all? She briefly considered joining them at *Nirgendwo*; after all, she hadn't forgotten why she'd kissed him: He understood her deflated hopes in a way few others could. Theo possessed a gravity she was unfamiliar with, but how much oxygen was there in his atmosphere?

Now, however, with Otto Steinmann's card in her pocket and an impending date with Mozart, she had other priorities. "Another time," she typed as she headed toward Marienplatz, Munich's main square, to crane her neck like the tourist she wasn't and watch the famous Glockenspiel. High up on the neo-gothic New Town Hall, wooden figures fixed stoically to a track passed the square again and again to play out a never-ending royal wedding and tournament of chivalrous knights.

January 27

Wotan, Fricka, Fasolt — the street names, from Nordic mythology, read like a Wagner opera. The houses were stately, older, some newly renovated, others weary, and the street was lined with large, bare oaks, dirty snow stacked at their bases. Sarah double checked her wallet to make sure she'd brought her American money. The twenty, five and three ones left over from her last visit to California paled like weeds next to the rainbow of euro notes.

She found the house, a centennial of average size and height dressed in inconspicuous beige, and pushed the button next to the sign marked 'O. & H. Steinmann.' *Bzzz!* The door creaked open a few centimeters, pulled by an invisible hand.

When Sarah reached the third-floor landing, he was standing at the open door wearing a traditional collarless Bavarian jacket in hunter green with embroidered copper accents and slippers that made his feet appear too big for his slight frame. Not quite clown-like but fit for a film set.

"Grüß Gott, Herr Steinmann."

"Please come in." He gestured to a wide cabinet with drawers at the bottom, a dim mirror and ornate hooks on the upper half. "You may hang your coat here and use the guest slippers if you like." In a tidy row under the cabinet, untrod on for months, perhaps decades, were several pairs of felt house shoes.

The entry led into a narrow hallway that opened into a sitting room lined with dark oak chests and bookshelves, the floors covered corner to corner with oriental rugs. She knew that odor from some-where — yes, the music shop, his apparent haunt. Paper preserves our histories but does not age pleasantly itself.

A grand piano in the same dark wood took up a good chunk of the room, camouflaged among the drab rugs and cabinets, except that the fallboard was open, the top raised halfway. The keys were made of real ivory, slightly rounded, not uniform in color. The alternating black and cream lines, crowned with 'C. Bechstein' in gold lettering on the underbelly of the fallboard, contrasted starkly with the pea, rust and sunset tones surrounding them. *Could it compare?*

"Ein Bechstein Flügel!" Sarah whispered, using the German word for grand piano, the same word for a bird's wing or the sail of a windmill.

Bechsteins were respected in the US but were rarer than other brands chosen for concert stages, like Steinways or Yamahas. She had only ever played two, and both had changed her. One had hidden the conductor's bottom half that evening, and had certainly not intended any malice toward her. The other Bechstein was one of Professor Rosenstein's side-by-side ivory-clad grands, intended for a hall and not a shoebox studio like his.

"Yes, the pre-war Bechsteins were particularly exquisite. This one used to belong to my mother." Herr Steinmann nodded toward his most treasured possession as if it were a 0-60-in-2.2-seconds Porsche in his garage. In fact, it was a model A-185, 185 centimeters long, Sarah measured with her eyes. Its legs and music stand were ornately carved, themselves pieces of art.

"Fortunately, the woman who lives below me is quite elderly and hard of hearing, so I can make use of the full range of the instrument," Herr Steinmann said with no irony.

Without his beret, he appeared frailer; hearing aids bulked up both ears. He had taken great care to comb his few remaining hairs, white and wiry, over to one side.

Curiosity stroked her; what did a pre-war Bechstein sound like? Still, she hoped he wouldn't ask her to play. *Professor Rosenstein would always be listening.* His theoretical disappointment at the dulling of her chops, the withering of her skill, weighed heavy; three short years divided her two lives.

"I don't drink tea," volunteered Herr Steinmann. "My late wife used to like the crap, but I have always been an avid coffee drinker. Would you like a cup? Please sit down." Two armchairs faced the piano, separated by a small marble-topped table, his steady spectators. "There were times, you know, when coffee was hard to come by."

Sarah nodded. Coffee was always a good idea; perhaps they had more in common than she'd thought.

He disappeared into the hallway. As the minutes ticked by, Sarah looked around. There was a black-and-white wedding photo on the wall, yellowed with time, the woman in a pale skirt and jacket, both smiling naively. Sarah's eyes fell on the Bechstein and they stared at each other until she looked away, turning her wrist to glance at her watch, inconspicuously as if not to hurt the piano's feelings.

A moment later, a flap in the wall swung down with a startling squeak. Herr Steinmann's face was framed in the square hole like a painting on the wall entitled 'Ancient Hobby Pianist Serving Coffee' as he pushed a tray with a pot, two cups, a flowered dish of sugar cubes, and a matching creamer onto the counter that had not been there a moment earlier. Sliding back to the sitting room, hardly lifting his slippered feet with each step, he placed the tray on the table as if in slow motion.

"We constructed the hatch when we bought this apartment in 1961. Ha! The East Germans were building a wall at the time, and we were poking a hole in one." He was delighted with his own comparison, then frowned. "What a ridiculous construction. It simply led to one catastrophe after the next. The world does not need more walls, for heaven's sake. If Germany had never been divided, we wouldn't have had to pay so dearly for reunification."

The canister rattled as the coffee flowed, pulled into the cup by gravity and some kind of miracle. He dropped two lumps of sugar into the black pool and pushed the bowl toward her; instead, she added a dash of milk, watching as white teardrops dissipated in the now caramel-colored liquid.

"Oh, of course, Frau Johnson. Or may I call you Sarah?" He pronounced her name in German, *Zah-rah* — her excruciatingly plain moniker dressed up like Cinderella in a ball gown — but continued to use the polite *Sie* form. "Before I forget, here is the score I promised."

Without standing up, he lifted the book from a stack on a chest next to his chair. "What a coincidence. I'm sure you know that today would have been Mozart's birthday: January 27, 1756." He continued wryly, "When he died, he was younger than my grandson is now — although Moritz most certainly hasn't achieved a fraction of what the composer did in his brief thirty-five years."

Would that make Herr Steinmann old enough to be her great-grandfather? She fumbled in her wallet to find George Washington's face. "Are you sure that just one dollar is enough? I'd be happy to pay you more." She reached for Andrew Jackson.

His grin took off a few decades. "I haven't seen one of these in over seventy years. Look at it. Quite the same, isn't it? Here in Germany, our currency changes with shifting borders and politicians' whims. We had the Reichsmark, then the Deutschmark, then the Euro. As long as I can buy bread with it, I don't care what they call it."

Slipping the one-dollar bill into his coat pocket, he peered intently at her as if through a window. "We agreed on one dollar. That is more than enough. It brings back good memories, and those are priceless at my age. But please do appease my curiosity. What is your plan for the score? You are a pianist without an orchestra, I presume?"

For once, Sarah didn't have a plan. "I did have an orchestra." She examined the ornate mustard and rust pattern in the rug. "I used to know this piece very well. I would say it's Mozart's greatest piano concerto. We had something of a falling out. And I think I need to make amends." *Yes. That was it exactly.*

"Pieces of music are like siblings. You go through a lot together. Sometimes you love each other. Sometimes you hate each other. But you never abandon each other." He pressed his fingertips together, then smiled. "I don't have any myself, but I assume that's how it must be with brothers and sisters."

Brian. He would be sleeping in, curled up in the cozy blanket of a pre-dawn Sunday as the sun inched over the Pacific. Being far away made it more okay not to talk that often. Sarah stood up to leave, forcing a smile even as a tear welled up in her left eye, born of melancholy or regret or just dust from the bookshelves. "Thank you for the coffee and the score, Herr Steinmann."

He didn't notice her intention, or he chose to ignore it. "I would not say that Mozart is my favorite composer. Certainly, the works of Beethoven or Brahms have an even greater depth. And Liszt and Rachmaninov are much more impressive — when performed by a real virtuoso, of course. But Mozart's virtue is his simplicity."

Dong, dong! Half past the hour, announced a slender grandfather clock in the corner.

"You know, Mozart was really an opera composer. *The Marriage of Figaro*, *The Magic Flute* — those were his masterpieces." The cup threatened to fly out of his hand as he spoke. Sweeping up a thousand shards of porcelain would significantly delay her exit.

"But some of his most enjoyable works, in my opinion, are his sonatas for one piano, four hands. Not many composers bothered to write for two pianists, but Mozart, you know, played with his sister." Gripping the armrest of his chair with both hands, he rose slowly to his feet. "You are a pianist without an orchestra and are seeking reconciliation with Wolfgang Amadeus. I am not exactly an orchestra, but I could quite possibly assist you with the latter. I propose that we meet again next week to explore Mozart's repertoire for piano four hands."

Sarah opened her mouth; her larynx was temporarily disconnected from her brain.

"Would next Monday at five o'clock suit you? I am generally too worn out on Sunday afternoons for such an exhausting activity, you know."

"Ah… I have a dentist appointment next week." A sorry excuse, except that it was true. She felt a rush of relief, then an unexpected dash of disappointment.

"Very well then, you can come the following week, if you like. I can use the time to get my fingers up to speed. And don't worry, I have all the scores here. I'm sure you are an excellent sight-reader and won't need much preparation." He scooted in a turtle's tempo toward the front door. "Don't let me keep you, Sarah." As if it were his idea.

Finally, she exchanged the borrowed slippers — gray felt flattened by two more feet, a hundred more words — for her own boots and coat in the entry. "Thank you again," she called over her shoulder as she navigated down the sagging staircase, trying not to let the steps creak. One floor down, a silver-haired woman smiled silently at her while she swept her landing, the welcome mat tilted up against the wall.

Outside, the winter wind whipped her calves and Sarah cringed. What had she just gotten herself into, there in that musty shrine to the 1960s with a lonely man practically old enough to be Mozart's brother? She simply wanted peace with the piece that had kicked her ass, to read through it a few times, like flipping through photos from the last vacation with an ex, and close that chapter so that when people like Theo asked about her music, she didn't have a gaping wound to re-bandage.

Theo. He kept insisting on meeting up again, and, as the days passed, their first date reshuffled itself in Sarah's head until she remembered the way he had looked at her when her fingers had fluttered on the table top and had nearly forgotten about sitting alone at the bar with her champagne.

FEBRUARY 1

"Madame." Mozart's eighteenth-century garb would have fit Theo's theatrical bow as he opened his door — white knickers, frills at the neck and a periwig rolled above the ears — but not the man. He was wearing jeans and a dark purple hoodie with 'Santa Barbara' in turquoise letters that were framed by a well-washed rainbow. His sleeves were pushed up to his elbows and that monkey was laughing, daring her to pet its tail.

Sarah felt overdone in her eggshell sweater dress; it was just dinner at his place. After making three or four excuses, she'd finally given in and agreed to come. A blend of curry and acrylic wafted through the small apartment. The walls were covered seamlessly with his paintings, creating a claustrophobic explosion of color. One corner was dedicated to photographs. While she studied them, he stood so close that she could feel the rise and fall of his chest on her shoulder blade.

"You worked with disabled children?" Sarah asked, pointing to a picture of Theo in the forest surrounded by teens, some in wheel-chairs, others with visible mental impairments; his hair, two shades blonder, had been pulled back in a haphazard ponytail.

"That was my volunteer year after high school. I loved being with those kids. They're not pretentious at all, they say whatever the fuck is on their minds. It's refreshing." He lowered his voice. "I guess I was drawn to them because my younger brother Malte was also born with mental and physical disabilities."

"Is he that boy there?" She pointed to a curly-haired teen and thought of her own younger brother, Brian, who had just started a PhD in computer engineering in Southern California. He'd always been the kind of guy to fit in with the cool kids, with everyone really, for whom being smart wasn't a liability.

"No, no. Malte's heart gave out when he was three. He passed away quietly in his sleep."

"Oh! That's so sad. What a difficult thing to go through." A sense of embarrassment seems to accompany the fact of death, as if she should have known, even though she couldn't have, as if accidental questions about the dead could become unsaid.

"It was hard as shit on my parents. I think they felt guilty that they were also relieved they didn't have to take care of him anymore." Theo shifted his weight, evidently eager to move on. He pointed to a group of jovially intoxicated guys in *Lederhosen* holding him up horizontally as he toasted toward the camera with a massive mug of beer, his hair cut short.

"That was Oktoberfest. It took eight of them to get me off the ground." He laughed lightheartedly and kissed her on the neck, catching her upper arms as she turned around toward him.

"Just don't go running off this time to fix something." *There was that.* She tried to sound flippant, forgiving. Losing a brother, learning to live with a chasm in the family and his parents' pain, must have taught him endless empathy, she calculated. Leaving her at the bar must have been a random mistake.

"Andreas always has a problem he needs me to fix. It's just his love life I can't do anything about. Unless you have a friend? No, seriously, he's not here. It's just you, me, a fruit forward Cabernet, and my favorite curry — which isn't ready yet. I hope it's good enough for a foodie like you!"

"A foodie? No, that's what my coworkers are. I just kind of fake it."

"Really? I figured you'd be an amazing cook since you work at that magazine."

"Yeah, *Fork & Messer*. Honestly, I couldn't cook to save my life, so thank God for German bakeries!" God, if he knew how many stale pretzels she'd eaten. A fraud. That's what she felt like at work every day. But she didn't want to talk about that now. "Your curry smells delicious."

Her stomach was rumbling like a second guest because she had skipped lunch to make room for whatever he was cooking. He went into the tiny kitchen and opened the wine with the finesse of a classy waiter. Certainly not a parsimonious one; his pour was heavy, and the cork disappeared on the crowded counter.

"To art, music and The Theo and Sarah Show." *Clink!* Their glasses collided. His agate eyes were grayer than she'd remembered. He opened a cupboard full of mismatched spice jars and, holding two jars in one hand, turned on LMFAO's "Sexy and I Know It" with his phone in the other and wiggle-danced back to the stove.

"Californian beats for your Californian guest? Very nice…"

"Old skool since you're into, ah, classics. And since you and Mozart aren't so tight anymore, I thought you might like something a little… dancier. How spicy do you want your curry?"

"I don't know. I'll try it however you like to eat it." Maybe it was the music, maybe the wine, but more likely his charisma: She was feeling daring. How spicy could a curry be?

"Make yourself at home. I'll just be a minute," he called over his shoulder as a burst of steam rose from the stove.

She took small sips of the Cabernet, picturing blackcurrants; too much on an empty stomach could lead to regrets, and she didn't need more of those. As he immersed himself in the chaos in the kitchen — cans, pots and vegetable trimmings piled up around him — she tried not to trip over anything in the living room: a Playstation tossed into one corner, cords tangled, next to two dumbbells; a bicycle leaning against the back of the couch; an oversized teddy bear propped against a bookshelf crammed with art history volumes, the complete Harry Potter series, several books on yoga and kamasutra. The song "Sexy and I Know It" ended and "Gettin' Over You" started.

"Great location you've got here." She spoke up over the music. "Apartments like this are hard to come by in Munich." Small, but newly renovated, just a short walk from downtown.

"My pop's helping me out with the rent until my posters really take off. I told him I'd sponsor a weekend home on the lake for him and mom when they do. Ha!"

He'd mentioned his father's generosity last time. Sarah's parents would have offered, even insisted, under similar circumstances, but she would never have taken their money. Not unless it were the last resort. She would do anything to manage alone.

Theo appeared with two steaming plates and set them on purple felt place mats on the coffee table. "*Guten Appetit!*"

The first bite exploded inside her head, scorching her cranium.

Water escaped through her eyes and she gulped her wine. Gradually, the burn subsided, and she became aware of a nuance of spices that she had never experienced before. "Wow!"

"The chilis and red pepper turn up the heat, but turmeric is the real goddess in the dish. It's hands down my favorite spice. You can put it in anything, it'll keep you healthy, and the color is amazing. Just look at that!" Theo pointed to his creation with his nose.

"Your cooking is way out of my league. I wouldn't even know where to buy turmeric."

"I can teach you to cook. It's easy. It's like art! You just mix together what you've got until you get what you want."

Art was easy? Not in Sarah's universe, and neither was balancing complex flavors.

Theo continued, "I got into Indian food after I spent a month there last year, traveling, chilling with some amazing people. In Pune, I met this street food guy who lived in a tiny shack with his whole family. He and his mom cooked like twelve courses for me. Best shit I've ever eaten. Probably ever will."

"That's funny, we have a special on Indian food coming up at work."

"Even if you don't cook, you must learn a lot about food at the magazine, don't you?"

"I probably could learn more at work, but a lot of what I do is admin. Emails and organizing and stuff. I'm not the one interviewing the chefs or cooking anything or, you know, *creating* anything."

"So why waste your time? You could do so many other things." Theo made it sound so simple, but he wasn't the one paying his rent. He put his knee up on the couch and turned toward Sarah, holding up his index fingers and thumbs in a square, framing her. "Why not go into TV? Be an actress or something. I'd bet my left testicle that you're a really good singer, am I right? Wait, I didn't see you on *The Voice*, did I? I mean, be honest with yourself. You're a performer in your heart and soul and bones. You just lost your audience."

And her orchestra. Not to mention her big time New York debut and the rest of her career. "I'm not a diva…"

"No, you're actually pretty shy for an American — in a sexy way. But there's a *Rampensau* in you that's dying to come out."

She snickered at the word — literally, 'ramp pig' — for the person people watched in a crowded room, the one magical being with the magnetic aura. Miss Piggy, the object of Kermit's adoration. "I don't know if I'd put it like that, but maybe you're not that far off." She paused. "Am I really that shy?"

Instead of answering, he leaned over and kissed her collar bone, then her neck, slowly running the palm of his hand from her shoulder over her breast and down to her thigh, fiddling with the seam of her sweater dress. Her fingers slipped between his jeans and sweatshirt. His waist was softer than she'd expected under his baggy clothes. Abruptly, he sat up on the sunken couch cushion and reached for his plate, taking a big bite.

She crossed her legs and tugged thoughtfully on her earlobe. "Why do I have the feeling you can see right through me?"

"Because actually I'm Superman and have X-ray vision. More Cab?" His face was stoic; should she laugh? He didn't wait for an answer, but went to the kitchen for the wine bottle.

"Sarah, relax. Have a little fun!" he called from the kitchen. The MBA student in graduate school had told her that, too, right before he broke it off. It may have been meant constructively, but she took it personally. Theo emptied the bottle into their glasses and, still standing, swooped down for a brief but heavy kiss.

Dammit! The digital clock on his bookshelf caught her eye; it was already past eleven. "I didn't realize it was so late! I have to get up early for work tomorrow."

"Case in point." He went over to the window, swung it open to forty-five degrees, and picked up a pack of cigarettes and lighter from the windowsill, replacing them with his glass. *Krrrshh!* The grating of the spark wheel; a slow, drawn-out inhale. He had told her he was a non-smoker.

"Only when I drink alcohol." It was an answer without a question. Theo sipped what was left of his wine. "This is usually the time I start to paint."

FEBRUARY 11

"You're as punctual as a German!"

"*Grüß Gott*, Herr Steinmann." Sarah nodded politely. "I try to blend in."

He chuckled and ushered her inside. "My forty-four years as a logistics manager with the German postal service taught me more about punctuality than the military did."

The coffee was keeping warm in a canister on the marble table by the armchairs, waiting patiently for its drinkers, waiting for the music to begin; the apartment smelled of waiting. The Bechstein, silent and still, bore it like a butler. Would it be gentle or bump her bruised memories?

Herr Steinmann resembled a tortoise with his thinning hair and round spectacles. Hunched as he shuffled to his chair, he gripped both armrests and plopped onto a pile of worn pillows strategically positioned to support his hips and back. Without prompting, Sarah filled their cups.

"I hope you have been enjoying the concerto." He reached for a yellowed, dog-eared score on the table between them: *W.A. Mozart — Original Kompositionen — Klavier zu 4 Händen*. "I thought we could start with the more cheerful Sonata in D major, if you have no objections."

"You've been rehearsing all week; I hope I can keep up with you." A whit of truth, a kernel of self-doubt. She rubbed her fingers together as if in front of a fire. She hadn't yet brought herself to open his score to the concerto. "In music school I used to sight-read a lot. I accompanied the voice students during their German diction course as an undergrad. Ten or twelve songs a week with next to no preparation."

"Aha! That explains your excellent German."

"I also studied in Berlin briefly, but the diction class improved my accent quite a lot. For many of the singers, it was just a required class, but I was interested in the language. I found arias boring because I never liked pretending to be an orchestra, but I loved the song cycles by Schumann and Schubert because the language seemed so much richer." Loved; love? Music school already seemed like a page out of someone else's biography.

"Those lyrics were written by Goethe, Heine, the best we have to offer." His voice quavered, but the melody was unmistakable: "*Ich grolle nicht, und wenn das Herz auch bricht, Ewig verlornes Lieb! Ich grolle nicht.*"[1]

"Schumann's *Dicherliebe* song cycle. Based on poems by Heinrich Heine." Sarah could practically feel that dusty brown Kawai grand from the diction classroom under her fingers.

"My mother was my first and only music teacher. She was a very talented pianist. She could play Schumann, of course, but also Liszt, Chopin, Rachmaninov on par with any of the virtuosos. But she loved Mozart in particular, like the great Clara Haskil, who was the same age as her. She appreciated his childish optimism, she would say."

He seemed to be visualizing his mother beside him, conjuring her up from another world, as he chewed a piece of nothing in his mouth, kneading his tongue in a way only babies and the most elderly do.

"My mother wanted me to be a pianist," he continued. "But after the war I needed a more reliable job. There's nothing more reliable than the German postal service." He raised a hand in a kind of salute, then looked at the picture frame on the table. "My daughter also works there, at the headquarters in Bonn. Good God, she is nearing retirement herself."

"You have two daughters and a son?" A boy and two girls smiled up from a picture frame on the side table. Hair slicked back with a comb and water, collars crisp, cheeks rosy; they ranged from around three to eight years old.

"My son was living in Berlin with his partner, but I haven't spoken

---

[1] I'll not complain, even when my heart breaks. Eternally lost love! I'll not complain.

with him in seven years." He pursed his thin lips, letting the bro-kenness hang in the air like fall's morning mist; ignored birthdays, missed holidays, irretrievable time. What about the second girl?

"Since you claim you are no longer a pianist, Sarah, what is it that you are doing in Germany? Studying again?"

"No, I…" At least she would always have a Bachelor of Music degree to her name, as worthless as it was on the world's grandest stages. For most jobs, too, but this time her German had saved her. After the botched concerto, Professor Rosenstein had given her the option of quitting — cutting her losses, as he'd put it — or tagging on a semester or two to see whether she could attain the level of perfection necessary to complete the master's degree and open the next door on her pursuit of a performance career: the audition for yet another degree program. The choice, she'd felt, had been made for her. "Here I work as a — well, as an editor at a food magazine." Saying it out loud felt like betrayal, but of what exactly? Herself, her dreams, truly good food that satiated rather than stressed?

"A food magazine! My wife Hannelore used to subscribe to some of those. Good grief, it didn't help her much. I, on the other hand, was always quite handy in the kitchen." He chortled, glancing at the flap in the wall to the kitchen as if remembering some of his best meals, or perhaps his wife's worst. Herr Steinmann, expertly slicing onions in his slippers and Bavarian coat, uninhibitedly humming Beethoven's "Ode to Joy" — it was a hilariously beautiful picture. "That certainly has nothing to do with music. What a pity. But I imagine it's a decent job."

"For now." Sarah didn't even sound convincing to herself. He wasn't the first to offer sympathy for her decision to put some space between herself and the piano. No one had died, for God's sake! They weren't the ones with the voices in their heads. *Go practice. You should practice more. NEVER STOP PRACTICING!*

Herr Steinmann moved slowly to the piano and lowered himself onto the left side of the bench. "I will take the *Secondo* part; you can manage *Primo*, I trust. Ladies first," he added in English.

She caught a whiff of antique aftershave, burned coffee and musty closets. A bony hip against hers; Sarah had to press up against him awkwardly so she wouldn't fall off the bench. Hello, keys. Hello again. She consciously avoided thought, lest the gargoyles pounce, instead cuing instinctively with a quick inhalation, setting a swift tempo; they were off. The opening was an exercise in scales and arpeggios until she leaned into the main melody. He breathed laboriously, keeping time with his slippered foot, matching Sarah's ambitious pace. His fingers proved surprisingly nimble for his age, and he clearly knew how to draw out the Bechstein's warm, clear sound.

The ivory, formerly tusks for digging and defense, were both soft and solid under Sarah's fingers. Her fingers moved sloppily, but the terrain was familiar, like a sleepwalker in her own home. The notes to the Sonata in D major, K. 381, had already engraved themselves in her inner ear, years earlier, like an ancient stone artwork blown over with sand. A once learned piece only needs a good sweeping before it becomes recognizable again. Playing the Bechstein was both new and known: Sarah couldn't tell yet how it made her feel.

She turned the pages with her left hand, typically the task of the *Secondo*, while holding on to the melody with her right. Approaching the somber minor section, their synchronization suffered, but they didn't stop.

As the first movement ended, Herr Steinmann raised a trembling index finger. "Not bad for a 'no longer pianist.' But we need a bit more — how shall I put it? — dance in our touch. Wouldn't you agree?"

"You play very well, Herr Steinmann." He was no Horowitz and time had begun its gradual corrosion of his skill, each day a wave against the rock, but to her surprise, his playing revealed a deep understanding of the music. He was certainly better than any other hobby pianist she'd heard.

"I'm not at my best today, you know. Thank you for managing the page turns." He shook his head. "Let us start again, a bit slower this time, and focus on our synchronization. You cue, and I will follow."

They repeated the first movement, reigning in the tempo, listening more. He squinted through his spectacles. Could he actually see the music, or was he playing from memory? As they reached the end of the movement again, bouncing their arms to over-dramatize the final cadence, he was panting.

"Mozart was an opera composer," he huffed. "You can hear the orchestra and the soloists in his sonatas for twenty fingers. My mother used to say, 'Otto, let your fingers sing!'"

"My piano teacher used to say that, too — Professor Rosenstein." He would wave his arms in huge arcs, tracing the slurs in the air over each phrase, as he vocalized the melodies of Sarah's pieces. Every instrument imitates the voice, while the voice can stand in for any instrument.

"Rosenstein... a German Jew?" He grunted. Such a blunt question. "We lost our best musicians, thanks to the National Socialists. They all went to America! Kurt Weill, Arnold Schoenberg, Erich Korngold. Fortunately for them, America was fertile ground."

He paused and blinked, looking upward, and changed the subject, picking up the tempo in his voice. "Mozart played the sonatas with his sister, you know. I played this one with my neighbor, Heinrich. My mother coached us, and we performed it at her birthday party. It must have been her thirty-seventh or thirty-eighth. She was beautiful, but I thought she was so old at the time. Ha! That was before the war."

Sarah was doing the math in her head until he added matter-of-factly, "Heinrich was killed in combat. In Poland. One of the very first casualties. He was three years older than me. He usually took the *Secondo* part."

Sarah had played this sonata in high school with her Chinese-American friend Cindy, who took lessons from the same piano teacher and was also three years older.

"The Second World War? Did you fight, too?"

"I was only fourteen when the war started. I didn't go to Poland, but I was sent to the front later." This frail man in fatigues, loading a rifle. *Chug-chink.* If he fought for Hitler's Germany during World War II, did that make him a Nazi? He pressed his fingers together on his lap. "Heinrich wanted to be a conductor. He would have been a very good one."

Herr Steinmann pulled a cloth handkerchief out of his pocket and coughed violently, his chest rattling, as Sarah looked away. Questions about the war would have to wait; it was growing dim in the small room as the fragile winter sun retreated.

"Shall we attempt the second movement before we call it a day?" He seemed to draw fresh energy.

In the Andante, the sixteenth notes in her left hand misaligned with the repeating eighth notes in his right hand, a tricky exercise in unison they would have to work through. His poky elbow and gaunt hip disrupted her concentration. The string-like accompaniment wobbled, his trills rattled, but the former logistics manager kept time like a metronome.

"We'll start with the third movement next week," he announced when they concluded the second, looking sideways at each other, both uncertain how much *ritardando* to take. He wiped his nose with his handkerchief as he stood up, supporting himself at the end of the keyboard. Sarah exhaled, both frustrated that she hadn't played better and pleased that it hadn't been worse.

Bing! Her phone chirped from her bag on the armchair. Was it Theo? She hadn't heard from him in a few days.

"Thank you, Sarah," said Herr Steinmann. "It's been a very long time since I've made music with someone else like that. And at such a… professional level. It's something I've missed very much. I would suggest you call yourself a 'still pianist' rather than a 'no longer pianist'." His eyes were watery, but not with emotion. "Same time next week?"

"*Ja*. Yes, okay." One more meeting couldn't hurt; neither would a little preparation. She would have to play through the Allegro molto on her own before they met.

She stepped out into the chill. Her stomach rumbled, but there was something else inside her besides hunger. She couldn't quite name it.

Hey gorgeous wanna come over? Theo was responsible for the interruption from her bag. People like people who are spontaneous, thought Sarah. But then, he didn't have a nine-to-five job. Or any real job, for that matter. Not answering his text was also an answer.

On the way home, she took a long detour and found her way back to the kebab shop where she and Theo had eaten, the entrance unlit only because the bulb had burned out on the sign. She ordered a beer and found a table in the corner, facing into the shop. Maybe it would taste less bitter this time. Her wrists ached from playing with with Herr Steinmann and she massaged them with her thumbs and forefingers. She'd have to concentrate more on relaxing next time. People came and went, and she created stories for their days and plans for their evenings.

He was right. She was shy — she liked the term 'reserved' better — but there was also a whiny diva under her skin. Are all humans full of contradictions? She didn't know anyone else who was, but maybe she didn't know anyone well enough to be able to know whether they were. She'd drifted away from the piano, but the void was a spreading mold, and her Schimmel wasn't helping with its nagging. Could Herr Steinmann's Bechstein fill the hole? Sarah drank until the beer's initial chill had warmed, then returned her glass, half-drained, to the counter and left.

February 12

Sarah was tapping a silent, arbitrary melody fraught with sixteenth notes on the conference room table, syncopated because the tip of her ring finger was cracked.

"Listen, people, what we need is something new, something fresh. I don't have to tell you how saturated the market it, how tight the competition is. What I want is less of the same and more of something different. The palates out there are jaded, so bring me new ways to tempt them, okay?"

As her staff fidgeted, Stefanie scanned the group like a rotating fan, without making eye contact. "Ok, then. Think about that, people. Right now we need to start talking about our upcoming summer specials." From June to August, *Fork & Messer* focused on cuisine from the region and maintained partnerships with several local tourism organizations. "I want to put together a small team to spearhead our spread on sweet classics from Austria. Who's interested?"

Franziska, a stocky, ashen-haired editor in her mid-fifties, raised her hand, index finger pointed, the class smarty pants. She was originally from Linz in Austria and used a strong dialect that was a whirr to Sarah.

Christoph stuck his ballpoint in the air and smacked his lips. "Hm, *Sachertorte!*" If he'd been a singer, he would have been a baritone. Instead, he was the picture editor, a tall, lanky German with ears that stuck out over the arms of his conspicuously stylish glasses. Sarah admired the ease of his standout accessory; on her, they would look pretentious.

"Sarah, what about you? You managed to come through on the

March feature." Stefanie's words felt like a scoff, but she knew it was the closest she could come to praise. The replacement author hadn't delivered yet, but Sarah had commissioned her to do a very promising interview with an Indian-German restauranteur in Munich who was using revenues from her popular restaurant to support asylum seekers in the city. Sarah remembered Theo's curry and her mouth ignited.

"Ok, I'll do it." Did she have much of a choice? She had tried *Sachertorte*, the chocolate bomb from Vienna with a thin layer of apricot jam in the middle, but when she treated herself to a dessert, usually after a big workout, she tended to choose ones that didn't land heavy as a rock in her belly.

"Why don't you three do some brainstorming and submit your project proposal by the end of next week." Stefanie cast yet another glance at her phone, perpetually laid out in front of her as a conspicuous badge of importance, then gathered up her papers and left the room, wobbling on her high heels.

Sarah sighed as she trudged out of the conference room, relieved that the meeting was over and no one had called her bluff, uncovered her as a fake foodie. Back at her desk, she felt a pang of guilt when saw the signature at the end of her emails:

Sarah R. Johnson
International Food Editor
Fork & Messer

It was a slow day. She squirted an oversized dollop of hand lotion onto her palm, rubbing it for several minutes until it was finally absorbed into her chronically chapped skin. She went through her list of contacts, then scanned LinkedIn for potential new authors. Boredom, her faithful but faceless office mate, steadily set in. Her thoughts drifted like wispy summer clouds, fragmented and in motion. Munich's city maintenance trucks, small and narrow by American standards, clearing speckled snow in front of her building this morning. Ice cream. Coffee ice cream. She could bathe in it right now. At least in the thought of it, especially if it were hot. Not an *Eiskaffee*, though, because that was made with vanilla. Her mom used to swing the carpool by Baskin Robbins on random Mondays. "Mondays are for mocha almond fudge," she'd say. Mondays fun days. Monkeys. Who the hell draws a monkey on their body? Why the hell not? A giraffe on her calf. A lion on her ass. Lions eat zebras. Black and white. Sia's face-veiling wig singing "The Greatest." An invisible *Rampensau* was a self-contradiction. The oceanic drift of Rachmaninov's second piano concerto, played by Peter Serkin. Her high school piano teacher's favorite recording. Her aspiration. Too late now. Seven years. What could make the chasm between father and son so wide? And what about Herr Steinmann's younger daughter? He hadn't said a word about her.

Knock, knock. Her office door. Christoph opened it with his elbow, balancing a cappuccino in each hand. "I brought you something." His voice cracked slightly with over-eagerness.

"You are my hero!" It was close enough to coffee ice cream for the time being. How did he know? The office only had a splattered drip coffee maker, stained with the residue of cheap grinds and middle-age frustration, but there was a gourmet espresso stand on wheels, Bavarian Brew, that parked in front of their building three times a week.

Christoph handed Sarah the coffee and sat on her desk, stretching his long legs out in front of him. Royal blue with orange polka dots — he must have a whole closet of statement socks at home, rolled up like Yule logs and lined up in a rainbow, ROYGBIV.

"Go team *Apfelstrudel!*" He tilted his head and gave Sarah a fist bump. "We'll just have to deal with Franzi, but it's a home game for her."

One one thousand, two one thousand — he was still looking at her. His ears and rectangular thick-framed glasses were prominent, but his cheeks, nose and lips were comparatively slender. His beard would be patchy if he grew it out. A few premature gray strands peaked out around his temples, wise rebels among his short, straight, umber hair.

"Can I make a confession, now that we're doing this project together?"

Sarah feared for a moment that he was going to suggest dinner. He was the only coworker she could have a normal conversation with, but she'd suspected since she joined the magazine two years ago that he wanted to be more than office buddies. She just couldn't quite picture wearing his t-shirts, rubbing his feet on the couch, sharing a spoon.

"Sometimes I feel like a total imposter here. When I photoshop all the pictures of rare steaks and exotic spices and perfect plating, I want to puke and go get a pizza at Valentino's down the street. That's honest food."

Sarah exhaled a relieved laugh. Thank God she didn't have to find an excuse for Friday night. And did he really just admit that they'd been a secret pair of pretenders all along? "I… seriously? I thought you were like them. You want to know something? I don't cook either."

"No way! Then you're damn good at faking because you always seem to know what you're talking about."

"I'm not kidding. You want to know what I ate for dinner last night? Frozen vegetables with cream cheese on them and a pretzel from the bakery." For the third night in a row, she didn't add.

In Christoph's face, Sarah read relief mixed with the glee of discovering a mutual truth and felt her back muscles loosen against the office chair.

"I really thought that the Austrian sweets project would out me as a non-foodie," she said. "Franzi is constantly dropping her haute cuisine vocabulary. You know she apprenticed with a top pastry chef in Vienna? But now we outnumber her, we outsiders. Doesn't it bother you, though, to feel like an outsider at work?"

"No, not really. If you think about it, aren't we all outsiders in one way or another?" He tipped his cup into his mouth with two fingers, then looked at Sarah understandingly. "The way I see it is that we can either get hung up about feeling like an outsider and miss getting real with people, or we can just get over it." *Like deciding between wheat or rye.*

He swirled his coffee, welding the last bit of foam to the espresso. Then he emptied the cup and backed out of Sarah's office, mumbling something about vegan bread spreads and a meeting in a few minutes, and leaving her to process his revelation.

Just get over it. His words echoed in her ears; she stared at her computer screen without seeing what was on it, letting the pixels fade into each other. Music had been her connection to others, the piano her interpreter, converting to sound the feelings she didn't want to talk about. But it was also a noble cloak to cover her discomforts. Now without the piano, she had to choose between disrobing, or clinging to her outsiderness like a toddler with a toy.

February 18

"*Hundewetter!*" Herr Steinmann threw up his hands as if the weather was his fault, the countless liters of cold water, the wind heaving it into faces.

Sarah left her umbrella on the landing in front of the door, hung her dripping coat on the rack in the foyer, took off her boots, and slid into the gray felt slippers she had worn twice before. The coffee was already on the table, but she had to pee, damn those high-waisted jeans.

"May I use your *Toilette* before we start?" The German word was so much more graphic, more candid, than the mis-named American 'bathroom' (a bath is for bathing, not pooping) or 'restroom' (waste removal isn't exactly a hammock in the shade).

He directed her to the end of the hall, where she found a dimly lit room tiled in military hues — olive green and dusty brown — as if to camouflage the sagging nakedness it witnessed. There was a small sink with a simple, unframed mirror above it and a bathtub with a cracked sliver of soap in the built-in dish. Feeling awkward, she hastily wiped the toilet seat, placed a layer of paper on it, and emptied her bladder as quickly as possible.

Blop-blop-pshhh! The faucet only offered a meager stream of water to wash her hands. In the mirror she saw tiny, crooked lines below her lower eyelashes and wiped the runaway mascara with her finger. She envied women who could get away with no makeup.

She sighed, glad to have a moment to herself before encountering the Bechstein's grandeur again. As she turned to leave, the two shelves on the wall next to the mirror caught her attention. They held four bottles of medication with names full of Xs and Ys, a brush made of wood and animal hair, a flat rectangular tin of hair wax, a glass bottle of men's cologne, a nail file with a wooden handle. Each was turned precisely so their labels could be clearly seen, as if they had been arranged for a museum exhibit entitled '1954: Men's Bathroom Paraphernalia.' At the end of the row there was a ring made of three strands of braided leather, too bulky for a finger, oddly out of place.

Closing the door behind her, she made her way back to the sitting room. The dark hallway between it and the bathroom was lined with thin golden picture frames, all of equal size, hung in perfect alignment. In one, Herr Steinmann's round face and prominent eyebrows were unmistakable. He must have been in his early thirties, even though his hair was already starting to thin. Dressed as a clown, wearing a tiny off-kilter top hat and an oversized ruffled collar, with circles painted on his cheeks, he had been snapped mid-dance, a knee in the air and an elbow at half-mast. He was encircled by more clowns, who were clapping and whistling.

Sarah returned to her seat; Herr Steinmann hadn't budged. "I noticed the photograph in the hall. Was that *Fasching?*" Bavarian Mardis Gras, a contradiction in terms.

He laughed like a boy. "Yes, yes, it was."

"You must have been quite the *Rampensau.*" Would he be offended by the word?

"*Ach,* perhaps I still am. Don't we musicians all have a bit of *Rampensau* in us? We always looked forward to *Fasching.* Imagine dancing and drinking on a Tuesday morning rather than going to work!" He raised his cup in an imaginary toast, sloshing a drop onto his lap, but didn't seem to notice.

"So you won't be there tomorrow?" The bakeries had been selling every conceivable variety of cream-filled donut in the run-up to *Fasching* — apricot jam, tiramisu, 'hot love' with vanilla cream squirted into one half and raspberry purée into the other; streamers in primary colors dressed up shop windows.

"No, no, not at my age. We met up with the same group of people in the photograph at Viktualienmarkt for over thirty years, until the first friends passed away. Franz had a heart attack at fifty-eight. Then Ingrid died of some kind of cancer. Heinz-Peter had been a heavy smoker, you see, and then my Hannelore. I am the last one left, I'm afraid."

Sarah tugged on her earlobe, paralyzed by the gap between them. For her, death existed in a future so distant that eternity lay ahead of it.

"We would drink liters and liters of beer. Oh goodness! We'd start Lent every year with a hangover so bad that you wouldn't even want to touch a drop of alcohol for the next forty days." That boyish laugh again. Herr Steinmann drunk? Sarah couldn't imagine it. Or, then again, maybe she could.

"That photo was from 1957." He glanced toward the hall as if expecting someone to emerge from it. "My wife Hannelore had just given birth to our second child, but that was no reason to miss out. She was the one who took that picture. The baby was in the pram, and she somehow managed at the same time to hold on to our oldest daughter so she wouldn't get lost in the crowd."

Bam bam ba-pa ba-pa. The lurch of kitschy folk music and stench of spilled beer (not unlike urine, unless perhaps it was) had made Sarah feel extrinsic when she observed the *Fasching* celebration at Viktualienmarkt last year. "Hannelore must have been very coordinated!"

"Yes, Hannelore was the most amazing woman I've ever met. I am just an ordinary man, but she made me feel like I was one-of-a-kind. Hannelore always encouraged me to keep playing the piano. She wasn't particularly musical herself, but she was artistic. She was an excellent photographer." He held his own hands, not knowing what to do with them. "Allegro molto — but we can leave out the molto for our first attempt, what do you think?"

"Starting slowly is always a good idea," agreed Sarah. Especially when you're just getting reacquainted with the instrument and a composer that had stabbed you in the back. "We can speed it up later."

They found their seats at the piano. Sarah stared at the Bechstein's ivories for a moment — simultaneously friendly and foreign — before she set a moderate tempo. The opening chords gave way to a quick twist of sixteenths. They both played the notes and dynamic markings on the page, but one plus one didn't equal a whole, as it should have. Instead, cacophony.

"*Oje!*" He cupped his ears. "Playing the right notes is not enough in a duo."

"Let's slow it down a bit more and go through it note for note," she suggested, looking at Herr Steinmann's hands, withered in the many decades since the photographs on his wall had been taken. Hers would not be spared the same weathering of time.

"You remind me of my mother. She was always keen on meticulous practice techniques, and she forced Heinrich and me to listen to each other. Teenage boys are not known for being the best listeners."

"Just playing is always easier than playing and listening at the same time, isn't it?" In music school, her fingers and forearms, but also her ears would be spent after a long afternoon of rehearsals.

"To listen you also have to hear." He patted down the disobedient hairs on his bald head and adjusted one of his cumbrous hearing aids. "But I refuse to see music as a young man's sport."

They painstakingly took the third movement one phrase at a time, repeating each one over and over. Decelerating to a snail's pace, they locked each chord into place, aligning the runs. With each repetition, Sarah heard new weaknesses and ordered countless do-overs without looking to her left. Herr Steinmann nodded each time as he followed her sharp gaze. Little by little, she felt her ears quickening, like muscles getting back into shape.

Finally, from the beginning again, she set a swifter tempo; apart from a few teeters, their unison improved.

The final chord was followed by a raspy cough, an alternative ending of sorts.

"Isn't it rewarding to approach perfection?" His voice was hollow and sapped, but he was smiling through his exhaustion.

February 25

"I hope you don't mind," — Herr Steinmann didn't sound particularly apologetic — "but last week, you left before we could agree on our next piece. I took the liberty of choosing another Mozart sonata, the C major, K. 521. That means I was able to prepare and you weren't, but that won't pose any difficulties, will it?" It wasn't a question.

He slurped his coffee, smacking away the heat. "The doctor says I should drink less of the stuff." He snuffed. "I would rather die early. I suppose it's much too late for that! But no coffee after six or I'll be awake all night."

Leaving her coffee half drunk on the marble table, she asked whether she could read through the first movement alone before they began. First, she raised the lid, feeling its weight press into her wrist as she put the prop in place. Settling into the middle of the long bench, she was arrested by a déjà-vu of being in Professor Rosenstein's studio, where she'd always felt the awe-encrusted contradiction of being part an elite club — he'd accepted her freshman audition tape, after all, and kept her on for the master's program — and also being a mere spectator. That magical door from music school to career pianist had never opened. Maybe it had never been within arm's reach to begin with. Maybe Professor Rosenstein had taken her on as a charitable project, to make the more successful students in his studio feel better.

Still partially trapped in her memories, Sarah perused the score. She lightly tapped through parts, visualizing the rest, as Herr Steinmann looked up from a photo album he'd been flipping through, a finger resting on his pore-spotted nose. A hundred pictures, a hundred memories, many hundreds of days were kept inside. He was older than present-day Germany itself, old enough to have begotten the chancellor herself; his history was also the country's history. The massive volume lay open on the table as he went to the piano. Sarah made room for him on the bench.

"Mozart's father apparently claimed his son invented compositions for one piano, four hands. Of course, a father's pride is unparalleled. I cannot blame him for stretching the truth, but Wolfgang actually learned it from Johann Sebastian Bach's son while visiting him in London." Was this going to turn into a ninth semester of music history? With no credentials except age and interest, his knowledge could rival that of most of the graduate assistants Sarah had taken classes with. He seemed glad to finally share it with someone who appreciated it. "We think of the musical greats as separate entities, as islands of genius, but in some cases they were more like a relay team, passing the baton to each other."

"And the piano is one of very few instruments that can be played by two people at once." Sarah had chosen it because it is, on the other hand, also one of very few instruments that is complete when played alone.

"With four hands, you are an orchestra!" he exclaimed dramatically. "Mozart designated this piece for two pianists and two pianos. That would have made it even grander. Unfortunately, I only have space here for one instrument. I always dreamed of having two grands, next to each other, but who would have played the other one? My children were never very interested."

Professor Rosenstein's side-by-side grands had been packed into his studio like in a suitcase ready for a flight, as if the inconvenience were only temporary. It must have been quite a feat to squeeze them in, legless and vertical. He passed away one month to the day after Sarah moved to Germany. A short time later, the movers would have revisited his studio to undo their work. What happened to that regal black Bechstein?

The Allegro opened forcefully, as if all instruments were marching in unison, until the 'horns' broke through with a delicate, mid-range melody. Synchronization was not the weakness this time, rather the dynamic range, the phrasing and, as always with Mozart, the tricky runs. There was a lot to be done, so they chose to read through the second movement before getting down to details.

The Andante was a preview of Mozart's famous *Eine kleine Nacht-musik*, a dry run for greatness, composed for chamber ensemble just weeks after the C major sonata in 1787. The middle section, the *legato*, was somber and gently tumultuous with its rolling minor arpeggios, giving way again to the placid opening melody. She stumbled though the rapid, light scales at the end of the second movement, but it was just their first reading. She would have another chance; rehearsals were a series of second shots.

He cleared his throat. She rubbed her eyes.

"Don't fall asleep just yet," he said. "I discovered an old photograph of Heinrich that I wanted to show you."

Only then did she see his cane with the gilded handle, like the Bechstein's fourth leg. Had it been leaning against the piano the whole time? He hobbled back to his chair with it and started flipping through the album.

Ding-ding-dong! Sarah jumped at the sound of the doorbell, too loud for the size of the apartment. Herr Steinmann had already lowered himself into his nest of pillows.

"Would you mind seeing who's there?" He didn't look up.

She pressed the buzzer and opened the door; an unusually tall, slender man in his late twenties was already standing there, holding a paper bag. *Oh!* Each of them was startled to see the other, she expecting to wait for the visitor to climb the stairs, he anticipating Herr Steinmann's unironed face.

"*Servus.* I live downstairs." A hint of a French accent shaded his fluent German. "I have some mail for Herr Steinmann, and his medication."

"Constantin! Please come in!" A hoarse voice came from the other room as the visitor entered.

"How are you feeling today, Herr Steinmann?" Constantin inquired like a doctor making his rounds at a hospital. "Here is the prescription you needed." He handed over a paper bag imprinted with *Siegfried Apotheke.*

"Sarah here is giving me quite a workout. We are rehearsing a Mozart sonata. Perhaps you would like to hear it next time. Right now I'm rather tuckered out. See, young man! I do listen to your advice once in a while." Between huffs and puffs, he smiled as if they'd just shared an inside joke.

Constantin reached out a hand to shake Sarah's with such a confident grasp that she wanted to keep holding on. "You're the *américaine*. He mentioned you." What would he have said? I met a girl seventy-five years younger and she comes over once a week (a Hugh Hefner he clearly was not). Or: Imagine, Constantin, I may appear to be just one old man, but now I am *the orchestra* for a used-to-be pianist who lost hers.

Constantin turned to his neighbor. "I'm glad you're playing again, Herr Steinmann, but remember, your heart will only permit so much, so please don't overdo it."

Two small, jagged scars marked Constantin's right cheek below his eye. A scar on the skin usually infers another beneath it. "I have a night shift at the hospital tonight — my fifth in a row. We're only supposed to do three or four at a time, but it never works out that way. *Alors*, I feel like a zombie, but, you know, Herr Steinmann, at least I get to see some sunlight on these short days. I can't complain."

After he'd left, Herr Steinmman explained: "Constantin helps me out from time to time. When I'm a bit under the weather, he's kind enough to pick up my medication for me and take care of other errands." He lowered his voice. "He comes from Chad, you know, though he has been in Munich for quite some time now. His family came well before the more recent wave of refugees. He is studying to be a doctor — a cardiologist, I believe. I am lucky indeed to have such good neighbors, living alone like I do. Have you also been as fortunate with your neighbors?"

Sarah considered the residents in her own building. Arne on the ground floor, a thirtyish German who covered his flabby belly in brands and parked his BMW i8 Coupe at a cocky angle in front of the house, had driven her to dinner one night during a lull with his twentyish girlfriend. He'd ordered for both of them without a glance at the menu at the kind of place downtown that offers a tiny, well-seasoned *ameuse-geule* and a slit of a parking space. During the third course (and as many paired wines), he'd told her that he had shot and killed his brother when he was three, the brother four, with a family heirloom hanging on the wall. It hadn't been loaded, he'd thought, hadn't even been touched in a generation. They were playing cowboys and Indians.

She'd never had much to do with the other neighbors: a single Bosnian man in his forties; a young Italian couple with two cats; a woman of unknown age, either Polish or Ukrainian; a German couple in their fifties with one spoiled teenager. She passed them occasionally in the hall or they would meet at the mailbox and exchange a superficial greeting, but she wouldn't ask any of them for a favor. It was different at home — the other home. On the cul de sac in suburban California where she grew up, neighbors were constantly ringing to borrow two eggs to drop off a child. Dinner would get delayed when parents chatted out front while their kids practiced wheelies in the street. It was named Pleasant Court. Right next to Hope Lane and Paradise Circle. A goddam hippie village for yuppies. Maybe that was why she left, but also why a certain home-sickness irritated her like spinach between her teeth.

"I guess I should take more time to get to know my neighbors," she said finally.

"I do believe people are thrown together for a reason." Herr Steinmann's face turned somber. "Living near Constantin and his mother has reminded me that sometimes we are the reason people must seek refuge." Was he making a confession? "Just as quickly, we can become the refugee, and just as easily, if we so choose, we can become the refuge-giver." He jolted, awoken from a daydream. "Where were we? Yes, Heinrich. Here we were in 1937. I was twelve, and he must have been fifteen."

He pointed to a yellowed black-and-white picture of half a dozen teenage boys, all wearing Boy Scout uniforms with light brown shirts and long black neckerchiefs. 1937? No, they weren't Boy Scouts.

"You were part of the Hitler Youth?" There was no diplomatic way to ask.

He chuckled reminiscently. "I see you are familiar with German history." Rewind. Stop. Play. He leaned back in his chair to watch the memories in his head. "We were boys. I know the youth today wouldn't quite understand. Especially not the Americans. You Americans see everything in black and white, do you not?" He nodded toward Sarah and poured himself another half cup of coffee. A drop splashed onto the edge of the saucer when he tossed in a sugar cube, leaving a dark brown streak as it rolled inward toward the middle. She looked at the photo again. The neckerchiefs were bound with woggles made of leather strands, three woven into a tight, thick braid. She'd seen one before, on his bathroom shelf.

"We were young, and young people looked up to their parents in those days. We had no choice. Everyone was a Nazi." He shrugged, studying the dull brown liquid in his cup.

Everyone? Bullshit. What about the White Rose, the group of Munich students that decried every German's complicity in the Nazi atrocities? From their leaflets: "Who among us has any conception of the dimensions of shame that will befall us and our children when one day the veil has fallen from our eyes and the most horrible of crimes — crimes that infinitely outdistance every human measure — reach the light of day?" The White Rose leaders were silenced by the Guillotine. *Woosh-krshhh!* Did fear of the blade give the coward an excuse for not knowing, or was it simply one more offense committed by the powers that be?

"Of course, you learned in school about the famous resistors, the few brave ones. But even the Bechstein family had Nazi ties, like so many other companies. Carl Bechstein's daughter-in-law Helene was a good friend of the Führer. Does that taint my instrument?"

Herr Steinmann didn't wait for a reply, but anticipated her questions. "The Nazis made many promises. Better infrastructure and good jobs, prosperity — and of course victory. Who doesn't want to be a winner? And then there were the threats. There was only one safe choice back then. Bad things happened to those who didn't become one of them. But in fact my parents believed Hitler's promises. My father designed airplane engines for BMW during the war — another tainted company — and was proud of his contribution. The triumph of the National Socialists was inevitable, he thought, and we had to do our part. He put on his white shirt each morning knowing that he would go to work with forced laborers in striped jackets, people borrowed from the camps. I didn't learn that until decades later, sadly. At dinner, he would only tell us how big the engines were and how quickly and effectively the workers built them. The Nazi faithful like my parents wanted to belong to a strong country again, to feel grand, be looked up to. And so did Heinrich."

He raised his index finger. Finally, someone to listen. "A country, like a man, in my opinion, should not strive to be great, but to be good." He paused to collect the memories, sift them, convert them from colors and sensations into syllables. "Heinrich was young, very young, but his family had been hit hard by the recession after the First World War and he had become quite political for his age. Politics, you know, tend to become perilous when mixed with the naivety of youth. 'We will show the world how smart and powerful we Germans are,' Heinrich told me the day he left. So proud; much too proud. He was wearing his uniform and bid farewell by giving me a '*Heil Hitler*' salute. No embrace. Not even a real smile, even though we had sweat through many rehearsals together with my mother, and our families had been acquainted since before we'd learned to ride bicycles, let alone play a minuet. That is my last memory of him. Of course, he hadn't yet learned much about 'the world' he was talking about, but he was very enthusiastic about going to fight for the Fatherland."

"And you, Herr Steinmann?" Sarah wanted to listen with her hands covering her ears. "What about you?"

"Me? I liked to go camping and hiking. We did that, too, in the *Hitler Jugend*. With my mother, I flexed my fingers. But a boy also has to get his fingers dirty. My father didn't do that with me, and I had no brothers or uncles. And yes, I did believe for a time, a long time, really, that we Germans, the true Germans, would take on unprecedented power in the world. It felt exciting! My children don't understand why I keep the photographs, but the past cannot — should not — be erased."

He sighed and looked at his palms and then the backs of his hands in his lap, turning them over several times, studying the lines on them. Not many more fortunes left to have told. "And even if all of it could be amended for, who should be the one to do that? At the time, I wasn't like Heinrich. I was young and didn't care about politics at all. I took it for granted that we would win the war quickly and live happily ever after in Hitler's paradise. It wasn't until the war progressed that things got worse for everyone."

"So you were sent to fight as well?" Her own grandfather, her mother's father, fought against the Japanese; there was a family rumor about a knife wound, a calf scar, an untold story of heroism because American soldiers were like knights out to rescue the damsel Freedom, to save democracy from demise. But, she always wondered, was he kept awake at night by the sound of grenades crushing trees, carving craters, breaking limbs? Her other grandfather had been too young for the draft by just a few weeks. Had he not been born prematurely, he would have been sent to the front, and Sarah may never have become a speck in human history. She'd heard her dad say that his father had carried guilt for staying home, while his older friends were losing their eyes and legs and minds and lives. Damned if they went; damned if they didn't.

"I was just a messenger at first, a boy's job. Things changed later, but that's another story for another day." He started coughing, phlegm and esophagus rattling, and reached for his handkerchief.

She took the cue. "It's getting late, Herr Steinmann. I'll just use the *Toilette* before I go."

On the way, she paused for a moment in front of the Mardis Gras photo. So carefree. She tried to picture him in a Wehrmacht uniform, his cheeks still smooth with youthfulness, doing a *Heil Hitler*, and cringed. He had no apologetic words for the maniac, but she couldn't overlook his voluntary salute. Sitting on the toilet, she looked up at the shelf with hair wax, cologne and the woven woggle. It belonged in the trash or a museum. Here, it stank of nostalgia rather than serving a *never again* collective memory, paying its dues by disgusting generation after generation of youths with the sins it had watched.

She thought of Professor Rosenstein, one man's family snuffed out in a few short commands, a loss immeasurable to him yet anonymous to its perpetrators, as she picked it up and turned it over in her hand. *Flush!* She wanted to throw the woggle into the toilet, watch it spin and gurgle like a captured spider. Instead, she washed her hands, turning the knob on the faucet to the left until her knuckles turned the color of cherries.

Ghraaa! A loud snore sounded as she turned into the sitting room. His chin was touching his chest, his nearly bald head tilted against the side of the headrest on his armchair. Should she wake him?

"Herr Steinmann?" He moved his fingers, playing the piano in his sleep. Leaving him there felt awry, but so did waking him.

She found a pen in her bag and looked around for a scrap of paper. The photo album was still open on the table in front of her; she couldn't resist another look. There he was again, young Otto, his right arm raised in a field of juvenile arms protruding like cornstalks. She wanted to vomit, but that would have woken him.

On the next page: Otto, a couple of years older, rifle in hand, dirty combat boots, sleeves rolled up. His appearance was weary, but his cheeks were rosy, his eyes bright. Alive. Whole.

She flipped through several more pages, crinkling the brittle tissue paper between them. There was the engineer in the white shirt, shaking the hand of a Nazi official. Behind them, rows of robot-like machines, metal cylinders and faceless workers. Repetitive shapes in shades of gray — squares and rectangles, curves and cones — like an outdated vision of a future that had already passed. Herr Steinmann's father was smiling enthusiastically at the official, pointing with a puffed up chest to disassembled airplane engines dirtied by the fingers of those called dirty.

Another picture had been labeled by hand: 'Benjamin West, 1946.' A Black man in a military uniform was sitting at a grand piano. Sarah stared. The Nazis despised not only Jews, but also people of color. She examined the photo more closely. The decorative slits in the music stand, the squarish carving on its sturdy legs. Could it be? Impossible. Yes, it was! She was sure: The piano was the very same Bechstein she and Herr Steinmann had been playing, the instrument that had belonged to his party-line-toeing mother. The man was grinning spiritedly at the camera, shoe over the sostenuto pedal, hands perched expertly over the keyboard, ready to strike. There was no score on the stand, so he must have been playing from memory or even improvising.

Who was he? He was clearly enjoying the instrument and Sarah realized that — perhaps just a little — she was, too. In fact, the very same one. That wonderment over gracefully twisting melodies and unexpected harmonic progressions was reforming itself in her, familiar, yet altered by its absence.

Herr Steinmann snored again and adjusted his head, succumbing fully to sleep's clutches. Sarah dug up a scrap of paper from the bottom of her bag and wrote:

Dear Herr Steinmann,
I hope your sleep was dreamless and peaceful. See you next Monday for more
Mozart.
    Sarah

As she left, she scanned the mailboxes in front of the house. Fliers advertising a nearby kebab delivery outfit were sticking out of some; a short stack of additional brochures had been dropped carelessly onto the ground. Kovac, Steinmann, Demirel, Bauer, Engelbert, Djabou. The last mailbox could be Constantin's. She ran her fingers over the letters. Their lives overlapped in their common foreignness, yet his wartime experiences in Chad — the kind of war deemed irrelevant to Western movie makers and curricula writers — dug a chasm between them. She hadn't had to come to Germany, but she wondered what things would have been like if she had.

Tweny years earlier

"Come on, Sarah, get your jacket! We're going to be late. Do you have your music book?" Her mom was fixing her makeup in the hall bathroom. Sarah was in the kitchen pouring a glass of milk. She was feeling funny, and not just because her opaque white tights were slipping down her bottom and her heels were rubbing on her shiny black patent leather shoes.

"Come on, Sarah, where are you?"

It felt warm first, almost comforting, before it burned, the backwards flow of her insides, unnatural but oddly relieving. She studied the mess around her feet. Were those Lucky Charms from breakfast? All the colors of the rainbow were visible in the lumpy mush. Patent leather could be easily wiped; thank goodness she wasn't wearing sandals.

"Sarah! Oh dear, are you okay?" Her mom rushed in, putting one hand on her shoulder, the other on her forehead. It was 1:30 on a Sunday. The recital was going to begin at two and they needed a good twenty minutes to get there. She had prepared Mozart's Minuet in D major, K. 355, a short piece with juicy chromaticism but little known history. Planted in her puddle of puke, she was still holding her book of music.

"I'm sorry, mom." Her mouth tasted like smoldering black licorice; she wiggled her tongue. "Now we'll be late."

"Was it just the butterflies in your stomach?" Her mom was on her knees with a wad of paper towels in her hand.

"I'm not nervous." It was her first recital after starting lessons with Ms. Wong a year earlier. Getting nervous hadn't occurred to her; she didn't know she was supposed to.

"Concert pianist," she told grownups who asked her what she wanted to be when she grew up; they would raise their eyebrow, laugh with disbelief or incredulity — some with jealousy, she presumed. Concert pianists, like athletes, were in control of their bodies and not bothered by annoyances like nerves.

"But maybe it was the butterflies." Honesty set in as paper-thin wings flapped inside of her. Did it feel afraid in the darkness of her belly, that butterfly?

"A little stage fright is totally normal."

"Barfing in the kitchen isn't normal!" Only babies were frightened of things. Stages — as abstract and mysterious as monsters or the dark — were supposed to be exciting, not scary. "Now we're going to miss it!"

She had been looking forward to wearing her new flowered dress and playing her minuet, which she'd practiced every day after school for the past month. Mozart was her favorite composer so far, and Ms. Wong had put a silver star in her book and written *Very good!!* for emphasizing the dissonance and delivering the unusual chord progressions with elegance and suspense. Piano was something she could do well, much better than softball or gymnastics. She had finally discovered her God-given talent.

Her mom grabbed a fresh paper towel, wet it in the sink, and wiped her shoes. The older students, who were playing things like sonatas and polonaises from memory, weren't smelling of stomach juices right now.

"Here." A glass of water; just what she needed. "Do you still want to go?"

"If we leave now, and you drive fast, Mom, we'll still make it." She put her empty glass in the sink and headed toward the garage before she could be talked out of it.

February 28

Sarah was holding her toothbrush when she noticed the Schimmel standing there like that, late on a Thursday evening. Not yelling this time, but beckoning, seducing her with its shiny edges and curves to come and touch it.

Her day had been tiring. So much typing gnawed at her tendons, and Stefanie's complaints about a lack of "scrumptious" descriptions in her authors' articles chipped at her self-confidence. She needed something to feel good about.

She placed her toothbrush on the edge of the sink, careful not to smear the toothpaste, and sat down on the bench, pulling it forward underneath her, then pushing it back again until the distance from the keyboard felt comfortable. *Twaap!* The fallboard hiccupped as she opened it and wiped her fingertips on her lap, making a mental note to dust the cover more often.

Herr Steinmann's score had been waiting for her, up there to the right of the music stand. The pages were tanned, just barely brittle enough to suggest the book came from a time long ago. A time that was done and over with.

Sarah massaged the muscle beneath her thumb and briefly considered starting with scales, arpeggios, a Czerny exercise to get the blood flowing and loosen her stiff joints. In music school, she had always begun practice sessions with a complete set of chromatic scales and arpeggios, owning the entire eighty-eight keys, rippling up and down the expanse of the keyboard like an ocean current.

Now, the technical exercises would only trip her up, shame her. She turned past the introduction in the score, where the orchestral part was reduced to piano accompaniment. There was no need to recollect the orchestra and its embarrassed conductor. She wanted to feel the yearning in the opening octave of the piano solo again.

Da-da-da-daa-da-daa. The simple, moving melody churned her insides as the Schimmel sang, its voice slightly muted, but its timbre rich nonetheless. There it was again. Her old friend. Her enemy. Her lost love. It seemed tamer this time, simpler and more ordinary. She played the first dozen bars over and over, each time a bit more imploringly, more delicately and, after a handful of repetitions, with greater self-assurance.

Finally coming to the sixteenth-note runs, she paused, then jumped right in. *Bash!* What a mistake. Perhaps she should have started with hours — or better, with days or weeks — of scales before she attempted to revisit this piece of all pieces. She went back to take the runs more slowly, locking her right and left hands together. Instead of making the keys sparkle, she felt knots pinching her wrists, squeezing her forearms. That night, the first movement had been radiant, nearly flawless. But even that had evaporated under time's rays.

Abruptly, she pulled her hands away from the keyboard and let the fallboard drop with a thud, sealing her weakness in its black box.

Sarah went to the bathroom, where her toothbrush was still wet, and sat down on the closed toilet seat to brush her teeth. Maybe she should give up on the piano altogether and do something she'd never be good at, like cycling or sewing or spelunking. Then *average* would be okay and there would never be pressure to be more. Now, though, she should get some sleep, if she could keep the gargoyles from disrupting her dreams. Tomorrow she had another date with Theo, and she wanted her head to be clear enough to see through the shellac of nonchalance he wore so well.

March 1

"The tree is really gorgeous, and the lighting is perfect," Theo said sarcastically, his hands on his hips. His dark sunglasses made the lighting relative.

The black-and-white photograph depicted a stoic, fully nude woman with voluminous curly hair standing next to a cherry blossom tree, although she couldn't actually have been next to it, because they appeared to be exactly the same height.

Sarah would have preferred to see the electric hues of the cherry blossoms in color. Theo was already moving to the next work, "Spheres." Three unclothed men were curled up in a fetal position next to three conspicuously round rocks of just the same size.

Lance, the photographer, was a British guy Theo had gone to art school with (Lance stuck around for the degree). His exhibition, *Naturart,* featured black-and-white nudes with conspicuously unkempt pubic hair juxtaposed with the outdoors.

"We humans forget that we are part of Earth, just like the trees and the rivers." Skinny from cigarettes, wearing a faded black t-shirt and black-washed jeans, Lance looked the part of the believer: Earth and art before self. He opened the vernissage with a few words, timid, but to the point.

"You just invited me because of the naked people," Sarah teased Theo as they grabbed drinks at the beverage table, Sarah a sparkling wine, Theo a matcha tea because his head was throbbing. A DJ was mixing New Age sounds in the corner, music like an e-cigarette, an ambiguous, addictive vapor.

"You Americans think nudity is sex. But in Germany, sex is a lot more chill, you know, and nudity is" — Theo was blushing in spite of his detachment — "nothing. Skin isn't ugly, but it's boring as hell because it's not the point. That's probably why it makes such a good canvas."

"It wasn't until I walked through the English Garden for the first time that I realized how unsexy skin is." Clothing is optional in one section of Munich's largest public park. She'd studied the sky instead, its voluptuous spring clouds, as she pierced the dewy grass with her heels. Sarah wondered whether the monkey was Theo's only tattoo.

"It sucks that it's too cold for that now. A naked nap in the park would be the perfect hangover cure." He rubbed his nose with his thumb and forefinger. "Remind me never, ever to touch whisky again."

"What did you get up to last night?" She tried to sound disinterested.

"A bunch of us were just hanging out at Sven's place, playing Playstation and drinking a few beers. Then Daniel came over with the whisky."

"Who's Daniel?"

"Daniel can get us a venue for The Theo and Sarah Show. He works at this concept store in Schwabing and they've got some sleek events going on. Fucking good way to sell stuff, entertaining people out of their money. And they have a piano. Or maybe it's a keyboard. I mean, is there really a difference?"

"I don't think Elton John would perform on a keyboard." Sarah was irked that he didn't know the difference. She tried to imagine Poulenc or Chopin without hammers and strings, among overpriced vases and socks, drenched in long drinks and *au gratin* with Theo's colorful quotes.

"So that's a yes?"

He stroked her hair, then slid his hand down to the small of her back.

"Yeah, I think so." She leaned into the curve of his arm, badly wanting his attractiveness to make up for his faults, wanting him to erase her aloneness. He pulled back and she nearly stumbled.

"Oh fuck, I'll be right back." Déjà-vu. This time, sparkling wine with Enya instead of drum and bass.

Standing alone, Sarah watched the other guests staring contemplatively at the photos, chatting subduedly in English, German, Czech, Portuguese. They were predominantly dressed in black, punctuated by bulky white sneakers, in solidarity with the artist and his chosen colors. Despite the relaxing music, she sensed tension between her shoulders and the base of her neck and consciously released it. She used to be much better at whole body muscle control.

Ten minutes later and a shade paler, Theo returned, squinting without his sunglasses, his irises rimmed with Cola brown.

"You didn't..." She was more disgusted than amused.

"Fuck Daniel and his whisky." He wiped the corner of his mouth with the back of his hand. "Don't you dare tell Lance I puked at his party."

MARCH 4

Sarah pushed the stop button with her thumb and put her ear buds in her bag. She hated to cut a song off in the middle, especially when James Bay was inviting her to put her hands on his body, but she was late. It was just past five and she didn't want to put a dent in Herr Steinmann's positive first impression of her punctuality if she could help it.

"Thank you for coming, Sarah." He was flushed under his ears and on the tips of his nostrils as he stood by the open door, leaning on his cane with both hands, the palm of one pressing on the back of the other.

They stood out immediately, the alstroemerias shoulder to shoulder with dahlias, a rose or two for good measure (orange, not red, of course), clothed in nameless greens. We admire flowers, like sunsets, because their perishability, unlike ours, is temporary: The plant reblooms, even when we do not.

Herr Steinmann would have to push the bouquet to the side to make room for their cups on the table. Sarah offered to carry the tray of coffee from the kitchen since he wasn't feeling "so perky."

"My drowsiness last time was certainly no consequence of your company. I do hope you weren't offended. My medication, you see. I'm terribly sorry, but I don't feel up to playing today." The concession was equally as hard for him as the musical abstinence.

Sarah was disappointed; Mozart would have been a rhinestone on her muslin Monday. He was paler than usual, his skin the color of rain-laden clouds, a faint white stubble covering his cheeks like fog.

"The bouquet is from my daughter in Bonn. Lovely, isn't it? Especially this time of year, when spring is taking its time. They haven't yet planted the flowers in the gardens at the Nymphenburg Palace down the street, so it's refreshing to have a bit of color in here." A card with a printed message was sticking out of the vase: *Best wishes from Silke, Thomas and Moritz.*

"She is very busy." A vicarious excuse in absentia. "They are restructuring her department at work again, I believe, and things aren't easy at home either. Moritz — that's my grandson — has had some issues with drugs and he is living with his parents again. And to think, he finally had a good job at Aldi. In my day, that was not something to throw away."

She couldn't console with more than "I'm sorry;" substance addiction was the stuff of hearsay. The police officers had come to her fifth grade class, filling up the threshold with their tight-sleeved blue uniforms. "Just say no," they'd urged, pointing to pictures of heroin-scarred faces. Converted and readied with role plays, Sarah had never had the opportunity to say no. The wrong crowd hadn't taken a chance on her.

"He is my only grandson."

"And your son in Berlin… he doesn't have any children?" Sarah asked cautiously. She sensed the strain between Herr Steinmann and his children, but couldn't yet place where it came from.

"Jürgen?! Goodness, no. He was married to a woman once, very briefly, in his late twenties. She was lovely, studying to become a chemist. But then he decided he would rather be homosexual, or had been the whole time, I suppose. I think he always thought I held that against him, when in fact I am the last person to think any less of him for it." A pause like a musical rest in the middle of a phrase. "He moved to Berlin to become a painter. He would have been a good father, but that door closed for him a long time ago."

"You mentioned you haven't seen your son…"

"Bavaria is too conservative for him."

"… but what about your daughter? Does she visit you in Munich?"

"The last time Silke came to Munich was… well, she came for her mother's funeral, of course. That was nearly ten years ago now. And once after that to check up on me. She does call about once a month, to fill me in on things at Deutsche Post, since she works for my former employer, as I told you." He looked out the window as a cloud drifted in front of the weak pre-spring sun. "She likes basket-ball, you know, from America. And jazz."

Sarah called her parents at least once a week, sometimes two or three times when her evenings gaped in her reticent apartment. They were displaced by nine hours. She often woke them, being the only early riser in the family, but they always said they didn't mind.

"Is Silke the older or younger girl in the picture?" Sarah pointed to the gold frame on the side table.

"Silke is the oldest. Jürgen is two years younger. And Gerda was our nest egg." His cup clinked against the saucer. "She passed away when she was three. Leukemia. Fortunately for her, it went quickly." A matter of fact, like his breakfast of rye bread with salami, a sentence from a history book he'd memorized and repeated, one answer to a hundred questions from a hundred mouths. He wiped his nose with his handkerchief, coughing into it several times. His voice softened. "Hannelore was never the same. You don't recover from losing a child. Gerda's death affected Jürgen much more than he would ever admit. He was only five at the time, but that is a very tender age. Silke was always the strong one, the oldest. She had to be there for her mother. Jürgen was the type to suffer silently."

"You have lost many people." Her chest tightened. Sadness would, one day, not skip over her either.

His smile was empty, his cheeks concave. "Time gives and takes, dear Sarah. You have already lost music, you say. With time, you will find it again, I am sure. Or it will find you. Getting to be as old as I am is both a gift and a curse. Others my age long for the past, but I don't do that. I miss Gerda and especially my Hannelore very much, but we will be together again soon. Very soon. Until then, I have no choice but to go about today, now do I?"

His eyes were glassy, nearly transparent, as he tapped his foot inaudibly on the charred yellow and orange pattern on the rug. "That is why I appreciate music. It only exists in the moment and then it is gone, not like a painting that you can stare at for hours and come back to and it is always the same. Music forces you to think about neither the past nor the future, and every time you play music in the present, it is slightly altered."

She had never thought about it like that. "You're right. Even a recording is played linearly and then ends." James Bay's body was suspended on her phone.

"It's unfortunate that we can't play today. But Constantin is right, I shouldn't overdo it. He will be a good doctor, that boy." He rose suddenly, but feebly. "That doesn't mean we can't listen! We don't have to neglect our Wolfgang. I have quite a lovely version of *The Magic Flute* here. Would you be so kind? It's on the second shelf from the top, the fourth record from the left."

There must have been a hundred records on the shelves that spanned from the floor to the ceiling, but Sarah found *The Magic Flute* exactly where he'd said it would be. She read on the flat square cover that Otto Klemperer had conducted the Philharmonia Chorus and Orchestra with Lucia Popp as Queen of the Night in 1964, the same year her parents were born. A time long ago when Mozart was already old hat.

"Without a doubt the best recording of *The Magic Flute*. Klemperer was a wreck by 1964, you know. He'd had a brain tumor and was paralyzed after a bad fall and from burning himself in bed with a cigarette and then pouring alcohol on the flames. Can you imagine doing such a horrible thing?! It is said that he was sharp-tongued and harsh, perhaps because his injuries forced him to conduct sitting down. But in my opinion the honesty and purity of his conducting is unmatched," said Herr Steinmann.

Sarah gingerly pulled the first record from the cover, as if it was by association also accident prone, unsure of where to place her fingers on the humungous chunk of vinyl. Even though she'd listened to dozens of records in the music school library, tediously navigating through the stacks to coordinates like H21.B67 or S8569-N, the obsolete discs still seemed like museum-worthy artifacts that should hardly be touched.

"Please play '*O zittre nicht, mein lieber Sohn.*' It should be among the first tracks." Herr Steinmann couldn't hide his eagerness. "It's not the most famous aria, '*Der Hölle Rache,*' as I'm sure you know, but it is quite beautiful nonetheless. The Queen of the Night is pleading with Prince Tamino to rescue her daughter Pamina, if you recall, who has been kidnapped by Sarastro."

Placing the record on the player in the corner of the room, Sarah lowered the needle ever so slowly, her hand shaking lest she miss the groove that held the product of genius. She would have made a poor surgeon. It struck her how being a listener used to be a tactile experience, but had become passive — a mere twitch of the thumb was hardly enough to command commitment all the way to the double bar line in a culture accustomed to zapping.

As it played, Sarah remembered that she was familiar with the aria; her left pinky had been the upright basses, her right the flutes for more than one aspiring Queen of the Night at music school. This time, however, one line of the libretto stood out in particular:

Zum Leiden bin ich auserkoren,
denn meine Tochter fehlet mir [2]

Sarah couldn't help but think of Gerda.

Herr Steinmann rolled his eyes and grunted. "Operas were the Hollywood of the era," he said. "Someone always needed to be rescued."

She snickered, picturing a plump diva singing a coloratura aria under a palm tree on the Walk of Fame. "But a magic flute would be a wonderful thing, don't you think? A flute that can change sadness into happiness."

"It would indeed." He rubbed the stubble on his chin with his thumb and forefinger. "But sometimes sorrows are more valuable than we care to acknowledge. We can laugh more sincerely after our tears have dried. Not that I would wish you sadness in your life, Sarah, but I've found that it is unavoidable."

They listened to the remainder of the aria in silence, sipping their now lukewarm coffee, careful not to drown out the vibrato with the *clink-clink* of their cups.

"May I ask you something, Herr Steinmann?" Her curiosity had dug under the fence around her thoughts, creeping in while she was answering emails at work, searching for sleep at night. "Why do you keep the clasp from your Hitler Youth neckerchief in your bathroom? Isn't it a reminder of so many other people's suffering? They had no magic flute."

He cleared his throat and stretched both of his forearms out onto the armrests, gripping them with his fingers.

"Let me tell you two stories," he began slowly. "The first is of a fourteen-year-old boy who was good at math and music and liked to read *Faust*. I'm sure even the Americans are familiar with Goethe, are they not? The boy couldn't kick a football in a straight line to save his life and could count his friends on one hand. Or perhaps on one finger, to be frank."

[2] I am chosen for suffering for my daughter is gone from me.

A fourteen-year-old boy named Otto Steinmann, she thought to herself, nodding toward him with a sideways smile.

"Then the boy became one of thousands, eventually millions, that put on the same uniform. Perhaps we'd been millions of outsiders. Or maybe the boy had been the only one. One night during a camping trip, I, I mean the boy, was sharing a tent with another boy named Karl Maurer. We had arrived after dusk as strangers, but had managed to set up the tent together in the dark without any help. It would have taken a monsoon to knock that thing over after we were finished with it! 'Otto,' he said just before we drifted off to sleep, after the birds and grasshoppers had stopped their chirping for the evening, 'It is good that you are here. Together, you know, together we can do great things.' I was an only child and hadn't experienced real camaraderie before. At that young age, I needed someone else to believe in me, someone who wasn't my mother, and I desperately needed to belong. I later learned that belonging is perhaps the mightiest tool in the world, a feeling so beautiful that it is nearly always abused by the powerful, the dictators and the tyrants."

Sarah opened her mouth, then bit down on her unspoken words, her hasty assessment, because she and the boy were not so dissimilar.

His gaze jolted from the photograph of his children to her. "Just look at America. You call yourselves the greatest country in the world, so that everyone feels like they belong to something extraordinary. But unless we understand that 'great' comes in many different varieties, our arrogance will be our downfall. We Germans know..."

We pay a lot more tax than Americans, Franzi had pointed out once to Sarah at work, but at least we get something for our money here in Germany, she'd said, tuition-free universities, well repaired roads, subsidy upon never-ending subsidy for having children.

"Many Americans think Germans are socialists, and many Germans think Americans are Bible-thumping hypocrites," reflected Sarah.

"Democracy has many faces. And ours bear scars. Both of them. I'll never forget the day I had to come to grips with what had happened. It was July 4, 1956. America's Independence Day, am I right? I was visiting my mother in the hospital. She had been ill for some time and passed away a month or so later. Just as I was leaving the building, an old neighbor of ours was walking in, Gerhard Schulz. He was about my age and was also there visiting his mother, or his grandmother, I don't remember exactly. I hadn't seen him since the war. He told me about his three children and his wife, a girl we'd gone to school with. Then I asked him about Simon, another boy from our neighborhood. They'd been close friends; they did everything together. 'Didn't you know?' he asked me, quite flabbergasted that I didn't. 'He was killed at Dachau. He and his whole family were taken there,' Gerhard said. Of course, I'd known, or heard, that he was Jewish, but..."

Sarah inhaled sharply. It wasn't a gasp; Simon's fate didn't shock her. During her second week in Munich, before she started her job at *Fork & Messer*, she had made a point of taking a guided tour of the memorial site in Dachau. There wasn't even a skeleton left of the former concentration camp, where over forty-thousand people lost their lives during the Holocaust. Barracks had been razed, but the gas chamber and incinerators remained as testimony to the lives they'd swallowed, the skin and bones they'd chewed.

"Dachau is so close. How could you have not known for over a decade?" Her question was provocative, even accusatory, but if silence was complicity, the accomplices had to answer for it.

He folded his hands in his lap. A prayer; a saint. His countenance revealed nothing in particular. "I knew that some of our neighbors were taken away. Of course we knew that. And I knew they did unspeakable things nearby in Dachau. But I didn't think about it. None of us wanted to think about it. That would have meant questioning everything, and what would we have had left? We suffered during the war, too. But that day I accepted just how evil we had been. I saw the humans inside those gaunt bodies wearing the striped suits and yellow stars. And I regretted" — was that a tear swelling at the corner of his eyelid? — "what I had not done."

He smiled grievously and raised a hand, vaguely gesturing toward the other end of the apartment. "You asked me why I keep the old woggle from my Hitler Youth days. A person is never just one thing, you know. That little piece of leather holds both one of the best and one of the worst feelings I've ever had. Bits of leather in and of themselves are neither bad nor good, but I don't want to forget either of those feelings."

Once again they sat in silence, this time without Mozart's coloratura to fill the void, until Sarah stood and wished Herr Steinmamn a good evening. The dichotomy of the braided leather could not be summed up tidily on a museum plaque, she thought as she tied her shoes in the entry, down on one knee. Her coat was tucked awkwardly under her elbow, threatening to fall onto the floor. She likely would have kept it, too, she thought as she strained her neck to look up at him.

As she plodded down the wide wooden staircase on her way out, she noticed that the woman who lived one floor down had placed a decorative pot of fresh lavender in front of her door, the sweet, earthy scent overwhelming the mustiness in the stairway. Sarah descended and pulled open the heavy door to the house.

Something kept nagging her and, standing by the mailboxes, she pulled out her phone to google the conductor, Otto Klemperer. Like so many great musicians of his time, he too had fled the Nazis early on, Sarah found, in 1933. His conversion to Catholicism hadn't been enough to ensure the regime would overlook his Jewish roots. Sarah also read that he'd lived in Los Angeles during the war, but never adjusted to life there. The musical ideas and ideals were too different, the sun too harsh, the smiles too fit for films. Just because he was forced out of his home country didn't mean he cherished his refuge, but did he ever feel at home again? Or was his home the baton in his hand?

Sarah put her phone away as she walked to the bus stop and watched the sky as dusk rapidly erased the colors of the day.

MARCH 11

Restlessness was jittering her joints like caffeine. Sarah's scowling Schimmel and unfed fridge were all that was waiting for her at home. What does a whole decade of aloneness do to a person? Did Herr Steinmann nag himself, mindfully keep his finger out of his nose, set a second plate at the table, as if it weren't so? It was after four on a Monday afternoon, but he had canceled with the only excuse that didn't scratch the holiness of their dates: a doctor's appointment.

"Hey Christoph, what are you up to?" Sarah was leaning back in her desk chair, stretching her arms, calling through the open door as he passed by in the hall without stopping. Christoph took two steps backward and stuck his head into her office, leaning against the door frame.

"Retouching the *Apfelstrudel* photos that Franzi took for our project. It might taste good with ice cream, but the stuff makes a shitty looking photo model." He planted both feet in her office. "I mean that literally."

"I believe it! Sauerkraut doesn't make for great pics either. I just finished editing that long read that Stefanie wanted at the back of the next edition. The one about sauerkraut in different countries. I mean, at least the Koreans managed to get kimchi on the superfoods list, but the Germans kind of dropped the marketing ball with their sauerkraut, don't you think?"

"Pairing it with sausage doesn't exactly give it a bikini-body image," agreed Christoph.

"After spending all afternoon nipping and tucking that article, the last thing I feel like eating is sauerkraut." And certainly not with a fatty sausage.

"I feel like almost all of the food pictures that go across my desk are too perfect. They look too fake to eat."

"They look like plastic. But with more calories."

"You don't have to worry about calories."

"Well, thanks, but…" But she was thin *because* she worried about them. "You know what I need right now is a change of scenery — you know, a *Tapetenwechsel*. Have you ever been to the Nymphenburg Palace?" The palace was Herr Steinmann's neighbor, a way to keep him company without intruding.

"Yeah, of course. Tourists go there by the bus load. Gardens, swans, statues. Hell, there's even a gondola I had to ride in once when my cousin was in town. I'm down for heading there now. Let me just send one last email and then we can skedaddle."

She hadn't necessarily meant to go *with* Christoph, but why not? "Okay, I'll meet you downstairs in ten." Done deal.

They got off the tram next to a small canal that led up to the palace grounds. The air was crisp — Christoph called it *frisch* — and the wind unkind, but the sky was warm with the promise of spring. Winter was looking over its shoulder as it turned to leave. The canal fed into a square pond in the shadow of the Baroque palace, where a dozen swans strained their necks against the gusts, anchoring themselves in the water that was tossing its white crest.

"Are swan like fish?" Christoph teetered as they stopped in front of the birds, hands deep in his pockets, shifting his weight from foot to foot.

"Pretty much. Except that they breathe air and can fly."

"No, no, I mean like deer."

"Yep. Except for the antlers and the legs."

"I just mean the word — one swan, two swan? Or one swan, two swans?"

"Oh, right! Swan, swans. Good question. I don't know why, but they both sound right to me." She would have to google the plural of swan later. "They can be mean, you know. I was bitten by one as a child."

"Ouch! What happened?"

"I was about four. It is one of my earliest memorics. I was staying with my grandmother for the afternoon. Her drinking got really bad not long after that and my parents stopped letting her babysit. Anyway, I gave that gorgeous, innocent-looking swan a piece of my cracker and it just twisted its long neck, snapped at me and drew enough blood to fill a few Band-Aids. It didn't even want my cracker."

"That must've been pretty traumatic at that age."

"I stopped feeding swans after that. Nana just wiped my tears and promised to take me to the *Swan Lake* ballet when I got older. 'It's about a princess who becomes a swan,' she told me. I found out later, at music school, that she's a swan because she's under a curse and was failed by her potential rescuer."

"That doesn't sound like much of a children's story."

"No, it doesn't." And not so unlike her unhappy grandmother, thought Sarah.

Several large busses were parked in the lot to their left, groups of tourists bunching their coats together at their necks as they kneeled to get closeup shots of the regal white birds. Did any of them turn back into princesses during the night, Sarah wondered. As she and Christoph watched from behind the visitors, two Canada geese landed on the rippling water, braking with their wings and skidding with their feet as if they were landing gear.

The palace looked smaller than she had imagined. A gilded main building zigzagged to the right and left, where it was flanked in a U-shape on either side by additional buildings in a similar, less pompous style. Mozart had kicked up this dust with his child-size heels. Did he chase the birds and jump in the puddles like other boys?

"Not bad for a vacation home." Christoph shrugged as they turned toward the palace, for decades a summer residence for Bavarian rulers, a quaint getaway from the pre-sewerage urban stench. Such Baroque pomp — even the bed pans were ornate — was a page out of a Brothers Grimm for a New World newcomer, something Sarah's parents and their neighbors would coo over.

They passed through the gate at the ground level of the middle building and entered the garden area on the other side. Tall wooden containers, protecting the statues within them from freezing temperatures, lined the staircase up to the palace and the square grass area beyond it. From the garden side, the U vanished and the main palace building was an architectural triptych with three burnt orange roofs shaped like pyramids. Winter had draped a veil over the estate, muting its charm, but not its kingliness.

"I used to come here to take photos." Christoph pointed to the left, beyond the canal that rolled out before the palace like a runway. Then he put his fist to his mouth, a fleshy microphone, for his sold-out tour group of one: "To your left, ladies and gentlemen, acres of forest are a haven for wildlife like deers — I mean, deer — now that no blue-blooded hunters are there to kill them. And to your right, an expansive botanical garden with trees, flowers and cacti whose names I should know but, sadly, have long since forgotten."

Tour over. "When the sun shines just after a snowfall, you can take some really nice photos here," he continued in his normal voice. "It was a good exercise in camera settings for me. Then I saw what some of the pros do out here. I'm talking light years away from my novice attempts. So I gave up and tried other motifs." There is always someone better, because perfection is not monogamous.

They walked along the canal, passing a number of after-work joggers and dog walkers. A family with a toddler in a stroller and two older children, a boy and a girl, had stopped to get a closer look at the geese plucking blades of grass at the water's edge. Silke, Jürgen, Gerda: They were about the same ages in the photo. The kids' father, on one knee, his head level with his daughter's, was pointing toward the birds, out of earshot for Sarah. What was it like to lose a child? To an abstract, unseen illness; to differences of character not compensated for by genetics.

"What's on your mind?" He broke the silence that hadn't been uncomfortable. With Christoph, talking and not talking were equally normal.

"Do you have any brothers or sisters?"

"Nope, only child. Can't you tell?"

"You don't strike me as an only child." Not that they were this or that. Only Theo fit the stereotype of the self-centered singling, although his only-childness was a matter of perspective.

"I spent a lot of time with my cousins, so it felt like I came from a bigger family. But, one day I'll have lots of kids. Ten, maybe twelve." His smile was sprinkled with a grain of truth, a speck of humor.

One boy, one girl, a perfectly squared family; that was Sarah's ideal, although *parent* was something other people were.

"Back in the old days, when the kings were living in this palace, children would die all the time. That was common, but how could a parent deal with losing so many children?"

"You lost me there."

"Take Mozart, for example. He had six children, but four of them died when they were infants." Her own existence was like a collision of asteroids in space, one in a million, billion — because a hidden virus or malformation claimed one child but not the other, because her great-great-grandfather was bursting at the groin on a Tuesday and not a Friday. Arne from the ground floor could just as easily have been the victim of his brother's bullet; fate twists and turns before it strikes.

"Mozart?"

"I've been thinking about Mozart lately." She wasn't making sense, but trusted that he could handle it.

"I don't know about Mozart's kids, but if they'd been born a couple centuries later, they could've just popped a few pills and Mozart would've had to buy the minivan after all. Still, it's not like we're invincible now with modern medicine. My grandmother died last year after getting some small infection."

"Sorry to hear that." There it was again. Death had a way of turning up everywhere. She thought of her own grandmother, her father's mother, who had left her a small inheritance. Was it really breast cancer, or had she helped things along like Odette in *Swan Lake*?

"My grandparents lived close to here," said Christoph. "When I was a kid, they would take me to the botanical garden over there. Boring as hell for a boy who just wanted to ride his bike and play Tetris. But my grandfather knew a lot about the plants — where this cactus came from, when the flowers bloomed on this tree or that tree. Now that he's gone, I wish I could remember some of it."

The canal came to an end and, as they turned to loop back down its other side, they could see the palace, framed in a corridor of bare trees, dwarfed by the distance.

"The view never gets old." He halted to rest in it, inhaling the chilly air, soaking up the shared experience. The tips of his nose and ears were painted pink by the cool air, except for the unmissable freckle on his left earlobe. "So you won't tell me why you're so obsessed with Mozart?"

"I…" Herr Steinmann wasn't exactly a secret, so why did it feel weird to be talking about him? "I meet up every Monday with an elderly man to play the piano — works for one piano, four hands, and so far we've only played Mozart." No need to go into detail about her previous misadventures with the wunderkind composer. "He had to cancel today's rehearsal."

"Well, I guess the palace isn't a bad substitute for Mozart." He could sense the underbelly of her words. Did he also see her aloneness — despised, yet desperately clung to for the comfort of its familiarity — in the way she adjusted her raisin-colored hair and tore furtively at her fingernails?

"So the elderly Mozart guy showed me old pictures of himself in a Hitler Youth uniform. He said he later fought in the war, too. Would you say that made him a Nazi back then?"

"You Americans love talking about World War Two. And we Germans can't shake it. Not that we necessarily should." Can't look, can't look away — was it the human fascination with horror, or the American obsession with its own self-righteousness? "Imagine having to salute the *Führer* at work and dress your kids in those uniforms, knowing every single neighbor in your building is a groupie. It's hard to picture now just how much power the Nazis had during that time."

"But the murders in their backyards? There's no excuse for ignoring them."

"No, there isn't. But was it that straightforward? I mean, were you either for them or against them? I'm sure there were people who didn't agree, but weren't brave enough to speak out. Otto Schindler and Corrie Ten Boom are famous because they were rare. I've wondered whether I would have been as brave as them."

"In Herr Stein… I mean, the man's album, I found a photograph of what I think is an African-American GI. The year 1946 was written on it, right after the war. He looks like a friend of his."

"So you mean he was a Nazi but not a hardliner? Or maybe he was a spy!"

"He said he wasn't political. He was young at the time. But he still joined, still saluted, still wore that uniform. How can someone be part of something so horrible and then do a total one-eighty? Can people change so quickly?" She remembered what Herr Steinmann had said about Helene Bechstein, who adored Hitler so much that she lived in Obersalzberg, the Führer's favorite place in the German Alps, after the war until her death, even after she'd been fined by a civilian denazification court. Not everyone changed.

A group of smaller birds waddled across the path in front of them, more like ducks than geese, except for their black, gray and white coloring.

Christoph tugged on his collar until it covered the back of his neck. "Don't underestimate what the war did to people. My grandmother donated money every month to some organization for mentally disabled children here in Munich, even after she had retired and was on a fixed income. She told me she did it because, when the Nazis were in power, a disabled girl lived next door to them. My grandmother was really young at the time, but she remembers that one day the girl was just gone. Disappeared. It wasn't until much later that she understood that the girl had been murdered."

"So she tried to atone for what happened?"

He ran his fingers thoughtfully through his short brown hair. "The thing is that my grandmother was actually a quarter Jewish herself. I think it was her grandfather who'd been a Jew. So her family spent the war posing as full Germans and hoping nobody found them out. It almost worked, too. But in late '44, her father was arrested on some bogus charge and she never saw him again. She never found out what happened to him."

"So she was actually a victim herself, but still felt responsible?"

"She wasn't just a German or just a Jew." A memory lit his face. "She used to make her own *Maultaschen* — those dumplings that are filled with meat and vegetables. I would sit in the kitchen with her and she'd tell me that in every batch she would make several different kinds — some with meat and vegetables, some with spinach and onions. And she would talk about how you have to bite first, and how you never know what's inside of a *Maultasche* or a person just by looking at them. It sucked for me though because I hated onions as a kid and never knew which *Maultaschen* they were in."

Sarah's Nana had never cooked, but her parents kept their visits so short that it wouldn't have been necessary. Instead of family recipes, her house had smelled of Nivea face cream, cigarette butts and stale rum.

"The Mozart guy said something like that, too. I should just ask him who the American soldier is, but I only saw the photo because I secretly flipped through the album when he fell asleep in his chair."

"So you're a spy." He smiled and raised a finger in a feigned rebuke.

She held up her palm in self-defense. "I was curious. He kept the leather clasp from his Hitler Youth neckerchief. It was shamelessly displayed on the shelf in his bathroom. I didn't have to snoop to find that. He said he kept it because being in the Hitler Youth made him feel for the first time like he belonged somewhere, but also to remind himself of what happened during the Holocaust, of what he didn't do."

"The world would be safer if we all could just shake that outsider feeling."

"I hear what you're saying," agreed Sarah. "Hitler… all the power freaks, really — just look at Russia or Hungary or Turkey or even *The President* — rise up because they preach belonging to a whole congregation of outsiders."

"Yeah. Maybe we'd all get along if we could drop the hyper emotional connection to each other," said Christoph.

They crossed over a short bridge where the canal intersected with a creek and found themselves back at the palace. The sky was dimming, clouds rolling in like high tide; a raindrop burst on Sarah's cheek, just under her eye. The family with three children was passing through the palace gate, the mother pushing the stroller, the oldest riding on a seat attached to it. The father was carrying the middle child, her face buried in his neck, either sleeping or pouting. Christoph would make a good father, steady, admirable.

Back at the tram station, the streetlights glowed like winter's fireflies, ignoring the last trace of sunlight. They watched the cars drive by as they waited for the tram, making a game of guessing the cities on the license plates, each marked with a one-, two-, or three-letter city code.

"What's BN?" Sarah pointed to a midnight blue Volkswagen Golf. "I see a lot of those."

"That's Bonn. You see them here because the Deutsche Post is headquartered in Bonn, so all their company cars have BN."

"Bonn. Beethoven was born there. Schumann died there. And that's where the Mozart guy's daughter lives."

"You really should ask him about the guy in the photo. There's gotta be more to that. My grandmother passed away and I wish I had asked her more. I guess I figured she'd be around for a while."

The tram arrived, opening its doors for a trickle of post-rush travelers.

"I'm going to walk home from here, but thanks for hanging out."

There was a thinness, a vulnerability in his voice.

She got on and stood by the door, looking back as it closed in front of her. In the dim light, Christoph's eyes were the color of walnut, his short hair more like oak. She waited until he was out of sight before she checked her phone, a reflex she hated but was unable to reprogram. It wasn't the phone she detested per se, but the perpetual hope for a message, the inevitable disappointment when one came. Theo had written for the first time in several days.

Hey Schätzelein, miss you, hope you had a good weekend. I was at my parents for my mom's birthday. Daniel's working on dates for our gig. I'm going to start painting some new stuff tonight. Can't wait to see you soon.

Schätzelein? A diminutive for darling, old-fashioned and ironic. *Schatz* would have been more typical, but only couples would say that. Which they weren't, right? Sarah felt chemically pulled to him, even to his unpredictability, in spite of herself.

She couldn't wait to take her shoes off, even though no one was waiting at home, no combustible curry, no wine-stained kisses on the couch. Maybe opposites really did attract. Theo's 'work' day — night — was just starting. What could she contribute to The Theo and Sarah Show, The Sarah and Theo Show? Brahms, Beethoven, Debussy, Poulenc — they all made her feel like vomiting in the kitchen.

She typed: **If you want company tonight, I...** Then she erased it and started over: **Happy painting; creativity is in the air. Can I kiss you on Friday?**

She hit send, put in her ear buds, turned on her favorites playlist, and stashed her phone. Damien Rice's "Cannonball" was knit sweater music. Her reflection stared back at her in the window; she tried to look through the pane at the passing houses and not directly at herself.

March 15

He hadn't been to her apartment yet, but then, the kitchen was more productive at his. Sarah was sitting on Theo's couch again on a Friday evening, fingering its canvas cover, watching the giant teddy bear in brown leather shorts. A bear had a hide; it didn't need a *Lederhose*.

Music! Was its absence more unsettling than the fact that they'd forgotten to turn it on?

Theo took their empty plates, smeared with his swear-by spice, to the sink and returned with the wine bottle. Their glasses half full again, the emptied bottle threatened to leave a red ring on the coffee table.

"Have you ever been to the Nymphenburg Palace?" Sarah asked, out of the blue. "I went there for the first time this week." Her walk with Christoph had left a sweet aftertaste.

"Yeah sure. Ace house with a nice yard. The tourists dig it. But I don't necessarily need reminders of monarchy. It's not like things were all *Friede, Freude, Eierkuchen* back then" — peace, joy and pancakes.

"Everything has its dark side." A coin has two sides, a dice six; or history is a sphere, gradual and nuanced, turning from the light side to the dark side without us knowing how it got there.

"You haven't shown me what you painted on Monday night."

Theo ran his fingers through his hair, pressing his palm against his head, and looked at her intensely. Sarah didn't look away.

"I'd sat down to paint a fucking simple 'Life's better at the beach' or some happy-go-lucky crap like that. But then this came out." He took her hand, leading her into his bedroom. The bed was unmade, jeans were slouching on a chair in the corner. No art was hung, but five or six paintings were leaning against the wall. He grabbed the outer canvas from the stack, laying it on the bed. It showed the back of a strikingly realistic woman; straight, dark hair, neither short nor long; her arms stretched out to either side, embracing an ocean in front of her.

"It's you. But it's not finished." The sea was just an outline, waiting to be churned by its creator; an ambiguous sky on a day that hadn't yet decided what mood it was in.

"Don't worry, I'm not a freaky stalker or anything." He put his hand on her hip, his warmth permeating her jeans. "I don't do people, so this was out of my vein."

"I've never seen myself from the back before." It struck her that he had spent Monday night with her hair, shoulders, elbows.

"The ocean is all of the options you have. It's big and mean and powerful, but you're ready to navigate it."

"And there are a million ways to cross an ocean," she realized. "No roads, no lanes, no stop signs." It dawned on her that she was completely alone on the canvas.

He brushed her hair behind her ear, kissing her deeply, filling her mouth with his. Feeling his fingers under her shirt, she unhooked her bra. He scooped her breasts into his hands, caressing her face. It happened in one phrase, under the expanse of a single slur, and then her torso was bare and she felt herself unbuttoning his pants, stroking the space between his pelvic bone and his waistband.

She pushed his jeans down to his knees and saw the second tattoo — numbers, letters, a couple of circles and lines. She slipped out of her pants before he was all the way out of his. They made love hastily on half of the unmade bed, a *ménage à trois* with the painting, still spreading itself out across the half creased by sleep.

As he plunged into her, she buried her nose in his chest. His skin was soft, squishy, odd smelling. A distraction. It wasn't the day's perspiration or acrylic residue; it was him. Like in the moment before a performance, or the corridor ahead of sleep, images strobed inside her eyes. Her third semester boyfriend with a disappointingly small penis and overcompensating ego; Herr Steinmann who possessed the liberating sexlessness of old age; the full lips of yesterday's bakery clerk that could grasp a cigarette, or theoretically her collar bone, but not an English *th*.

As Theo's breathing grew heavier, he leaned into her and she reached for the wall. His thrusts were confident, almost rehearsed, and he came coarsely, collapsing onto her.

She could have used more time; the white dildo under her bed never rushed her. Fingertips pressed into his back, she clung to the togetherness, trying not to inhale.

"You're just as hot as I'd imagined." He bit her nipples as he slid out, not noticing the incompleteness, one foot already on the floor. She had imagined it differently.

Sarah pulled her top over her braless breasts, her nipples burning against the cotton, and retrieved her panties from the floor. When she returned from the bathroom, she found him completely naked, standing at the open window in the living room, savoring his cigarette as if it were a praline.

He'd put on music by German electronic pioneers Kraftwerk. The ceiling light was harsh after the forgiving darkness of the bedroom. The unshaven hairs on his chest and belly had a reddish tinge, curling in all directions. She traced his tattoo with her index finger, curving around the left side of his waist at his lowest rib: 48°08'8.40" N 11°34'18.59" E.

"Where is it?"

"Right here. The center of Munich." He blew the smoke out of the side of his mouth and into the night, tapping the ashes onto the street below. "I don't need to stay in this city forever, but it needs to stay in me."

"Or on you." She envied his bond to a place, any place, trusted like a sandbox friend. She owned no coordinates of her own.

"And the monkey?"

"It's technically a lion-tailed macaque from India. They're endangered; they're practically all gone. All monkeys are fun and smart, but this one is especially awesome because it's so rare. They live at the tops of the trees, far away from us human polluters, and the silver mane makes them look royal. The fucking Prince William of the monkey world." He grinned at his arm.

"When I was seventeen, I wanted to get a sixteenth note on my ankle. Now that seems ridiculous." What would she have tattooed over it, covering it up like one of youth's many blunders? Taking her wine glass from the table, she swirled it and drank the last sip; the sediment had settled to the bottom and it tasted chalky.

"There's an extra toothbrush in the cupboard above the sink if you want to stay." He nodded toward the bathroom, brushing an unruly, sweat-dampened curl off his forehead.

Sarah swallowed a cough. "Thanks, but I think I'll head home."

March 18

The door was cracked when she reached the landing, but he wasn't there. An invitation or an accident?

"Hello? Herr Steinmann?" A sweet aroma — simple sugar laced with the anticipation of a pleasant surprise — greeted her first. He appeared, wiping his hands on a kitchen towel, as she hung up her leather jacket.

"I hope you don't mind, but I prepared something delicious to go with our coffee."

"Smells like something special!" Sarah followed him into the kitchen, which was long and narrow, a square wooden table and two chairs at the far end, a *Süddeutsche newspaper*, a magnifying glass, an empty coffee cup and saucer. One of each. A large, flat pan occupied the gas stove, drawing attention to itself with its perfume, holding what appeared to be a pancake that had sadly gone awry. What a pity.

"*Kaiserschmarrn!*" announced Herr Steinmann, pronouncing it slowly and rolling the double R, tasting each syllable. He plopped large portions of the golden chunks onto two plates and gave them a dusting of powdered sugar from a metal shaker — miniature models of Alpine passes, covered in late winter snow.

"It's actually from Austria, like our friend Mozart. Since you have a food magazine and a liking for Austrian composers, I thought you should taste the stuff."

Sarah was hungry, but she hadn't gone running in three days. A splurge wasn't part of her plan for today. She had sampled *Kaiserschmarrn* once in a restaurant; it was always a much too generous dish that was both main course and dessert, more for the palate than the eyes. "I could have sworn it was German," she said, swallowing the ball of stress that was rising in her throat.

"As they say, the most famous Germans are actually Austrians."

"Like Hitler." Christoph was right about those six putrid letters always turning up.

"And some of the most famous Germans became Austrians."

"Beethoven!"

"Exactly. Although neither Germany nor Austria existed as such back then, of course. Borders are bought with so much blood, you'd think they'd stick around for longer than they do. *Naja.*"

He smoothed his few wiry hairs, then took an unmarked jar of fruit puree out of the tidy, sparsely packed refrigerator, and carefully added a dollop to the side of each plate. "Homemade apple sauce. Of course, you can use plums or cherries or any kind of fruit, but I prefer apples."

He must have been feeling better; shopping, standing, stirring — banalities became generosities at his age. She carried both plates, which were wooing her empty stomach with their warm aroma. He trailed with a fork in each hand like tiny hiking sticks.

Coffee utensils were crowding the table, so Sarah balanced her plate in her lap while she poured both cups, adding two lumps of sugar to his. Then she bit into a cloud. Made with more eggs and milk than American breakfast pancakes, *Kaiserschmarrn* is fluffier on the inside, scrambled for a caramelized crunch on the outside.

She exhaled. Maybe she would skip dinner or run twice as far tomorrow; the dish was so heavenly, it wasn't just a splurge, but a necessity right now. It would have been perfect if it weren't for the raisins — treat for some, bane for others. She didn't discover them until the second bite, then tried to swallow them whole, their mass a disruption like hail in the cloud.

"I'm very impressed, Herr Steinmann. Delicious!" He hadn't exaggerated his kitchen skills, but he'd had a few years to practice.

"Hannelore loved *Kaiserschmarrn*. Once in a while we would make it for dinner, especially after the children left home. We would take it downstairs to the garden in the summer and sit there for hours, wash it down with a large beer, and watch the sun go down."

"That's a bittersweet combo." She wiped apple sauce from her chin with her thumb.

"Hannelore was like that." He chuckled, taking a large bite. "She had quite a sweet tooth, but she always enjoyed a good beer. She had her feet on the ground, as they say." He pointed with his fork to the wedding picture on the wall. "We were married for fifty-four years."

That was about how old Sarah's parents were, more than twice her age. "How did you meet?" She remembered Theo's fingertips on her elbow, the warm rush of a passing tram.

"At the wedding of a mutual friend. Weddings are romantic, but that had nothing to do with it. We would have fallen in love immediately even if we'd met in the street." His expression was two-fold, like the sky on a rainy day when the sun glares through the clouds, its light magnified by the drops. "We danced all night. Then we both knew we wouldn't be alone any longer."

"But how did you know?" She licked her spoon, pressed it into the powdered sugar on her plate, stirred her coffee with it. If she was going to eat it, then all of it.

"I never asked myself whether Hannelore was right for me because I was so convinced that night that there was no reason to ask."

Two raisins left on the plate were innocently overlooked, more would have been an unfair statement. She held the last unadulterated bite in her mouth, relishing it to the end. Herr Steinmann had stacked his dishes; he was rocking in his armchair, gathering enough momentum to catapult himself to his feet.

"I'm sure you have been missing Mozart. Austrian sugar is the perfect fuel for the Allegretto, wouldn't you agree?" It had been three weeks. If not fondness, absence can breed necessity.

"But how did you know you were in love with Hannelore?" Love at first sight happened in black and white, thought Sarah; it was passed down aurally like centuries-old myths told at silver and gold anniversary parties. She'd had three showers since Friday, but Theo still stuck to her skin.

"I knew. I knew that I knew. And I knew enough to know that I knew that we belonged together. It sounds like nonsense if you've never experienced it, like so many things in life. Love may begin with certainty, but it isn't a well to fall into, not a light that's turned on; it's what you create together over the years — no matter what else happens. Nevertheless, I do believe it's possible, even inevitable, that we will love truly, love deeply, more than once over the course of our lives. Perhaps we become the sum of those we've loved, because they make us the most vulnerable, and the most impressionable."

Sarah first thought of the piano, her first real love, rather than Theo. It had indeed left a mark on her vulnerable self. Herr Steinmann was already adjusting his hips on the bench and reaching his arms to the keyboard to test the distance as she finally stood up to meet it again, the formidable Bechstein.

"Come, Sarah." He ignored her hesitation. "Let's get down to business."

The Allegretto opened with a sweet sing-song melody, a gentle lurch that evoked a stroll through the park, an outing to the lake. It required the light touch that could only come with the security of knowing what comes next. They would have to go through it several times. Herr Steinmann provided the rhythmic foundation as they experimented with their dynamic range, breaking the almost naive simplicity of the main melody with forceful bursts of *forte*. The sixteenth-note passages slipped away from them both, but the long first note of the melody was an anchor. As they reached the end of the movement, Sarah relaxed even more, overdramatizing the quaint dance without poking fun, feeling reckless without letting things get out of control. A simple synchronous *forte* cadence, and the movement was over.

"Brava! That's it, Sarah. You seemed a bit more liberated toward the end, didn't you? I think Wolfgang Amadeus wouldn't have objected. And it certainly didn't hurt our synchronization."

"Sugar high." The tiniest morsels, now a paste, were still between her teeth. But he was right about her loosening up. Like with the idea of an unplanned dessert, she'd just needed a few minutes with the Bechstein to warm to it.

"I spoke with Constantin's mother this week. They live downstairs and can hear us sometimes on Monday evenings. The building is not as well insulated as I'd thought. I apologized, of course, but she said she really quite enjoyed it." He looked pleased with himself. "So I asked her whether she'd like to hear us properly from up here."

"You mean a little concert?" The prospect was immediately more appealing and less daunting than The Theo and Sarah Show. Two on 'stage,' two in the audience, just one piece and not a whole program.

"We could call it that. They would come up one of these Mondays for a bit of Mozart. We would have to choose an appropriate piece of music, of course. Besides the sonatas, Mozart wrote a lovely Theme and Variations for four hands."

"In G major, right?" The last piece in the book; she'd already flipped ahead. The piece appeared playable.

"Exactly." He stood up. "Let me put our recital date in my calendar. Say, four weeks from now? That should give us enough time to prepare." He scribbled in the diary lying open on the dresser next to the record player, pulling aside a crimson ribbon marking the page, the year's twelfth week.

Sarah took the dishes to the kitchen and placed them carefully in the empty sink. The flower design was not particularly beautiful, but the porcelain could have been thirty, forty, even fifty years old, by sheer coincidence or good fortune undropped in all those decades; she didn't want to be the one.

"Have a nice evening, Herr Steinmann." Her lighter jacket, zipped up to block spring's evening chill on her throat, made her feel more agile without the weight of winter.

She had already opened the door when he put his hand on her arm, reminding her of how he'd snatched up her fingertips all of a sudden in the music shop where they'd first met.

"Sarah, if you can't imagine loving him a century from now, when he's as old as I am, then free yourself for something better. And if you do love him, but the world can't imagine you together, then be assured that another, better love will come if you wait — perhaps even sooner than you think." He sure had an uncanny way of reading her. But who was he talking about? The world certainly didn't give a damn about Sarah and Theo, The Theo and Sarah Show, near stand-ups with spectators, Friday-night stands, unfinished portraits.

She turned from the sweet scent of the apartment, inhaling the dust from so many comings and goings on the stairwell. Outside, the sun had just set, caramelizing the sky. Constantin and his mother were a tiny audience in familiar surroundings — a safe cornerstone for her to rebuild on. It was a goal to work toward, the first goal, a safe one.

A squirrel scurried up a tree, startled by her; it was hurried but without a destination except to flee the abstract feeling of peril. She leaned against the oak to type a message:

Hey Theo, thanks for a wonderful...
Delete, delete, delete.

Hey Theo, thanks for a nice evening on Friday. I've been rethinking our collaboration. Not sure it's such a good idea. Let's talk later.

On the bus, she settled into her seat, her shoulders and back unwinding after maintaining piano bench posture. The thin clouds, hung low across the sky, had faded. She wished she'd asked Herr Steinmann about Benjamin; that would have to wait.

March 25

The bunny's back, covered in gold foil, softened under her fingers. It was the Monday before Easter. Once again, the front door was ajar when Sarah arrived, but only the familiar staleness greeted her.

"Herr Steinmann?" She strained her voice; had he turned off his hearing aids? The door to the sitting room was cracked, but she could see only a slice — the armrest and his slippered foot — as she hung up her jacket. Had he raced back to his seat after buzzing her in? A physical impossibility.

"Herr Steinmann?" A pressure swelled in her abdomen. Would she make an unpleasant discovery, be traumatized for life in the next few seconds?

"Benjamin, I have been waiting for you. I opened the door for you this morning, and I have been waiting ever since then. What took you so long?"

What?

She took her usual seat across from him, her bottom at the edge of the cushion, pushing the balls of her feet into the rug, ready to stand up again. Her fingers tightened on the bunny's back and the ten ovals deepened.

Not budging from his chair, he had the look of a man whose bus never came. Waiting, waiting; he wore the agitation of unfulfilled expectation. With his tan vest, plaid button-down and slippers, he was just as he always was. Still, something was very different.

"Herr Steinmann, it's me, Sarah."

"Benjamin, I haven't said a word to my mother. She won't be home until three o'clock." *Ding, ding, ding, ding, ding.* The grandfather clock was as punctual as a German postal worker.

Concern crawled over her. He was looking toward her, but past her, not registering her worried face, with her but not with her. However disconcerting, it was the chance to ask the question that had been nagging her since last week. "Who is Benjamin?"

He began gesturing broadly with his hands, fingers bent, knuckles large and craggily. "What will it be today? Gershwin again? No, let's hear some ragtime! That will get the bastards on their feet, ha ha!" He let out a cynical laugh.

"Ragtime? What happened to Mozart?" She wanted to ring the bell again, walk up the stairs, and find the Herr Steinmann she knew at the landing. *Redo.*

"Come on Benjamin, we don't have all day!" He put on a childish pout, genuinely annoyed.

A knot of fear tightened in her belly. First, that she had made a mistake, rung the wrong bell, found the wrong man, forgotten that her own name was actually Benjamin. Then, that her Herr Steinmann would never return from the depths of his own mind. Her grandfather had had Alzheimer's and called his own daughter, her mother, by the name of the next door neighbor. Sarah had been away at music school, and was spared the deeply personal injury caused by a cracked intellect.

She looked around the room, searching for help among the records and cabinets, for the ghosts of the people who'd loved him, who were not there to rescue him — or her. The Bechstein stood quietly with the fallboard closed; the record player was silent in the corner, its needle returned to its resting position. She was alone.

No, there was Constantin!

"Herr Steinmann, just stay here, I'll be right back."

He protested as she stood, setting the chocolate bunny on her seat, and hurried toward the door, careful not to let it lock behind her. Please, God, let him be home; the quietly whispered prayer was amplified in the stairwell.

"But Benjamin, we have tea and one square of chocolate left in the cupboard. I don't feel like waiting any longer, and my mother will be home soon. You really are being impossible today!"

She knocked on Constantin's door so urgently that her knuckles ached. His mother opened it.

"I'm Sarah from upstairs, I mean, I don't live here, Herr Steinmann does, but I play the piano, I used to be a pianist, I mean, I play the piano with Herr Steinmann, he's upstairs with himself, with Benjamin, who's Benjamin? What I'm trying to say is — something is wrong." She released an incomprehensible stew of syllables.

"I've heard about you, Sarah. What's wrong with Herr Steinmann?" Mrs. Djabou was unshaken as she put the pieces together and turned to find her son, who appeared next to her.

"What happened? Has he fallen?" Constantin's broad shoulders filled the doorway. "Should I come up with you?"

"He didn't fall, he's just being…" What, exactly? "He's talking about Benjamin and his mother and Gershwin."

"He's delirious?" Constantin took the stairs two at a time, propelling himself upward with his elbows, as Sarah did her best to keep up, rubbing her sore knuckles. "I'm always worried that he'll fall and hurt himself. That could be pretty dangerous for him, all alone up there."

Relief! He was still in his chair, opposite the bunny, a smile frozen on its golden face, the red bow around its neck garishly out of place. Herr Steinmann was now waving both arms wildly and humming. *Rhapsody in Blue*? Something akin to it. Constantin was on his knees, his hand on Herr Steinmann's forearm.

"Benjamin." He vaguely addressed Sarah again, "It's about time you came back. I've been so looking forward to seeing you. Did you bring your orchestra?" He gestured toward Constantin, who stood up, diagnosis complete.

"This has happened before. Once." Constantin turned to Sarah, speaking softly, as if he'd rotated the dial to their personal wavelength, unreceivable by the patient. Sarah wondered what shape his mouth made when he spoke French, whether his pitch was higher or lower than when he spoke German. "I think he may have accidentally overdosed on his medication. I fill his pill boxes every week, but one time he forgot he took his pills and thought I'd forgotten to fill the box. Then he took a double dose."

"And that can lead to *this*?" Last week, he was giving Sarah relationship advice, now he had walked through the wardrobe and into the past. "Will it get better?"

"Yeah, it should. The meds just have to wear off. And rest — rest is the cure for so many things." Constantin thought for a moment. "Maybe you can help me get him into bed."

"Sure." This could get interesting. He wasn't a large man, but he was stubborn — not to mention breakable.

The patient was still conducting an imaginary orchestra, but his tempo was waning. "Herr Steinmann, it's me, Constantin, and this is Sarah. You know Sarah; you play the piano with her on Mondays, and today is Monday." Constantin supported him by the elbow and lifted him to his feet, gesturing to Sarah to take his other arm. "We are going to take you to your bed. Rest is the best thing for you right now."

Upright, Herr Steinmann was irritatingly asymmetrical; he had missed a button on his floppy cardigan. The trek to the bedroom felt like a field day sack race, narrated with incoherent references to Benjamin, Herr Steinmman's mother, and various forms of jazz.

"To hell with them all if they hate it!" he cursed vehemently. "And let them burn if they hate you. Because I swear to God we will keep playing!"

They couldn't fit three abreast through the hall without knocking the picture frames off the walls, so they walked sideways, a trio of dancing crabs.

The bedroom was sparse, walls void of coverings that would have distracted from the thin cracks in the ivory paint, jagged like rivers on a map. Hannelore smiled lovingly from a simple gold frame on the nightstand next to a short stack of books: Günter Grass's *The Tin Drum*, a biography of Scott Joplin, the Bible. Sarah became a trespasser, a thief of secrets.

The blanket was turned down on one side of the bed; the sheet was crumpled. He let himself be laid down like a drunk who knows he's *non compos mentis*. His words — each one with a meaning of its own that was lost in combination with the next — kept flowing.

Then, — *ghraa!* — the breath that is not yet a ripe snore but a mere sign of sleep; his slippers were still on, the blanket at his ankles. Constantin removed the footwear and fixed the comforter with the ease of someone who has wiped another man's ass, borrowed blood, collected urine in clear bottles.

They tiptoed back to the parlor like new parents.

"Has he ever told you about Benjamin?" asked Sarah. It could only be the man from the photograph.

Constantin shrugged. "He mentioned him before, just once. An American who played the piano. That's all he said. Like you, I guess. And he was someone he used to know a very long time ago, someone who meant a lot to him."

Sarah nodded. That was a start. "What now? Can we just leave him here?"

"You can go home. I'll come back up and check on him in a couple of hours or so. Don't worry."

The bunny was still there, looking perpetually content, but rather lost, as Sarah closed the door behind them.

"It's really nice of you, you know, to play with him." They descended slowly, taking the stairs one-by-one this time; Constantin was smiling in a way that was trying not to smile. "I've never seen Herr Steinmann this… *alive* before. At least not since his wife died."

"You're the one who's doing what a son would do. He's given me more than I have given him. A new reason to play."

Her dollar had bought the Henle edition of the concerto that she'd been after, but there had been much more to their trade. What was Herr Steinmann really looking for in return? Sharing an instrument like they did, even a bench, requires a physical negotiation unknown to trios and quartets. It means rubbing buttocks, overlapping runs, rude reaching for page turns — professional intimacy like that of paired ice skaters. Was it musical closeness he wanted? No, it was more, and she was sure that it in some way involved Benjamin West.

Constantin held the key in the lock at his own door. "In Chad, people respect the elderly more than they do in Germany. Here, you take up space and aren't supposed to bother anyone until you die. I don't think it should have to be like that." Time is linear, but humans are not: The old forever see themselves as sprightly youths, while the young forget that they, too, will take a turn at being old.

Constantin was two, maybe three years younger than Sarah. What of Chad did he bring with him to pristine Germany; how long had he bled when his face was gashed? As she opened the heavy front door and stepped outside, Sarah thought of Benjamin, who, so she'd been told, was just like her.

Six Years Earlier

ppp — *pianississimo.* The music disintegrated in her fingers, barely audible as she pressed the final chords. The Bechstein maintained its rich sound even with the lightest touch. She released the final F-sharp major chord, suspending her hands millimeters above the keyboard to give silence the last word. Professor Rosenstein was taciturn for twenty or thirty seconds as the resonance faded completely.

"Schumann, you know, was already in the insane asylum in Bonn when Brahms wrote this homage to him and dedicated it to his wife Clara Schumann." He was leaning back in his leather armchair, his fingers curved over the armrests as if they were keyboards. "The closing variation falls apart like Schumann's mind did. It's really quite poignant considering how young Schumann was and how close Brahms was to the family. And to Clara, of course. Maybe Schumann lost his mind because of syphilis, maybe he was bipolar. We will never know for sure."

Brahms, Schumann and the other German Romantics: Sarah felt a certain mutual understanding with them. Brahms's *Variations on a Theme by Robert Schumann*, Op. 9, was utterly personal, straightforward, laden with pathos, and particularly up her alley.

It was nearly six on a Monday evening, dinner time. She had just a few more minutes with Professor Rosenstein and was fading quickly. Sarah was more of a morning person and would have preferred an early bird time slot, but he didn't teach before noon (artist's prerogative), so she had to energize herself beforehand with hasty macchiatos at the hole-in-the-wall coffee shop between the practice room and the studio, where she avoided her face in the crooked mirror hung to make the joint look bigger. Then, with gum between her teeth to calm her nerves, she visualized the first few bars of her assigned piece as she hurried to her lesson.

"The sixteenth variation" — he stood up, but was hardly taller — "needs more tragedy, more sincerity, more humanity. You are still being too careful. Losing a human soul is not something to be careful about. It's…" — he thought for a moment — "raw." His German R made the word sound like it was stuck inside of him and he was prying it loose.

"I'm just trying to follow the dynamics in the score as closely as possible."

"Do that, too, but subconsciously. Perfection is never something we achieve at the conscious level. If you strive for perfection you will lose your humanity." But how was she supposed to manage her conscious and subconscious simultaneously and also deliver a mistake-free performance?

He looked reflectively out the window of his ground-floor studio; outside, a ponytailed freshman was wheeling her double bass to a rehearsal or lesson.

"I remember a time, when I was a boy, when society thought it could achieve some kind of self-defined perfection. Not only was there no such thing, but they lost their humanity — lost reality — in the process."

"You mean the Holocaust?" Was it okay to say that word in his presence? The *Shoah*. She was going through the chords of the last variation in her head, searching for the five-step plan to subconscious flawlessness.

"I don't mean the good music and art that the Nazis banned, but the whole idea of perfection. It is a lie. Truly good music is human, and humans are strong and weak and everything in between." He looked back at Sarah. "That's what you need in this last variation: weakness. Schumann lived for another two years with his terminal illness, and Brahms foreshadowed everything."

She put the score in her backpack and got out her water bottle; the lessons inevitably made her thirsty.

"When exactly did you leave Germany?" That was a safe enough question.

He rubbed the lenses of his glasses with a white cloth, around, around, around in precise circles, long after their transparency had been restored. "It was in 1938, right after *Kristallnacht*. Maybe you've heard of the Night of Broken Glass? Things were bad for us Jews before that in Munich, but that was — how do you say in English? — the last straw for my parents."

"And you came to New York with your family?"

He hesitated, carefully positioning his glasses on his nose, trying out his fresh view of the world, before he spoke. "My parents made it out with me and my sister. But my grandparents, two uncles and three cousins were taken to Dachau and later to Auschwitz." He let out the guttural cough that buys time and fulfills the obligation for a facial expression but is not physiologically necessary. "Only one uncle survived. He went to Israel, so I have no one left in Germany."

Sarah's red sneakers suddenly looked frivolous. The rug under the pedals was threadbare and patternless in two heel spots. She stared at the floor for lack of words. "It must have been difficult starting over in the US." It was something to say.

"In a way, my heart is still in Germany, even though my country wanted me dead at one point." It was as if he were talking about someone else. "I had become an outcast there, although I was just a boy, so being a foreigner someplace else was not so bad. America is a wonderful place, but certainly not the grand paradise it is often painted to be. Anyone who thinks their country is better than all others is treading on dangerous ground."

The campus clock tower chimed the hour. His face lit up as Sarah slung her backpack over her shoulder and stepped toward the door. "I would love a good *Weißwurst*, though! They are hard to come by in New York."

"Maybe you should go back for a visit sometime." Closing the studio door, she bit her tongue, clenching her jaw in shame at her privileged naivety until she tasted iron.

MARCH 29

"Should we grab some drinks here?" Theo suggested as they passed a tiny take-out joint a few blocks from the English Garden. A picnic blanket with a mandala in shades of purple was peeking out of his rucksack.

It was the middle of the afternoon on Good Friday and unseasonably sunny for late March. Winter, it seemed, had treated itself to a well-deserved long weekend, but spring was still young and fickle. A low-key coffee downtown had been Sarah's suggestion, but Theo insisted on relaxing at the park. Seize the day, he'd said, you never know when the sun might come out again. She was disappointed with herself for giving in, bending in his breeze again. He had a way of taking the upper hand, even when she didn't mean to give it to him.

"I got it." Wallet open, she stepped forward as he put two *Russ* on the counter. It seemed odd that the Germans, of all people, would condone the mixing of wheat beer and Sprite.

Where the pavement acquiesced to the park, a crowd had gathered at a steep embankment above the Eisbach, a thin arm of the Isar River. They stopped to watch surfers — covered from head to toe in neoprene, anonymous and genderless — brave the single man-made wave that coiled in front of a bridge. Munich's little Half Moon Bay.

"It looks dangerous!"

"Yeah, a buddy of mine slammed into the concrete on the side of the river, split his noggin wide open." Theo exuded vicarious pride. "He had to get twelve stitches. The dickhead tells chicks it was a fucking shark bite, and those who believe him get laid."

They continued into the park, teeming with holiday strollers that had peeled off a layer or two, baring forearms and shoulders, wan like a tree under its bark. They followed the creek until they found a shady spot at the edge of the brook to spread out Theo's blanket. He kicked off his Chucks without untying them and peeled off his t-shirt before settling onto the blanket, legs crossed and outstretched, leaning back on his elbows. Sarah traced his tattoo with her eyes; the ink was stark against his pale skin, meters away from the location it marked. His belly was soft, but his chest was taught, freckled and fair.

Dammit. Sunscreen would have been sensible; the first rays of the season were always brutal, especially to the tip of her nose. She was still young enough to prevent wrinkles and old enough to want to.

Theo closed his eyes, tilting his face toward the light, filling his lungs with the friendly air. "It's an oasis." He turned toward Sarah. "Except for the hundred thousand other people here, but what can you do?"

"I don't mind all the people. On days like these, everybody is in a good mood." She knew what she wanted to say next, just not how. She fidgeted with the grass next to her, until roots came up with a single blade and three squirming bugs that preferred the dark. Hastily, she returned them to their home.

"And so are we." He leaned over onto his elbow to peck her on the arm, then opened his beverage by hooking their bottle caps together until they loosened and popped off.

"I'm not so sure…" She didn't know how to end the sentence. Meaning exists outside of words, but not without them.

"About your mood or your *Russ*?" His bottle was tilted at sixty-five degrees, held by three fingers high up on the neck. He was the spitting image of carefree.

"About this. About us." Squinting at him, she gauged his reaction; beating around the bush would have been a lie. The Sprite-beer was half sour, half bitter, half okay.

"If you're nervous about The Theo and Sarah Show, we can postpone it. No biggie. Summer's a shit time for events. Everyone's on Bali or *Malle*." *Malle*, Mallorca, Majorca, the Spanish vacation island so popular among Germans that it had been dubbed Germany's seventeenth state.

"No. I mean, yes. It does make me nervous. Kind of." She was getting off track. She uncrossed her legs and pulled her knees up, hugging them.

A couple next to them tossed a towel on the ground, took off their shoes, and waded into the water. Arms up, they squawked like awkward birds, flightless ostriches, even though the ripple only touched their calves.

"Being nervous means you care." He tucked his hands under the back of his head, crossing his feet and closing his eyes as he lay back.

The pair in the water found their footing and stopped flapping. She had her hands in his back pockets and they kissed in the cold current. He stumbled on a rock and they caught each other by the waist, shrieking and laughing. Next to them, a toddler in just a diaper and water wings was testing the temperature with his hand as his dad, squatting beside him, gripped his upper arm, dithering between holding on and letting go.

Two teenage boys emanated German rap like body odor as they sauntered past with a beer crate in tow. The one holding the phone turned boom box beat the air with it.

"But I mean us."

"Just relax, Sarah, and let it happen." He didn't open his eyes. Then, all of a sudden, he sprang to his feet and pulled her up by the elbow. "Come on, we're going in!"

Here he was again, calling the shots. As they waded into the water, his hands were on her fingers, above her shoulders in a marionette dance. Sarah dropped her arms, freeing herself from his grasp, and rolled up her jeans, which were already wet at the hem, before she went further.

"It's so cold!" she exclaimed as he sloshed water onto her naked knees. She made a brief but unsuccessful revenge attempt before her bare foot slipped on a smooth stone in the riverbed — *splash!* Her groin grew icy, the water enveloped her chest, rippling at her collarbone; at least her head was spared.

Theo roared, crossing his hands over his belly before scooping her up under her arms, lifted up from above like after her first ski accident. She was center stage again, spotlights glaring, a mute audience — were none of the loungers even paying attention? Being rescued by Theo was far more embarrassing than being seen by them.

On her feet again, the *faux pas* had passed, but now she was soaked. The March sun was too weak to dry her blunder away. She would have to go home for fresh clothes. Even worse, she couldn't get her words out; they were a foundered pudding, uncongealed and non-cohesive.

"But it's just water," he protested.

"We'll talk later. I really have to go."

He said he'd stay in the park, dunk his feet again, soak up the rays, catch some Zs, while Sarah dripped a river of her own all the way home.

A crowd of goosebumps joined her as she walked, her soaked jeans chapping her inner thighs. She would have to hang them up in the bathroom and hope they dried before they started to stink.

APRIL 1

It was always supposed to be relaxing, healing, artistically inspiring. In her mind, Sarah could sit in a café for hours, undisturbed by frivolous conversation, 'productive' written on her forehead, reading the latest bestselling memoir or inking her dry hands with the *Süddeutsche*.

The reality was distracted aloneness. The couples paying together after lingering; the laughs and snickers of the girlfriends that came in table-sized packs of four and wearing flowing blouses; the hot server sipping a Coke by the register with a hand-rolled cigarette behind his ear. Not just her fingers, but also her tongue was stiff from lack of use that day. *"Einen Cappuccino bitte."* Three words were all it had made.

Sarah never managed to stretch her beverage for more than fifteen minutes; an empty cup risked having her legitimization cleared away. Still, the caffeine jolted her creativity and the loneliness awakened her *ennui*, and it was in these moments that she would miss music the most. Melancholy can be as addictive as joy.

The café around the corner from Herr Steinmann's wasn't busy and her cappuccino arrived quickly with two skinny packs of sugar on the saucer. She put them next to the unlit candle on the table and ordered a piece of cheesecake before the server had a chance to turn around. She was feeling generous with herself. The cake was two days old, a mediocre cheat treat, but at least the foam on the drink was enjoyably lightweight. A tiny spoonful dissipated in her mouth. Milk without air was merely a children's drink.

Theo would have been a sore thumb here. It wasn't fancy; it just wasn't him. Did he even drink coffee? They'd had no morning after to find out. She didn't want to be his girlfriend, that much had become clear, but did he think she was or not? So much for German directness. He wasn't upfront and her attempt to be had flopped. In the wet, wet river.

Ten euros minus her tab of €6.70 made for a very generous tip in this country of modest round-uppers. The server thanked her with a little bow and a *"Dankeschön!"* as she pushed her chair in and left.

Sarah should have rung first, but she hadn't seen him since he'd called her Benjamin. The day after Easter was a public holiday, but chances were good that he'd be home, considering that he was estranged from his living children and unlikely to have embarked on a long hiking weekend in the Alps along with the rest of the *Münchner*.

She pressed Constantin's bell first. No answer. *Bzzz!* The door opened when she pushed the button marked 'O. & H. Steinmann.' Upstairs, a woman in her early sixties was waiting. Her salt-and-pepper hair was stylishly short, and she was wearing a carefully tied flowered scarf over a pant suit and expensive ballerinas instead of homey felt house shoes.

"You must be Sarah?" She pronounced her name like an American would, letting it jut out from the German sentence. "I'm Silke Steinmann-Mohr, Herr Steinmann's daughter." She opened the door and stepped aside so Sarah could come in, but remained in the entry.

"Yes, I'm Sarah Johnson. How is he doing?" Why was Silke here? A fall, stroke, heart attack, sudden inexplicable death in his sleep? The possibilities at his age read like a medical textbook.

"I heard you were here last week when he had an — ah — episode. Thank you for helping him. He's been admitted to the hospital, but he'll be fine."

"The hospital?"

"The delirium was just an issue with his medication, but he caught a bout of pneumonia after that. That can be serious at his age, but he's improving. Always headstrong, my father."

Sarah pictured Silke behind a large desk rimmed with tidy stacks of papers, her fingertips pressed together, leaning back in a Hollywood-worthy executive chair. She was cordial, but professional, as if Sarah were a new hire and they were reviewing numbers on a spreadsheet, 4s and 7s and 3s and 0s — especially 0s; the non-number is always the most important one.

"Will he be okay?"

"Father always pulls through. He just needs a lot of rest — and heavy-duty antibiotics, of course."

Sarah heard jazz music playing. Was that John Coltrane? *Impressions*, first recorded in New York in 1961, the year the Berlin Wall went up, the year the Steinmann family bought this place and cut a hole in the wall to the kitchen. The music was coming from a laptop perched on Herr Steinmann's chair, as incongruous as a cowboy hat on a robot.

Silke's face warmed. Her neutral-toned makeup was heavier than it had looked at first, the nude hues masking the wrinkles around her eyes and mouth. "I was actually surprised he got sick. He's had more *Pfiff* since he started playing the piano again."

How would she know? Constantin, the better son; Sarah, already closer than his own daughter. "Mozart will do that! Your father is really good for such a…" Sarah cut herself off.

"Mozart, yes, he taught me to play Mozart when he had the time. Usually, he was busy reading the newspaper in his favorite chair or listening to opera instead of playing basketball with me or helping us with homework. Mom did that. Mom did everything. But jazz always had a special place in his heart. It was his bizarre personal obsession. He never wanted to share it. If he'd made the effort to teach me jazz, maybe I would have kept it up as a teenager." She drew a line with her hand as if to underscore the universal difficulty of adolescents.

Jazz? Sarah only remembered him talking about jazz when he was delirious.

"How long will he be in the hospital?"

"Another week or two. I have to get back to Bonn tomorrow. But I know that Constantin and his mother downstairs will look after him."

Sarah started to leave, but stopped with the door handle in her hand, turning on her heels. "Can I ask you who Benjamin is?"

"*Ach*, that was such a long ago. Benjamin — I'm surprised he hasn't told you yet about his old friend." Silke crossed her arms and turned up the corners of her mouth, looking at her, or rather through her. "He was an American pianist like you. Except that he was a jazz genius. My father always said he had fingers like a gazelle."

APRIL 8

Sarah's brain was dull, not because it was Monday morning, but because she and Theo had been texting all weekend. She felt hungover from poor sleep: weakened muscle synapses, throbbing head, parched throat.

I wanna touch all of you woke her with a beep at 3:12 on Saturday morning.

Now followed at 3:14.

Daniel brought whisky again and says I should be painting instead of texting you at 3:23.

He wrote nothing on Sunday. She didn't reply. He'd allegedly been visiting his parents in Augsburg — Sunday roast and red cabbage, his boyhood bed, he'd texted before he left. The words she wanted to write him streamed through her head like the intro to *Star Wars*, repeated ad infinitum, aligning themselves into lengthy quasi sentences. Words are sleep's nemesis.

Sarah's Sunday was spent with Chopin's *Nocturnes*, marked up in her book with red, gray and blue scratchings in an array of scripts — hers from middle school, high school, music school, fingerings from her teacher in California, a rare slur or circled hidden motif from Professor Rosenstein. She dedicated an hour to the left-hand part of the D-flat major, Op. 27, No. 2, taking the leaps quickly and slowly. The twenty-one *Nocturnes* were not imitations of operas or orchestras, but pure piano candy.

"Bavarian Brew ran out of beans!" exclaimed Christoph, who was standing unannounced in Sarah's office doorway. Her tunnel vision was still focused on a poorly written text about the most popular sausages on German barbecues. She'd started taking pleasure in the arduous task of whipping an article into shape and — to her own surprise — reforming it like a piece of music. But this topic was not at all whetting her appetite.

"What?" Sarah turned blankly toward Christoph. "It's going to be a long day." She sighed with her whole body, water welling in each eye.

"Just kidding!" He stepped into her office, holding up two cups like freshly caught fish writhing on a line. "I didn't mean to scare you. I didn't think you'd believe me!"

She felt annoyance and relief in equal parts. "Extra foamy double cappuccino." He handed her the cup with *Sarah J.* written on it with a black felt tip. That was not the work of Bavarian Brew, which prided itself on *not* being Starbucks. It was Christoph's handwriting, the squarish, genderless script of an aesthete.

"Not a great weekend?" It was half question, half conclusion.

"The weekend." Her head navigated its way out of the *Bratwurst* and back to herself. "You won't believe it, but I practiced the piano for longer than I have in a long time." She pulled the lid off her coffee and tilted the cup way back, oblivious to her foam mustache.

"Mozart?"

"Yeah, Mozart; then Chopin. It sounds nerdy, I know, but it was — fun. Yeah, fun."

"Cho-paing. The Polish composer who was also French?" Christoph exaggerated a nasal French accent.

"A lot of classical composers had lives in more than one country. For love, music or war."

"Like you — except for the love, music or war part." Christoph adjusted his glasses. "Do people ask you often if you want to go back?

"All the time! And it's *when* and not *if.* If I had a nickel for every time someone asked me if — no, *told* me that I must be missing California…"

"You wouldn't be working here, that's for sure. You would buy a surfboard and pretend that you were still in California."

"And drive a Tesla wearing flip-flops. But seriously, for everyone back home it's just a matter of time." She held a sip of espresso and milk in her mouth before swallowing, remembering the near-perfect cappuccino she'd drunk last year next to polo-shirted Twitter employees at the tiny but trendy Blue Bottle Coffee on Market Street in San Francisco. "Maybe I just want to prove them wrong."

Bing! Her phone illuminated.

"You strike me as one of those people who could learn another language and fit in anywhere — Brazil, Japan, South Africa." He ignored the device. "Does being a chameleon make fitting in at home even harder?"

It was rude, she knew, but she read the message anyway. Theo. Finally! But there were no words, only a YouTube link. "The Thrill Is Gone" by B.B. King. Really?

Dumped with a song. Sarah stared at the screen in case her Monday brain had missed a catch, a relevant nuance that negated the obvious. After all, until early Sunday morning, he had still been game. Or Daniel's whisky was. But now, taking this at face value, he'd changed his mind.

Hang on a second. If anyone was breaking up with anyone, then *she* was with *him*. Right?

"When you do move back to California, take me with you." Christoph swirled his half-full cup. "But I guess you'd have to marry me because I'm not a *Glückspilz*. I can't even win a ridiculous teddy bear at Oktoberfest. My chances in the green card lotto are zilch." His cheeks turned the color of raspberries.

"What the hell?"

"Sorry, I was just joking!" He seemed genuinely alarmed.

"I didn't mean you." Christoph had a way of always showing up when she had something to say, but no one to say it to. She was fairly certain that he was flirting with her, that he desperately wanted to be more than her coworker, so it felt awkward to include him in this moment, but here he was. "I've been seeing this guy. I tried to end it last week, but he wasn't listening. I thought he was still into it, but he just sent me this video."

She pointed her phone toward Christoph and he grimaced. "He sounds like a dick with no balls. Guys like that make us all look bad."

"He's not. He's..." What was Theo? "Nice and funny and..." Arne downstairs was also nice and funny and a whole bunch of nothing. She fiddled with her earring; a large turquoise teardrop framed in Southwest-style silver.

"That doesn't make him good enough for you." Christoph shifted his weight onto the other foot, looking like he needed to pee. If only she hadn't looked at the message. Sarah wished she had left Christoph with his coffee offering and encouragements out of the whole thing.

"I finally realized he's not a commitment kind of guy. Know what I mean?"

"That sounds like a lot of people I know. The curse of our generation? We're not all like that."

"I need things to be clearcut. That makes me the odd one out, I guess." Sarah looked straight at Christoph as the thought crystallized in the space between them.

A timid smile curled onto his lips. "I can totally understand that. At least you know what you want."

"He just thought he could pre-empt me."

Christoph turned to leave, but looked back over his shoulder. "It's okay to want what you want, Sarah. You're normal."

Normal? No one had ever called her that before. As Christoph disappeared into the hall, she put on her headphones and turned the volume up, first on Ravel's glistening *Miroirs*, then on her German pop favorites playlist. It was the only way she could finish the sausage text, tidy up her inbox, and pre-edit a piece on how to make authentic Austrian *Kaiserschmarrn* for the upcoming special. The secret, the author wrote (as Herr Steinmann must have learned decades ago), was to tear the pancakes with a fork, not cut them cleanly, then thoroughly caramelize.

It was just after four when Sarah left the office, the time she typically made her way to Herr Steinmann's. The hall was nearly empty, her co-workers making the most of their flex time. In the elevator on the way out, she pasted a YouTube link of her own into a reply: "Du weißt nicht was Du willst" by Revolverheld, a ballad for on-the-fence lovers. She could play his game.

With no internet connection in the lift, she had a few seconds to reconsider and erase. He'd chosen her poison, perhaps she should choose his instead:

Give me now leave, to leave thee, from *Twelfth Night*.

Backspace, backspace, no. She wouldn't stoop to his level. Some things didn't merit a response, and Sarah decided this was one of them. She opened her phone book and scrolled down to S. It rang four or five times before she heard, *"Djabou bei Steinmann."*

"Constantin! This is Sarah." A voice, at least; someone. His French accent sounded stronger on the phone. "I'm glad I caught you, but I hope I'm not interrupting. I wanted to check in and see how Herr Steinmann is doing?"

"Very weak, but he's better. I just gave him his medication, and the pastry and coffee he ordered from the bakery down the street. The man hasn't lost his sweet tooth! Here, I'll give him the phone." She heard a grunt in the background as Constantin explained to Herr Steinmann who was on the line.

"My dear Sarah, it is kind of you to call. Our audience is waiting for Mozart's Theme & Variations, you know." His voice was tired, but familiar.

"It's taken me some time to be ready, Herr Steinmann, but I am now. Are you ready, too?"

"Constantin here is taking quite good care of me. I'll need to get my chops back up to speed. Give me a few weeks. Then we'll make Mozart magic!" It was such a beautiful thing when words were combined to create comprehensible meaning.

"See you then, Herr Steinmann. See you then."

II. ANDANTE

MAY 27

Dong, dong, dong, dong, dong! There it was, the familiar but unplaceable gong that had hammered in Sarah's sleep over the past few weeks, that was dug up at 3:00 a.m. as if excavated from the chambers of her most distant memory. She'd wondered whether it had been the clock tower at college? Perhaps the centennial clock in her home-town, restored with cookie sales, on the relic of a post office turned trinket shop, the last building for miles with a history? No, Sarah realized as she heard it chime the fifth hour again, awake, the dream disruptor was a more recent acquaintance of hers. It had been keeping the Bechstein company in Herr Steinmann's living room, where she found herself once again.

"Ambitions should serve us, not the other way around, so we are free to revise them when we see fit, I do believe. Not that we should set the bar lower for ourselves, but there is a time for everything — and it doesn't always have to be now."

Herr Steinmann was sitting in his same armchair, looking like the Abraham Lincoln Memorial, evaluating whether his dearly bought wisdom was taking root. She'd been practicing more than ever since leaving music school, she'd told him; some days with *élan*, other days with a can of chickpeas in her hand, this close to bashing a descend-ing F-sharp major scale on the Schimmel. Her playing still never felt good enough, and not even half as good as before. What if the piano could exist outside the realm of emotion and simply make calculated sound, free of expectations? Then, she knew, she'd hate it like put-you-on-hold music. The price of music was experiencing the whole gamut of emotions, and a certain dissatisfaction was necessary for progress.

She looked around: a silent record on the turntable, three children on the coffee table, the loyal Bechstein. Nothing had changed. *Doch.* There was one small thing: The window facing the street had been tilted open, inviting in the occasional *bzzz bzzz* of a bee and the friendly spring air that had touched someone's arm or tousled someone's hair en route. American windows didn't do that, pretend to fall on you when you pull the handle, then catch themselves before finishing the deed.

"Tell me what you've been playing," he asked her. "More Mozart? Or rather the *Romantiker?*"

"Most recently, Mussorgsky's *Pictures at an Exhibition.* It's not something I played at music school." At times, she purposely relived past lessons, concerts and practice hours; at others, she chose the freshness of untouched music, though shaping it entirely alone — no frowns, no disappointed sighs, no hummed vibrato — was a challenge.

"A brilliant work, isn't it? It's so visual and so Russian. The Russian composers managed to combine perfection with pure passion, even better than the Germans and Austrians, I think. It is not very common for a piano work to be adapted for orchestra."

"The orchestra version by Ravel is the most famous." Sarah had first heard it in a quiet cubicle in the music school library, her nose buried in the piano score, her ears completely covered in large Sennheiser headphones — not how it was meant to be heard.

Playing it now, turning those painted pictures into sound, was her way of getting back at Theo the artist for his crude breakup. It was over, just as she'd wanted, but she hadn't gotten to have a say in how it ended. With just a YouTube link, B.B. King was really the only one who'd *said* much of anything at all. **I agree. Thank you nonetheless for the fun and the curries**, Sarah had finally decided to text Theo. And that was it. After a few weeks, he was already someone she used to pass by on the street, like the businesswoman walking her Dalmatian or the city sanitation worker with the dreadlocks. His unused ear holes, the ink spot on his hand, his nondescript eyes — they were a blur. Only the precise scent of his skin returned to her nostrils from time to time like a recurring motif.

"I've read through the D minor concerto; it doesn't sound like much without an orchestra. But it doesn't seem so important anymore." She sunk back in her chair. The more that separated her from that fateful performance, the further away it seemed.

"I hope you are still willing to play in our upcoming performance. Constantin and his mother are still interested, of course, and I think it would be very nice. Constantin has been such a help to me in the past few weeks." He was wearing too many clothes for the warmer temperatures. A plaid button-down shirt and a brown cotton vest hung looser than they did in April. The heat brought color to his temples, at least, if not his cheeks and hands.

"As long as you're feeling up to it." She poured the coffee into the same flowered porcelain. Chrysanthemums, without milk or sugar to fertilize them with. "Should I get you some sugar from the kitchen?"

"Oh dear. Constantin says I should use less sugar, bless him, but to be honest, I simply forgot it. It's fine, I'll take my coffee black today. I'm out of milk, too, come to think of it."

The liquid in her cup looked like sweet raisins, like her hair, but was as bitter as licorice. She winced as it hit the back of her throat.

"Constantin says I've been getting more forgetful. *Pustekuchen!* Hannelore would tell you I've always been a bit absent-minded. Ha! It's the musician in me." He looked down at his knotted hands. "Growing old is a paradox, Sarah. It means losing and finding yourself at the same time. You wake up and don't recognize yourself in the mirror; your arms and legs grow heavier, like you're moving under water. I do hope that heaven really is in the clouds, where everything feels lighter! But on the other hand, aging is predictable. You've already seen it happen to your parents, your friends, and your own spouse by the time you get around to accepting that you have no excuse for being caught off guard. And by that time, I suppose, you are already old."

Brahms's Schumann Variations played in her head — the final variation, the disintegration of his dear friend's mind. At forty-six, he had been much too young to lose it, much too unfinished to die.

"Hannelore never had a problem with getting older. She didn't care about gray hair or wrinkles. That made her even more beautiful." It was an excuse to say her name. "Yes, I will make sure I feel up to it. But I wanted to tell you that I'm glad we are able to meet again; it's been a long time. I'm afraid it would be best if we set our appointments for every second Monday from now on, so it doesn't become too taxing. My health, you see. Constantin keeps reminding me to slow down. He knows I don't want to hear it, but unfortunately it's true."

He leaned his head back to down the last sip like a shot of schnapps. "Would you be so kind as to help me to the piano?" He smelled different, like a bouquet that had overstayed its vase.

The theme began with her simple, naive melody, ornamented with trills, as he plucked a *piano pizzicato* accompaniment. Yes, the strength in his fingers had waned, but his spirit and desire for precision were still intact. The quiet Andante opened purely, the *Primo* and *Secondo* parts so sparse that they almost sounded like one. The variations grew in intensity, if not volume, so organically that the gradual transformation was hardly noticeable until the key signature changed to G minor in Variation IV, and somber chromaticism marked the first *forte*. There was a loud caesura after the fourth variation as Herr Steinmann reached for his handkerchief, coughing violently and gripping the side of the keyboard with his left hand. He'd spent every ounce of his energy on the music.

"Are you okay, Herr Steinmann? Can I get you…"

"I'm fine, don't you worry. The most important thing is to keep playing."

She did worry, but also didn't want to hurt his feelings by dwelling on his frailty — on the fact that time takes *and* gives, but sometimes it feels like it takes an arm when you give it a little finger.

"It's interesting that Variations IV and V alternate twice." Sarah pointed to a kind of *da capo* preluding the real finale in the continuation of Variation V.

"They say that history always repeats itself, but I would say, rather, that we often hear its echo," Herr Steinmann ruminated into his handkerchief.

"Did you play this with Heinrich?" She turned toward him, leaning her wrist on the open fallboard.

"No. We ran out of time, I suppose." He tidily folded the handkerchief into eighths and slipped it back into his pocket. "The shortest years were the ones we'd thought would go on forever."

"Herr Steinmann… who was Benjamin?" Her voice sounded loud, like a cadenza to a concerto, all alone on stage.

"Benjamin! That was a very long time ago."

"You were talking about him that day — when you weren't feeling well and Constantin came over. You seemed to think I was him."

He snorted. "Ha! Yes, Benjamin. He was an American pianist

like you."

"That's what everyone else has said, too."

"Perhaps that is why I haven't mentioned him. Playing with you very much reminds me of playing with him. Even though you two are very different, of course. As you already know, some of our most precious memories can also become the most painful."

"Hm. Would you like to tell me about him? I'd be curious…"

"Where do I begin? The war turned everything upside down, you see. When it ended, the world turned again, but in a different direction. Maybe it really is a cube and not a sphere, as the ancient Greeks said." He laughed cynically at his own joke. A Rubik's cube, thought Sarah. "Things were not normal. But they weren't all bad. We Germans had lost. We became foreigners on our own soil. You Americans had been the enemy — and then, during the occupation, you were suddenly everywhere. Grinning victors bearing gifts of coffee, canned meat, sugar and powdered milk."

"So Benjamin was an American GI?"

"He was a musician, first of all." He raised a palm to differentiate, not disagree. "He was not a soldier at heart. But who is? None of us were. He was stationed near our home for a while. One day, he knocked on the door and said he'd heard we owned a grand piano and whether he could play it for a few minutes. He was very polite, but he knew, of course, that we couldn't refuse."

Sarah was tapping her fingers lightly on the open fallboard, biting her tongue. She didn't want him to stop talking.

"My mother was furious. He was a Black man, after all — a Black man with the name of a Jew, for Christ's sake! And she hadn't yet come to grips with the fact that Hitler had not conquered the world. Thank God for that — though I think she regretted it until the day she died."

"And you? What did you think?" From Hitler Youth to Wehrmacht soldier to best buddy, his seemed to be a curious evolution.

"Whatever thoughts I had were reset the moment Benjamin started to play."

"You spoke of Gershwin…"

"He mainly played ragtime. His favorites, he said, were Scott Joplin, Jelly Roll Morton and others. They sounded so exotic. It was scandalous — and sensational!" His eyes lit up; enthralled with the memory, he clapped his hands with a startling burst. "But he was also a jazz virtuoso and loved Gershwin. His fingers flew like… like cheetahs on the hunt. I'd never seen anything like it." He stared at the keyboard, imagining Benjamin's racing digits, then ran his own knuckles across the keys in a slow, silent glissando. "He would stop by a couple of times a week when my mother was out. She knew he came, and she hated it, but she also knew she couldn't stop him. She would wipe down the keys every afternoon, whether he'd been there or not."

"And she could have stayed for free concerts."

"I'm sure Benjamin was happy to spite her. In your country — that is, in his country — he couldn't even ride the bus with white people. In the very country that had condemned Hitler for its racist policies! But here in broken, racist Germany, he could do whatever he wanted. And that was music, most of all. I don't think things were easy for Benjamin. He couldn't go to music school at home because they wouldn't accept Black students, even though he was the best around, I tell you!" Indignantly, he pounded a fist on his lap. "Music school would have been too rigid for him anyway. I don't even know whether he could read music — he never had any. Everything he played came out of his head. But he always wore a smile. When it was raining, when it was sleeting — which it does often here in Munich — and when he handed me one American dollar at the end of every month for the privilege of playing our piano."

One dollar. The price she'd paid for the Mozart score, a price, she realized, with more value for the seller than the buyer. It had been an invaluable replay, a role play. *He was an American pianist just like you.*

"A smile isn't something you see that often in Germany." It was a generalization, she knew, but one she'd experienced. Christoph had told her they smile more often in Munich than in other parts. Maybe it was that more people smiled at *him*.

"He'd seen plenty of men die, as we all had. I believe he'd even been at the Battle of the Bulge, which seemed to leave a deep impression on him. He must have experienced horrible things there, though we never shared our combat stories. We wanted to forget them as quickly as possible. We had each killed the other's brothers, I in Russia, he in Belgium. That's not something you talk about."

"In Russia?" Sarah asked quietly, giving him the option to hear her or not.

"Now it is called Volgograd." Herr Steinmann quickly returned to his friend. "Benjamin was stuck in crippled Germany. But he still acted like every day was the first day of spring. That's what made him so conspicuous."

He turned to heave himself up from the piano bench, reaching for his cane as Sarah leaned over and supported his elbow.

"Let me show you a photograph of Benjamin." Holding the album with both hands, he plopped back into his armchair with a grunt and flipped through the pages until he found it, the image called up again and again by the 3:00 a.m. gong in her head.

"I think it was your Secretary of State Colin Powell who said that Black American soldiers in Germany were freer than they were at home. Powell was in Germany years after Benjamin was, but things didn't seem to have improved much over there. The irony!"

Benjamin did not wear the expression of a man who had been trodden on back home, dodging bullets and mines for years. The straps of his combat helmet dangled under his chin; the standard-issue jacket was missing a button; was it thick enough for Belgian or German winters? Nothing could have been. One hand was stuffed in his pocket, the other raised in a gesture, a simple gold ring shining from his pinky finger; he'd been snapped mid-phrase.

"I had just returned from the front myself," he continued, "and not with the badge of victory every soldier dreams of. But I was alive. That was more than I could say for Heinrich and most of the other boys in our neighborhood. I was alive, and that was a damn good reason not just to smile, but to dance." He wiggled his hips in his chair ever so slightly, then scooted a few centimeters closer to the edge, as if he were about to stand up.

"One day," he said, lowering his voice with a mischievous smile, "he was playing a rag — I think it was actually called 'The Naked Dance' by Jelly Roll Morton — and he suddenly stopped and jumped up from the piano bench as if he'd been stung by a bee. He grabbed both of my hands and sang the rest of the rag as we danced all around the living room. Ha! I was a stiff German; he practically had to drag me the whole way. I'd never danced anything other than the waltz before, or picked my feet up so high!" Nostalgia settled as a film over his eyes; he smiled into the space in front of him.

"The ugly thing about war is that it makes enemies out of those who would otherwise be friends. But without the war, I never would have met Benjamin. His hometown, Raleigh, in the state of North

Carolina, was another planet for me — and maybe for him too after spending so much time in Europe."

She was standing behind his armchair, peering down over his shoulder at the picture of the grinning GI with the magic fingers. "It's harder to dance to Mozart."

Herr Steinmann ran his finger over the photo. "I didn't know until I met Benjamin that music is much more than Mozart. Perhaps it can be for you, too."

May 31

"Hard at work, I see?" Christoph wagged his index finger.

Daaa-da-daa. Sarah had been humming the second movement of Beethoven's "Appassionata" Sonata and scanning biographies of the composer online when Christoph knocked on her open door.

She was twirling a pen in her left hand as she turned toward him. "Yeah, but on good stuff. You know what? When I can't stand the *Schweinshaxen* and *Quark* anymore I've started looking at ways to incorporate my expertise in my work. Then maybe I wouldn't feel like such an imposter."

"You mean music? Tell me more."

"Well, did you know that Beethoven moved to Vienna just a year after Mozart died? Everyone thought he was going to be the next Mozart. I'd say that Beethoven more than filled those shoes."

"Ok, but I don't quite see where you're going with this."

She ignored him. "One reason Beethoven stayed in Vienna was the war in France."

"Maybe he just liked the *Apfelstrudel* there."

"Those musicians all had their nomadic tendencies."

"That would put you in good company, wouldn't it?"

"But outside forces were always steering them, weren't they?"

"Fate? God? Most people play video games on their phones to avoid doing work and you are googling Beethoven and pondering the powers of the universe?"

"But it is my work. Remember what Stefanie said about taking a new approach and bringing in creative ideas? I want to integrate my music background into an upcoming special, so that I can feel like I know what I'm talking about. Do you think she'll go for that?"

"You're asking the only other non-foodie in the team what our Queen Bee will think?"

"Wouldn't you be curious to find out what Mozart ate for breakfast?" It was a half-serious suggestion with potential. The most banal topics were the most popular. Everyone eats like everyone poops, and everyone likes to read about themselves. *We are Mozart.*

"I'm guessing it wasn't espresso and croissants," said Christoph. "Pictures for Instagram could be a challenge."

"True." Sarah tugged on her earlobe. Her own Instagram-unworthy breakfast had consisted of two cappuccinos and a heel piece of bread blanketed with the last slice of cheese imprinted with a square pattern from the bottom of the plastic package.

"A historical look at cuisine from the region would be interesting. I don't think we've covered that before," said Christoph.

"And I guess no one wants to read any more about those *Mozartkugel* candies." Sarah remembered the chocolate slivers stuck to the corners of Herr Steinmann's mouth as they ate them together.

"Speaking of historic refreshments, some of us are going to meet up at the *Biergarten* in the Hirschgarten for some brewskis at around six if you want to come." His second foot and other hip shifted into her office.

She absent-mindedly scribbled a square onto the notepad next to her keyboard, coloring in half of it with her black felt tip, even though she knew it would seep through onto the page underneath. "Historic?"

"I think it dates back to Mozart's time. At least the park does. The biergarten is the biggest in Europe."

"Okay, why not? It's too nice out not to be sitting outside." She tossed her pen onto her desk and put her hands behind her head. She had no other Friday night plans. How embarrassing. It was too late for a coverup, but it was just Christoph, so why should she care?

Sarah had spent two and a half years at *Fork & Messer* without a single happy hour with coworkers. Was it her or them? If they didn't get too close, they wouldn't find out she had a complicated relationship with food: She didn't want to be pressured into eating their cream sauces and éclairs, even though sometimes she was famished for them. Chance mid-day meetings in the office kitchen, restrooms, elevator, focused predictably on the length of the morning meeting (perpetually too long) or their summer vacations to Majorca and

Crete (nice, but too short).

It was just after six when Sarah finally arrived at the crowded Hirschgarten, a hop and a skip from Herr Steinmann's apartment. She didn't like that sunglasses made her feel anonymous, but the glare left her no choice, so she put hers on. Entering the park, she watched through the mirror-coated lenses people laughing, shouting, dancing with arms linked at the elbow, kicking balls, turning skewered meat on portable barbecues, kissing on blow-up chairs. As she kept walking, she passed impromptu soccer games, pinkening flesh on blankets, bottles clinking bottles, bike baskets spilling picnic spreads. It was promising to be a friendly summer.

Tidy rows of long wooden tables, bobbing with heads, rose out of the grass. Next to them, a dozen deer, naturally camouflaged, meandered behind a fence. Two young boys were sticking orange, purple, and yellow carrots into the enclosure, speaking Japanese with their grandmother and fluent German to each other.

The older boy, who was eight or nine, showed her his carrots. "The deer like the orange ones the best," he said.

"And which color do you like best?" she asked him, surprised at the children's ease with strangers.

"Purple is my favorite," he answered without hesitation. His grandmother smiled silently at Sarah. The animals were elegant and vulnerable, satisfied but fettered.

Near the deer enclosure there was a simple stage, a wooden box large enough to hold a ten-piece brass band. *Baaah-ba-bah!* She imagined the ring of the absent horns, reflecting the sun rays at random angles, and pictured bare-kneed musicians dressed in leather shorts and high socks.

"Sarah!" Christoph touched her shoulder. How had he found her in the crowd? "We're over there," he pointed and she recognized a few of her coworkers, also disguised in sunglasses. "We have to get our drinks this way. I was just going to stand in line."

"Perfect timing!" She was relieved that she didn't have to comb the countless rows to find them. As they queued, Sarah peered over the other customers' shoulders at the wares, inhaling the hearty scent of sizzling oils and roasting meat. "Those pretzels are huge!"

"Want to share one? You know you have to drink a whole *Maß* here. No wimping out! First round is on me." One liter of beer meant a hundred bitter swallows.

At the table, gaps closed on the bench as hips touched to make room for the two of them. She didn't recognize the woman across from her, but quickly learned that she — Lauren — had moved from New York to Munich three weeks earlier to start as a features editor. Her strategically messy bob and tiny but tasteful gold jewelry made her glamorously urban.

"And what do you do?" Lauren was halfway through her giant mug, which looked like an overdone souvenir in her slender hand. Had she poured the five hundred milliliters into that bitty handbag?

"I'm…" Sarah's mouth was full of saliva-soaked pretzel. She coughed and took a swig of beer so she wouldn't choke. First-time introductions were a chore. Why not meet someone by asking something else. *Hello. How organized is your underwear drawer?*

Christoph interrupted. "Actually, Sarah is a pianist." His bony elbow poked her ribs. Lauren seemed impressed.

"Sarah's always got the best story ideas. She'll show you the ropes," Alex called from the middle of the table. She bumped into him in the kitchen most days at noon, both of them grabbing their lunchboxes from the communal fridge to eat them at their desks, joined by the hum of the computer monitor, the next email to answer one-handed. But what did Alex do there the rest of the day? Sarah didn't know.

"And you don't want to be one of Sarah's authors. She'll crack the whip if you miss a comma." Beatrix was roughly her age, wore her bangs slashed off in the middle of her forehead, and worked as Stefanie's assistant. She flicked her imaginary whip Indiana Jones-style and smiled. Sarah had discovered grammar was her biggest strength on the job, but hadn't realized anyone else had noticed.

"Now you know everything about me." Except that her underwear drawer was the least tidy in the whole dresser. Sarah grinned at Lauren and reached over Christoph's arm to tear off another piece of the head-sized pretzel. It was crisp on the outside, doughy on the inside, just as it should be.

Her coworkers respected her even without top food credentials. Maybe she'd never been included in their semi-regular get-togethers because they assumed she'd say no. Maybe they thought she thought she was better than them. If only they knew.

The early evening sun was gentle on her forehead. She laid her sunglasses on the table and rubbed her nose in case they'd left a pink dent. The beer grew warmer with every sip, but neutralized the salt, stuck a stick in time's gear. She would stay for a while, she decided, uncrossing her legs under the table, and get to know them a little bit better.

June 10

Herr Steinmann stood in the threshold resembling a ticket taker. Passed time hung between them like chewing gum between fingers, unbreakable but warped.

Sarah slipped her sandals off at the door. She should have brought socks. Sweaty feet in felt were a distraction.

"Are you ready for the last variation?" asked Herr Steinmann.

"Don't you think we should warm up by going through the theme first? Look, I brought us something. I hope they haven't melted in my bag." Sarah presented a small box of *Mozartkugel* pralines marked with the expiration date June 30. They'd nearly gone to waste behind the can of chickpeas in her cupboard, but it was starting to feel like Mozart deserved the luxury of indulgence, even at the cost of extra calories. No, not just Mozart, but music in general.

"Lovely! I've been craving pistachios." Pistachios contain anti-aging antioxidants, like chocolate, like coffee. How many *Mozartkugeln* would one have to eat to be born again?

"I always thought the red and gold candies were the originals." They had taken their seats, assumed their rehearsed positions and familiar angles. The milk in her cup clung to itself before surrendering to her whirlpooling spoon. "But then I discovered these with the blue and silver wrappers when I went to Salzburg."

It was just before Christmas with her friend Abbie from sophomore year, who was doing Madrid, Marseille, Milan, Munich; a straight-talking medical student Sarah had met when she spilled salad dressing on her in a tiny café on Broadway. They bonded over a shared appreciation for cheap Bordeaux and Wim Wenders films. Salzburg received the two young Americans wearing its charm like a collection of flashy shawls, layering Wolfgang Amadeus Mozart with Alpine countryside, *The Sound of Music*, and holiday kitsch.

"Konditorei Fürst, yes. A reminder that, if you invent something delicious, you should always get it trademarked. These are certainly the best ones."

"Trademarked or not, being copied is the biggest compliment, isn't it?" Her feet were sticking to the slippers. She'd have to pick felt fuzzies off her toes later.

"If only compliments could pay the rent." He bit into his ball of chocolate, marzipan and pistachio, a dark brown smidgeon hanging precariously from his lip. "Mozart did spend a great deal of time in Salzburg, but he was unhappy there, in such a small town, where there was no opportunity to perform his operas. That's why he had to move on to grander Vienna."

"Musicians are migrants, always following the audience." Talking with Christoph had reminded her of that.

"Like you, Sarah?" He wiped the chocolate off his lip with his pinkie, emptied his coffee cup and reached for another candy.

"When I was growing up, I liked to be home. My brother was always out with friends and I figured my parents could use the company. But when I was home, I thought about faraway places — Paris, Munich, Prague, Warsaw." A tiny drop of blood ballooned on her thumb as she tore at the loose skin around the nail, dead when detached. "At some point I realized my parents probably would have been happy being alone with each other."

"I can't speak for your parents, but musicians aren't known to be the happiest people on the planet, now are they? I suppose that hasn't changed much since Mozart's day, when you read the news about drug overdoses and suicides in the industry. It's very tragic." He frowned, as if taking partial responsibility.

"Or maybe depression is just as common among non-musicians, but the media only reports on famous people." Even *Fork & Messer*, which claimed to present the names of tomorrow, stuck to the chefs, trucks and bistros that already had a following.

"What made Benjamin so happy?" She thought of her own unhappy grandmother, always dressed for the couch in her velour loungewear. She didn't have her instrument to brighten her TV-filled days.

His smile was closed-lip. "Benjamin was a dramatic showman

who loved to share his music, but he did not need an audience — not the way you and I do." He watched for a reaction, but she showed none. "He enjoyed music for its own sake, no strings attached. And he knew music could make other people happy, too."

At the top of the classical music world, lip-service was given to music being something artistic, emotional; in the end, success was purchased with velocity and technique.

Still riding his own train of thought, he leaned forward in his chair, straining a whisper. "Benjamin is the only person I've ever met that managed to live without giving a thought to the future — though I sometimes wished he had. We would get so wrapped up in talking and playing that I would always have to remind him when my mother was about to come home. He would give me a pat on the shoulder, say, 'Stay eager, beaver, until next week,' and dash out the door with a hop, skip and a jump. On the days he ran into my mother coming back from the neighbors', he would wave at her unabashedly as he left."

Herr Steinmann leaned back in his chair. "A war may force you to ignore the future, but we Germans like to worry about all of the bad things that could happen no matter the circumstances. Now we live in peace and still worry about how expensive bread is getting — I remember a loaf costing 50 deutschmarks! — and whether our pensions are safe, and whether we'll get hit by a car if we cross an empty street on a red light."

That bad crossing-on-red habit she'd picked up in New York City. There, a matter of survival. Here, an invitation for public scolding.

"What do you worry about, Herr Steinmann?"

"Me?" He chuckled as he made his way, unassisted, to the piano. "My children, of course. That's every parent's burden, no matter how old they get."

"So Benjamin must not have had any kids?" She joined him, flipping through the book of music on the stand until she found the Theme and Variations, K. 501; the taillight piece.

"He did later. A German baby, in fact. I'm sure he had a lot of admirers back home in Raleigh — he was a dish, that boy, he was — but he fell in love with our neighbor, Ilse. I'd say she got the long end of the stick in that duo, allow me to be frank. In any case, it certainly ruffled some feathers, especially her father's. The neighbors would shake their heads when they saw her. They knew the baby in her growing belly didn't look like them."

"And you never kept in touch with Benjamin after that? Did you meet his child?" She got comfortable on the bench; he opened the lid: white-black-white-black-white-white-black, an imperfect pattern.

"He was transferred to Nuremberg in 1947, and I lost him. I tried many times to find him and his child, but to no avail. Ilse and her parents left before she had the baby. They said they were trying to find work in the North, but they were also ashamed for the neighbors to see her in that condition, and then what would they do with the baby? It seems not everything during that time, just after the war, was written down fastidiously." Regret pulled down his jowls; decades of wondering, the list of scenarios piling up only to be waste-paper-basketed again and again.

They began the theme wordlessly, cueing with a barely audible breath. The dance was carefree, innocent, but gradually gained the weight of experience as the piece progressed. Variation V marked a return to G major, a firm rediscovery of upbeat stability and speed. Sarah kept the thirty-second-note runs in check, milking the chromaticism, until she handed off to Herr Steinmann, who contrasted with rather uneven triplets in the left hand.

He leaned toward the score, blinking to focus his watery eyes. He left out the right hand so he could concentrate on securing the bass. Would he have done that a few weeks ago? His coordination seemed weaker; his dexterity shakier.

The piece concluded, not with bravura but with a restoration of the theme — not a repeat, but an ornamented echo, richer for what had been heard in the meantime.

Bam-thud-bam-thud! In the final two measures, marked *pianissimo*, the G only sounded half the time, the hammer dully striking the string in the other half. She replayed her part, careful to make each note audible.

"Anyone can be loud," susurrated Herr Steinmann. "Playing softly is the real art."

June 19

"If I close my eyes, I almost feel like I'm back in New York." Lauren had ordered a double espresso at Bavarian Brew. Were the people who drank their coffee without milk or sugar on a diet, did they want to appear tough, or did they truly enjoy the bitterness?

"Except that it's quieter here." She opened her eyes.

"People here call Munich a big village rather than a big city." Christoph swirled his double cappuccino. He never stirred.

"New York City is amazing, sure, but it's also overrated. I drank a lot of bad coffee when I was studying there," Sarah recalled. "Just because you find something in New York, doesn't mean it's better."

During her first three months in the city, she'd gripped the pepper spray in her pocket, thumb on the release button. During her second year, she deliberately took a walk through Harlem (in the middle of the afternoon) to see for herself what it was really like. Nothing notable happened, which was both a relief and a disappointment.

"I definitely don't miss the madness, but Munich hasn't exactly been a piece of cake." Lauren reached for the canister of whole-fat milk and added a drop to her drink. "I didn't expect it to be so hard to meet people here."

"Germans are tough nuts to crack, aren't we?" Christoph squeezed his hand over an imaginary nutcracker.

Sarah nodded. "A lot of Germans here speak English, but you won't really get to know them without your German being pretty fluent." Did that make her sound arrogant?

"It'll take forever for my German to get as good as yours!" Lauren threw up her hands in resignation. "So what's the deal with apartments here? I had to buy the kitchen from the guy who moved out of the place. It cost a ton, but there's not even a garbage disposal in it. And there are no screens on the windows and I keep getting bug bites!"

"It's a jungle out there, you know." Christoph was really dishing out the one liners. He stood a head taller than the American women; his face could have been cut out of any black-and-white photo labeled "Germany, 1924" or "1947" or "1969" and technicolored. The structure of his skeleton was apparent in his cheeks and wrists, which made him look honest. Even his skin had little to hide.

"You're right. Who likes wiping food gunk out of the sink? And we get flies and bees inside this time of year, but I think the spiders in the fall are much worse!" She used to pay her brother Brian fifty cents to clear the bathtub of spiders. When he raised his rate to one dollar, she got braver. "But we humans can get used to anything if you give us enough time."

With another American, the English words rolled over Sarah's tongue freely, comfortably; her English, when spoken with a German, would ingest their accent like light laundry washed with new jeans.

"So you studied piano in New York? That's so interesting!" Lauren's hand wrapped around her now cold espresso with whole milk; her fingernails were uniformly long, unpainted but perfect, her skin smooth.

"Yeah, it left a… dent," replied Sarah. A dent dips then rises to the starting position, but leaves the object forever changed.

"How's that?"

"In a roundabout way, it brought me here." She thought of Professor Rosenstein and how her connection to Munich began long before the city had become her address.

"When I was in culinary school, I thought I'd end up in France," said Lauren. "Then I went back to school for media production and saw the job opening at *Fork & Messer*. I wasn't sure about it at first. Everyone seems so stuffy and…"

"Boring?" Christoph dared to say it.

Sarah sighed at the thought of culinary school plus media training. Lauren brought the whole package.

"I wouldn't have put it that harshly. But, yeah," Lauren agreed. "I'm happy you guys are here — some younger faces with new ideas."

"I just pitched a new idea to Stefanie about including Mozart in one of the fall specials," shared Sarah. If she was going to find her footing at *Fork & Messer*, this was the chance.

"That's great that you went ahead and asked. Fingers crossed that Stefanie will agree to it," said Christoph.

"It sounds like you're the right person to write about that," said Lauren. "I'm just glad there's another American on the team. Someone who's on the same wavelength."

But were they? Theirs was a bond based on Nickelodeon and Kool-Aid, turkey sandwiches and mid-summer fireworks, a bond that wouldn't have existed had they met in another time, another place. Lauren still had so much to learn in Germany. But something about her openness, her good-natured naivety, made Sarah long to wrap herself up in her own culture again. *Home* was far away.

"Do you still play the piano? Where can I hear you play some Mozart?" asked Lauren.

"Yeah, where? I want to come too." Christoph piped up.

"I do play, but mostly… for myself." In music school, Sarah had never intended for that to happen. The scales, the exercises, the countless hours at the keyboard — they weren't an after-work hobby, they were to achieve artistic excellence, and that only existed in the ears of others. She heard the click of a twisting Rubik's cube and pictured a muddled up rainbow on its side.

"I don't mean to be the party pooper here but I've got a deadline to meet with some bland pictures of white rolls. Should we head back?" Christoph was already carefully stacking their used cups at the side of the counter.

"Sure. I've got an appointment with the girl from tech to answer all my questions about our crazy content management system." Lauren rolled her eyes.

"That thing was definitely not built by an editor." Sarah realized how many workarounds she'd picked up in her two-and-a-half years at the magazine. "You guys go ahead. I'm going to stay for a bit more fresh air."

Twenty-three minutes without a screen check; after Christoph and Lauren left, Sarah satisfied the craving and discovered a message from Charlotte Lagherty, a soprano she'd accompanied during music school.

Everybody knew Charlotte was a big deal. She was cast as Queen of the Night in *The Magic Flute* as a sophomore; her predecessors had all been graduate students. Her performance schedule was bringing her to town next month, she wrote:

It must be amazing making music in Munich! I'll be on the run as always — you know how it is, Sarah, Berlin is waiting — but let's have tea after my concert.

June 24

Eight minutes and three seconds, no intermission: It was a short recital.

Herr Steinmann bowed like a tortoise, dropping his chin without moving his torso, staring for an appropriate four seconds at the rug beneath his slippers. Wax had been combed into his countable hairs, a crimson handkerchief folded into his jacket pocket, and he smelled faintly of oranges.

Sarah dipped to a practiced ninety-degree angle, her hands sliding down to her knees. It was borderline acrobatic, but not awkward. *Clap clap clap* as enthusiastically as four hands could manage.

Snippets of memories flashed as she saw her feet: Sarah in front of the full-length mirror in the practice room after a lonely four-hour session, watching herself bow, her own audience; the stiff leather of Professor Rosenstein's bench, pressed by so many prize-winning bottoms; being blinded by the spotlights in the largest concert hall on campus; drops of sweat spilling into her bra, the dam behind them threatening to break. In the cloth-paneled practice cubicles, which had heard an inestimable swath of music, she had envisioned rows so deep they seemed endless and the whirr of applauding masses, not a smattering of hands.

Sarah hadn't expected this to feel like a real performance, but it did. She saw the satisfaction in Herr Steinmann's upturned lip, the way his hands shook, not only with the increasing weakness of age, but also with residual adrenaline. It didn't matter that the runs were choppy or that the second-to-last chord didn't sound. They'd done justice to the Theme and Variations; everyone in the room was wealthier for it. *Click click*, went the Rubik's cube.

"Please have some more loz." Mrs. Djabou held up a plate as Constantin and Sarah sat down on the wooden chairs they had brought in from the kitchen; Herr Steinmann relaxed into his pillows with a sigh.

"Thank you for baking, Frau Djabou," said Sarah, still a bit breathless from being on 'stage.'

"Oh, please call me Iris. 'Frau Djabou' just makes me feel old." She looked festive and fresh in her bright green blouse with an intricate circular pattern in orange and purple hues, paired with a long denim skirt and white indoor crocs, a blend of times and places.

Sarah nodded and reached for another sugar-coated ball with a pistachio on top. "Tell me again what's in them, Iris?" They were pralines without chocolate. A pattern was emerging: Music was sugar-coated, a luxury she'd earned, or rather didn't have to.

"They're mostly almonds, pistachios, loads of sugar, and a couple of secret ingredients my mother passed on to me. Constantin loves them, too," Iris added with a mother's pride, her hands folded across her lap. "He'll eat the whole batch if I let him!"

Sweet and sticky, all their tongues were tied. They chewed, staring into their coffee cups as the clock tick-tick-tocked in a quiet continuation of the concert. Sarah bit the pistachio off the top. It was the same nut buried in the *Mozartkugeln,* but she liked these better: They had nothing hidden inside.

"Food is one of those things that keeps you connected with home," Iris reflected. "If I stopped baking Chadian sweets, Constantin would forget what they tasted like."

"Which foods do you miss, Sarah?" Constantin stretched his long legs, crossing his feet, clad in classic Adidas slip-on sandals.

"The few American recipes I've tried here don't seem to turn out." *Few* was an exaggeration; she'd only baked once in Munich. Her mom had sent her a care package with a bag of Hershey's chocolate chips; the result was flat and gooey and too sweet for the German palate, said Arne downstairs.

"But in California, we have really good Mexican food. What I wouldn't give for some homemade enchiladas." Every so often, between fourth and eighth grade, a pan of corn tortillas hugging cheese and pork would show up on the kitchen counter. From Alejandra next door, her mom said, she couldn't make just a few. It had been friendly, filling food that didn't yet threaten her discipline or appearance.

"Don't most good things come from our neighbors?" Herr Steinmann exaggerated a nod toward his.

"Well, I, for one, know that something very good comes from upstairs, Herr Steinmann. Your playing is amazing!" Iris put her hands together in a mute applause.

"They say it takes ten thousand hours of practice to do something well, right? At your age, I'd say you've mastered the piano ten times over!" Constantin slapped him on the shoulder like a buddy.

Herr Steinmann was visibly pleased with the compliments and stuttered his reply. "I have had some very good teachers over the years. My mother taught me to keep my intentions simple, and to listen to the silence between the notes." He reached for a candy, cradling it in his palm before biting off the top half. "And Benjamin, well, he showed me that music sets you free."

After a double round of good evenings and well wishing, Sarah followed Constantin and Iris down to the ground floor. They exchanged more farewells and compliments as the key clink-clanked in the lock. Through the doorway, Sarah noticed the eclectic couldn't-decide-so-take-them-all colors, dominated by the warm tones of poppies and sand, that she hadn't seen before.

Music, the liberator? Benjamin, himself an emancipator despite the bonds an ignorant society had shackled him with, was freer than ever at the keys. How free was she? Like food, music intertwines itself with both pleasure and necessity.

July 2

Step, step, step, stop. Out here, Sarah wasn't alone and was in no hurry to get home at quarter to six. The sky was cluttered with bulging clouds, all drifting in unison, looking for the best spot to release their tepid summer rain.

Sarah tucked her sweater into the crook of her elbow, pausing in the middle of the Ludwigsbrücke to look over the island that split the Isar into two rivers. She imagined the dual waters flowing through her as they mirrored a blurrier, larger version of the city. Her German self paralleled the American Sarah; the pianist raced the editor.

The thick air made her sweat, then cooled her damp skin. She crossed the second river and veered to the left to avoid the busy Isartor square, absent-mindedly scanning the license plates on the vehicles that sped by. B for Berlin, BB for Böblingen, M for München, MM for Memmingen. The streets grew narrower but fuller, patios filled by early diners, late coffee drinkers. Sitting under that sky was a gamble with unfavorable odds.

She found a small table at an inconspicuous café; its legs rattled off-kilter against the pavement until she slipped a cardboard coaster under one of them. She knew what she wanted but had nevertheless memorized the drinks menu by the time the server with a messy man bun finally arrived.

"*Ein Glas Rosé, bitte.*" California Zinfandel was the only one on offer. Three minutes later, a coaster was flipped onto the table, a chilled glass placed on it. Its deep grapefruit color was a work of art, coquettish and cheerful, though the drink itself was mild and ordinary. Wine was a treat for body and spirit that seemed classy but not too decadent; it was neither hard liquor nor particularly caloric.

"If it starts to rain, I can open the umbrella for you." The server was balancing a tray full of large beer glasses, some erupting foam out the top, others spotted with it on their empty insides like a rash. Were man buns still trendy or was he balding early? Sarah's workday was crumbling off her like a crust of mud; his was just beginning.

Catch up on the news, start the Colin Powell memoir she'd downloaded after Herr Steinmann had mentioned his time in Germany — she had planned a semblance of productivity. Instead, she put her phone face down on the table and stared at the people walking by. Munich, everyone said, was infatuated with fashion. It was true, she thought, as two Furla bags strolled past. And were those Valentino shoes on a teenager? Munich was a stage, though it was the performers that double-dutied as the audience, those few a ripple in the sea of otherwise average people. Sarah was one of those now; she missed standing out, not with collars and cuffs but with artistic prowess.

Her German teacher in college had told her Germans were hard to get to know. Population: eighty-three million, and how many of them could Sarah count as a friend? Was Christoph a friend? He knew more about her than Theo did, except for the texture of her skin.

She liked to know where she stood, which is what had always made performing so stressful. Audiences only became honest at the highest echelon, where a boo fell within the budget of a career that wasn't at stake. Below that, she tended to refashion the generic 'good jobs' and 'well dones' in her head, perpetually presuming criticism: 'You'd better have a Plan B, Sarah.' 'Nice, for an amateur,' they must have meant.

Theo had been hot until he turned cold; she couldn't blame him because hot and cold yield lukewarm, and that's what she had been. She wasn't sad that it was over, but she missed his energy, which had tugged her like the steady current of a river, threatening at times to cover her head. He didn't need her (like she needed to need someone), but the few men who did had been decidedly boring.

His tongue against the inside of her cheek, the warmth of his fingertips through her jeans, through her panties, on her nipples; she felt a vibration in her legs. Then the odd scent of his skin filled her sinuses. She hadn't eaten since the banana and walnuts she'd called lunch; the rosé was watercoloring her thoughts. She was alone without an alibi phone or book but let them pity her.

A plump raindrop landed in her wine glass, splashing the last beads of Zinfandel against the sides. No need for an umbrella, just the check please.

Heading toward the closest tram stop, she adjusted her ear buds: Listening to pop music felt frivolous but also freeing, unburdened with past baggage, and Ed Sheeran was a good companion on days like these. Going home, not going home, home-home — the other home. She didn't know anyone her age who'd died of an overdose or already gotten a divorce, but "Castle on a Hill" still infected her with its homesickness. If the remedy for homesickness is going home, then we are not homesick, but *awaysick* and *homewell*. There are castles in California, just not old ones, not German old, not Old World old.

Thulp! The bottle exhaled as it lost its hat. A quarter bag of marshmallows, the remains of her mother's last care package, were next to the Bordeaux on her shelf. Wine was supposed to be drunk dry to sweet. To hell with that; the squishy white cylinders would make up the difference. She turned on the television: some hoarders-versus-declutter guru, and clicked down the volume. It was only Tuesday. Damn.

She should pursue her hobbies outside the office, Stefanie had said about her idea of mixing in Mozart. They couldn't start doing articles on badminton or stitchery, now could they? Sarah googled *What did Mozart eat for breakfast?* Capon, she read. The man started his day with castrated cocks; a fucking breakfast of champions. Clearly, she'd been doing it all wrong.

Her glass was empty, save the chalky residue at the bottom; she should have eaten something, anything, other than the marshmallows. She went to the kitchen for a refill instead, tossing the cracked cork, a blood-like stain marking one end, into the trash.

July 6

Sarah bit into her Florentine. Milk chocolate stuck to her lip, an almond sliver sailed like a summertime snowflake. She picked up the stray pieces from her saucer, dabbing them with her fingertip.

"Do you like them as much as I do?" Christoph asked. Sarah nodded with a full mouth, planning to cut the carbs from her dinner later, then deciding that it didn't matter. They were standing at a table at Viktualienmarkt, Munich's central market square, a bustling ant hole on a warm but overcast Saturday morning. Another day, another shared cappuccino, none the stranger without the office at their backs.

"*Dürfen wir uns dazustellen?*" A young couple with a baby set their espressos on Sarah and Christoph's table, taking for granted that conversations would be overheard. A chubby, crumb-crusted little hand reached a soggy cracker toward Sarah. The baby was nine months old, maybe ten, the rest of it wrapped expertly in a sling on her dad's breast. No thanks, I'll stick with my grown-up cookie, said Sarah's smile.

"They call them Florentines, but I'm pretty sure they don't come from Italy," conjectured Christoph. An expansive indoor Italian market was a few steps away, the land of pizza and gelato just a few hundred kilometers away, lapping over its melodious syllables and aromatic starches.

"Well, I don't know either, but French toast doesn't come from France, that's for sure."

"Food is a bad geography teacher, isn't it?"

Sarah took another bite. "Maybe we're all too obsessed with labels." American. Pianist. Food journalist. Immigrant. She could think of quite a few that could apply to her, but did any of them really fit?

Christoph's spoon was unused, the foam in the cup piled up like sooty street-side snow. Sarah hated to see it go to waste; would he mind if she dipped her spoon in? Instead, she scraped the last smidgeon of milk crust off her own porcelain and caught herself staring at his hands, slender but strong.

"Did you know that the May pole was stolen not that long ago?" Its blue and white stripes swirled like a hookless Bavarian candy cane. Christoph swallowed his last bite of Florentine and pointed to the slender mast in the middle of the square that bore images of historic beer makers and revelers. Each municipality in Bavaria had one, Viktualienmarkt being home to the pole for downtown Munich.

"The getaway car must have been a semi."

"It was a bunch of — what do you call those male student groups in the US?"

"Fraternity guys?" Her only experience with the Greek system was a fraternity-organized Halloween haunted house during her freshman year. *It only costs a couple dollars, Sarah, come on and have some fun!* She'd been talked into it by two braver piano majors and two predrinks. The result was two months of nighttime visits by a calf-grabbing zombie Santa in her dreams. By second semester, she'd stopped crossing the street when she had to walk past the frat house.

"But they're not Greek; the *Burschenschaften* are very German. It sounds like a bizarre crime, but stealing May poles is a tradition. There are even rules for stealing it."

"Of course there are rules for breaking the rules in Germany!"

"They didn't steal it directly from the Viktualienmarkt, but from a warehouse. When you take a May pole, you can hold it ransom for beer."

"That's frat boy currency everywhere."

"In this case, as far as I know, the guys got their beer and gave it back in time for the May First festival, so I guess no one got in trouble."

"Sounds more like an April first prank than a May First party." The fun factor got lost on Sarah.

Blue and white was camouflage against the sky as the clouds drifted apart, growing wispier and less threatening. The pole's predecessor was visible in Herr Steinmann's *Fasching* photo, with young

Otto kicking up his feet, cheeks rosy beneath the painted red circles on them, a smile like Benjamin's.

Sarah had been meaning to update Christoph. "At the palace, I told you about my Monday Mozart guy and the photo of the American GI."

"Did you find out what his story is?"

"You were right; I'm glad I asked. Herr Steinmann sounds smitten by him. Benjamin West from Raleigh, North Carolina. That was his name." The faded handwriting in the album, a steady hand. "He would stop by regularly to play ragtime on his piano. Apparently he had a child with the next door neighbor, a German girl, but Herr Steinmann lost touch with him when he was transferred and the girl's family moved away."

"Benjamin West is a name with celebrity potential, don't you think?" Christoph's German nuances on the J and W made it even more stage-worthy. He scratched his temple. "Brown Babies — that's what they called the children born to Black soldiers and white women during the war. There were a lot of them; my ex-girlfriend's dad was one. She knows nothing about her grandfather, since he didn't stick around. That was hard for her. I think he's the reason she moved to the UK, since he was British. And just because her skin was a little on the darker side, people here would ask where she was 'really' from. She grew up in Augsburg — she couldn't have been more Bavarian — but she liked to say she was from Wakanda." Those confused looks she must have gotten. *Sounds familiar, Sweetie, is that in Nigeria or New Jersey?*

An ex-girlfriend? Sarah's flushed cheeks embarrassed her, deepening her blush. Jealousy can appear unannounced and uninvited. Christoph in a twosome, waking up to pre-toothpaste kisses, coordinating a grocery list, spending Sundays with someone else's parents. Sarah was tempted to pry, but didn't.

"I'm sure a lot of people lost each other because of the war," she said. "So much displacement. I know I should feel lucky that I chose to move to another country. I can't imagine what it would be like to be forced to."

"I've chosen change, too. Stefanie doesn't know this yet, but I've applied for a new job." He lowered his voice, pulled his red bomber jacket across his crisp white v-neck, and put his hands in his pockets.

"Seriously?" Since Stefanie turned down her pitch, she'd been starting to think that her days at *Fork & Messer* were numbered. Now Christoph was about to jump ship before her. He, she realized, had been a fixture there, a rock in the sand.

"*Fork & Messer is nett...*"

"But *nett ist die kleine Schwester von Scheiße* — nice is shit's little sister, as you Germans say." She was buying time to figure out how she felt.

"Ha! I mean, it's been fine. But I can't grow there." He shifted his weight, put his elbows on the table. It was a decision with roots. "A friend of a friend founded this digital travel startup and they're looking for an artistic director. The idea is to offer travel deals, but then support the customer in every aspect of their trip, from how to pack your suitcase, to insider guidebooks, coupons to local restaurants, stuff like that."

Change suddenly seemed like an oasis. Another burst of jealousy flashed through her. It wasn't the novelty of the startup — did the world really need another travel app? — but the unwrittenness of a beginning.

"They have to see whether the funding comes through, though, before it becomes official."

"We'll really miss you!" Yes, it was true. "Can you take me with you?" She tried to make it sound like a joke.

"That's what I wanted to ask you. They're also looking for a music manager to do things like curate playlists for each city, recommend concerts and create music-related content for the destinations. They're filling a bunch of positions right now — *if* the funding comes through — and being a native English speaker will definitely get you brownie points."

Sarah looked around. Was anyone listening? The couple with the baby had left. Who should care that she was courting professional infidelity? "That sounds like it could be a good fit. What are the chances that they'll get the funding?"

"Fifty-fifty. I'm only telling *you* about this for now."

"You were the one who told me that my future at *Fork & Messer* wouldn't be a long one. And you're probably right." She looked down at her fingers resting on the saucer, claiming her empty cup, her right to stand there. "Remember when we met at the Hirschgarten *Biergarten* and ate the giant pretzel? Alex and Beatrix said kind things about my work. I never knew that anyone noticed."

"If you're that good at something you feel like you have to fake,

Sarah, think how well you'd do at something you know you're good at." He hunched his shoulders as he put his hands in his pockets.

She stared at the May pole, a jester's toy, a reveler's accomplice, bearer of the brewer's patron saints. "You're right, Christoph," Sarah said finally. "Working with music again could be... let me think about it. Maybe I'm afraid that if I start walking toward what I want, it will turn out to be a mirage again."

July 8

Sarah couldn't look at Herr Steinmann without seeing it, but she couldn't look away. That reddish stain on his shirt; Bolognese, soup or watermelon?

"I'm curious, Sarah, what have you been playing at home this week?" He was unaware of the distraction.

"I needed to shelve Mussorgsky for a while. Or maybe I'm done with it, actually." An on-the-spot decision. "I needed something edgier this week, so I picked up Ginastera — his *Danzas argentinas.*" The work opens jaggedly, the left hand only plays black notes, the right hand only white notes; it is deeply unsettling. Despite its own aggressions, the Schimmel lacked the teeth the piece needed.

"The great Argentinean! Many Germans moved to his country after the war. He, on the other hand, came to Europe at the end of his life, you know. To Switzerland, I believe."

"The piece is hard on my hands." Rubbing her palms together, she heard the dense chords jolt in her mind.

"Then Mozart will be a well-deserved vacation?"

"He's certainly never been that before." Mozart, a three-tiered fondant-covered cake; Mozart, a summer morning in the palace garden; never Mozart, the island hammock and cocktail.

"Benjamin used to do stretches for several minutes before he sat down to play, like a long-jumper or a runner. He would stretch his hands and arms, of course, but also his back and legs." Herr Steinmann shrugged his shoulders up and down in a mini warm-up. "The first time I saw him do it, I thought he was going to do a back-flip right there in our family room. He probably could have. He was quite athletic — unlike me."

"Playing an instrument is more physically demanding than people think." She pressed the thick part of her palm beneath her right thumb. "Music schools should add yoga or Pilates to the curricula. A lot of musicians hurt themselves, but no one ever talks about it. And no one wants to do anything that takes them away from practicing." Tendinitis, back aches, neck strain. A musician who admitted to being in pain would be presumed to have poor technique, even though no instrument is capable of an ergonomic miracle for eight hours a day.

"Benjamin told me a gunshot wound he'd taken early on in the war had stiffened him up, though he never said where he'd been shot." Cup emptied, he folded his hands reminiscently in his lap. "You know, he was the first Black man I'd ever spoken with. That sounds absurd now, but Germany was a different place back then."

He was already en route to the piano before Sarah could reply, limping as he leaned on his cane. Was it English or German that he had spoken with Benjamin? Or hand gestures with random remembered words: *Musik, Klavier, Liebe.* Jazz, at least, was shared, from *jasm*, English slang for energy, gifted to the world along with its syncopations, its steps, its celebrities. Herr Steinmann kept talking, more to the instrument than to her.

"I suppose he helped change it, though. Change Germany. I don't mean how you Americans helped us rebuild things and get our economy off the ground. But his optimism was contagious. We had just surrendered to the Allies, you see, and saw nothing but rubble, limbless soldiers, sonless mothers. It wasn't exactly a cheerful time. Benjamin showed at least this grumpy German that you can choose to be joyful, no matter what life deals you." He coughed and touched his handkerchief to his eyes and nose. "And he gave us a child. I never met his son, of course, but I always wondered whether he carried on his musical talent."

"And you never found out what happened to him?" Sarah scanned the stack of scores on the piano: Mozart Sonatas for piano solo and duo, Chopin Nocturnes and Bach Partitas; sheet music to Gershwin's "The Man I Love" and Joseph Lamb's "Top Liner Rag" on top.

"When Gerda died, I spent months trying to find Benjamin's son. Nothing. I found nothing after Nuremberg. It's as if the records vanished, as if he never existed." He threw up his hands. "I liked to think he and Ilse went to the US. I hoped they didn't separate, so that he didn't have to lose a child, too." He opened the book of Mozart sonatas for piano duo, flipped through a few pages, and stopped at F major, K. 497. "Hannelore would have liked Benjamin. I met her just a few weeks after his last visit." He nodded toward the score. "It begins with such melancholy, for F major."

The opening Adagio meandered; their synchronization broke down on the first read-through. They had to repeat it three times before lurching from 3/4 to *alla breve* in the Allegro di molto, which opened with six measures of rests for Herr Steinmann, a slow start for *Secondo*, a chance to find his bearings. He still stopped short after his first phrase with sound.

"Let's go back to the Adagio. I'm not at my best today. It needs to be weightier, more contemplative." He smoothed his hair, then rubbed his chest.

As they concluded the Adagio for the second time, he sighed heavily. His hands, still curved as if holding a tomato, slipped from the keyboard to his lap, weary and pale, his skin the color of egg whites. Time was quickly dulling his skill. Sarah knew her chance to produce perfection was not an endless expanse, but a book whose pages turned one by one. One day, the back cover would fall shut. She felt a tightness in her throat telling her to hurry. *Quick!* The piano would not wait for her forever.

"My grandson is also quite musical. When he was very young, he asked me to tell him stories about Benjamin over and over again. He especially liked to hear about the time when Benjamin stopped in front of our house to share a small piece of chocolate with three or four boys playing ball out front. They were rather afraid of him, but they wanted the chocolate so badly that they ran up and grabbed it out of his hand. Then they jumped back two meters and kept watching him."

"That means you used to spend more time with your grandson?"

"When they lived here in Munich we were... closer, you could say. He plays the bass, the electric bass. It can be a very loud instrument, I'm afraid, but bass players have to be very good listeners."

"I would miss playing the melody, I think." As a child, Sarah had dreamed of becoming either a singer or pianist; the first door never opened, the second was closing so slowly she couldn't hear the latch fall.

"That's the thing about the bass. You never play alone. We pianists can allow ourselves to isolate; that is not good for our music, let alone our souls. His band produced an LP a few years ago. Not a fancy new MS3 or ML5, or whatever those digital things are called, but an old-fashioned record. They figured out that, when you find something good, it's worth sticking with it."

"You mean MP3? If Benjamin only knew what an impact he had on a young German, two generations down the line."

"Yes, it's unfortunate that Moritz and Benjamin never met. Maybe the impact would have been much larger. Of course, I hope that Benjamin had grandchildren of his own, perhaps even a few more than I did." He smiled weakly with surrogate regret.

"I'd better get going and let you get some rest." She felt guilty for not leaving earlier.

"I'm always happy to have you here, Sarah. Wouldn't it be nice to be twenty-seven and full of energy again! We could have kept playing." *Wouldn't it be nice to be old and not give a damn about shirt stains?* He wiped his nose again as he saw her out.

Outside, the summer sun was shedding its strength, too tired to be fierce. A group of teenage girls bounced by on the sidewalk in front of Herr Steinmann's house, bare stilt legs attached to taught belly skin by strips of denim. They were holding hands or had cast their arms around each other's necks like one creature with many limbs, a colorful, lime-scented caterpillar. Sarah fell in step with them for a block or two, then split off and doubled her pace.

TEN YEARS EARLIER

Sarah had writer's block at ten on a school night. The first three college entrance essays had written themselves in an hour, all variations on 'What do you want to be when you grow up and why?' That was easy: a concert pianist, to share something beautiful with people.

The fourth — What would you do if you couldn't fulfill your career goal due to structural changes in society or personal injury? — wasn't flowing. It was an unfair question: True ambition didn't allow for a Plan B.

"Dad and I are going to bed now. Don't stay up too late." Sarah's mom came in to give her a quick shoulder massage, her strong thumbs digging into her flesh. Not the good kind of hurt. "Maybe you should take a break and come back to it tomorrow when you're fresher."

"Ouch, mom! Not so hard!" Sarah also had a major exam in advanced chemistry (her worst subject, though she was still getting an A-) at the end of the week and a recital later that month. She really wanted to get this out of the way.

She took a quick break. Brushing her teeth gave her a two-minute excuse not to think. Just as she was sitting back down at her desk, her laptop *wooshed* with a new email.

Dear Ms. Johnson,

While your interest in my studio is appreciated, it has been full for months with superb young talents that already have extensive concert schedules of their own. The waiting list for my studio is equally comprised of major prize winners. The best only take the best. If you haven't learned that already, you soon will.

Yours sincerely,
A. Mynne

She read it four times, the knot in her stomach growing tighter each time. Incoming music majors were supposed to reach out directly to the faculty they wanted to study with on an individual basis. The music instructor had the stand-by-you intimacy of an athletic coach, a sculptor forming its protégés in its own image. At best. They were also show-off lines in the biographical blurbs found in future concert programs and — optimal, though rare — cognac buddies with the judges of the top competitions.

Some of the faculty, like Andrej Mynne, were literally world famous inside the snow globe of classical music. Though he was well over seventy, maybe eighty, he still made regular solo appearances with orchestras from San Francisco to Tokyo, and also toured with his chamber trio. Not that he would get stopped at Starbucks for an autograph — not Justin Bieber or even Lang Lang kind of famous. Not that he went to Starbucks, because not being recognized would shatter his ego.

He was out of her league, she knew that. But wasn't she supposed to shoot for the stars? Hell, why not the next galaxy? She was only seventeen, but everyone — her parents, her Sunday school teacher, even her third-grade softball coach — had guaranteed that limits were nothing more than figments.

Feeling relieved that she didn't have to study with a superstar after all meant she had thought it was a possibility. How embarrassing. If music school was full of arrogant assholes, did she really want to go at all?

She closed her laptop and changed into her cloud-print pajamas. The fourth essay could wait another day.

July 14

The walls were the color of ferns and a magnificent crystal chandelier dangled above their heads. Sarah and Herr Steinmann were trapped in the middle of the row of armless chairs, in the left hook of the U-shaped seating arrangement. Every seat was full; the room was pregnant with the anticipation of the soloist's entrance, tense with the self-restraint of the spectators. He was breathing laboriously, too loudly, next to her, his hands crossed over his lap.

Charlotte Lagherty had offered Sarah two tickets to her performance in the Hubertussaal, a four-hundred-seat hall within the Nymphenburg Palace. Herr Steinmann had been overjoyed at Sarah's invitation.

The stroll to the palace grounds had been strenuous and slow. They arrived just seven minutes before the Sunday matinée was scheduled to begin. A pale yellow handkerchief peeked out of the breast pocket of his Bavarian coat. He appeared shorter than usual, one gray head among many. His cheeks had taken on some color from the walk, but his hands were still mottled with their usual shades of taupe.

A door opened; applause; *clack-clack-clack*. Charlotte and her pianist entered from behind the grand piano on the shallow stage. Just a few steps, her heels were meant to be heard; she held up the front of her ballooning emerald skirt. Her dark hair was piled high on her head in a dramatic up-do; her corset-style dress suited the historic setting and accentuated her bouncing bosom. Eight-hundred hands wound down uncoordinatedly, but she wasted no time: her right hand on the top of the piano, a focused look at the floor, a nod to the pianist. Ready, set, go.

Sarah felt the want titillate from her toes to her split-ends. She had always relished the millisecond before delivering her first note in a performance, the one that took command of the room or lost it. Charlotte took it — even more so than Sarah had remembered. Her presence was so consuming, she nearly forgot that Herr Steinmann was there next to her. The silence around her grew palpable as Charlotte's voice filled every corner of the room, richer than it was loud.

> *Ein Veilchen auf der Wiese stand,*
> *gebückt in sich und unbekannt;*
> *es war ein herzigs Veilchen.*[3]

The words belonged to Johann Wolfgang von Goethe, the music to Wolfgang Amadeus Mozart; it was a deceptively simple song detailing the trampling of a heart as fragile as a flower. In hardly two minutes, the deed was accomplished.

> *Ach, aber ach! Das Mädchen kam*
> *und nicht in acht das Veilchen nahm,*
> *ertrat das arme Veilchen.*
> *Es sank und starb, und freut' sich noch:*
> *und sterb' ich denn, so sterb' ich doch*
> *durch sie, durch sie, zu ihren Füßen doch!*[4]

Charlotte touched a clenched fist to her painted lips in a silent

---

[3] A violet in the meadow stood
stooped in itself and unknown.
It was the sweetest violet.
[4] Ah! But alas! The maiden came
and no heed to the violet paid,
crushed the poor little violet.

It sank and died but was happy still:
and though I die, I shall have died
through her and at her feet yet.
The poor violet!
It was a dear sweet violet.

https://lyricstranslate.com/en/k-476-das-veilchen-violet.html

cough, nodding her head to each prong of the U. Sarah surveyed the wrinkled faces that had seen three times as many years as hers. Mozart was twenty-nine when he wrote the song they'd just heard, just a couple of years older than she was. Could he have dreamed his audiences would be so much hoarier than he'd ever become? The palette of lined up hues spanned the entire grayscale, from off-white to dusk, painting the shadows in the fern-walled woods.

"It's quite masochistic, really." Herr Steinmann leaned over to Sarah during the applause, the back of his hand in front of his lips. "The poor violet is so in love with the shepherdess that it rejoices in being killed by her. A bit twisted, if you ask me, but that is our dear Goethe."

The violent end to the fragile violet was merely the beginning. Charlotte hardly waited for the clapping to dwindle before inhaling and exhaling the next work on the program that mixed Mozart's songs for soprano with a few arias. By the intermission, she was pink-cheeked, her breast heaving, while coughs burst from the U with increasing frequency, like the pops of corn kernels on a stove, as background noise overcame the applause.

Herr Steinmann picked up his cane as they filed out for the break and stood in the drinks line, an unlikely pair in a cloud of Chanel No. 5, because the older women get, the more perfume they squirt. He bought two glasses of sparkling wine and they found half a bar table, dressed in a white tablecloth, to rest their flutes. For how long would he be able to stand, even with the cane? It was nearly noon.

"I used to especially enjoy accompanying singers. I would memorize the texts and pretend my piano keys were speaking them, too," Sarah said. She would secretly sing them in front of the mirror, heard only by absorbent practice cubicle walls, chin dropped, hand rising, for once the one that looked at the (imaginary) audience and not ninety degrees away from it.

"The voice is perhaps the greatest instrument of all. But God either anoints you with one or..." He tipped a third of the elixir down his throat.

"... or not. Charlotte has a magical instrument. She was born for the big stage." Sarah sipped her drink slowly, holding the glass with three fingers, daintily, politely. Herr Steinmann rested both wrists and the hook of his cane on the table.

"With composers like Mozart, the line between vocal and instrumental music blurs, I like to think." He peered toward the ornately decorated ceiling, jutting a hand upward. "Mozart played right here, you know, right here in the Hubertussaal of the Nymphenburg Palace. He was just a boy."

"Mozart, the *Wunderkind*." She looked around at the soaring ceilings and paneled walls with a fresh sense of awe. "I didn't know that, actually."

"The world knows at least one German word thanks to him. *Wunderkind*. Mozart was still a child, so it must have been the early 1760s. He and his sister were here to play for Elector Maximilian III Joseph. It was the summer, and this was the summer residence of the Bavarian royalty."

"The city must have smelled atrocious during the summer. No wonder they wanted to get away." Sweat spilling over dried sweat, layer for unshowered layer. "Nowadays people complain about not having air conditioning here in the summer."

"Air conditioning is like pain pills, in my opinion. It alters reality. Why would you want to do that? You're only really alive if you let in both the wonderful and the horrible." He scoffed, opening and closing his mouth as if he'd eaten a spoonful of peanut butter. Was the sparkling wine already flowing though his veins? "It was Elector Maximilian III Joseph who ornamented the Great Hall of the palace. It's quite exquisite. But there was no money left over to offer the *Wunderkind* a job." He pushed his empty glass to the center of the bar table and leaned on the edge with both forearms. "*Ach*, the things you pick up when you live near the palace as long as I have."

"I always thought I could practice really hard and make up for the extra bit of talent I wasn't born with. But if even Mozart stayed poor…"

"Success, dear Sarah, almost never has to do with talent, even though you certainly have the latter, and I'm sure you will find the former."

As the stoic herd of spectators filed back into the green room, he tipped toward Sarah. "I'm so sorry, but I'm afraid I'm not feeling well. I think I'll go home now. Please tell your friend Charlotte that her concert was exquisite. I particularly enjoyed the opening song, '*Das Veilchen.*'"

"Of course, Herr Steinmann. Let me walk you home." She didn't want to miss the second half, but she also didn't want to find him later in a pile somewhere near the palace, swans curiously poking their beaks into the pockets of his Bavarian jacket.

He feigned reluctance before relenting. She offered him her elbow without giving it a thought as they crossed the palace grounds: a novel posture, a familiar arm. A few months ago, she'd walked here with Christoph, elbow to unhooked elbow, pieces of Herr Steinmann's Nazi past between them as they'd talked about him.

As they walked, like grandfather and granddaughter, great-grandfather and great-granddaughter, the sun grew more intense. Sarah was sweating in her blazer. With one hand on Sarah's elbow, the other on the neck of his cane, Herr Steinmann could have used a third to wipe his brow with.

Vrrr! Packs of cyclists zipped by, making the most of the Sunday at the park, portable barbecue equipment and packs of meat strapped into bike baskets. A brass band played traditional Bavarian music in the distance, a jarring shift from Mozart's delicate violet. She deposited him at his door like her first boyfriend had done when they were fourteen: with a warm nod and a well-wishing. "See you next week, Herr Steinmann."

"Thank you for a lovely concert, Sarah." As he turned into the house, she saw that the white hairs at the nape of his neck, a few more than at the top of his head, had grown long enough to turn.

She took off her blazer, folded it over her elbow, and raced back to the palace. Charlotte had agreed to meet her after the performance for hot tea, liquid gold, or whatever it was that professional singers allowed to flow past their instrument.

Applause enveloped Sarah when the heavy door to the Hubertussaal opened, the kind that ebbed and flowed but whose end seemed unwritten. It had been so long since the roar, never quite as loud, had been hers; would she ever own an applause as full as this?

Charlotte put one hand to her chest as she accepted a summery bouquet from a gray-suited employee of the hall, an eye-catcher in the muted moss-colored room. Sarah didn't bother taking her seat again, but pressed herself against the back wall like a spore. Charlotte's pianist was standing with his hand on the edge of the keyboard, morphing with his instrument in his simple tuxedo as the soloist continued leaning toward each side of the audience — not too far down; a wardrobe malfunction would not be a boost in this kind of business.

The door was opened behind Sarah, and guests began to shuffle. She was the first in the foyer, stepping into a corner to text Charlotte: "There's a quirky café very close to the palace. I'll wait there for you. Come when you can."

She had only been inside the hall for a few minutes, but her eyes had adjusted quickly and she was blinded when she stepped out and left the palace grounds. The café was garishly accented in hot pink, a fluorescent sign in the window, a striped awning. Dozens of elaborate cakes were on display at the front. Inside, the walls were lined with historic photos, some dating back a century. A café that was even older than Herr Steinmann — inconceivable. Pictures on the walls showed women in high-necked dresses pushing prams with huge wheels, men in hats and mustaches. The storefronts would, just a couple of decades later, surely all be bombed to smithereens.

The concave pull of hunger in her middle, Herr Steinmann snoring restoratively in his trusty armchair, breaths manifested in the sway of his eyebrows, the sparse stubble on Christoph's slender chin: Sarah was daydreaming when Charlotte finally walked through the door, her hair and make-up still in place, a cotton scarf wrapped around her neck despite the warm weather. She was wearing yoga pants and an oversized t-shirt and pulled a small red suitcase behind her. A brief but audible hush fell over each table as she walked by. She wasn't extraordinarily beautiful or tall, she simply had a way of casting a spell on people, even — or perhaps especially — strangers.

"Sarah, it's so good to see you again!" They embraced; Charlotte faked three French-style cheek kisses.

Sarah ordered a second cappuccino; Charlotte asked in English for a *heiße Zitrone* — hot lemon juice with honey.

"Your cappuccino looks amazing. I'd much rather have one of those, but the milk traps phlegm in my throat. That's the last thing I need." She stirred the honey into the steaming yellow liquid until it became invisible, glancing at Sarah's cocoa-dusted cup. "And the traveling, you know, it really gets to my voice. I can't afford to come down with something."

Sarah took a sip, and the scorching cappuccino burned her tongue. She flexed her fingers on her lap under the table, feeling them loosen up. "I really enjoyed the concert. I was only able to see the first…"

"Great that you could make it!" Charlotte cut in. "You know I'm really here in Europe to audition with some of the bigger opera companies. I arrived from Milan earlier this week."

"But the Nymphenburg Palace is not a shabby gig. Your show sold out." Sarah rested her forearms on the table.

"Yeah, I was really lucky to get booked there. The place is a much bigger deal than I am at the moment. It's gorgeous and when you think of all the royalty that has been there."

"And Mozart, too."

"Yes, exactly, which is obviously why they wanted an all-Mozart program. But you know I'm more of a Carmen." Charlotte woke up her phone, lying face up next to her cup, with a tap. No notifications, only a wallpaper photo of her as Aida in thick theater makeup. "It's just been harder than I thought to land a big role since music school."

"It's so competitive…" Charlotte *was* the competition, thought Sarah. It was hard to imagine her being turned down.

"Crazy competitive. Especially New York. Sometimes I wonder why I stayed. There's always someone better, and it's probably your next door neighbor." She laughed cynically. "Mine is actually a first-chair oboist. I envy you for coming here and getting out of the city. You must really like it here. Munich is such an inspiring place, isn't it? Are you playing a lot?"

"Yeah. Yeah, I am." Was that an eggshell white lie? No, it was the truth. Every other Monday with Herr Steinmann, every other day with her Schimmel; it wasn't a professional's schedule, but more than nothing, more than before.

"How are the gigs here? Good pianists must be a dime a dozen in Germany." The lipstick stain on her glass mug gave the liquid inside an orange tinge.

"I recently played a small house concert." Including an after-show reception with refreshments. "But you — you're doing the big leagues, living the life we all dreamed about. Are you happy?" It was a question only Christoph would ask, thought Sarah, smiling inwardly.

Charlotte looked toward the wall-sized mirror behind Sarah's head. "Happy? I'd be really happy to land a big role. My boyfriend just moved out and I can't afford the rent on my own, so I'm going to have to move anyway."

"Nikolai, the conducting student? I thought you two would be together forever." Even on a student's budget, Charlotte and the Bulgarian cellist-turned-conductor had managed to host simple but legendary dinner parties during music school, where the guests were ninety-five percent European or Latin American, the meal was never served before ten, and the wine flowed until dawn.

"Yeah, well, having music in common wasn't enough. I should look for a scientist, or an NBA star or something. At least someone who makes tons of money and doesn't get so... obsessive. Or I have to start screwing a music director," she said flippantly, but not without a trace of seriousness.

"I'm sorry about Nikolai." Charlotte remained silent; Sarah didn't exactly have BFF rights to pry.

"This place looks like it's from another time, doesn't it?" Charlotte's eyes drifted to the photos on the walls.

"I'd never been here before, but living in Munich has made me appreciate old things."

Charlotte pulled a large wallet out of her bag, a holder for everything, bits of paper sticking out on all sides. She tucked a five-euro note under her saucer. "It was so nice to see you, Sarah. My train for Berlin leaves this evening. I'm going to try to catch an hour of sleep. Thank God for late checkout."

Sarah wished she had stayed longer, but Charlotte had always been abrupt, off to more important things. She watched the singer make her exit, maneuvering her red suitcase through the door as she slid a pair of oversized sunglasses onto her nose. Charlotte was the kind of person who left a dent.

Sarah gave a generous tip when the server finally came.

"Is she famous?" the woman asked with a hand on her aproned hip.

"Yes," said Sarah, still looking through the glass door. "Almost."

JULY 18

Félicité had to have almond hair and wear silk blouses. That's how Sarah pictured the Paris-based author when they phoned. Calls were stressful because she had to wing it, covering up her uncertainty over cooking techniques by being a tad too strict about the things she knew.

Can you extend the deadline two more days? — Absolutely not.

Of course that's a proper English word! — Not according to Webster.

Email, on the other hand, left time to weigh her words and room between the lines. But in the office, she couldn't just ignore the penetrating *dingelingeling* of her telephone.

Christoph rapped his knuckles on the doorframe. Sarah raised two fingers and mouthed "two minutes." She was just about to green-light Félicité's pitch for a portrait-based story on the different kinds of bread Parisians with non-French roots eat and how it differs from the local *pain*. The article would be on her desk an hour before deadline with gaping grammar flaws and a crappy headline, but with edgy, personable interviews and mouthwatering descriptions only a true foodie could come up with.

While Sarah was deliberating about whether she could possibly clean the piece up enough to impress Stefanie with it, she scanned her sparse desk: a postcard-sized map of the Munich subway system, a dish of paperclips she never used, two giveaway pens.

Five minutes later, Christoph's foot was in the door, which he closed behind him. "They got the funding." He bubbled with anticipation.

Who got what? It took her a millisecond to find the context. "Damn! That means you're really leaving?" That travel startup was taking off after all. She felt a stab of disappointment, a prick of envy.

"You're the first person I've told, so it's not official yet." His hands were in his pockets. Were they shaking? "The question is, are you?"

"Well, congratulations, first of all." She gave him a wide-armed, celebratory hug and felt the sinewy muscles in his shoulders. He smelled faintly of sap — woody, woodsy, and sweet.

"It's not like I've made myself at home here." She waved toward the empty space on her desk. "But I don't think the startup is right for me. I need something more…"

"Your own. I know."

"Yeah." He got it. "You're right."

"I didn't really think it was your thing, despite the music connection, but I would selfishly love to keep working with you." He pulled his hands out of his pocket and rubbed his palms together. There was a one-inch scar between his right pinky and wrist. The color rising in his cheeks, Christoph hastily changed the subject. "By the way, have you tried looking up Benjamin West from Raleigh?"

Sarah felt her mouth dry up and a tickle in her belly as Christoph's half-way admission of affection dissipated from the space between them. "No, no — I didn't want to meddle in Herr Steinmann's business."

"Don't you wonder though?" Christoph's dimples shone through a suppressed smile; he definitely had something to hide.

"Sure, but…"

"I may have found something. I don't know whether it's really him because I didn't contact him, obviously. I'll leave that to you. Let me double check the details and I'll send you an email about it in a couple days."

Who had he dug up? Could it really be Benjamin West, the jazz angel — *the* Benjamin?

He turned to leave, but stopped, looking at her thoughtfully, intentionally. Four seconds, five seconds. "And, Sarah, as much as I'd love to keep you in this city, I'd bet my first paycheck that you'll be someplace else next year."

She wanted to say how much she loved Munich, how well she fit in. Here, where the Aldi wine was more plentiful than the drink dates, the nine-to-five a costume that was cracking. *Mozart also failed to find his dream job in Munich. Repeat: Mozart failed. Mozart failed on repeat.*

"Don't forget." The scar on Christoph's hand turned white as he gripped the door frame, one foot already in the hall. "You could always take me with you."

Would he really follow her around the globe? Sarah wondered as he left. The thought was flattering, even exciting. Change was a fast motorcycle that packed risks in its side car. Should she get on and get going? She turned back to her computer and finished the email accepting Félicité's pitch. Sure, she could manage the edit, and so what if Stefanie wasn't happy with it.

July 22

Flower coffee, the Germans call it, *Blümchenkaffee*, so weak that the blooms at the bottom of the cup shine through it. Herr Steinmann's porcelain did have chrysanthemums, but not on the inside. Despite heat and humidity, he looked pale in his short sleeved button-down and tan cotton vest, gray skin sagging from his upper arms like an elephant's.

"It's been eleven years exactly since Hannelore left us." He wasn't enunciating.

"A very long time." Sarah felt the helplessness of someone for whom death is the coffin in the storefront next to plastic irises.

"Not for her, fortunately. Not when you have eternity. Only for us. Yes, for me." He folded and unfolded his hands in his lap. "But one good thing about the anniversary of her death is that my daughter Silke phoned me. Good God, I thought someone else had died!"

"She was just thinking about you?"

"Yes, I suppose so. And about her mother. They were very close, you know. Much closer than she and I were. It was the longest phone call we've had in many years. She's always so busy. They seem to be constantly restructuring her department. She usually manages to come out with even more employees under her each time. Or at least more meetings."

He reached for his cup, took a generous sip, grimaced. "*Bah!* Not my best coffee, I'm afraid." Sarah tilted her head in wordless agreement.

"Silke also mentioned that my grandson just spent a few days in the hospital. It seems he had gotten into a disagreement with some ungentlemanly characters near the central train station in Cologne.

They left him with a black eye and a broken rib."

"I'm sorry to hear that. You said he had some issues with drugs?" She cradled her cup in both hands.

"He was trying to get clean, but fighting an addiction is one thing. Changing your entire social milieu is another." His breathing was strained. "I worry about that boy every single day." They swallowed their thin brown liquid reflectively, listening to the glug of Adam's apples, until Herr Steinmann suddenly heaved himself to his feet.

"If I keep sitting here, I will fall asleep." He shuffled to the piano without his cane.

"Benjamin," he said, lowering himself onto the bench, "also got into a serious altercation."

"He sounded like a very peaceful guy."

"Of course he'd just spent years lobbing mortars at us Germans, and I'm quite sure that he was a very good shot, but a fist fight is different. You have to look a man in the eyes when you hurt him. You get his blood on your knuckles."

Sarah opened the book of Mozart sonatas, stretching the binding at the first movement of the F major. She cringed at the thought of Benjamin's aching hands — such a strong, but delicate and invaluable body part. She cracked her left knuckles in empathy, then quickly rested her hand in her lap. A pianist didn't crack their knuckles.

"Let's begin directly with the Allegro and skip the Adagio," inserted Herr Steinmann. "Benjamin didn't start it, of course. Two white soldiers, Americans, got very drunk one night and attacked him in the street after dark. I think maybe one of them was also in love with Ilse, but that is only my personal theory. Benjamin never said anything about that, only about how interested he was in her."

"After winning the whole war together, an American attacked an American?"

"In your country, Benjamin was still a second-class citizen, don't forget. And in Germany, the war was over, but there was no real government yet. There were no viable rules except the ones enforced by the Americans. And apparently the good old US military looked the other way. Martin Luther King, Jr. was still a very young man at the time if you'll recall."

"Was he badly hurt?"

"They broke his nose and several ribs, bruised him up quite a bit. But he went down swinging, that boy. I suspect he put up a better fight than they'd anticipated. He didn't come around to play the piano for three weeks after the incident. He was clearly still in pain the first time he came back, but they hadn't punched the smile off his face — which is probably what they were out to do in the first place." A look of pride ironed a decade or more off Herr Steinmann's cheeks. Sarah gently rubbed the joints in her fingers.

"I think the attack had something to do with why he was transferred to Nuremberg, though I don't know whether perhaps he requested the transfer himself because of the brawl. We didn't talk about military affairs. After all, I was still *ein Deutscher*, still the enemy in a way, and that was work and not music." As if it were a dirty word, a German.

She cued and they jumped jauntily into the Allegro di molto, leaning into the *tenutos* and running away with the scales.

The mood turned minor, and his fingers fell abruptly off the keyboard. "I need a moment to catch up." Huffing, he pressed his hands into his thighs like a runner after a race.

"Benjamin, you see" — he found his breath again — "was disciplined for being involved in the fight, even though he was outnumbered two-to-one. However, he never saw himself as a victim, and he never spoke poorly of any of his white colleagues."

"He sounds like a very good man." She wondered what Christoph had managed to dig up. "I used to think that being a good person, caring about my audience, would make me a better musician."

"Yes, he was both. Even though being a good person and good musician never brought him success, at least in the short time that I knew him." Not when music schools couldn't see past skin. Would audiences have been blinder if they'd had the chance to listen?

Sarah dropped both hands into her lap with a thud. "But the assholes, the egotists — I've met plenty of them with sold-out concert schedules." She thought of Professor Mynne, fêted on the world's biggest stages, but insecure enough to insult a teenager.

Herr Steinmann exhibited the wry smile of experience, one that would make any teen roll their eyes. "My dear, I'm afraid that is something you may learn many times over in the decades ahead of you. Some of the world's greatest pianists, and all kinds of high achievers for that matter, have been assholes, as you call them."

"*Naja.*" Yes and no at the same time; the most necessary of words. The wounds that molded her were not as unique as she liked to think, but tiny pieces of the human experience; it was like discovering Herr Steinmann also had a spade in his deck.

"Mozart himself was very likely one of those genius assholes," he speculated. "It would be a shame if he were, of course, but that wouldn't make his music less worthy, would it?"

"Mozart will always be Mozart. I try to follow the composer's musical instructions and overlay them with my good intentions when I play. I like to think that the music becomes mine. Is that naive?" The key to — the joy, even — of classical music was infusing a work with herself. But how far had that brought her? If offering an audience herself wasn't enough to be successful, she doubted not only the extent of her talent and the efficacy of her rehearsing, but the core of her being.

"Once in a while, Sarah, it's better to be naive."

Taciturnly, they picked up the sonata where they left off, stumbling here and there, leaving out entire runs when it became too brisk, seeing it from the minor trenches to the F major resolution at the end of the first movement.

July 26

The sun should have pinkened their naked limbs. The statues of Greek and Roman gods that lined the garden at the Nymphenburg Palace were unboxed and bared.

Thud-thud-thud. Sarah's quick tempo underlined their contrasting immobility. A swath of forest with a lake extended beyond the palace garden, inviting her to run further than she had intended, but it was Friday evening and she had time.

One waddled right across her path, traversing her trajectory, as she trotted back along the canal leading to the palace gate. Up close, a surprisingly pure, snowflake white. She'd forgotten to look up the plural of swan(s) after her walk here with Christoph, months or maybe lifetimes ago? She looked around, but the family of five she'd watched that day must have been elsewhere, seated around spaghetti and meatballs, or pushing swings at the playground.

Her house key was drowning in her sock as she stepped onto the tram with sticky skin and salty lips. Thirty-two degrees Celsius; no air conditioning. Everyone else was red-faced and damp, even without a strenuous jog behind them.

The shower could wait. She arrived at her apartment energized by the exertion. There was work to finish before rewarding herself with a rinse. A sports bra and sleeveless spandex were perhaps the more appropriate rehearsal outfit anyway. She gave Brahms' A major Intermezzo, Op. 118, No. 2, a rather athletic treatment, and her remaining strength, dropping her arms to draw out the richness of the poignant harmonies (within the Schimmel's capabilities), and extending her elbows to embrace the width of the range. She focused on the expansive leaps in the baseline and, after forty-five minutes, was sufficiently satisfied with the ocean-like swell she had brought to flow. The piece threatened to become choppy if she didn't maintain long phrases and play the sea rather than the water.

Sarah let the resonance fade, closed the fallboard (it didn't quiet the constant calls to practice, but it did muffle them), and stood up to look out the kitchen window. She could only glimpse a snippet of the Isar River in the winter, when the trees were naked. It was the main reason she'd signed the lease, but it wasn't the ocean. When she was growing up, her family would occasionally go down to Monterey, where the water made her bones shiver, but also made her long to belong to it, in it, not as a garish fish, but as an invisible sea cucumber tucked into the sand, free from snorkelers' stares, silently withstanding the weight of the sea on her back.

Her grandmother loved the ocean so much she wanted her ashes thrown into it when she died, Sarah's dad had told her years earlier, wistfully staring into the Pacific when they pulled over at a lookout point near the Golden Gate Bridge one afternoon after another audition or youth competition. "Your Nana had a hard life. Her father was especially hard on her, and I don't think your grandfather was, well, the husband she needed. Perhaps she should have been born as a mermaid."

In one of her alcoholic dazes, Sarah's grandmother told her before she died that she'd written Sarah into her will. The money was intended for her first piano when she had a place of her own. "I won't live to see you play in Carnegie Hall," she'd slurred, "But maybe I can help you get there."

Freshly showered and shampooed, Sarah tied up her damp hair and put on her summer pajamas. Braless and sockless, she placed a chilled glass of rosé and half a cantaloupe on her desk and opened her laptop. Carefully carving out each orange bite with a soup spoon, she opened the email she'd received earlier:

Hey Sarah,
   I found a Benjamin West that could be relevant. The ball is in your court. Swing!
   Yours,
   Christoph

There was a link to a faculty biography page at a renowned music school in the Midwest: Otis Benjamin West, professor of composition. In the position for seventeen years, originally trained as a cellist, regularly received commissions from around the world. Pictured was a man, evidently of African-American heritage, with white-streaked hair, mid- to late-fifties, burgundy turtleneck and brown corduroy jacket. He had a friendly, portrait-appropriate smile, that of an artist, an intellectual — more of a Rosenstein than a Mynne.

But he was not the soldier in Herr Steinmann's album. Otis Benjamin West was either his son or someone else entirely.

Sarah sipped her wine and wiped the dew from the glass on her pajama shorts. Here she was, a spy, ashamed at the possibility of knowing something of such great significance to Herr Steinmann. But that's all it was: a possibility. The name, the *métier* — it could all be a coincidence.

What if Benjamin didn't want to be found; what if the fascination wasn't mutual? What if he'd forgotten the stiff German boy with the Bechstein? Being forgotten was both a matter of course and Sarah's biggest fear.

She'd taken guest lessons with the renowned pianist Leigh Ann Bussolo from Berkeley, an acquaintance of her teacher's. Her dad drove her to Berkeley three times that summer, once on her sixteenth birthday. Leigh Ann had praised her poise, helped her visualize a successful performance, encouraged her to pursue piano after high school. A degree meant shooting for the big leagues (the degree itself, she later found out, was only one screw on the rocket). A star, whose too-red lipstick glowed from event posters the world over, had told her fortune.

Five years later, Sarah was a sophomore in New York City and Bussolo a soloist at Carnegie Hall. When it was over, Sarah waited for half an hour by the backstage door, squeezing a small bouquet of orchids and statice, pinching herself to be in such proximity of *the goal*, if only as a flower holder. Finally, she appeared. Sarah shook her cool hand, passed the flowers, explained breathlessly that she had taken her advice, already had two and a half semesters under her belt. Leigh Ann's reply was the polite smile of a performer; there was no recognition in her eyes.

Sarah stood up to pour more wine into the now room-temperature glass. Cold wine quenched, but not thirst.

If she didn't put herself out there, she would never discover anything. And if Herr Steinmann really had been cast aside, she would bear the burden of keeping it from him. Returning to her laptop, she clicked on the email link on Otis Benjamin West's profile, and typed:

Dear Professor West,

Even if you find my email odd, I assure you, it is not spam. I recently learned of a Benjamin West who was stationed in Munich as a soldier after World War II. He was a talented jazz pianist and befriended a young German named Otto Steinmann, an acquaintance of mine with a beautiful Bechstein, who does not know that I am writing you.

Could Benjamin West be your father?

A brief note about myself: I am an American pianist living in Munich. Mr. Steinmann and I meet regularly to play Mozart's works for piano four hands. Benjamin West left quite an impression on him. Because of him, he keeps Jelly Roll Morton scores near his piano and smiles at strangers.

Sincerely,
Sarah R. Johnson

I am an American pianist. Letters on the screen, five As and four Is. What would she have to do to become one? Start putting it like that, for one thing, even if the title felt like a scratchy winter sweater in April. She chose to add her middle initial because Professor Otis Benjamin West also had a middle name. Nobodies don't have middle names. In school, she had never been the only Sarah in her class (always Sarah J.); the username sarahjohnson was always taken. Her parents should have made Reina her first name, Sarah a middle name at most.

She hit send and typed a reply to Christoph:

Hey Christoph,

I only get the eighteenth-century British-American artist when I google Benjamin West. Thanks for scrolling through more pages of search results than I did. I'm serving!

See you,
Sarah R.

July 31

Toto wasn't usually on Sarah's playlist, but it was her birthday. The last day of the month, the beginning of a new year, the end of another one. The song that was much older than her, but kept turning up everywhere, making her feel young. A deep longing to go to Africa, to drink the African rain, to go somewhere, anywhere, and fall madly in love there, welled inside of her like indigestion.

Instead, a frowsty mélange of exhaust and other people's perspiration filled her nostrils on the crowded Munich subway. As the stations flew by, recent memories popped up like flying photos on a screensaver. Theo's unsatisfyingly impatient penis and the coordinates not far above it; the swans at the palace that belonged to her and Christoph, their ancestors to the wunderkind; the narrowness of half a piano bench, Herr Steinmann's bony elbow poking hers.

A heavy bag in each hand kept her balanced while standing in the train. The pressure on the inside of her knuckles made her uncomfortable, as if it would numb her fingers forever. There were nineteen cupcakes in one bag, two bottles of sparkling wine (*Sekt*) in the other. She would have to put them in the freezer when she got to the office, then remember to take them out in time. A Vesuvius in the kitchen would not elevate her reputation. Fulfilling her cultural duty of baking on her birthday could, especially at a place like *Fork & Messer*.

Last year, she'd conveniently flown to California for her birthday week. Her mom had made her a confetti cake from a mix, a sweet throwback to her elementary school years when she'd requested it every year, more for the rainbow than the taste. The cupcakes she'd made from scratch — her coworkers would spot a mix a mile away — but halved the sugar, even though the recipe had gotten five stars online. Just to be sure she wouldn't overwhelm any German tastebuds.

"These are delicious!" Stefanie said when the editors had gathered in the conference room later that morning.

"Thanks Sarah!" Alex was talking with his mouth full. "That diet I was going to start today can wait until tomorrow, right?"

"The first of the month is always a better start date anyway."

July 31, on the cusp, was an ideal time to be born, she felt. Her due date had been August 18, incidentally the birthday of Mozart's supposed rival Antonio Salieri, but Sarah chose her own month, her mother liked to say, she was in a hurry to move out of the womb.

"A July birthday means you were always on summer break as a kid, right?" asked Alex, looking awkward in his trekking-style sandals. Toes are such an intimate body part, never pretty, but even uglier under exposed socks.

"That's right. I got to spend my birthday on Maui a few times when I was growing up." The island was her parents' favorite getaway. Her family would spend half their vacation snorkeling, which she loved, and the other half boogie boarding, which she never quite got the hang of.

"So, how old are you turning?" Christoph knew the answer already.

"Twenty-seven is almost thirty!" Sarah put her hands over her eyes in feigned anguish.

"Does that make you the youngest in the room?" Stefanie looked around inquiringly.

"I turned twenty-seven in February," Lauren volunteered as the others nodded.

"My twenties were exciting, but my thirties were much better," said Franzi, crossing her ankles as she leaned back onto the table, looking like she had a thousand secrets she wasn't going to tell.

"Your twenties are for figuring yourself out, and your thirties are for finally living as yourself." Alex's mouth was still full, full again. "Don't worry, you don't get old until forty." He surveyed the response, chuckling under his breath, as "Hey!" echoed through the group.

"That's something to look forward to!" Christoph chimed in, sitting on the conference table, one ankle crossed over his thigh, revealing a moss green sock with gray owls on it. He raised his glass: "To

Sarah!"

"*Prost! Zum Wohl!* Cheers!" rang the chorus, cheerfully, if lacking exuberance. Sarah blushed under the attention. A crowd of a thousand would have phased her less. The significance of an audience is never proportional to its size; one is most intimate, while the individual is infinitesimal among many.

A dozen strangers, save Christoph. Miraculously, she had pleased their tastebuds. Maybe they weren't quite as picky as she'd thought. But maybe pleasing them wasn't quite as important as it had seemed. Christoph was right: This would be her last birthday here.

Twelve years earlier

The September sun was still broiling down dry like a summer barbecue. A Friday ripe with expectations: the first home game of the year.
Football was a big deal at Sarah's school; the team had made it to
the league finals last season; the coach's brother was a former NFL
player. Earlier that day, campus abuzz, she had overheard groups of
girls, flashing slices of bare bellies, as they talked about which outfit
they'd laid out for the evening and which players' rears looked the
best in tights.

Sarah had other plans. She had just gotten home from school.
Her mom had to pick her up; she still had a whole year until a license
of her own. She counted three plain rice cakes from the package and
sliced a cantaloupe in half. Perched on a bar stool in the kitchen, one
foot on the floor, she ate quickly, then looked at her watch, took it
off, put it in her pocket. Watches and rings were big no-nos for her
piano teacher. They impeded her freedom of movement, he would
say, waving his hand in the air.

It was 3:39; she was running late. Dinner was at half past six and
she needed to get a good three hours of practice in before her lesson
early the next morning. She and her dad would have to leave the
house at eight, while her classmates were rolling over, adjusting their
pillows in darkened bedrooms.

She sat down at the small Steinway grand her parents had purchased three years earlier. A good investment for their retirement,
they'd said. Her dad had built a tall, slender cabinet next to the
piano for her scores and the handful of plaques she'd earned at competitions: Honorable Mention at the Young Chopin Competition,
Second Place at the Bay Area Baroque Festival.

Ten minutes in, on her second Czerny exercise, her mom interrupted. "Hey Sarah, Dad and I were thinking about going to the game at school tonight. We'd love for you to join us."

Sarah would score exactly zero cool points for being seen there with parents. Didn't her mom get that? Not that Sarah belonged to any in-crowd, but that was all the more reason not to jeopardize her invisibility, the second-best alternative to popularity.

"Mom, I have to practice! He's expecting the first movement of the concerto tomorrow." She was annoyed — at her mom for suggesting they go to the game together, at herself for not having anyone to text her meetup spots or coordinate colors. It wasn't that she didn't have friends, but Candace volunteered at a church group on Friday evenings, and Lily worked at the snack bar at the stadium to earn the extra cash her parents couldn't give her.

Todd, the intriguingly quiet guy from advanced history and her occasional daydream, hair perpetually dented by his hat — what did he look like in shoulder pads and a tongue guard? She would never know.

Sarah tossed Czerny onto the floor next to the piano bench; now for the Bach Concerto No. 1 in D minor, BWV 1052, a densely layered work, weighty and intense on a modern piano. Just five weeks and two days; then she'd perform for a blind panel of judges behind a screen, no faces to play for, no human hearts to move. Still so much to be done.

"Okay, we're going to take your brother and his friends Jake and Leo" (the twins from down the street) "and leave around six. Let me know if you change your mind by then. There is leftover minestrone in the fridge if you decide to stay home. I've been craving a hotdog lately!"

Great. Her parents were going to have a date night, a sunset cuddle under a blanket on the bleachers, bellies satisfied after splitting a hotdog and jalapeño nachos (their usual), while she heated up last night's dinner and practiced until her eyes grew blurry. Her eighth-grade brother — who had older friends in band, in the IT club, on the wrestling team — would be partaking in the high school activities she was missing. Friday nights were supposed to be different at fifteen, right? Maybe if she had a boyfriend who could drive, things would be better, but there were no prospects in sight. Boys were intimidated by good grades and high-brow hobbies.

Todd didn't listen to Bach, obviously. Sarah charged into the opening theme, marching forward with inertia, sinking into the keyboard as she heard the orchestra play in her head. She stopped and reached for her metronome in the cabinet (the old-fashioned kind that waved its wand like a wagging finger), turned it on, and started again. Tears threatened; playing from memory, she saw a kaleidoscope of black and white.

She couldn't blame Todd. She was the one who'd have to google a 'down.' The line of scrimmage had been drawn in her social life, and she was on neither side of it.

August 2

"What?" Christoph's lips brushed Sarah's ear. It was more the full-body vibration of sound than the volume that hindered her hearing.

He tried again. "I'm going to go get us a couple of gin and tonics, okay?"

She pointed her thumb toward the ceiling and drifted toward Lauren, who had planted herself close to the wall where it was quieter. Neuraum had been Lauren's idea, Munich's largest club — buried not far from the central train station, over thirty feet underground, a futuristic bunker pulsating with mainstream EDM. Sarah felt her arms and legs moving, propelled equally by the music and the current of bodies around her.

"They get really big names here." Christoph handed Sarah a per-spiring glass. "Paul van Dyk and Steve Aoki have headlined."

"Paul van Dyk — the DJ that fell off a stage a while ago?" She was picking her brain for relevant conversation starters.

"Yeah, that's right. I think he was injured pretty badly." Christoph rubbed his chin.

"Those DJ stages can be really high," added Lauren.

"There was that Australian DJ who died in Bali trying to help his friend who'd fallen off the balcony, remember that?" said Christoph. The trio was leaning in on itself, looking like a half-time huddle, trying to hear each other.

"I think his name was Adam Sky, wasn't it?" EDM wasn't Sarah's forte, but she loved the DJ's name jealously. Adam; the beginning, the original. Sky; vast and never ending.

"And Avicii. He committed suicide, they say. He was so young." Lauren slurped her drink, already down to ice.

"Sounds like a really dangerous job." Christoph raised his eyebrows behind his glasses. "But I still would've done it if I'd had a big break."

"Wait, you're a DJ?" Lauren scratched an imaginary record in front of her. "That's awesome!"

Christoph a musician, a used-to-be musician, a wanted-to-be musician? A shared disappointment bonds more firmly than a common joy.

"It was a long time ago. I pretty much stopped after high school." Was he blushing? It was too dark to tell. "I decided a life of drugs, sex and dangerously high stages wasn't for me. No, seriously, it was a dream with a dead end. And I was better at photography anyway." He swerved away from the topic. "What I love about this place is being so far underground." Dark windows above their head revealed an upper level. On the other side, revelers were bouncing to different sounds, some staring down on the enormous wiggling pit below, crisscrossed by Batman-like spotlights.

"Being underground makes you claustrophobic though, doesn't it?" said Lauren. "But in a *geil* kind of way — like how some people get turned on by feeling like they're suffocating."

"Like shades of…?" Sarah didn't finish; an elbow pushed past Christoph, and he stumbled into her, apologizing. She didn't feel claustrophobic because she wasn't alone. Christoph found his footing, his arm still brushing against hers; she didn't pull away. Redwood tickled her nose.

"What are we drinking next? This one's on me." Lauren was already pulling an itty-bitty coin purse out of her Love Moschino handbag.

As she disappeared toward the bar, Sarah spotted familiar blond curls from behind. No, it couldn't be. Would he show his face? Then he turned, stooping to plant a kiss on the forehead of a shorter, brown-haired woman, his hand on her shoulder blade. Sarah was sure; Munich was the village it was said to be. The same purple hoodie and Chucks — he was a replica of the Theo she used to know, undone and remade by passing time, him but also not him.

"If you start daydreaming here, you might fall into a trance and we'll never get you back." Christoph nudged her.

Sarah let Theo fade into the crowd, stuttering to Christoph, "I thought I saw someone I knew."

"An ex?" He was dancing hesitantly, one hand in his pocket, feet kicking like a seal's to his very own beat. A couple next to them was grinding absent-mindedly, their eyes scanning the crowd with their hands clamped firmly on each other's gyrating rears.

How did he know? "Yes. No. I mean, we weren't actually together."

"Oh *that* guy."

"I told you about him, didn't I? It probably wasn't him anyway." Or it was, but it didn't matter.

Christoph took his hand out of his pocket. "I wanted to ask you a favor. Since you're going to California for a whole month, do you think you could bring me something?"

Sarah had booked her flights back in January, when Munich was at its bleakest, before Herr Steinmann had shown up, before Christoph had become a... what was he becoming? Not knowing the answer trapped the air inside of her. She'd taken most of her vacation allowance at once and was leaving on Sunday for five weeks at home, the other home. She needed a break from *Fork & Messer* — more so now than back in January — but it was going to be a long time in a place where she had roots but no branches, night after night in her childhood bed. A long time without the two men that were making Munich harder to leave.

"Yeah, sure, I can bring you something," she replied to Christoph. "Unless it's a surfboard or an In-N-Out burger. I don't think I could get those on the plane."

"I'd love both of those. But no, I was hoping you could bring me a tiny bit of sand that has touched the Pacific Ocean." He was bashful, as if he were asking her to the prom; dipping his head down to speak into her ear, pulling it back in case his breath smelled unpleasant (it didn't). "The furthest west I've been is South Korea. Wait, is that east? Either way, it doesn't officially touch the Pacific Ocean anyway, the waters mix with the Sea of Japan and East China Sea. It would just be magical to touch the Pacific Ocean."

Lauren emerged like a nymph from the murky water in her strappy top, except that she was awkwardly trying to balance three glasses between her hands. Neuraum didn't seem like the place for a geography lesson.

"I promise I will," said Sarah to Christoph, accepting a glass from Lauren.

"I figured we couldn't go wrong with a drink called Munich

Mule," announced Lauren.

Sarah sloshed a large drop onto the ground as she took her first sip. The cucumber and ginger beer were earthy, herby. Maybe she would like it more after two or three sips. The music evolved gradually; the rhythm grew faster, the strobe lights shifted from orange to white.

Christoph leaned into Sarah to whisper, "It also means we'll have to meet up when you get back. You can't email sand. I won't be at *Fork & Messer* anymore, but I'll still be here, okay?"

August 5

"Oh fudge!" He scrunched his nose and squinted his eyes, looking over the rims of his glasses as he leaned toward the score. "I've lost my place."

The second movement of Mozart's F major sonata had begun with a paced timidity, as second movements of the era so often do — a timidity that is never the end of the story but dissolves with the transition to minor. The relaxed tempo of the Andante meant they could focus on shaping the tender phrases the first time through, rather than grasping for the notes, holding them together like a burrito threatening to drip salsa verde. As they landed firmly in B-flat major and the rhythm grew jauntier, mixing in dotted sixteenth notes and a triplet of eighth notes, Herr Steinmann's hands had fluttered away from the keyboard to hover, shaking slightly, in the air.

Sarah took two and a half measures to reign in her momentum. "Should we go back?"

"No, no, we need to bring this movement to an end. Let's start at F," he said. Amusement parks used animals, colors, cartoon characters; chamber music marked meeting points with the alphabet. She didn't want to embarrass him by letting his blunders take the limelight, didn't want to remind him of his increasing frailty. Or she didn't want to remind herself that the very same fate awaited even her own fingers and eyes and muscles and tendons one day.

"I always found the classical ornaments challenging," Sarah said truthfully.

Turns, trills and grace notes dotted the score; slow movements retained their edginess and forward motion with bursts of glitter. The movement concluded simply with a chromatic scale, each hand claiming a single note. He observed the quarter rest on the final beat of the last measure, lifting his hands from the keyboard more or less in time. She held her B-flat and D a millisecond longer.

"The rest is necessary to prepare for the Allegro. Otherwise, the element of surprise is lost." He was nearly whispering. Sarah felt a sudden cold against her leg: Herr Steinmann had stood up.

"We will have to save the Allegro for after your return." He was making his way back to his cushioned armchair, clearing his throat, hardly lifting his feet from the floor as he walked. He gripped both arms, lowering himself into the seat a centimeter at a time until he reached the tipping point, abandoning all efforts at a controlled fall. *Grunt!*

"San Francisco… it's a pity you'll be so far away. For such a long time. We were just getting to be a real duo, you and I. I was going to suggest we go on tour." Herr Steinmann cut a wide smile to show he was jesting, revealing all of his aged teeth. Despite his facetiousness, Sarah sensed a genuine sadness to see her go.

"You're right, it's far." She thought of her parents' lovely Steinway and suddenly wished she could transport Herr Steinmann to their living room. Not because she couldn't stand five weeks apart, but because she felt an urge to share the building blocks that had constructed her, because he and his Bechstein were also becoming ones.

"I don't think that San Francisco is as European as people say it is," he speculated. "If it were, why would all the Europeans go there on vacation?" It was clearly a rhetorical question, meant to avoid uncomfortable emotions, though he wrung his hands and peered at Sarah. "It's a shame I won't get to see San Francisco before I die. It seems like such a conflicted city, but one that was kissed by the gods: the Gold Rush, the tech boom. Does it have good music, too, or just keyboards with letters on them?"

"Music in San Francisco? Absolutely." She felt an unexpected surge of local pride, although she had never actually lived in the city. "The Fillmore district has always been a major jazz hub." She recited what her dad would tell her on their drives to auditions, chamber rehearsals, master classes. Jazz had been like Hungarian to her, an extraordinarily difficult language even though it used the same elements as others: letters A through G and punctuation — meters, slurs, rests.

"Benjamin would have felt at home in San Francisco, I imagine. The South was not friendly to him." He pressed his fingertips together thoughtfully. "I, on the other hand, would stick out like a checkered dog with my poor English — like a German shepherd with polka dots."

"I don't think so." She shook her head. "San Francisco is diverse. German shepherds with polka dots are nothing new." Had Benjamin's son, in fact, moved from the South to the Midwest, and could her email have landed in his spam folder? So much time had passed.

"I don't like to dwell on what would have been, but I hope Benjamin found someplace to feel at home." He stared past Sarah, as if at a baseball game playing on the wall in a sports bar. "That reminds me" — he shifted in his chair, focused on her again — "I wanted to ask you whether you might be able to bring me something back from America. Something simple; I hope it's not too much trouble."

"No, of course not. What would you like?" Another souvenir request: She was going to rattle like a tourist when she boarded the plane back to Germany.

"A box of sweet powdered milk, like we used to get from the *Amis* in CARE packages after the war. We had a grand piano, for heaven's sake, but nothing in the pantry. The meat in those CARE boxes wasn't exactly top quality, but it kept us alive, especially during that first horrible winter." He stared at the imaginary television screen again. "We would read the labels on the cans and try to pronounce the English words with an American accent. They sounded foreign and exotic, like how Humphrey Bogart and Cary Grant must have spoken. We'd spent years fighting the Americans, and here they were, sending us food halfway across the globe."

"And the powdered milk?" The local supermarket closest to her parents was unlikely to still stock the 1946 version.

"Of course, you would be right to say my fondness for the stuff had something to do with the desperate circumstances of the time. It very well may taste like cow farts now. But I still think it's what heaven is made of." Nostalgia and anticipation clinked together in his chuckle.

She gathered up her things to leave. A time gap multiplies the miles. She would miss him in the coming weeks; she would check her watch, add nine hours and imagine what he was doing: lunch, nap, Bechstein, coffee. The two of them had become united in their very different solitudes.

"You take care of yourself, Herr Steinmann." She felt tall in her shoes as he slouched in his slippers. "I'll be back before you know it and we'll pick up where we left off."

She heard his door click closed and echo in the stairwell only after she'd reached the ground floor. Constantin and Iris's apartment appeared quiet. She considered knocking to say she'd be gone for a while, but glanced at her phone instead.

Finally! She had nearly given up on Otis Benjamin West, until she saw his email. He kept it brief. There was more in what he did not say than in the disappointingly few words on the screen. Was it a dead end after all?

Dear Sarah,

Thank you for your email. Indeed, my father was stationed in Munich many years ago. However, I have never heard of Otto Steinmann. Shall we arrange a phone call anyway? Perhaps we will both find what we're looking for. Please have my office set up something that works in both our time zones.

Kind regards,

O. Benjamin West

III. PRESTO

SEPTEMBER 8

The Schimmel greeted Sarah with a silent stare when she opened the door, its whimpering muted by the unbecoming layer of dust it had collected during her absence and by what she had found out while she was away.

Her backpack slung over one shoulder, a wheeled suitcase still attached to one hand, she flipped up the fallboard and tinkled a D major scale. Gratefulness clashed with bitterness in her. She'd been given everything — the best teachers, the best instruments. That was more than she could say for her grandmother. But with so many privileges, Sarah had only herself to blame for her broken dream.

She put down her luggage and pulled the letter out of her backpack, opening it on the Schimmel's music stand, pressing the paper flat against the lacquered wood.

"I finally went through that last box of Nana's stuff in the attic," her dad had said over soft tacos three weeks earlier. "This had your name on it, so I didn't open it." He'd handed her an unsealed envelope with purple irises on it, kitschy stationery the color of her velour loungewear.

Sarah had taken a small bite of her dad's homemade guacamole and chewed it before reading the note to herself at the table. "Her first and last letter to me."

"She was a lot smarter and wiser than she let on." Sarah's mom sounded apologetic.

"On her good days," her dad added, shaking his head sadly. He'd been only eight when her drinking got really bad. "Most of my childhood she spent brooding in the back room while Pop cooked us sausage and sauerkraut for dinner."

Sarah's voice echoed against the high ceiling, reverberating life back into the apartment and the instrument after their weeks of isolation. She read the letter aloud off the Schimmel, imagining her grandmother speaking from her sunken couch, a tall glass of 'iced tea' in her hand, her fingernails perpetually the color of red zinnias.

Dear Sarah,

I'm sorry for what has become of me, even more for not telling you earlier. Not even your father knows much about who I used to be — before all this. Perhaps I was never able to get too close to you because we are too similar, you and I.

Many years ago, I was a violinist. A very good one, in fact. I dreamed of London and New York, where you were able to study. I longed for spotlights and applause. Most of all, I adored the music. Beethoven, Bruch, Berg — but especially Mozart. I even performed his D major Concerto (No. 4, K. 218) with a small orchestra when I was eighteen. It was the most glorious day of my life.

My father had been there. He'd listened stoically when my teacher said I should be auditioning for music schools around the country. That night, he emptied his brandy glass earlier than usual. I was still on Cloud Nine, cleaning my violin when he came into my room, grabbed the instrument out of my hands and smashed it against the bed post. I wished he'd hit me instead. I was a selfish brat, he said. Classical music was fine as a hobby, but I had responsibilities and couldn't be running off to other cities. He expected me to find a husband and cook him dinner every night until I did.

It was 1958. My mother had already passed away and I didn't have any money for a new violin. I didn't know better and didn't have much choice, so I did what he said. My first husband, whom I married three days before my twentieth birthday, was an honest roofer, but a monster at home. He forbade me from even talking about the violin. Now I understand that he and my father felt threatened by a woman who was good at something they knew nothing about. My father had lost three fingers fighting the Germans in the war. He couldn't have made music even if he'd wanted to. Those Germans should have taken the rest of that evil bastard, too.

My first husband died unexpectedly after falling from a roof, thank goodness, otherwise I may have pushed him at some point. I was twenty-two, broken and stigmatized as a widow. Your grandfather, whom I married not long after, is a decent man who, frankly, has bored me to death for the past fifty years, bless Ed's heart. He had nothing against the violin, but it was too late.

I had your uncle and your father soon after marrying him and found myself stuck in the kitchen once again. How boys can eat! Time kept passing, sucking me further and further away from the violin and further away from myself.

The cancer will take me soon, Sarah. I am in constant pain and cannot sleep. Less sleep, my dear, means less life and not more of it. I do not want to die because I don't feel like I ever really lived. You are still young. I envy the chance you have to make your own choices. At least you have a good father who drove you to lessons and listened to you play. I should have taught him more about music. And you, too, if he hadn't kept you away from me when you were older. But music was stolen from me. Shame on them! You can take

Unfinished and unsent, like her life, but not discarded. The letter stopped there without a full stop, no *Love, Nana*. She never would have signed off that way; she was never the sentimental type, not even the grandmother type. Sarah's dad had decided that she should be called Nana, perhaps to uphold the semblance of one, to pretend yet again that his mother was like the others. She probably would have preferred just Stella.

They would have had so much in common if they'd been able to talk about it, two used-to-be-musicians. Her faith that Sarah would one day play at Carnegie Hall was now more than just the naive rambling of a couch barnacle.

But were they so similar? Sarah felt little empathy for the woman who'd let her sons raise themselves. She pictured her grandmother with a reddish circle on her neck, the violinist's tattoo. The violin would have suited her.

Da-da-da-daaaa-dada. Sarah touched her own instrument, made in 1993 just like her and bought with Stella's money, drawing the opening solo of Mozart's D minor concerto out of the Schimmel. It was time to have it tuned agan.

Music was in Sarah's blood after all, in her genes like spontaneity and freckles. She always thought she'd been the only one in the family, Mozart's only divorcée. But the weight of Stella's lost love, in another time, another place, was too heavy to bear. The box of wood and metal in front of her could not mend the soul of a dead woman. Music, it seemed, was like sex or champagne: Life's greatest pleasures can cause the most devastation.

A salty tear dripped onto the envelope as Sarah folded the letter back up, smearing the S in her own name. She retrieved the box of multicolored pens from her desk and opened the top of the Schim-mel. Inside, on the bare, untreated wood, she carefully drew a rain-bow no larger than her fingertip, each half-circle a thin line tucked up against the next. Now it was scarred with peace. She couldn't let music, no matter what color it took in her life, pull her down, couldn't let regret prey upon her for decades. If selling her soul to her piano in a kind of Faustian deal meant she'd lose one when she lost the other, then what good was it to give her all for her instru-ment?

Sarah leaned the envelope up against the rainbow, hiding its hues, and closed the lid. She had a goodbye letter of her own to write.

September 11

She had been very young when the airplanes flew into the Twin Towers and the Pentagon, but it seemed strange to Sarah that, this year, September 11 was a day of new beginnings. The air was still warm, burnt around the edges like her mother's apple pie crust.

She touched the envelope in her bag as she walked into the office marked by a fork and knife, a no-frills logo because food should speak for itself. It was just after eight in the morning. Stefanie never arrived before nine. Sarah leaned back in her chair, surveying the space around her as her computer purred into action. After over a month away, being in her office was like putting on shoes she hadn't worn in a while; the soles suddenly feel compressed in places unnoticeable before.

Bzz bzzz bzzzz! A fly rammed the window, again and again, not learning. She tilted the pane toward herself, offering an opportunity to escape.

Three-hundred-seventy-eight, her inbox told her. Most of her emails were no longer relevant. An hour later, there were eighteen that required quick replies, only five that would need more time. She would be caught up by the end of the day.

But she couldn't get started before dealing with unfinished business.

Stefanie still had on her red leather jacket and a large bag slung over her shoulder; her back was toward the door. Her boyishly short, dyed chestnut hair was tousled in the back, as if she'd only brushed what she saw in the mirror after getting out of bed. She was chatting with her assistant, Beatrix, in the anteroom next to her office.

"I don't mean to interrupt."

"Sarah! Welcome back!" Stefanie ushered her in, tossing her oversized bag onto the white sofa, and took a seat behind her desk. Despite the posh couch, she preferred to hold meetings buffered by a table, computer and countless doodads.

"It won't take long." Sarah took a seat at the edge of the square armchair, which was more for the eyes than the rear. Three thick volumes on digital media, ironically printed on paper, populated the bookshelf behind the desk; badges from bygone conferences were pinned to the edge of the shelf, a show of self-relevance like stacks of raveling music festival armbands on a teen's wrists. Sarah leaned forward, her hands folded over her knees and her legs crossed.

"How was your time in California? You're looking tanner than usual." She was moving papers on her desk, busy, busy like the fly in Sarah's office. It was true; Sarah didn't tan easily but had made a point of absorbing vitamin D while she had the chance.

"Really nice, thanks. But actually, I wanted to see you because I've decided to leave *Fork & Messer*."

Stefanie's hands froze on the important papers; her fingernails were short and unpainted; a nail biter, evidently, although Sarah had never seen her do it. She wasn't wearing a wedding ring today; there was no rhythm to when the inconspicuous, inexpensive looking silver band appeared on the fourth finger of her right hand.

"Are you going to work with Christoph? I know you two were close."

Close? The words in someone else's mouth made them sound true. "No, no. I know Christoph has already left. I was sorry I missed his last day."

"So where will you be working next?" Stefanie started fiddling with a pen. "Or do you plan to… finish another degree?"

Sarah floundered. She hadn't anticipated so many questions, certainly not a salt jab into the wound of her unfinished master's degree. "I… actually, I'm not sure yet. I have a few ideas, but…"

"That's very, ah, courageous of you. So, you'll be with us through the end of the year then." It was not a question.

"Yes, here is my letter of resignation." Three months' notice was typical in Germany. That would still give her time to think, to decide, to see what else happened. Because something needed to happen.

"I'll pass this on to Beatrix and HR. Then, all the best, Sarah." Their conversation was over.

That was it? She wasn't expecting Stefanie to break down in tears at her news or offer her a raise. But deep down she'd wished she'd asked her to reconsider, told her she was making a huge mistake, that she had a glowing future at *Fork & Messer*. At least Sarah was sure now: She'd made the right decision.

"Thanks for everything," Sarah muttered under her breath as she slowly returned to her desk.

The fly had found the fresh air or died alone behind the heater. The still felt equally agitated without it.

And just like that, everything was different.

Christoph was gone, if only from the building. He had constantly been on her mind, and she had sent him a few photos from California — the double cappuccino from Blue Bottle Coffee, the Golden Gate Bridge from the Sausalito side — and carefully collected his sand. Each grain originated from a different stone, a different wave, a different millennium, joined together randomly as a new entity. He'd responded with a photo of the milk foamer attached to the fancy espresso machine at his new office, captioned, "Almost as you like it: dense with no air bubbles."

She needed him to fill up the door to her office, stick a foot and shoulder in, lean on the door frame, tell her she'd done the right thing by quitting. There was no one to agree that she had been brave — courageous; Stefanie's mockery also held truth. Maybe the always-prepared Germans were right. No plan B? Idiotic. She still had three months of work, a bit of savings. Three months seemed shorter than they had twenty minutes ago. She sighed, leaned back in her chair, scanned her inbox.

Work was now aimless; when was it ever meaningful? Three months — that much longer to no longer care.

She googled '*Klavierstudium München.*' Stefanie was rude, but maybe she wasn't entirely off base. The Hochschule für Musik und Theater offered a program that would complement her bachelor's degree in piano and make up for her wasted graduate study, but she'd have to audition — with more than Mozart sonatas for four hands. How many Professor Mynnes would she encounter along the way?

She paused, fingers suspended above the keyboard — a measure of rests. Then she googled 'music management jobs in San Francisco' and found a lot of internships and opaque job titles containing terms like 'head of partnerships,' 'curator,' 'program manager.'

During the past month in California, she had gone into San Francisco twice, playing the tourist. There was the mall on Powell and Market, the ice cream at Ghirardelli Square, the bubbling lobster pots at Fishermen's Wharf, the sea lions at the pier. French, Russian, Chinese, always a crowd of cameras, map-studiers, pointers.

There is a busker at the wharf who hides behind a leafy branch and scares passersby to entertain onlookers in exchange for a few ones or fives. They had screamed in unison, Sarah and her mother, when touring the city fifteen years ago; she had fallen prey countless times since, even this summer, caught unaware and unprepared. In San Francisco she was a regular, not a local, still an outsider, a newcomer, just as she would be in Rio, Tokyo, Cape Town or any other town.

Nevertheless, gravity was pulling her away from her *status quo*. Without a *status quo ante*, she could only put up her sails and submit to the wind, because every direction was forward. Theo was right about crossing an ocean.

Sarah had made her decision to resign while on the airplane on Sunday, between complimentary glasses of red wine; the plastic bottles promised it came from Napa Valley. Airplanes are greenhouses for sentimentalism and melancholy, either because of the whirr of the engines or the solitude of twelve hours between strangers.

After shelving the job search for the time being, she dug in her heels and answered the most crucial emails by lunchtime. Alex was also in the kitchen, washing his single-serving tea pot in the sink, when she came to collect her Tupperware from the fridge, just bread, cheese and a banana.

"Haven't seen you in a while. Have you been away?" She didn't remember Alex being prone to small talk.

"Yeah, actually I was in California for over a month." She closed the fridge and stood there gripping her box in both hands like a child asked to carry something carefully.

"Good to be back in the Old World?" *Bshhhh.* He left the water running as he talked.

She smiled. "Yeah. I guess it is." Munich, with its scrapbook-like juxtaposition of past moments on every street corner, its jumble of tech giants and Dirndl makers, its self-confident individuality. Alex would find out soon enough that her return to the office was short-lived.

"We're glad to have you back." He nodded amicably as he picked up the wet sponge.

September 13

Just four more minutes. Why was Sarah nervous? It wasn't like she had an audience.

She was sitting on her couch, one ankle crossed underneath her, staring at the black screen on the phone in her hand. Her left foot fell asleep; she uncrossed her legs and put both feet flat on the floor.

Weeks had passed since her initial email exchange with Professor West. He had been out of the country, his university office said, and the secretary wouldn't be available during the summer recess. Their phone call had finally been scheduled for today at six. She pictured him in a minimalist chair of Scandinavian design, wearing a simple dark sweater, the classic artist's turtleneck, sleek loafers, like the composition majors at music school. She'd had little to do with them, except for debuting a challenging trio by one. A 'world premiere' as it were, for piano, cello, and percussion comprised of a triangle, typewriter and stainless steel pot. How difficult could that be? No one knew what it was supposed to sound like; no one had ever heard it. The composer looked dismayed, a bit teary eyed, after the spotty applause had ceased. There were so many rests in the piano part, the shifting time signatures had made it impossible to count; treating the piano like a percussion instrument was disrespectful, Sarah decided in self-defense, although the composer's disappointment later cost her a package of Kleenex.

Ring, ring, ring, ring, ring. She was about to hang up, try again in five minutes; maybe his clock wasn't his phone, maybe he wasn't under the influence of German punctuality.

"Hello?" His voice was low and hurried, but not unfriendly.

"Professor West? This is Sarah Johnson. I'd written you about your, um, father." Her own voice sounded strange, younger than it was.

"Yes, I'm glad we've finally connected. I've been away, you see, working on commissions in San Diego and Buenos Aires." Professor West was distant, as if he hadn't totally returned, and sounded older than Sarah had anticipated. "You had written something about a Mr. Stone?"

"That's right, *Herr*, um, Mr. Steinmann. He's an acquaintance, um, a friend of mine, and he showed me a picture from 1946 of his good friend Benjamin West. They used to play the piano together when Benjamin was stationed in Munich after the war, um, World War II." How to explain Benjamin in just a few words? "Herr Steinmann lost touch with Benjamin, but he still means a lot to him. We found your biography on the university website and thought you might be related." "We" was just Christoph, but there was no reason to complicate things.

"My father was named Benjamin West, yes." His voice was low and solid, resonating like a cello. "He passed his name on to me and I was told he insisted on giving me the first name Otis, though I've always preferred to go by Ben. But I don't know whether I can help you, Sarah, because, you see, he passed away fifty years ago." He was professional and reserved, as if giving a lecture at the university.

Her tongue was parched. "Oh, I'm sorry." She wanted to hang up as quickly as possible; she was just wasting his time. But then she remembered that he'd written in his email that he was also looking for something.

The silence was awkward as he cleared his throat and suddenly sounded vulnerable. "You see, he took his own life when I was a teenager. I wish I'd known more about him." His tone grew thin with uncertainty. "I do know that he was stationed in Munich for a time, but he never mentioned a Mr. Steinmann. And, to be honest, he was never particularly fond of the Germans. He said they were rigid and close-minded."

There was a slight affectation in his pronunciation, as if he'd lived in England or Canada for a time. His description didn't align with Herr Steinmann's picture of a life-loving musician who smiled in the wake of war and danced in the enemy's living room. And was their fondness not mutual? Or were they speaking about two different Benjamin Wests?

"Herr Steinmann thought the world of Benjamin. He even started talking about him recently during a bout of delirium." It felt improper bringing up his moment of embarrassment with someone else. "And he certainly broadened his musical perspective."

"My father was a pianist, and he loved jazz." The sentimentality in his voice revealed a great desire to talk about him. "He would have been very pleased that music became my livelihood, although I don't think he would have understood or even liked the music I create. Formal training was never an option for him back then, you see." There was bitterness in his words — at the systemically racist society that limited Benjamin West, or at the abandonment of a boy who was still defining himself?

"Tell me more about him." Her foot was tingling from waking up. She leaned back on the couch, ready for a story, emboldened by the professor's openness.

"Well," he hesitated, "I remember him as a joyful person. He worked as a bellman at a large hotel in Raleigh and would come home, sometimes very late at night, with a smile on his face, humming a song to himself, even though it was hard work and he'd been on his feet all day and his back ached. On good nights, he'd give me a dime from his tips and tell me to save it toward something special. I did, although he never got to see it. I got a number of scholarships, but I put all that change he gave me toward college, toward the musical training he was never able to get for himself. Sundays were our family day when I was a child. My grandparents would come over and make Hoppin' John and the best sweet potato pie in the state and he would play the piano. All the jazz standards entirely from memory! I haven't had a single student who could do that. He couldn't read music, you know, but he did love it. Especially Joseph Lamb, Jelly Roll Morton, the ragtime greats. He would get so into it that he would push the bench aside and play standing up and then dance around the room and pull my grandmother to her feet. Those were the good times."

He paused. "Things started to change when I was ten or eleven, although I didn't realize it at the time. 'Music is freedom,' he would tell me, but I think he stopped believing it himself, if he ever really had. There was this other, more complicated side to him, a melancholy facet. Looking back, I'm sure it had always been there. Perhaps all of us musicians have it, if you know what I mean. You studied music yourself, didn't you say?"

Sarah muttered a quiet "yes," recalling the background murmur of the tiny television in Stella's living room.

"Then you know that even cheerful music isn't possible without a certain human sorrow. Maybe it was also the war. Who knows what kind of violence he saw or committed himself? Or financial struggles, or his unhappy marriage to my mother, or just being a Black man in 1960s America. The sick irony of a Black man hanging himself, I hope you understand. In the end — it's not as if life wasn't hard — but I'll never know exactly why he left my mother and me. I spent many years searching for his last straw, but maybe there never was one."

Sarah soaked up his words, let the passing seconds flow over them. "Professor, can I ask you one thing? Is your mother's name Ilse?"

"No. It's Janet." His words fell like a mallet on a gong. "She passed away several years ago."

"Oh, I'm sorry to hear that." Sarah's voice cracked with embarrassment. "Benjamin — I mean, Herr Steinmann's friend Benjamin — apparently had a child with a neighbor in Munich named Ilse. He said they were very much in love. I'm sorry to waste your time. I mean, I'm sorry for your loss."

He grunted, confused and disheartened. "I don't know anything about an Ilse. Listen, Sarah, I'll tell you what. There aren't many people left who knew my father, except for my Aunt Rosemary, and we haven't been in touch in a few years. Let me see if I can find out more from her. Did you say you were in Munich? I'll be there in January for the European premiere of my orchestral suite. Maybe I can meet with this Mr. Steinmann. There are too many coincidences to let it go. I'll send you an email if I find anything more." He was back to business again.

Sarah thanked him and they hung up. She sat for a moment, staring at her screen until it darkened. Had she nudged a stick into the rear of a sleeping bear? A father who took his own life, an estranged aunt — this man's family history was better left untouched. Like her grandmother's.

She went to the kitchen and opened the refrigerator: two yogurts married at the lid, a half-empty carton of milk, a wilted cucumber, several sprigs of grapes. The cold, garishly lit box mirrored her empty feeling. How could such a light-hearted musician grow so tired of life? Was it not the very essence of music to shine a ray in dark places? No, she thought, music existed without strings attached. Music itself was perfectly free but was not the liberator it was promised to be.

Sarah never ordered takeout, but tonight was a good time to start. Black beans and grilled veggies from the burrito joint a few blocks down. It couldn't be that bad, even if it wasn't Enrique's Tacos at home. The walk would clear her head, unravel the knot in her gut. She could pick up a bottle of red on the way back; she'd be awake for a while still. Slipping into her Birkenstocks at the door, Sarah dropped her key into the pocket of her jeans. If the professor's father was the Benjamin she was looking for, Herr Steinmann would be thrilled to meet his other son, but the price would be enormous: He would be crushed to learn of his suicide.

SEPTEMBER 16

Sarah pressed the button again. Herr Steinmann sometimes needed a few minutes to get to the door. She counted to ten, then eleven. A third ring. Still, nothing. She'd watched him note the date of their next meeting in his calendar before she'd left for California. Could he have forgotten?

She shifted her weight as the worry creeped up her legs, traveling through her muscles and ligaments, and she imagined the worst: a three-week-old corpse, stiff and gray, lying next to framed Hannelore, slumped over the kitchen table, flopped into the flattened armchair pillows. Had Constantin not been checking in? She didn't want her name in the coroner's report (was there a line marked 'discovered by'?), didn't want that to be their last encounter.

When she rang Constantin's bell, the front door was buzzed open within a few seconds. Iris was in her doorway when Sarah entered.

"Sarah! I thought you might come by. Haven't you heard?" She spoke before Sarah had even closed the front door.

"Heard what? What happened?" Concern pricked her gut.

"Herr Steinmann has moved into a nursing home." Iris was clutching her own hands, standing on her front mat with the door half open behind her. The scent of roast and onions wafted into the hall. It smelled more of fall's arrival than of the summer that was dwindling.

Sarah wasn't sure whether to be upset or relieved. Iris continued: "He slipped in the bathroom and otherwise just wasn't… he's been deteriorating, you know. His daughter came down about three weeks ago and moved him in."

"I should have called him from the US." She felt guilty that she'd been savoring a semblance of home while Herr Steinmann was losing his.

"Look, I'll give you the address. Herr Steinmann asked me to let you know if I saw you. He was very fretful about you finding him." She gestured for Sarah to step inside the apartment as she reached for a pen and paper in the kitchen. "It's not far from here. Please give him our best and let him know that we're looking after his flat and collecting his mail." Iris handed Sarah a Post-It with an empathetic close-lipped smile.

"Thank you, I will. And say hello to Constantin, too." Would it be the last time they saw each other? Would she ever again pass the Djabous' door to ascend to the awaiting Bechstein, Mozart's playful sonatas ringing in her ears?

The women filled up the small entry, which smelled of rain; Iris reached for the front door, pausing thoughtfully. "And Sarah, in Chad we say, 'Look for misfortune, or it will track you down first.' Coming to Germany and leaving my home has taught me that our paths will always be rocky. But sometimes the biggest misfortunes turn out to be our greatest treasures. If we don't welcome them with open arms, they will bite us in the rear as we run."

Herr Steinmann was not running anywhere; Iris could only be talking about her. A failed music career, dashed childhood dreams; was her pitiful discontent so conspicuous or was it something that Herr Steinmann had told her? She remembered his gnarled fingers pressing hers in the music shop many months ago.

Sarah had inherited Stella's blood, but not her fate. Iris raised a hand in farewell. Sarah stepped across the threshold, slowly pulling the heavy door to the house until it fell into the latch with a click.

SEPTEMBER 17

The air inside was dense from collecting lives, observing countless goodbyes, forbidden from rushing past trees or carrying birds.

It felt strange to be going to see Herr Steinmann on a Tuesday after so many Mondays together. The caregiver escorted Sarah to the sitting room, where several pale couches framed a broad stone fireplace on one side; a handful of residents were playing chess, reading books, slouching with visitors at tables on the other side.

The building must have been born around the same time he was. Extra high ceilings were laden with elaborate stucco decor; heavy curtains hung across the long, narrow windows. The interior was clean and tidy, a 1980s refurbishment — a decade she only knew from pictures.

He was sitting alone on the couch, facing the extinguished fireplace. It would be several weeks before fires became desirable. He looked like he was about to go out, with a kerchief carefully tucked into the pocket of his Bavarian jacket, but his hands were folded across his lap and his eyes were closed.

"A visitor is here to see you, Herr Steinmann." The caregiver gently brushed his shoulder, bending toward him to ensure the message was received.

He opened his eyes without moving any other muscles, smiled, adjusted his jacket, and touched his hearing aid. "Sarah. I'm glad you found me. I'm very sorry for the trouble. I certainly wasn't expecting to be here. If the bathroom hadn't been so slippery, you see." He was a variant of himself.

The caregiver disappeared through the tall double doors at the back of the room. What should Sarah say to a man who had been removed from his own home, no longer capable of bathing by himself, his dignity dealt an irreversible blow? At home he could drink from the same cups Hannelore had drunk from, play his mother's piano, entertain the illusion that the past would go on forever, like a playlist on repeat. This place, tasteful and pristine, was separated from life by a one-way turnstile; he had passed through without a hand stamp.

A young couple with a baby — gurgling with five months of life, maybe six — pushed a resident in a wheelchair over to one of the tables. The woman parked the stroller, her movements squirrel-like amid the static of the room, moved a chair aside to make space for the wheelchair, and retrieved her infant. She couldn't have been older than Herr Steinmann, the resident, his new neighbor, but she looked much frailer. *Death is a continuum.* Nevertheless, there was a glow in her cheeks when she beheld the baby, a girl in a superfluous pink headband and frilly white dress. Her hands were folded limply across her lap; a long twist of white hair had fallen from the bun on the back of her head that had been wound and pinned up by less-than-agile fingers.

"I brought you something." Sarah sat down next to Herr Steinmann, pulling two boxes of powdered milk out of her bag, their corners dented from her suitcase.

He let out a gleeful chuckle. "Ha! That is the good stuff. Of course, the brand and the packaging are different now, but I'm sure the recipe hasn't changed much since then. It's just good old American milk, isn't it?" He cradled a cylindrical package in each palm like an egg, or a hand grenade.

"The food here is quite good," he said, as if they were on holiday, had just sat down at a local restaurant, and were perusing the wine list. "But the coffee is atrocious. Really, I don't know how they can call it that. You, my dear, have brought back one small memory, even if it is a bit frivolous."

She hoped she wouldn't have to destroy another of his memories. How long would it take Professor West to find his long lost aunt? And would she know anything?

He carefully placed the containers on the table next to the couch, turning them so he could see the Carnation logos. A plain white, hospital-style coffee cup already occupied the table. Two opened packs of sugar had been discarded next to the cup; tiny white granules were scattered as if an hourglass had broken.

"I wish I could have brought you more." She crossed her legs, sliding a few inches away so she could turn and look directly at him. "How are you doing… in here?"

"The piano here is quite unfortunate, to say the least. Perhaps it had its time, but that time has long passed." His wobbly finger pointed toward the opposite side of the room. The walnut upright with golden decals was so inconspicuous that Sarah had overlooked it. "The sound is rather hollow, and I've requested three times already that it be tuned, though I'm not sure that would help much. The staff told me it is tuned at the beginning of each new year, so they don't see a need to make an extra appointment now, but they are not experts, of course. Maybe you'd like to give it a try? I wouldn't attempt Rachmaninov on that thing, if I were you, but perhaps a bit of Schumann or Schubert?"

She typically didn't like spontaneous requests to play in public places; she wasn't a dog doing a trick or a child reciting the alphabet. But here and now, it seemed like the only natural thing to do.

"Schumann's *Papillons — pour vous*." She made a slight bow before taking a seat, adjusting her posture, and rotating at the waist to loosen up. "I picked it up while I was home." It was a suite of jovial dances, reminiscent of a masquerade.

The piano, like the curtains, had known thousands of faces that no one would ever see again. It had never been particularly valuable and, unlike the Bechstein, did not age with grace. The keys were plastic, still white but lacking the weight and mildness of ivory. A handful of them didn't sound at all; with the others, the hammer struck the string, but fell flat, hardly resonating.

Her octaves were crisp, her wrists loose, and her fingertips light and weighty at the same time. The piece poured out of her with control and wit. Despite the instrument, it felt good, but she sensed how out of place the cheerful music was in this place and stopped after the first four waltzes, just short of the polonaise. A smattering of delighted, uncertain applause came from the half-dozen residents, slumped and silver haired, and their bewildered visitors.

"Even harpists transport their own instruments, and bassists, too." She sat down on the stiff sofa next to him. "A pianist always has the burden of playing someone else's."

"I'm anxious to return to my dear Bechstein, as you can imagine.

I am not particularly fond of playing someone else's piano."

But would he return? His shoulders were narrow and sagging, his body deflated like a balloon days after the party. "I imagine the Bechstein is feeling lonely without you," said Sarah, thinking of the Schimmel waiting for her at home. "Iris said your daughter came to move you in?"

"Yes, yes, Silke was here for two days. It was very good to see her, even though the circumstances could have been better. A pity she couldn't stay longer. She could have slept at my apartment and worked from there, but she preferred to get a hotel and had to fly back for some important meeting. Of course, every meeting is important." He stared through the dark mustard curtains at the garden in the inner courtyard, which was smudged with rust and brown.

"But Jürgen, my son, is coming to Munich! I couldn't believe my ears when he told me. I thought he would never set foot in this city again. He said he is showing some of his work here. I'm not sure I will be strong enough to attend the exhibition, but perhaps he will come by with a few paintings so I can see them in person." A crispy orange leaf, freshly fallen, blew against the windowpane, sticking for a second or two before spinning to the ground.

"That's fantastic! You haven't heard from him in what…"

"Nearly eight years. That is too long. And now we don't have much more time. Soon I will be with Hannelore and Gerda, but first I need to be with Silke and Jürgen, even just very briefly." The resignation in his voice was heavy and unfamiliar. A moment ago, he'd mentioned going home, now that seemed out of the question.

"When did you say Jürgen is coming?"

"I believe he said October." Herr Steinmann slowly ran his fingers across the few stray hairs on the top of his head, his nose wrinkled in confusion. "October? Is that next month?"

"Yes." Saddened by the question, Sarah spoke deliberately, as if to affix the answer to his brain. "It is still September."

The mother across the room, tired under her skillfully applied rouge and eyeshadow, turned the baby on her lap to face the old woman; it kicked its tiny legs, stretched its arms, basked in the smiles, its hands folded up into fists. A granddaughter, a great-granddaughter, a great-great-granddaughter?

"Don't you worry, Sarah, I will dig up some good music for your next visit." He pointed across the room. "Something suitable — for us and that quasi piano over there."

"As long as you feel up to it, Herr Steinmann." She was too junior for such a motherly tone. "In the meantime, you enjoy your powdered milk with your coffee." She should have crammed a hundred boxes of it into her suitcase. How many could he consume until he stopped consuming anything at all?

Thank you very much, but he would stay in the sitting room, he said, when she offered to accompany him back to his room on her way out. Maybe he didn't want her to see the guard rail on the bed, the call button in the restroom; maybe he was self-conscious of his weaker gait.

She was blinded by the low-hung sun when she stepped outside; two bicyclists whizzed by, a jogger turned the corner ahead. A harried mother in a pant suit and chunky heels was frantically pushing a mewling toddler in a stroller bulging with sand toys and groceries. It took Sarah a moment to find her bearings and make her way home.

September 21

"It's good to see you, Sarah. Really good." She felt the intensity of Christoph's eyes on her as she stirred her cappuccino, listening to the spoon strike the porcelain.

"It feels good to be here," smiled Sarah as she took in his face again, familiar despite the weeks apart. She had missed their talks.

They sat for a moment, listening to their breathing amidst the rustle of chatter and clinking dishes, their eyes shifting from each other to their surroundings. Coffee sacks were pinned to the walls in the tiny café in the trendy Schwabing district, a show of appreciation for sustainability; jewelry made by the relatives of coffee bean harvesters in Vietnam, Columbia, Ethiopia, was displayed in overturned wooden crates. Thirty-somethings, some with small children, sipped pour-overs and cold brews around them, breakfasting on mini crostinis and fancy porridge.

"I finally spoke with that composition professor you found, Otis Benjamin West," began Sarah.

"Really? What did you find out? Is his father your old guy's friend?"

"Our phone call left me pretty confused. Some things do line up. His father was musical and loved jazz and ragtime. He was stationed in Munich and lived in Raleigh. But he never mentioned Herr Steinmann — and didn't think much of the Germans."

"We're used to that. And it's not surprising, I guess, considering that they shot at him for years and murdered people that looked like him." He put the cup to his lips, rationing the sips.

Sarah raised her spoon like a wand. "And the professor's mother wasn't Ilse, the neighbor that Benjamin was involved with."

"Are you going to drop it? It was a long shot, I know."

"The professor said he'd look into it, talk to his long lost aunt, and get back to me. He seems to think his dad might be our guy after all, and I have the feeling he's desperate to learn anything about him. I guess I'll wait and see." She balanced her spoon on the edge of the saucer. Should she bring up the rest? "The thing is that his father committed suicide fifty years ago. Herr Steinmann described him as such a radiant person. How could that be? Benjamin, his Benjamin, found solace in music — that's how it sounded — and preached that music could be liberating. Even if the professor's father is the right guy, I'm not sure Herr Steinmann would want to know the truth. He puts Benjamin on such a pedestal of... joy." Her brow furrowed; she hated the vertical line that split it when it did. "But, I've been thinking, maybe it's music itself that doesn't belong on a pedestal."

"One phone call and you're losing all faith in music? That wasn't my intention when I started digging around. There are lots of possible explanations for the things that don't line up," speculated Christoph. "Ilse left Benjamin early on and the professor is the son of his second wife. Maybe his little friendship with Herr Steinmann wasn't as mutual as he'd made it out to be. Or maybe there were two Benjamin Wests on the planet that played *The Entertainer*."

"Part of me would rather not know more." But was that true? Curiosity was a termite, burrowing deeply, clandestinely. Now it was in the professor's hands.

"Do you want to do something spontaneous?" He downed the last drop from his cup irreverently.

"I guess it depends on what it is." She'd been the one to make that proposal last time, taking them to the Nymphenburg Palace.

"We can't sit in a dark café on one of the last nice days of the year. Let's head down to the lake. It won't take us long to get to Lake Starnberg from here."

"That would give me an excuse not to do housework today. I think the S6 train goes to Starnberg."

"We can take my car. It's parked in front of my apartment building just a few blocks from here." He was already returning his wallet to the back of his pants, slipping it into the permanent crease it had made in the pocket.

They strolled the few blocks quietly, hands in their pockets, taking in the noises of the city — cars, scooters, babies crying, people laughing, others shouting. Art for a composer like John Cage.

Instead, Baroque music was emanating from an open window, from a recorder. They heard a sudden pause, then a repeat from the beginning of the phrase.

"Do you hear that music?" Sarah asked. "I always thought the recorder had an odd sound, but that's probably because we had to play a plastic one in school." The unseen player could have been slender or round, early twenties or late eighties, brown or white. "But there is something powerful about the Baroque repertoire in general — the complexity of the fugues and counterpoint."

"Everybody has to learn the recorder in school here, too. Well, *learn* is relative. I don't remember playing any fugues," confessed Christoph.

"You'd need a few recorders to play a fugue. In one of my music school lectures I remember hearing that American kids have a German composer to thank for having to learn the recorder. Carl Orff was from Munich, come to think of it."

"Which isn't necessarily a claim to fame in and of itself. You remember a lot from music school. That means you must have really liked it."

"I only remember Carl Orff because there was some talk of him being a Nazi sympathizer." That word again. But Christoph was right. "I did like it. But I'm not sure playing the recorder in elementary school inspired any of us to pursue music, although I can't speak for the others." There was Gabriel, the goof-off who always called her Miss Goodie Two Shoes; quiet Kim, who wore dresses made by her mother; Sanjay, the first to come to school with his own cellphone. She regretted that she didn't know how any of their stories had unfolded after fifth grade.

Christoph's yellow Peugeot was parked on the street in front of a four-story house dressed in a pale blue façade that had seen two world wars, depression and economic boom, and four soccer World Cup trophies. He pulled the key out of his pocket.

"I live at the top. No elevator, but they say stairs are good for your butt, right? Moving out will be a bitch though." Sarah let her eyes drift down to his slim rear, hugged by tight Levi's, as he opened the passenger door for her.

"It must be useful to have a car here," she admitted as he settled into the driver's seat and pulled into traffic.

"Yeah, well, everybody calls it a *Montagsauto* — a Monday car."
He looked over his shoulder before changing lanes. "But it's been a
reliable set of wheels for the past eight years. The drivers in Munich
are crazy. If you can get by without a car, I'd do it if I were you."

"I've gotten by pretty well so far without a car. My California
license isn't valid anymore in Germany, so I'd have to pass the written and behind-the-wheel tests. To be honest, that's daunting; I've
never driven a stick shift before." The foot-hand coordination should
be easy for a pianist.

"If you want, I can teach you how to drive a stick. It's not as hard
as it looks." His long leg dug into the clutch each time he changed
gears as they wove through the city streets.

"Maybe I'll take you up on that another time. I know it sounds
strange, but not having a car makes me feel more independent. No
payments, no repairs, no accidents." Sarah looked out the window.
Just outside of Munich, the views quickly grew greener, the trees
denser, the houses shorter and sparser. "Plus, I'm not sure how much
longer I'll be here."

Christoph shot her a glance as he pulled onto the freeway. "What
did I tell you? This isn't your forever city. And it's not mine either."

"I turned in my letter of resignation at *Fork & Messer*. It's funny,
the first thing Stefanie asked me was whether I was going to work
with you." The tips of his ears burned. "I told her the truth. I have
no idea what I'm doing next. Absolutely none." She kneaded her
sweaty hands in her lap.

"That's not very German of you. I bet Stefanie couldn't deal with
it, right?"

"She called me courageous, but she meant stupid."

"Don't let her get to you."

"I don't have to for much longer. So how is your dream job
going?"

"I thought the startup would be a lot more intense and fast-paced,
but honestly it's just like any other office. People take cigarette breaks
and call in sick and work from home." He adjusted the rearview
mirror and changed lanes. "But it's still better than *Fork & Messer*.
There is more creativity, even though it can get chaotic at times. And
I have a lot of freedom to work whenever I want, which is nice. I
would say I enjoy it… enough." He pulled into the far left lane. "I'm
happy for people that love their jobs, but I've learned that my job

will never be who I am. I'm much better off taking photos of my own on the weekends rather than spending my life searching for artistic fulfillment at work."

"It's easy to envy the people that make money doing the things they love the most." She saw Charlotte walking out the café door, all eyes on her, scarf wrapped tight, on her way to another stressful audition, then home to an empty, overpriced apartment.

"Even if you had become a concert pianist, work will always be banal. The sooner we embrace its banality, the more life we have left to enjoy, right?"

"I spent the past month eating avocados and getting sunburned and you spent it figuring out the meaning of life." She laughed.

"Well, you know my head." A grin crept into the corners of his mouth. "I can't turn it off, even when I want to. And believe me — I want to a lot of the time."

"I know. But I like that about you." The words protruded from the traffic sounds around them and echoed in her head.

He broke the bulging silence. "So my new company is working on expanding to the US. I've already told them that I'd go in a heartbeat."

"Wow! That would be exciting." She turned the vent toward her until she felt air on her flushed neck. She was hit with a sudden fear of seeing Christoph go, but also disappointment at not having a similar opportunity herself.

They pulled off the freeway into the calm perfection of suburban streets, unpolluted by city dust or loud trucks, residential rows like Sarah's parents' neighborhood. *Scuff, scuff, chiss, chiss;* their four soles hit the pavement as they strolled to the lake, hands in their pockets, faces craned — toward the sun, the laundry strung on balconies, the ever shrinking house numbers.

The promenade at the lake, in contrast, was teeming with the thrill of final hours with the warm rays. A certain end upvalues the moment. The path rimmed the northernmost part of Lake Starnberg, a long, slender body of water that pointed like a mittened hand toward the not quite visible Alps to the south.

It was Saturday. The flow of walkers wasn't hurried, particularly behind a purposefully directionless toddler. His grandparents took turns grabbing his hand, but he pulled away, pointing out a car or bird; footprinted slugs on the path were more interesting.

They passed a gift shop, a restaurant, a beach bar with sand strewn out under lounge chairs and umbrellas; then the food and drink offers stopped suddenly and the path continued next to the still, clear water. Two swans drifted by, eyeing the visitors: Who might spare a crumb? One submerged its head and neck, jutting a white tail into the air. The toddler stopped to watch; grandma's hand closed quickly over his.

"Didn't we see swan last time we went for a walk?" asked Christoph.

"You mean swans?" Sarah teased. It seemed like such a long time ago.

"A lot has happened since then."

"Before I forget, I brought you something from California."

He smiled with anticipation. "How fitting to be given sand from the Pacific Ocean while I'm looking out into the water. There's something claustrophobic about lakes, don't you think? They're traps for melted snow; they're predictable. The ocean is unrestrained."

"And there are a million different ways to cross an ocean." Fleetingly, she wondered whether Theo had kept his painting of her. Then she produced the tiny vial that she'd picked out at a craft store to impress Christoph's artistic eye. Her handwritten tag around the bottleneck read: 'Made in the Pacific Ocean'.

He studied the gift, reading the words out loud. "You're right, it's the water that creates the sand."

"Thousands of years in the making."

He slipped the sand into his pocket and looked at Sarah. "Thank you."

"You're not the only one I brought something back for. My elderly Mozart man, Herr Steinmann, also had a special request: powdered milk. It reminded him of the CARE packages the Americans sent the Germans after the war. I'd never thought I could make someone happy with powdered milk!"

A bench facing the water invited them to stop. An elderly couple, each balancing a cane on their knee, was huddled on one side, their thighs, hers wider than his, pressed together. They sat silently, gazing at the swans gliding through the water.

"My grandmother told me about those CARE packages." Christoph sat, stretching his legs out, folding his hands across his middle. "I think she would have been happy to see me move to the US. She actually believed for decades that Americans made the best chocolate in the world because those CARE boxes had chocolate bars in them."

"That makes me wonder what it's like for Herr Steinmann to eat a Mozartkugel today." What would a real shortage feel like? Not the picked over shelves at the discounter on Friday afternoons, having to settle for overripe bananas instead of fresh strawberries; rather carrying the growing stone of hunger for days, weeks, months, no end in sight.

"Are you still playing Mozart with him?"

"He moved into a nursing home while I was away. There is a piano there. A crappy upright, but he wants to keep playing. Even though" — she reached down below the bench and picked up a smooth, round stone — "it seems like he's got one foot in the grave. I don't want to rattle his world with sad new information about Benjamin. What would that do to him?"

"I don't know, Sarah. But I think the truth is always worth telling."

"Maybe you're right." She stood up, crossed the footpath, squatting to skip the stone across the surface of the calm water; it bounced twice, hovering for a fraction of a second above the lake before becoming part of it.

The elderly woman next to Christoph reached for her husband's hand, wrapping it in her fingers, not taking her eyes off the water. Christoph had stretched out his arm across the empty side of the backrest. When Sarah sat down, filling the bench, she inhaled his familiar woody scent and felt his warm slender torso against her elbow.

"I used to think that music was inherently full of life and that it was such a wonderful thing to breathe life into the works of dead composers for new generations." She inhaled the lake air; the well-traveled breeze was tamer than a seaside gust. "But now it somehow seems very fitting to play music in a place where people go to die. That must sound macabre."

His fingertips brushed her shoulder. "Maybe music is just something to enjoy now, in this moment, without worrying about life or death."

"And maybe I should stop expecting so much from music."

"Even Mozart will be replaced one day," considered Christoph,

"So is he that important?"

The couple next to them stood up slowly, carefully keeping their balance, the very act of moving a rebellious claim to personal liberty. Each gripping a cane, they continued six-legged along the promenade, away from the town, their shoulders, precisely the same height, glued together.

"I guess Mozart is a blip in human history," she agreed. "But some things seem like they deserve to last forever."

September 30

Celestial freedom was wafting from a small speaker at the front desk when she arrived. The receptionist was mouthing the lyrics to Reinhard Mey's 1970s chanson "Über den Wolken" and typing with two index fingers, moving her eyes from the screen to the keyboard and back again. Above the clouds, the song goes, big and important things become small and futile.

S.R. Johnson. Sarah autographed the visitor list, smearing her left palm with the black ink, before she was directed to the sitting room. *Ding, ding, ding, ding, ding.* A grandfather clock against the wall praised her punctuality, a familiar tone in a strange place.

Herr Steinmann was seated like a balding Forrest Gump on the sofa, holding a book of music instead of a box of chocolates. His palms were cupped, fingertips touching the paper. As Sarah sat down next to him, his eyes remained focused on the window, through the pane, on the oaks shedding their clothing. The sun rippled like a wave over the rusty leaves, some glistening like gold, the others left dull. Was he sleeping with his eyes open like a Mallard duck?

"It's not as cheerful as *Maple Leaf Rag*, but there's something about a fugue, the density of the counterpoint, that makes you feel complete." He turned only his head toward her, tapping an index finger on the score on his lap: Mozart, Fugue in G minor, K. 401/375e, for four hands.

"Benjamin would have appreciated the complexity of the fugue. Though I'm not sure he ever played in a minor key." He chuckled reminiscently, his shoulders sagging under his wrinkled button-down shirt and tan vest. "I don't know why he didn't finish it. Maybe he knew he was a genius, but no Bach."

"Benjamin or Mozart?"

Confusion added more creases to his pale face. "Benjamin would have had hands big enough to play it, that's for sure. But the rest of us mortals have to rely on an organ with foot pedals or a second pianist." He waved toward the insignificant instrument against the wall. "As you can see, we'll have to take the latter." Reaching for the cane resting against the end table, he heaved himself to his feet, handing her the book and gripping his crutch with both hands. *Benjamin.* His adoration made her uncomfortable.

"Did you bring this from home?" She pointed to the score as she stood up, instinctively putting a hand in the air beneath his elbow, not wanting to seem like she was helping, but genuinely concerned he might topple momentarily.

"Bring? I didn't bring anything. My most important things are all still at home. Silke didn't know what to send. No, I asked Constantin to dig it up for me. This and Joseph Lamb's *American Beauty Rag*, which I haven't had a chance to play through." Joseph Lamb. Professor West mentioned him, his father's soft spot.

Thud! Herr Steinmann's cane fell to the floor when he tried to lean it against the piano. He paid no notice as he held onto the fallboard, lowering himself onto the seat, right of center. It was a conventional bench, made for one pianist, so Sarah pulled up a chair, leaving a gap between them. She had room to move her left elbow, there was no bony hip poking hers; the unfamiliar distance was disorienting.

"I thought I would take the liberty of playing the *Primo* part this time. The *Secondo* part is quite likely more difficult. I thought it would be better suited to you. Mozart, you know, wrote the bass and tenor lines with such large intervals between them that we mortals with modern instruments need another pianist." His gray eyes glimmered faintly. Did he realize he was repeating himself, or were his thoughts spinning like spheres: no beginning, no end, no time? "So it's a good thing I'm still here."

"Didn't Mozart's fortepiano have narrower keys?" It was like a toy piano, she'd thought from the second row during a concert at music school of Mozart sonatas on a period instrument.

"It had only sixty-six keys, rather than eighty-eight, and was smaller all around, but so were the people back then." Herr Steinmann would have fit right in in the eighteenth century. "The white keys were black, you know, and the black keys white. That looks odd to us because we like to think the world has always functioned as it does now, when at any given moment we only see a tiny sliver of an ever changing reality."

He began without cuing the tempo; it was an insecure start. *Primo* played solo for the first four bars before Sarah entered, echoing the Baroque theme as the layers of the cannon thickened, propelled forward by dotted quarter notes and occasional sixteenths. His could have been crisper — cleaner, one would say, as if he needed to take bleach and a rag to them.

He nevertheless held his own through the contrapuntal forest without listening to his left, his breaths heavy and irregular, incongruous with the emphatic, staggered rhythm of the piece.

She reached for the lower right corner of the first page, which already had a crease in it, just as he dropped his hands from the keyboard to cough uncontrollably. Blood is a harbinger — of birth, of death — immodestly abandoning the covering of our bodies.

"Should I get the nurse?" He didn't hear, didn't choose to hear, didn't want to be the reason.

"I always saw fugues as brick walls," he said hoarsely, wiping his mouth. "Layer for layer, interlocked, until they become so thick and heavy that they're impenetrable."

Herr Steinmann wasn't okay and wasn't going to be okay, said the pit in Sarah's stomach. She'd reached out a hand to cover his forearm, but quickly retracted it. She should just let him be. "The theme always turns up somewhere all by itself. Like a door in the wall, I suppose. I know G minor was Mozart's favorite sad key. He wrote his first piano quartet and his Symphony No. 40 in G minor. But this still doesn't really sound like Mozart, does it?" she asked. "Do you think that's why he didn't finish it? It just wasn't him?"

"We leave so much in life incomplete." His voice was a distant whisper and his cheeks sagged. "There was coffee in the coffee maker when I was brought here. It was my last good cup, you know. I had put on a lively ragtime record before I fell in the bathroom that day. But do you think anyone here has ever heard of ragtime?" His smirk was lacking enough energy to be indignant. "That life has now passed, and the time has come." He sounded like a priest, emceeing at his own funeral.

"Is there anything I can bring you from home?"

"It's not so much the things as the familiarity of it all. Hannelore and Gerda are waiting for me. I would have preferred to meet them at the home they knew."

Sarah's grandmother had called her at college, which she never did, several months before she died. She didn't explicitly bid farewell. "Keep it up, Sarah, and never look back," she'd said with strained cheerfulness, sounding surprisingly sober. Now Sarah wondered why she'd never finished or sent the letter. Had she been overcome by her jealousy of Sarah or just forgetful?

"At least I can see Jürgen. He's coming to Munich very soon. But Silke...I will have to leave them. Perhaps they will forget me quite quickly, but that's nothing that more time would change."

"You're still here now." He'd just moved into the home; it wasn't time yet for goodbyes.

His nose was almost touching the keyboard. "We all have unfinished business. Except when you're young. Then you always think you can go back to it. Perhaps Mozart thought that about this fugue. Maybe he simply intended to do it later." Both palms on his lap, he turned his head slowly toward Sarah. "There is something you could bring me from home. Next to my bed, there is a framed picture of Hannelore. I would very much like to have it with me."

"I can do that."

"There is one more thing. In the drawer of the nightstand you'll find a black folder. That's all. Constantin and his mother have a key to the apartment."

"I'll talk to Constantin and bring you those two things next time. Would you like to finish Mozart's unfinished fugue now? If you feel up to it." She readied her hands, pointing toward the score with her chin.

They took another go at the first page; Sarah savored the dotted rhythms, accentuating the start of each theme. His fingers were heavier in the keys, tidier, and the fugue became richer. The magic of music is in planned repetition.

Just one page and his exhaustion was spelled out in his breath, in the dip of his shoulders. There was no need to overdo it. On her way out, she walked him to the dining room, which was emanating the honest, timeless aroma of roast and potatoes.

"I'm not very hungry," he protested.

"But you need your strength." The price of age is being mothered by childless youths; he complied as she shooed him in.

Outside, the clouds were dimming from below, though the retreating sun still highlighted a few spots from above, as if the sky were a two-story house and the guests at the party were lingering upstairs for one last digestif.

Sarah zipped her coat up to her throat. When it came to retrieving his precious possessions, he called on her and not even his own children. Gradually, yet quickly enough to blur like a rolling tire, she had become something like family to him. While that felt comforting, his haste to bid forever-farewells was not. She reached for her phone and called her brother. When had they last talked, just the two of them? She couldn't remember. One, two, three, four, five. She counted the rings; she didn't want to seem pushy. It was Monday morning in California. Maybe he was still sleeping or had an early lecture to attend. Not that be had ever been an early bird. He would see that she'd called, and she could try again tomorrow.

OCTOBER 3

It could have used a little WD-40; the door squeaked intrusively as Sarah pushed it open. Time's perspiration wet the air. Christoph turned the handle slowly, letting the latch fall, sealing them in.

Then, silence. It was five o'clock, the hour that was both afternoon and evening depending on the time of year, but the grandfather clock in the corner was mute, not having been wound in weeks.

It was *Tag der Deutschen Einheit*, German Unity Day. Shops were closed, families were out together, riding bikes or kicking up leaves, going for walks, lunching on restaurant filets. There were no parades or brass bands, not even flags. Outside, it was like a typical Sunday.

Inside, everything was just as it had been. A newspaper, pinpointing a single day, perhaps the day of *the fall*, was folded on the coffee table; Herr Steinmann's pile of rumpled pillows was pressed into his favorite chair; a record lay on the turntable, the ragtime album he'd mentioned.

The grand piano hadn't moved a millimeter, resting like a faithful dog that had fallen asleep awaiting its master's return, eager to jump into his lap when he came. The fallboard was closed, the score to Mozart's Sonatas for piano four hands open on the music stand.

"This is it," said Sarah, to break the silence as they stood, as if sitting would break the chair.

"A place with a million memories." Christoph stood close to the wall, hands in his pockets. "Would you play something for me?"

Play? Her first reaction was to decline, say that she was too tired or hadn't practiced lately, but when she saw the Bechstein, she realized that she had missed it severely — that curving brown giant that had patiently drawn her to itself, bit by bit on Mondays, had hammered away her self-doubts with every measure of Mozart.

She sat down on the right side of the bench, opened the fallboard, and flipped through the book of sonatas until she found D major. Inhaling a superfluous cue, she played the first page, *Primo* only, with gusto, aware of her audience, comfortable in the familiarity of him and the ivory. The treble half was energetic, its cheerfulness not out of place as the autumn sun poured in, brightening the amber hues of the decor. It was beautiful to touch the Bechstein again, to feel her fingertips against the worn keys, struck so many times before — by Herr Steinmann, his mother, Benjamin, and now Sarah. But the sound was conspicuously incomplete, void of any bass tones, like a portrait that had been cut, neatly and horizontally, across the nose of the subject.

"This was the first piece we played together," she turned to tell Christoph, whose smile was an iceberg, glimmering on top, fragile, with considerable hidden depth.

"You're amazing, Sarah. I can tell that you don't just play the piano, you give something from deep inside of you."

Relief washed over her as she felt in her palms, in her core, how nervous she'd been to play for him. At least he didn't think she was an imposter at the piano, too. Her fingers were much more agile now than the first time she'd played the D major Sonata with Herr Steinmann, her wrists more fluid, her shoulders more relaxed.

Christoph took a seat next to her on the left side of the extra- long bench, placing his fingers on the keyboard, tinkling a few of the keys in an atonal arpeggio. They were so close that she could see his dark eyelashes, unusually long, and the two dozen freckles on his cheeks.

He looked at her as if seeing her the first time. "Maybe you could give me a lesson one of these days. Mozart would be a whole new kind of music for me."

"You wouldn't have to start with Mozart." His fingers were long and graceful for a man. She envied his reach. He could easily grasp an interval of a ninth, even a tenth if he practiced. "You have the hands of a pianist." Then she pointed to the scar near his right thumb, which was not a tidy slice from a surgeon's knife. "What happened there?"

"Oh that?" He turned his hand like a watch reflecting the light. "Pretty stupid, really. I was about sixteen and had been asked to DJ at a private party. They wanted cheap beats and I thought I'd hit the big time. Between my sets, one of the guests was really drunk and started getting rough with his girlfriend. It looked like he was going to punch her. I thought I was brave and tough, like most sixteen year olds, and went over to help. Then he threw a bottle at her. I went to catch it, but the neck had already been broken off." He ran his left thumb over the line. "Fortunately, it didn't hit the girlfriend or damage any nerves in my hand. But that was another reason I got out of the nightlife business."

Instead of replying, her lips were on his, she was leaning over and stretching upward to reach his mouth. He placed one hand on her cheek and neck, not to guide her, but to gauge her reaction. He tasted woody, sweet, comforting, like an extension of herself. She rested her hand on his sinewy thigh and traced the shape of his mouth with her lips. The kiss had been fermenting for months, ripening to become itself more every day, without spur-of-the-moment haste or groping hands.

"My company has approved my transfer to New York City." He swept the back of his index finger across his lips as they separated, a flush dawning with graduating tones like a sunrise on the tops of his ears and neck.

"So, you're leaving?" She slid away from him on the bench.

"You said *Fork & Messer* wasn't your future. But maybe New York is?" His walnut eyes, warm and unchanging, were full of hope. "My company is still hiring like crazy if you change your mind about working for them. They're especially looking for people who are fluent in German and English. But in New York, you can reinvent yourself any way you want, right? Maybe not Sarah the concert pianist, but what about Sarah the cupcake-baking music historian?"

"Or Sarah the German-speaking piano teacher?" In graduate school, she had given piano lessons to undergraduate string majors for whom learning a second instrument was a degree requirement.

The abyss that was January — when she would be unemployed and directionless — was looming. She considered for a moment that there were handfuls of categories and capabilities that, in certain combinations, only belonged to her. But could she make a living with them — in New York City of all places?

"New York is a crazy place," Sarah said.

"I'll fit right in then."

That city, that restless Apple, can be lonelier than a graveyard, its thrill in that it will make or break you. She had vowed never to move back alone. *Rush!* Adrenaline, libido, body chemicals coursed through her at the thought of returning so soon. She was leaving *Fork & Messer*, that much was already clear, but could she leave Germany so easily?

"I like Munich. I do. A lot, actually. But watching Herr Steinmann decline, visiting him in the home, has made me think about where I would want to die. I don't think I want it to be here. What about you? Where would you like to die?"

He had crossed his lanky legs, pinning his knee against the piano just below the keyboard, his socks a solid grassy green. "Actually, I wasn't planning to." He put a hand to his heart and looked heavenwards but was completely serious.

"That would be nice. Though I suppose we all have to die to get to heaven." She stood up and gestured widely with both arms, as if the furnishings were made for dolls and she was about to pick them up. "It's easy to say that it's fine for someone to die when they've reached a certain age. Like, oh, he was ninety-seven, so what can you expect. But I'm afraid Herr Steinmann is going to die anytime now, and it feels completely wrong."

He spun forty-five degrees on the bench to face her. "If dying ever felt right, I'm not sure living ever could. People say death is just a part of life, but I always felt like we were made for a lot more than a century here and that's it."

"So you believe in heaven?" That wasn't a question for Germans, she'd found; God was a crucifix, a stained glass window in a centuries-old stone house sponsored by historical foundations, a box they unchecked on their tax returns to save a few hundred euros of down-the-drain donations.

"Absolutely." As if everyone did. "I wouldn't say I'm in a hurry to get there. But I know it'll be amazing when I do."

"That will finally feel like… home." She'd read *The Chronicles of Narnia*, a read-aloud going-to-bed ritual when she was nine, again by herself at thirteen. Heaven was a place where a loving but unpredictable lion reigned over a land of fantasy creatures and wardrobe-exploring adolescents, not a long-term resort for family and friends, people she actually knew.

"In German, we call it *Heimat* — that feeling of home, of comfort and belonging. But I think it's overrated. I'd rather live in many places and do what it takes to feel comfortable there than spend lots of time in one place and become too attached to it. But who knows, maybe I will get attached to New York. Maybe you will, too."

"I'd thought I felt at home being an outsider here, as ridiculous as that sounds. But I don't think I do anymore. There's a piece that's missing. A piece of my roots. A piece of what made me." She ran her fingers over the fallboard, collecting a thin film of dust.

"Stronger" by Kanye West blasted from a car stereo in the street below, pouring electronic sound into the still room like wine into water, fading as the engine revved and the light turned green.

Sarah stood up abruptly to change the subject to something less personal. "Should we go find what we came for?"

Christoph gently closed the lid over the ivory before getting up from the bench. "You lead the way."

They tiptoed down the hall, examining the pictures on the wall without turning on the light. Was it weeks or years ago that she had first seen the faded photo of the clown — tipsy young Otto and his little hat?

The bedroom door was slightly ajar; Sarah was relieved she didn't have to open it. Christoph stood at the threshold as she went in to collect the picture frame and folder. The sheets were crumpled, the winter comforter slumped over to the side. There it was, the frame alone on the nightstand.

As she picked it up, she heard a fluttering sound from the other room, like falling leaves, then *pflup!* The noise startled her, and the frame slipped, ever so slowly, all the way to the rug, which failed utterly as a protective buffer from the floor. The crack in the glass was like the line on a seismograph or the border of a country.

"Oh!" Sarah groaned.

"What was that?" Christoph ducked out and reappeared in the doorway seconds later, looking bewildered. "The music book fell off the piano."

"The Mozart sonatas for four hands."

"Are you sure there aren't any ghosts around here?" He smiled uneasily.

Sarah was more concerned with how she would explain the broken frame to Herr Steinmann. Then she saw the other photographs, exposed on the rug, peeking out behind Hannelore. Christoph came around to survey the damage.

"What are these other pictures?" After unsticking Hannelore, a radiant toddler smiled up at them, full of life despite the aged shades of gray that were once black and white, laughing in her mother's embrace, mouth wide open. They were outside, sitting on the lawn, arms uncovered in short-sleeved dresses.

"Her name was Gerda." The girl was beaming with the joy of the moment, the unhindered trust in her parents that only small children have. She had never become capable of hurting him, like the others.

"There's one more." Christoph laid Gerda and Hannelore to the side to reveal a third image, noticeably older, enclosed in a wider, yellowed border.

Benjamin and Otto, a very young Otto, were sitting side by side at the piano. Benjamin was open-mouthed and pointing toward the camera; Otto had his hand on Benjamin's arm and was smiling up at him admiringly, enthralled by his seat-mate, oblivious to the camera.

"Is that the piano in the living room?" Christoph had an eye for detail. "It's funny how these old black-and-white photos can seem more real than digital ones."

"Yes," mumbled Sarah as she turned the photograph over, looking for a date.

On the back, hand-written in faded black ink and hardly decipherable, was a message:

Dearest Otto, It will set you free. Yours affectionately, Benjamin.

The former Hitler Youth and the Black GI were bantering like brothers, like lovers, at a time when the price of freedom was measured in liters of blood and ultimately overlooked millions: the East German, the American of color.

She hastily shoved the three photos back into the frame, ashamed at having brought his treasure into the light, the very one he wanted to die next to.

There was one more thing. *Creak!* She opened the narrow, rickety drawer of the nightstand. The black folder inside, marked with gold foil letters — *Testament* — couldn't have contained more than a few pages.

Christoph held up the cloth tote bag Sarah had brought, the one she otherwise used for pretzels and wine, as she slid the broken frame and the will into it. She took the bag but left her thumb on his hand, tracing the scar.

"There was no bottle and no bad boyfriend. That is my canned explanation when people ask," Christoph confessed in a whisper. "I cut myself. It was another time, and I was in another place. I can't lie to you, Sarah. You're the only one who knows."

They knelt in the entry to tie their shoes, then left quietly, before the stillness overtook them. Sarah knew she would never be back again.

Four years earlier

A. A. Aaaaaa. The A below middle C. The first rule of accompanying was knowing which tuning tone to give to each instrument. Sarah relaxed her shoulder, letting her arm turn to dead weight, sinking into the pure sound.

Carlos's left ear was nearly touching the fingerboard, his back to the piano, as he adjusted his cello; tuning was an art in itself, somewhat mysterious to Sarah, who was served eighty-eight fixed tones.

He was a short, slender, bespectacled performance diploma student from Ecuador; she'd accompanied him occasionally over the years and had agreed to be his regular pianist this semester. Extraordinarily erotic, some said, the sway, the embrace; the tenor resonance of one of the most vocal of instruments had appeal. In her next life, she would be a cellist. In this life, she could play vicariously, in her head, her fingers touching keys and strings at the same time.

Carlos didn't talk much; when he did, with a Latin lilt. He mastered his craft vigorously and was a good rehearsal partner: punctual, prepared, precise about his vision for the music.

Sarah was a guest, a necessary gawker at Carlos's Thursday afternoon lessons with Professor Imamoto, entering the inner chamber that, for cellists like Carlos, required a golden ticket — an audition.

A few minimalistic Japanese paintings hung on the walls, along with a large poster announcing a 1993 performance at the Lincoln Center featuring the Tokyo Trio. A younger Professor Imamoto (longer hair, rounder glasses) was pictured with a violinist and pianist. Now, he was a small man who sunk into his armchair, but commanded attention by exuding calmness and experience — the antithesis of Professor Mynne.

After a silent nod from the armchair, they lurched into Beethoven's Cello Sonata in F major, Op. 5, No. 1. The Adagio sostenuto flowed with singular intent: They were the smallest of orchestras. They couldn't make eye contact but didn't need to; a musician doesn't listen with their eyes.

After the first page turn, Sarah's jitters waned. She was having fun. Yes, *fun*; there was no better word. Other people played video games or shot baskets. This was the dividend for the lonely practice room hours — 8:00 a.m. on Mondays, 8:00 p.m. on Saturdays — for the scales and the score studying in the library cubicle. She pressed on, careful not to let giddiness disturb her concentration, shaping the long phrases as if bowing them, too. Wrists up, elbows out, fingers firm.

He held no score in his hands, just closed eyes and decades of rehearsals, students, stages. The professor didn't stand up when the first movement ended or offer an expression for a good twenty seconds, until the resonance had fully dissipated from all the strings.

"You both have a very light and lively touch, like a deer that knows when to run and when it's safe to sit. And you are a good chamber music team. You use your ears." He spoke slowly, evenly but melodically, uttering his sentences like musical phrases. "Keep playing together and you will become a true duo."

Praise was a luxury good in this business; the professor didn't seem like one to dish it out gratuitously. Relieved, Sarah glanced at the trio's poster on the wall: a chamber ensemble with a name. What could she and Carlos call themselves? Despite their handful of past rehearsals, she didn't know much about him except that he was a diligent musician, quicker to laugh than to speak; he drank liters of tea from a thermos and had a picture in his instrument case of his late mother playing the cello, her hair so long it touched the sound board.

"Don't shy away from the Allegro. Beethoven performed this for the royal court in Berlin. It can be bolder, more regal. More German." Such an extensive international career, residencies here and there, a professorship in New York City; his Japanese accent was faint, but it lent his words authenticity. He pointed out a few passages from memory, where their dynamic balance could be improved, and corrected Carlos's bowing technique in another several places.

Next week they would offer the second movement; there were

only two in the piece, one of Beethoven's earlier works — unusual for sonata form. As the heavy wooden door closed behind them, Sarah blinked under the industrial neon lights in the hall, as if exiting a movie theater but without the sticky soles.

"Thank you, Sarah! Professor Imamoto was pleased — and you know he's not easy to please. I'll see you Tuesday, okay?" Carlos smiled, holding up one hand as he slung his cello case over his shoulder with a little hop.

"Looking forward to it!" She waved back.

They turned in opposite directions down the hall. She walked alone, replaying the opening of the Adagio in her head, mimicking the strokes of his bow with her right hand, not caring that someone, even a real cellist, might see her. Would she ever read *Sarah R. Johnson, piano* and *Lincoln Center* on the same poster?

October 6

It was just going to be salmon, rice, a simple green salad with store-bought dressing; Sarah and Christoph had agreed to make it together at her place, so that neither of them would bear the blame alone if the fish came out on the dry side, the rice a bit too sticky.

Sarah had spent the past hour straightening up, dusting the Schimmel and her bookshelf, and washing the new wooden cooking utensils she'd bought for the occasion. Arne's BMW was parked outside. She secretly hoped that he would notice her date coming to the door and ringing her bell, though he was more likely glued to his flat screen.

Christoph arrived wearing a button-down shirt and holding up a large maple leaf that was tinged with crimson and gold.

"What's this?" Sarah asked as she accepted the leaf and drew him close to her.

"I know I should have brought you flowers, but I spotted this near my place this morning. I hope you don't think it's silly, but I've never found such a perfectly intact leaf on the ground. And maple trees, you know, stand for strength and endurance. They can adapt to different soils and climates. Somehow it kind of reminded me of you."

"Hm… and its color is already starting to change." It was an unusual, but thoughtful gift. She touched it to her nose, like a bouquet; it smelled of early October, the beginning of a new season. "Thank you."

Sarah put the leaf on top of the stack of music books weighing down the Schimmel's shoulder. Christoph looked around curiously, taking in her simple but unique furnishings: the rectangular ocean-blue couch, the ornate second-hand desk, a small boxy television.

Then he approached the piano and lifted the fallboard. The keys seemed stark compared to Herr Steinmann's ivories, white as blank printer paper.

"If I asked you to play here, you'd have to play both halves of the piece this time, right?" He smiled.

The score to the D minor concerto was holding up a book of Chopin Nocturnes and works by Schumann. She opened the Schumann book, flipped to the Brahms *Variations on a Theme* and hesitated. Another performance? She hadn't touched the instrument since yesterday.

"Only if you want to play." Christoph sat down at the edge of the couch, eager to listen.

With him, she didn't need to hold back. Besides, the opening theme was not virtuosic; she wouldn't strike any wrong notes. Playing it well was measured in degrees of pathos.

As she progressed through the simple but poignant chords, her arms fluid and her fingers nimble, she saw him in the corner of her eye, elbows on his knees, watching her intently. The flash of the spotlights, the hush of the auditorium — in an instant, she felt transported back to the stage, except for one major difference: He wasn't there to judge, so she no longer had to either.

She concluded the theme tenderly on an F-sharp minor chord and stopped. Just a few bars, but that was enough for now. It felt good to play again for this audience of one, for Christoph. If the feeling was a house of cards, a stack of tuning forks, she didn't want to topple it by overplaying.

"Beautiful, Sarah. It's like you're in another world. Your piano is different from Herr Steinmann's. Do you like it just the same?"

"A new Schimmel and an old Bechstein can't be compared. But both have their baggage, I guess you could say."

"You make it sound like they're people." Christoph sounded confused.

"Sometimes I feel like the piano is like my lover. Ex-lover."

"Not your husband? I mean, you've been together for a very long time."

"But sometimes it feels much too fickle. Or maybe I've been the fickle one all along."

"But you're still playing. Or playing again. So how does that fit?"

"It's becoming something different now." She thought of the

rainbow she'd colored on the unfinished wood on the inside. "But I still hear so many mistakes. Sometimes I think I should go do something I've never been good at and never will be. Just to see what it's like to have no pressure to be perfect."

"What did you have in mind?"

"I don't know — maybe golf or badminton? But those would bore me. I've always wanted to try fencing. Those mesh masks hide your face."

"On my way here, I saw that the gym down the street is offering a free trial month. What about trying a new sport or class there?"

"That's not a bad idea." She stood up to turn on some music. "What do you want to listen to? You can pick anything but Mozart."

"Anything at all? Then play something you used to listen to when you were a kid."

That was easy. Her parents had played Simon & Garfunkel constantly, first tapes, then CDs. Their poetic tunes were on in the evenings so often that they infused themselves into Sarah's dreams. She clicked on "America."

"I wanted to ask you, just to get it out of the way…" Christoph began uncertainly. "What made you kiss me last week? You know how long I've… I mean… did you mean it, or are you playing with me?"

Playing? It had taken months to germinate, but how could she tell him that, when they were together, she felt like she could exhale without losing a part of herself, that he seemed like the only steadfast thing in her life?

"I did mean it… I do… I… it just felt right." Her words came out like an echo, and she instantly knew they were true, even if they were not yet tried. Uncertainty rides as a hitchhiker on all new beginnings.

He stood up just as she was going to sit down next to him on the couch and their kiss met in mid-air, suspended at a half-squat until they both rose, interlocked in each other. She felt the pull of his familiarity, comforted by how well she knew his face, his shape. But she was equally intrigued by what she did not yet know of him; people are small and finite in the scope of things, although the soul of the beloved is eternally deep. She wanted to ask whether he was now her boyfriend, but the German word — *Freund* — was the same for platonic friend. For the first time in a long time, her language skills failed her. Maybe it was better to wait and see.

As he kissed her ear, they folded themselves onto the couch, like a single writhing being with four arms and twenty exploring fingers, gravity pulling Sarah on top of Christoph. Dinner didn't seem so important for the moment. The salmon had nowhere to swim off to.

October 10

Both hands full, the bag dug into Sarah's wrist as she slipped off her shoes in front of the door, put her folded umbrella under her arm, and fumbled with the key. The automatic light in the hall switched off; a punishment for being too slow. She sighed, two fingers on the key, two more feeling for the keyhole; there would be a red mark at the base of her thumb from the shopping bag.

The apartment was heavy with dusk and a day of waiting. She turned on lights everywhere except the bathroom, although they couldn't extinguish the burning silence. The place felt emptier since Christoph had been there. She had picked up a new knit dress on the way home, hunter green with long, extra wide sleeves, an impulsive purchase. He would like it, and it looked good enough on the mannequin; she hadn't bothered to try it on, size S usually fit and dressing rooms were always too dark to make an informed decision.

Sarah tossed the dress on the bed and put her purchases in the fridge — one carton of milk, three plums, four passion fruit yogurts, one small loaf of bread, one bottle of white wine still at shelf temperature. She washed a plum and ate it over the sink, watching purple streaks drip onto the metal.

After drying her hands, she went to the Schimmel and held the book of Chopin Nocturnes on its spine, letting it fall open to a page marked up with red and gray pencil: Opus 9, No. 2 in E-flat major. Her high school piano teacher's handwriting; a few fingerings, a metronome speed in gray, pedal markings and slurs in red. A couple of crude scribbles were her own. *Slow down! Enunciate!* Fourteen-year-old Sarah's boxy, juvenile script.

The shopping bag had left a faint crease on her arm and slightly numbed her right hand. She made a mental note to stop lugging so many wine bottles and started with just the left hand, striking the bass note, holding it, waiting, then jumped at lightning speed to the next chord in the middle register, cementing the large leaps in her muscle memory. Playing everything over and over at tempo would only increase the probability of errors. "If you repeat the wrong notes, you will learn them," her teacher used to say. Practice only makes perfect if you practice perfectly.

She paused for oxygen before switching hands, listening to the sound of hushed voices in the stairwell, the rustle of coats, the jingle of keys. The BMW hadn't been out front since Christoph had come over; Arne was evidently on again with his on-off girl, so it could only be the middle-aged bachelor on the first floor with a guest.

Slippery runs and trills made the right-hand part the star of the piece, though it was technically simpler than the left hand. She hummed, then belted from her diaphragm, projecting the melody with her fingers into the dark far corners of an imaginary concert hall.

It was going to be beautiful again. Later, another day, she would put the hands together, but she could already hear it. She had first played the Nocturne at age sixteen, at her teacher's annual Christmas recital. She had struggled with the lurching rhythm, misjudged a few of the left hand leaps. The result was dissonance, parents' bottoms shifting in folding chairs, coughs as if to right the wrong notes for her.

That had been one of the few recitals Stella had attended. Sarah's dad had driven her up from San Luis Obispo for the holidays. Nana wouldn't know the difference between Mozart and Méssian, she'd thought. How wrong she'd been. Her grandmother had arrived in oversized sunglasses (sixties Hollywood glam) and a mid-thigh Versace dress from TJ Maxx, too short for her age. Afterwards, Sarah didn't know what she was more embarrassed of: her wrong notes or Stella.

Once she'd found an amber block of bow rosin in the drawer next to Stella's couch. "What's this, Nana?" she'd asked. She'd looked for a mosquito inside; did it contain dinosaur DNA? "Put that back!" Stella had snapped, uncharacteristically.

Sarah stared at the letters in front of her: S-C-H-I-M-M-E-L. She traced the S with her eyes. S for Stella; S for Sarah. She remembered the pieces of paper behind the wood — the wood her grandmother had bought but did not own. There was supposed to be something holy about musical instruments, not only because of their crafts-manship, but also because of the music they held — in most cases, only theoretically. But was music so inextricably bound to wood and metal?

Woosh! The wind, a single gush, came from the kitchen. It was just her phone announcing a new message.

Hope you're having a relaxing evening xx.

Christoph included a selfie of himself with one arm outstretched, the other bent like a bolt of lightning, with a guy she didn't know, in front of the movie poster for the latest superhero flick. "xx" — kisses, *bisous*. Much sweeter than canned emojis, those two little letters.

She unscrewed the lid, watched the white wine swirl and splash up the sides of the glass as she poured, then opened a box of *Schaum-küsse* — chocolate-covered marshmallow domes. One, two, three, four, five, six in a dish. A nice round number. Some people still called them *Mohrenköpfe*, 'Moors' heads.' Did they really not see the racism, or simply not care?

Chopin is relaxing for the audience, not the pianist. Enjoy the action! xoxo S.

She snapped a photo of the score and sent it, too, then took a large sip of wine and dug her navy NYC zip-up sweatshirt out of her closet. The Riesling hadn't been in the fridge very long, but it would chill her before it made her warm again. She put another handful of chocolate marshmallow kisses in her dish without counting them this time.

It took several scans of her bookshelf to find it because she'd never looked for it before: *Twentieth-Century Jazz Hits*. It was the kind of book anyone might get for Christmas ('I've been meaning to learn the piano'), not something a pianist would buy, and had been lying around her parents' house for years. How did it end up here? She flipped through the volume printed in an extra-large font, stopping to add a crease to "Georgia on My Mind."

Stumbling through the piano part, she crooned the lyrics, uttering pitches not among her eighty-eight, reorienting herself now and then with the aid of the keyboard. Her voice echoed against the high ceiling, rebounding back to her like a boomerang. She had never been to Georgia, but she suddenly felt like maybe she should go.

OCTOBER 14

Herr Steinmann wasn't alone when she arrived.

Drip, drip, drip. Rain, from the window frame, not the sky, was pounding the pane at a metronome speed of approximately seventy-two, keeping time perfectly. Sarah folded her umbrella and wiped her wet hand on her coat. Was that a Mozart opera playing faintly in the background? She hadn't heard music here before, apart from their own.

It was as if he hadn't moved, never moved, sitting there on the sofa, a creature of habit. Two men were seated across from him, blocking his view of the window. They'd pulled chairs over from the other side of the room, the kind with generic metal frames that Sarah knew from contemporary American church services held in industrial buildings. They extended their hands politely as she approached.

"I'm Jürgen." A friendly but formal smile. He could have been Elton John's brother with his thick, straight hair, carefully swept to one side, his round, wide-rimmed glasses; he was wearing a black blazer with slim, gray-washed jeans, trendy white sneakers, puckered holes in both ringless earlobes.

"This is my *Lebensgefährte*, Peter." *Life companion*; while English flirts with ambiguity, the German word for partner makes it clear the relationship isn't about business. "And you must be Sarah. My father was just telling us about you."

He spoke so softly that she found herself leaning toward him, but he had a vibrant energy as if constantly in a state of active creativity. Peter was younger, perhaps by ten years or more, taller and trimmer than Jürgen. He was dressed more conservatively: khakis, gray sweater, brown loafers.

"Herr Steinmann had said you were coming." How could she have forgotten? "I'd be happy to come back another day if that would be better."

"No, no, no," protested Herr Steinmann. "Please do stay! Jürgen was just showing me some impressive photos from his exhibition. Have a look."

Jürgen pulled out his phone and retrieved the images. "These are from the vernissage on the weekend. It's a mixed media show. I have always been a painter, but I've also been sculpting quite a bit lately."

He swiped through the album, tilting the screen toward her. The paintings were wall-sized, abstract, extremely vivid — a cross between Jackson Pollock and Gerhard Richter. The sculptures — he showed her three or four — were of nude males doing everyday activities. One man was on one knee, tying his dress shoe (his only covering), his belly bulging from the crease that was his waist, his penis dangling awkwardly between his legs. Another was sitting on a toilet, elbows resting on his knees, holding a fork in his right hand, his weary eyes full of resignation.

"Jürgen's works speak to everyone, I think." Peter rested his forearm on the back of Jürgen's chair. "He sold several pieces this weekend already." He beamed at his partner; Herr Steinmann was smiling, too — they formed a glowing triangle of admiration.

"I'm very impressed, Jürgen." His eyes were directed at the space between them; the faint voice of a father who hadn't rehearsed.

Gratefulness and regret reddened the rims of Jürgen's eyelids. "You've never said that before." Then they came, the tears she'd anticipated half a minute earlier, a lump of vicarious embarrassment in her stomach. Fortunately, they couldn't fall to the floor, or dampen his shirt, caught instead in his large pores, absorbed back into his body, where they'd resided for decades.

"I'm proud of you, too." Jürgen removed his glasses, putting his thumb and index finger in the inner corners of his eyes, pinching the bridge of his nose. Peter handed him a Kleenex, rubbing his knee firmly as if to anchor him. *Your father*: They'd had those late-night red-wine talks, the *I'm fucked up because of my childhood* conversations only lovers have.

Herr Steinmann cleared his throat, Peter parted his lips to say something, but the silence between them remained. They had chosen very different words, yet interpreted the same meaning, the two Steinmann men. How could a father stay tight-lipped after years of longing for his son?

Finally, pointing to the air because she meant the background music, Sarah asked, "Is that *Idomeneo*?"

"Apparently, we can request music to be played in this room. So I did. It's been playing all afternoon, and no one has complained so far. This is already the second time today that I've heard Act III." That matter-of-fact tone he liked to put on when it came to his family. She saw right through it; his hands, like leaves in the breeze, always gave him away.

Idomeneo. Charlotte Lagherty had played a lead role in a particularly elaborate production at music school. Idomeneo, King of Crete, is rescued at sea by the god Neptune and vows to pay him back by sacrificing the first living creature he sees on land. A tragedy incomprehensible to the modern psyche, suitable only to the stage: It is his son, Idamante. But the rule doesn't have the last word, isn't absolute. In the end, Neptune himself — not entirely unlike the God of Abraham and Isaac — finds another way and Idamante not only lives but becomes king.

"*Idomeneo* was commissioned and premiered here in Munich." Herr Steinmann was more comfortable as a well of knowledge.

Jürgen had dried his eyes and slid the soggy Kleenex into the tight pocket of his jeans. "Excuse me, I'm sorry. It's been a very long time; now there is such little time left." He shifted in his chair as if his blazer were one size too small and turned to Sarah, eager to change the subject: "Mozart. My father said you play a lot of Mozart."

"Yes. Mozart. We've only played Mozart so far."

"I'm sure you're very busy. That's so kind of you." Jürgen made it sound like she was spreading mayonnaise on bologna and wheat bread at the local homeless shelter.

"It's, no, it's really..." It felt harder to explain than it should. Why did she go there every Monday? "Actually, Mozart and I — the piano and I — had a falling out. Your father has helped reconcile us."

There was sad irony in Jürgen's thin smile.

"It looks like goulash soup for dinner." She tried to lighten things up. "Should I take you over to the dining room?" It was nearly six. She needed a way out; they all did.

"My mother made excellent goulash," said Jürgen.

"Bah." Herr Steinmann looked disgusted — by the cafeteria or the memory of Hannelore's cooking? "And I was just going to get another cup of coffee. But I suppose it's too late for that."

"Jürgen is a fabulous cook, too, like his mother was," added Peter. "When we first met twelve years ago, he could hardly make scrambled eggs, but now... he's recently been exploring Central African cuisine." He stood up and offered to bring coffee for everyone.

"No milk, two sugars," Herr Steinmann ordered. "It's not like it will keep me up all night. And even if it does..."

Jürgen and Peter agreed to take him over to the dining room after they finished their coffee, before it closed at quarter past seven. They had to get to a dinner engagement of their own after that. Sarah excused herself — the men surely had more catching up to do — and, after a polite round of handshaking, stepped into the drizzle and unfurled her damp umbrella.

She put her earbuds in and searched for the final aria from *Idomeneo*, "Torna la pace" — peace comes again. Luciano Pavarotti; who else? She put her hands in her pockets as the wind picked up and the waning sun finished its final business for the day.

Peace can feel a lot like turmoil, she thought, even in E-flat major, and wondered whether Otis Benjamin West had ever composed anything in that key.

OCTOBER 17

"Are you having a baby?" On the phone, Vanessa sounded convinced.

"What? No. No, I'm just...moving on." Sarah knew Germans could be direct, but she wasn't prepared for that question, not from her wine writer.

"Oh." As if she knew better than Sarah, because *there had to be a good reason*.

If she had a dime for every time she heard, 'Maybe you should keep your stable job until you find another one,' she wouldn't need another one. Advice came more quickly than encouragement when it concerned her immediate future. 'How exciting that you are free to forge a new path,' said no one.

Now that she and music could be in the same room, she didn't want to leave without it. But would making it her job be like going into business with a father-in-law? Never as good an idea as it sounded. The US had been tugging before Christoph suggested sharing the same city again. It wasn't the 24/7 grocery stores or the free refills. Certainly not the traffic or the cardboard bread. Not the flagpoles on manicured lawns or tri-level tract homes. That naive, everything-will-work-out optimism — she hated it, quite frankly, for stabbing her in the back. But it was undeniably a part of her like the peanut-shaped birthmark behind her left ear.

"Thanks for reviewing my edits carefully. I'll look forward to your updated draft by Monday." She tried to wrap up with Vanessa quickly and avoid more personal questions. The author had a way of deflecting critique, depriving it of air; there was an unfounded self-assuredness that oozed out of her monthly wine column and glued readers to her. Sarah envied her ability not to reflect on herself. The arrogant are not burdened by the need for self-improvement.

Knock-knock. The door was already half open. Lauren skipped in hectically like a leaf blown down the sidewalk.

"Oh right, it's two o'clock already," Sarah mumbled.

It was the first of their handover meetings. Lauren was going to take over managing Sarah's pool of authors after she left. But could she fertilize a network of writers with thoughtful compliments and plausible noes, train it like a high school football coach; slash, scrunch and twist an article so excruciatingly well that the stringers would want to hug her for it? That was the part of the job Sarah could now manage, the part she'd gotten better at, even if it wasn't edible. Maybe even Stefanie would miss her way with words and freelance authors when Lauren took over.

"I almost forgot," Lauren announced as they were wrapping up their business of laying bare the strengths and weaknesses of authors Lingendorf, Madison and Nellen. "I'm going to have to reschedule our next meeting for O to Z because Stefanie is sending me to Hamburg at the end of the month to work on the new film project." Lauren glanced at her phone, clicked her pen closed, and stood up to go.

If video killed the radio star, did it also slay the wordsmith? That was their biggest fear, those old-school texters on the editorial team, still committing their genius to print with two index fingers. That's why the publication had been sluggish about moving images, even though food is never stationary: farm, vendor, buyer, cutting board, plate, table, mouth, belly, toilet. Stefanie was finally catching up and boosting online performance with a play button. Sarah was the last to know.

"Film project?" She had no right to be irked, she knew, but saying goodbye to *Fork & Messer* was starting to feel like peeling off a scab.

"Oh, you hadn't heard? Instead of just the recipe demos we've been posting, Stefanie wanted us to produce an original mini-feature. It's going to be a fifteen-minute documentary on the sustainability of Germany's fishing industry. It's a pretty short format to go water to table, but we'll see what we can do."

Was Sarah leaving at just the wrong time? Probably. But it was thrilling to be so unwise after so many years by the book — and it was too early for regrets.

Lauren whirled out.

Sarah put on her office-issue headphones and turned on Mozart's Piano Concerto in D minor, the first recording she could find on YouTube. It had been a while. Like shaving her legs, she knew each vein and freckle in the score; it felt like it was flowing out of her own head into the headphones, draining herself of energy and desire. She scanned her inbox — an empty gesture for the walls, the dead fly somewhere behind the heater; there was no one else to impress.

The final cadence sounded to boisterous applause. There was something both wrong and refreshing about recording a live performance, eternalizing a fleeting moment. She wrapped the cord around the headphones, tucked them into the drawer, put on her coat without buttoning it, and left the office. The fall chill tickled her ribs.

NYC... she started typing to Christoph.

The light at the corner turned green, a little man walking. She looked up from her phone, erased those significant three letters, and wrote:

I miss your face in my office doorway.

OCTOBER 20

Sarah plucked slick chestnut-colored leaves from the soles of her Asics with Billie Eilish's "Everything I Wanted" still ringing in her ears. The lull of her music made her melancholy and didn't improve her running tempo, but she couldn't help coming back for more.

Still breathing hard, she reached down, pulled her black leggings over her ankle, and found her slippery apartment key in her sock. Eight kilometers. Not much for a pro; not bad for an amateur. They'd singed her thighs, which tingled with the seasonal clash of warm and cold as she climbed the stairs to her apartment.

Throwing her clothes onto the bathroom floor, she turned the shower on extra hot. She sang quietly about standing on the Golden Gate, dreaming that she'd gotten everything she wanted, as if someone were listening, as the mirror fogged up. Then she turned the water temperature down until she shivered, turned the faucet off, and hugged herself in the towel Christoph had used earlier that morning as the melancholy from the song evaporated. She buried her nose in it before draping it over the shower door and putting on her pajamas and NYC sweatshirt.

After filling up a water glass at the tap, she slathered herbed cream cheese on a soft pretzel. Gourmet cooking for one or even two? That wasn't going to happen anytime soon, but it didn't need to. The way to Christoph's heart was not through his stomach. Biting into her simple salty creation, she felt the guilt lift from her gut. She didn't have to be something she wasn't. And soon she wouldn't have to spend every day with foodies reminding her of what she couldn't do.

She opened her laptop and saw the name she'd been waiting for: Otis Benjamin West.

Dear Sarah,

    It seems that you did not reach out in vain. My aunt is quite senile and was hardly willing to talk about my father, but I managed to soften her up with shortbread and sherry. I wish I'd had an occasion to badger her about him earlier, but his death drew a line between me and the rest of his family. She would have taken his secrets to the grave, as he did. Indeed, she confessed that my father was briefly married to a German woman named Ilse, but she apparently stayed in Germany after their son died in infancy. This had been kept from me for sixty-four years. My father never got over losing them, she said. I presume he never told me about his time in Germany, Mr. Steinmann, and my half-brother because the memories were too painful for him. The others likely thought they were fulfilling his wishes by not bringing up his great loss, or maybe it was simply no longer relevant after he was gone.

    My aunt rambled something about the war and a horrible incident at the Battle of the Bulge. I suspect it could have been friendly fire, but perhaps your friend Mr. Steinmann will know more. When someone close chooses death over you, you never stop asking why — until the day death chooses you. I will be in Munich, as I mentioned, at the end of January. I would be grateful if you would arrange a meeting with him, ideally on January 27, following the performances of my orchestral suite, since I fly back to Indianapolis on the 28th. I don't expect the full truth — that lies buried with my father — but I do hope for some closure for myself and liberation for his memory.

    After we first spoke, I had a feeling that you were on to something. You were right about Benjamin West being my father. Not every story ends the way it should. Nevertheless, thank you for reaching out. Even if it is tragic, the truth is always worth knowing.

    Yours sincerely,

    O. Benjamin West

Finally. She read the email again. Herr Steinmann and Benjamin shared more than they ever knew: the death of a child. Then Ilse — lost to the wishes of her parents, to the norms of the time, or to youthful indecision. No happy ending; no American Dream. The man who'd spewed joy and preached the power of music, ultimately defeated by so many sorrows. Losing Ilse and their son had made Germany a source of pain for Benjamin. Now she understood why he'd never told of his time with Herr Steinmann.

Sarah leaned back in her chair. She was anxious to share the story with Christoph, who had nudged her down this path to begin with. She swirled her water glass as her eyes drifted to her desk. The picture frame on the desk was a kitschy collage in black plastic with a treble clef in the upper left corner, a bass clef in the lower right; she'd bought it in a trinket shop in Half Moon Bay in high school and had never changed the photos. There she was at twelve or thirteen in a pink and white dress, clinging nervously to the rim of a grand piano, about to bow under a garish spotlight. Christoph had said she looked "exhilarated." In another picture, she and Brian were screaming, hands raised in unison, stars haloing above their heads on Space Mountain at Disneyland; elation on his face, fear on hers. He took after their mother with his lighter, wavy hair and tan skin. She had her father's side in her; she couldn't deny Stella's raisin hair and moon skin. Black Irish, it was called: She'd been Byrne before Huxley before Johnson.

Sarah stood up, reached her arms above her head, then used the wall to stretch her arms, chest and back; she tended to hold tension in her shoulders after a run. Still standing in front of the desk, her muscles now loosened, she scanned the professor's email a third time. Herr Steinmann would be overjoyed to hear that Benjamin's son became a respected composer, but that knowledge came with the price of learning that music had not set his beloved friend free. The price was too high for a man that might not even make it to January.

October 28

Another man had parked his walker and was lifting a dripping tea bag out of his cup on the side table. He was sitting in Herr Steinmann's usual spot on the sofa when Sarah arrived.

She found Herr Steinmann at the piano, not playing, but staring at the score on the music stand, fingers moving in his lap. She sat down next to him and handed him a small, handled shopping bag containing his request, the two objects that would send him off, that he wanted but couldn't take very far.

"I'm so sorry, but I… the score fell…"

"The frame is not important," he assured her, surveying the contents of the bag. "Only the images matter to me. I see their faces in my mind every day, but my memory is starting to fail me." He was like a traveler embarking on a long, but remarkable journey, anticipating the adventures ahead, wistful about what was being left behind.

"We should complete the fugue today," suggested Herr Steinmann. "That is, complete our reading of it. It was Maximilian Stadler who completed the composition Mozart began; I found out with a little help from the nurse and her smartphone. Stadler was a priest, you know. That's fitting. Fugues can be quite spiritual, don't you think?"

For piano students, there was Bach's *The Well-Tempered Clavier*, a book of twenty-four preludes and fugues. She had played them at age eleven; they were a down-to-earth exercise in coordination. But yes, many fugues were composed for church, The Church. "The theme is usually pretty simple until you layer it, if that makes it spiritual."

"Most things in life, and I suppose in heaven as well, are not as complicated as they appear." He was distant, as if speaking on the phone.

"Spirituality should simplify things — even though it often tends to complicate them instead, but a fugue does that, too."

"A matter of interpretation."

First his, then hers — each hand entered with the theme in a canon, the layers stacking one on top of the other. A sluggish, but less hasty run-through to balance the four voices and emphasize each entrance, although the decrepit instrument didn't leave much room for dynamic variation.

She turned the first page; his breathing grew more labored, his forehead moist, but he trudged onward like a hiker with the summit in his sights. She let him take the lead, injecting a trace of musical expression here and there. Their sound was unified, but tired.

Eighty percent in, the counterpoint dissipated and resolved in a D major chord held on a fermata.

Waiting.

E t e r n i t y.

Then the theme again, naked at first, one voice at a time until all hands were busy again.

Just before the end, there was a disintegration of sorts, an unlayering, the lowest voice holding down the bass tone, abandoning the theme until the whole short piece resolved. Then a sunny G major triad, as if nothing had happened; the moment when the sun peeks out from behind a gray cloud.

A smattering of hesitant applause broke out from the tables on the other side of the room. A draft nipped at Sarah's ankles. The G major chord faded. They had forgotten that they weren't alone.

"Bravo! I would clap if I didn't have to hold on to this damn thing with both hands." The man from the sofa was standing next to Herr Steinmann, his pale knuckles gripping his walker. "I have lived here for two years and have never heard this unfortunate instrument played like that before." His eyelids hung like curtains over his eyes, still glimmering with enthusiasm; Sarah saw two gaps in place of lower first premolars.

Herr Steinmann wiped his forehead and nose with his handkerchief and caught his breath, running both hands over his head, powerless to tame those hairs.

The man continued. "I was a violist with the Munich Philharmonic for twenty-seven years. We had some brilliant conductors, you know. Sergiu Celibidache was quite demanding, as you can imagine; then I retired under James Levine. It's a pity, because I would have liked to play with his successors, Arne Thielemann and Lorin Maazel. But, one cannot play forever."

"You've had quite a career!" A career, thought Sarah. Doing the same thing for days and years, better and better; being a Google search result, a Wikipedia page. Would she ever? She wasn't expecting to find a career musician, an expert, an artist — not *there*. Nursing homes made people into bodies, nobodies.

"Do you have your viola here?" Herr Steinmann asked curiously, as if about to pin the man down for regular rehearsals, even though they both knew that wasn't possible.

"No, no. It is with my other things. My children and grandchildren are all musical, but none of them were interested in the humble viola." His voice quivered like a string student learning vibrato.

"I would like to play very much, but we violists are not *Rampensauen* like you pianists. I have no orchestra, no chamber ensemble. I miss the music, but I don't need the audiences. Most of the others in here are too tired to listen or can't hear well enough anymore anyway." The longer he stood there next to the piano bench, the further he hunched over his walker; dilapidated, yet unexpectedly sprightly; enamored with music, yet not enslaved by it.

"Yes, I've been called a *Rampensau* before." A boast. "But that's why all pianists should play chamber music. It grounds us." Herr Steinmann nodded toward Sarah. They were being watched by twenty eyeballs, maybe thirty.

"How wonderful that you two found each other." Still smiling, he shuffled back to his — Herr Steinmann's — seat on the sofa.

"Yes, it is wonderful," echoed Herr Steinmann, boyishly. "Look, Sarah, we have a fan club."

Yes, indeed, *we do*. The fugue had dried her mouth. She dug her water bottle out of her bag on the couch. Sarah, the accompanist: She had been the background for dozens during music school, a chamber partner for handfuls more. With none of them, not even Carlos, had she become *we*. They'd been good together for her first year of graduate school, until Carlos found someone better: Sung-ho, another of Professor Rosenstein's students, an undergrad prodigy known for performing Liszt's *La Campanella* flawlessly his freshman year. They both stayed on to complete a master's degree. Carlos had traded up. Sarah certainly couldn't blame him for it. He was now getting first-chair offers from Amsterdam to Cleveland and compliments from the Professor Mynnes of the cello world.

With Herr Steinmann, the tables were turned and she had the upper hand. She was — had been — the almost professional, he the passionate amateur. She hadn't traded up, not because she couldn't have found a better duo partner, a better substitute for an orchestra, but because being a *we* made music worth making.

NOVEMBER 2

The purple and orange athletic sneakers made her self-conscious; everyone else was rocking on stiff cycling shoes. Sarah's first time and she was just in time. Only three bikes were available, in the last two rows.

She picked the one next to the glass separating the spinning room from the rest of the fitness studio. It was a wallflower's nightmare, an extrovert's sweet spot. As Christoph had pointed out, the gym near her apartment was offering a no-commitment free month — free except for the sales talk at the end of the trial. She'd give a vague excuse about leaving town on short notice. Would that become the truth? She wasn't entirely sure yet.

The bike, hers for the next fifty-five minutes, had levers and knobs she hadn't seen on its outdoor cousins. The room was whirring as other riders warmed up in the saddle, spinning their wheels, chatting with their neighbors. Was that an unborn baby; a belly? Its wearer was an athletic looking woman in the row in front of her.

"Your first class?" One bike over; he smiled and dismounted, wearing spandex cycling shorts, revealing well worked quadriceps and a nicely rounded rear. His sleeveless, wide-neck tank top read, 'Half Moon Bay.' His dark chest hair was already damp and lay flat on his skin, curling in every direction.

"Here, try this height." He raised the seat a few inches. She climbed on; he tightened a knob to secure the seat, then moved the handlebars closer to her.

"Thanks! It would have taken me a while to figure this thing out."

"Are you new to the gym? I haven't seen you here before." He was in the narrow space between their bikes. One subtle, transparent hearing aid wrapped around his right ear.

The chiseled instructor — wearing black, ankle-length leggings with mesh cutouts, a turquoise workout bra and a sassy pixie cut — was adjusting her headset. Get ready, get set.

"Yep. It's my first workout here. And my first spinning class, but I guess that's pretty obvious." She pressed the pedals with the balls of her sneakered feet. *Bah-bah-baaah-baaah.* Twenty-five cyclists synched their step to the beat for the warmup as a welcome to regulars and newcomers sounded in the speakers. Spinning Guy grinned as if to say, hold that thought.

She could keep a beat. She'd played works in 9/8 and 4/16 time. Simple 4/4 was a piece of cake. Cake. After this, she would have definitely earned a piece. She could almost taste the vanilla-lemon accent in a good *Käsekuchen*, until her lips turned salty.

"Okay, let's pick things up," piped the instructor. Weren't they already breaking the speed limit? Sarah's seat felt high. Did Spinning Guy really know what he was doing? Rihanna's "Don't Stop the Music" began. Pixie Bra Top told the riders to stand, then sit at certain intervals. Sarah's thighs blinked, then burned. Only twenty-four bars had passed.

Ms. Prego was matching the pace. Some stamina! But wasn't it too loud for the baby? There was something remarkable (both natural and alien) about women's bodies that could carry a whole baby in a tidy little ball in front without bulging anywhere else. A soccer ball under their shirt; it would never stay in place, like a tennis ball in her hand when Sarah touched the keys. Mozart wasn't Rihanna; yoga or Pilates would be calmer in a hundred years, in her next life as a mother.

Sweat was collecting in tiny drops between the hairs on Spinning Guy's legs. Had he actually been to Half Moon Bay in California or just known someone who had? She hoped he'd felt the chill of the breeze exhausted by the Pacific (she shivered despite the rising temperature) and dusted California's arid, fertile dirt off his flip flops (her pedals tripped up; it took her six bars to brake and restart).

Now it was dripping from his elbows, creating small puddles on the black mat beneath the bikes. His movements were precise, as if he'd measured out the exact distance to raise his rear from the seat each time, never deviating a centimeter. Sarah felt her legs cave; next time she would focus her movements better, like him, next time she would eat an energy bar before the class. She retied her sagging ponytail, dug in her heels, and chased the beat.

Today she wasn't *the pianist*, not *the used-to-be pianist*, especially not *the food magazine editor*. Just another mediocre indoor cyclist; the new girl. Aspirationless and middling, it was fulfilling to spend so many calories on going nowhere. She turned up the resistance until the sweat spilled from her brow into her eyes, her lips as briny as French fries.

Finally, the cool down. "Don't forget to breathe, people," ordered Pixie Bra Top in her coconut voice. "Visualize that beer you've earned later." Sarah was relieved. For her, tomorrow's reward was not a Hefeweizen but a new understanding of her muscular geography. And that piece of cake. Wobbly on her feet as her wheels slowed and halted, she dismounted. There were tiny pools on the floor next to her bike, too.

"I'm Cem, by the way." He was wiping his face and head with a towel imprinted with the name of the gym. "A few of us usually grab dinner after the Saturday class if you want to join." *Us* seemed to include Ms. Prego, who turned halfway to wave. "When Sandra comes, we all drink less beer."

Inhale, exhale; Sarah willed her voice not to shake from breathlessness, like her hands during a performance. "That sounds fun. I'm meeting up with someone after this, but maybe I can join you next week."

"Sure, okay." He drained his water bottle into his mouth without touching his lips to it. "British?"

It was not the first time she'd been asked. "American, actually. I'm originally from California." It always drew a reaction, the Golden State, the slew of stereotypes. He was German, she deduced, but also Turkish.

"Seriously? Where the sun always shines! I really have to get my ass there one day." His solid brown eyes widened as he paused, towel and empty water bottle in one hand. He waved as he maneuvered around the bikes to the door. "Catch you next time, Miss California!" A cute compliment that was both flattering and dissociating.

She was meeting Christoph for dinner at seven. That gave her an hour to shower, dress, recalibrate her pulse. They hadn't decided yet where to go; she would be hungry after this, would push for Neapolitan carbs. Christoph was less of a gym rat, he'd said, she should go ahead and try the class without him. That made her look forward all the more to seeing him later.

She tossed around the term in her mind: *Christoph's girlfriend.* They knew each other so well that it made sense, sure, and it also felt right. Still, she couldn't quite shake the fear that he would drop her suddenly like Theo, or trade her in for someone better like Carlos, or simply get bored with her like that MBA student. It seemed too late to tread slowly, but she didn't want to get burned again.

In the locker room, Sarah peeled off her sticky clothes; her pale skin, blotchy from the exertion, stared back at her in the mirror. She saw her protruding hip bones and soft abdomen, more with skin and essential organs than with fat, camouflaging any muscles underneath. Her legs were slender, but it bothered her that her thighs met each other when she stood up straight, even though Christoph had whispered that she had beautiful legs, when theirs were interlocked on her couch.

Sarah spent ten full minutes under the shower head, warm water running over her eyelids, down her face. She opened her eyes as Ms. Prego stepped into the shower area, looking more cumbersome than she had on the bike; her belly formed a perfect curve, void of freckles and stretch marks. Was it a boy or a girl?

Sarah lathered up, rubbing extra soap beneath her small breasts, between her legs, watching the suds form a tiny whirlpool as they gained momentum around her flip flops and dashed down the drain.

NOVEMBER 11

A dinosaur, a pumpkin, Spiderman, stars — the homemade lanterns
glowed, bobbing on sticks and lurching with the children's irregular
gait.

"C'mon dad, hurry!" A boy, six or seven, eagerly grabbed his
father's hand, catching up to half a dozen of his classmates ahead.

It was just before five on St. Martin's Day; the lantern-lit pro-
cession was about to start. Afterward, there would be a man on hor-
seback, playing the part of the monk who shared his cloak with a
beggar on an icy fall night in the fourth century.

Sarah watched a floating stegosaurus and a shooting star disappear around the corner before she stepped inside, where she heard
a familiar tune from a different generation. The woman at the front
desk swayed her shoulders to The Scorpions' "Wind of Change."

It was out of place, verging on poor taste, that anthem of youthful hope that was retroactively made the soundtrack to the fall of the
Iron Curtain. Unlike the Soviet Union, no one moved out of here;
no one moved on. The woman, broad-shouldered and in her early
fifties, wore inexpensive polyester tops with animal prints that added
a decade or so; her long, lavender bangs were cut asymmetrically.

Sarah was a regular now: no sign-ins, no bureaucracy. She found
him in an oversized armchair by the fireplace, flames crackling, her
numb fingertips burning. An empty coffee cup and saucer, a pill
box and the picture frame from his bedroom were on the small side
table next to his chair. The yellowed photo of Benjamin and Otto
was visible behind the crack, their smiles conveying a lightness that
was strange next to the stone fireplace and autumn dimness at the
window.

Something was different. A pair of Bose headphones stretched over his bare head and there was a cell phone in his hand. He pressed the screen and slipped the headphones off one ear when he saw her, letting them hang askew, the bulky earpiece clamped behind his hearing aid. He grinned sheepishly as if he'd been caught with a *Playboy*. Sarah pulled up a chair.

"My grandson was here yesterday. He brought me the headphones, and this gadget so I could listen to music in here. Whatever music I wanted, he said. His mother must have given it to him. He doesn't have the money for this kind of thing."

She glanced at his screen; *Maple Leaf Rag* was on pause. A second glance and she saw that two men were sitting at the piano in the YouTube video. It was a version for four hands.

"You saw your grandson?" That was an even bigger surprise than the headphones.

"Silke didn't come. It's a shame. I would have liked to see her one last time. To tell her..." He locked his eyes on the fireplace, pressed his lips together. "But Moritz appeared yesterday. I didn't know he was coming. He took the bus here." His tone grew earnest. "The bus, for God's sake. That must have been horribly uncomfortable. Buses have always made me ill."

"And he showed you how to work this thing?" Impressive. But then, Herr Steinmann had been taken away from his piano and his record player; his motivation for music was enormous.

He lifted the phone, turning it to view every angle as if it were a meteorite. "My first cell phone, at my age!" he snorted. "But it's a phone that can't make calls. It can only play music, he said. I told him, fine, that's the best kind of phone. And who would I call anyway?"

Pulling the crooked headphones off, he placed them in his lap. Shadows from the fire hollowed out his cheeks as the last of the sunlight resigned.

"I'm sorry that I cannot play today. The nurse has said I need to rest more. Not that I listen to her." The shadow doubled the size of his eyelid when he winked.

"Then it's best for you to take it easy." Sarah was let down. She had been looking forward to the fugue. The somber counterpoint mirrored the season, its voices piling up like fallen leaves.

He cradled the headphones in his hands. "Mozart died so young;

he knew he was taking half his genius with him to the grave. I, on the other hand, am so old that my work here has long been completed. At least what was in my power to complete." He smiled peacefully. "Gerda and Hannelore have been waiting long enough for me. I could not locate Benjamin on earth. I can only hope to find him on the other side."

"Herr Steinmann, Benjamin..." No, halt. She wasn't ready to bring it up, to admit to meddling in his memories, to report that everything he feared had come about. "... will be the one at the piano, laughing his head off." It wasn't untrue: Benjamin was already on the other side with his first son, there, where there is no sorrow.

He touched the frame, avoiding the crack. "This was taken the day before Benjamin was beaten by those white American soldiers. It was mail day and he had just received a letter from his mother in Raleigh. She had gotten a new job doing the laundry at a hospital. It paid well, apparently, and took a huge burden off the family. His sister had just had a baby. His spirits were high."

"I can see that." Two smiles, two unburdened faces, two minds imprinted with war, twenty nimble fingers. "And who took the picture? Your mother?"

"My mother? Heavens, no. She was having tea with the neighbor and probably discussing how bothersome the Americans were. She must have brought the tea since rations were still very tight. No, it was Ilse. She and Benjamin were already — how should I say? — quite close. He was smiling at her." The glass reflected the dwindling flame in the fireplace, turning red and blue as it petered out. "In those days, the afternoons were gloriously long. Then for much of life they become very, very short until they get unbearably long again. The pendulum always swings back to a slightly different place." His voice was melancholy, but not sad.

"All the better that you have music now." She nodded toward his phone.

"Would you help me find the Mozart fugue on this thing?" The composer, the man, the device: each separated by over a hundred years, brought together by necessity. "It's not such a common work, I don't know whether you will be able to find an adequate recording of it."

Paul Badura-Skoda and Jörg Demus — a quick search led her to the Austrian pianists, both recently deceased, both in their early nineties.

"Just press here when you want to listen."

"If we can't play the fugue today, then I'll listen to it once or twice before dinner. Though I hardly eat much these days." He was already pulling the headphones over his ears.

"Goose and dumplings were on the menu when I walked in. You're not going to want to miss the special St. Martin's dinner." The meal was a Bavarian tradition honoring the saint, even though generosity requires someone else; selflessness another self; can it be celebrated alone, one bite of bird at a time? Sarah considered asking the staff whether she could stay to eat with him (a bit of protein for once) but didn't want to tax his energy even further.

Out on the sidewalk, her feet flattened brown leaves that had already welded themselves to each other. She found the same fugue recording on her phone; it was just several minutes long. A lone star oscillated along the other side of the street, steered by the silhouette of a child, and she wondered which images had shone from Christoph's lantern when he was young..

Her back to the nursing home, leaning against the wall, she listened to the end. She hadn't known Herr Steinmann for very long but, watching him slip away, it felt like her anchor was being yanked up off the ocean floor. She thrust her hands deep into her pockets and found her way home.

Eleven years earlier

A blob of raspberry sherbet corroded, suspended in the Sprite like a pink buoy. The same plastic punch bowl with the fake crystal details, the same chipped ladle. The table was cluttered with a box of Oreos, a bowl of Cheetos, and a dozen paper plates loaded with sweet and savory treats Sarah didn't recognize: nearly translucent dumplings, crescents of fried dough, homemade cookies topped with a single almond, blackish spotted rectangles that looked like seaweed smeared into asphalt. Sherbet dripped down the side of her paper cup as she scooped the punch.

She was eighty percent satisfied. It had been better than mediocre, but there was still a shadow of disappointment with her performance of Beethoven's "Pastoral" Sonata, No. 15 in D major, Op. 28. She was careful not to smile too broadly, not wanting the others to think she hadn't heard her own memory slip, her unplanned improvisation; she knew, they knew, it could have been better.

Another audience wouldn't have noticed, but the parents of her high school piano teacher's other students were intimately familiar with the standard repertoire; they heard it at home for three, four, five hours every afternoon, every day of the week. They prodded from the kitchen, from the den, "Not too fast," "Clean up the runs," memorizing and repeating the teacher's admonishments.

She had been placed two-thirds of the way through the spring recital program, after the intermission; enough time for her hands to grow stiff and slippery. Her mind wasn't nervous, but her body knew better. The leather gloves never helped much, nor did the hot water bottle.

Cindy was last on the program, as usual, with her virtuosic

Chopin Études: C-sharp minor, Op. 10, No. 4, and C minor, Op. 25, No. 12. How did she do it? The impossibly long wait, then the flawless performance in a dress with pink bows like a toddler's. Maybe it was a strategy: The younger she appeared, the more impressive her playing seemed — except that she didn't need a bag of tricks to enhance her skill.

Mothers, fathers, younger siblings were teeming in the teacher's kitchen, which was laden with the welcoming scent of ginger and cloves. Voices crescendoed in surround sound, parents speaking Mandarin, children answering in English spiced with tonal phrases from their mother tongue.

Sarah sipped the sugar bomb and surveyed the small space. She and Mikhail, whose parents were from Russia, were the only students without a Chinese background. It was difficult to join a conversation when she only understood thirty, fifty, sometimes zero percent. She put two almond cookies and three slices of melon on her paper plate.

She and Mikhail didn't look like them. She had never noticed that until now; it had never mattered. No one here was going to call her unspeakable names or tell her to go back to her country like they sometimes did to the other kids, the *different* ones. She could enjoy her outsiderness comfortably like a favorite t-shirt; it fit perfectly and was always waiting for her to put on whenever she chose. It was a privilege to walk out the door and take it off again.

Squeezing herself through the kitchen, she brushed past Cindy's mother. She turned and said in nearly flawless English, "Beautiful job on the Beethoven, Sarah. The Pastoral was always my favorite early Beethoven Sonata."

Thanks, thanks a lot, thank you. Sarah fumbled the words, embarrassed but bolstered by the compliment. The woman had heard her mistake but chose to overlook it.

Sarah pressed into the family room, where the Steinway B was rimmed by rows of now mainly vacant folding chairs. Her dad was filling up one, holding a paper plate up to his face.

"These sesame bars are really good. You should try them." He bit into the black square. They chewed slowly, repositioning their bottoms in the plastic seats. *Squeak, squawk!* She returned to the kitchen for a final half cup of pink Sprite (the sherbet was long gone), folded a mystery square up in a napkin and put it in her bag. She would try it later, at home, where she could quietly look up what they were called in Mandarin and spit it out if she needed to. Everywhere she went she was an insider on the outside, or rather an outsider on the inside? Piano was the reason, but also the excuse.

In the car, with her dad, the volume up on Ravel, she started feeling better about her performance. The glitch was further away, shrinking in the rear view mirror. Tomorrow it would feel even more alright.

NOVEMBER 13

"You're still here?" Alex had been scribbling on his notepad when Sarah walked in. *Still.* As in, would you please leave already? Or, so glad I didn't miss saying goodbye?

"Five more weeks."

"Oh good! I just haven't seen you around that much. I thought maybe you'd left." He was genuinely glad to see her, she decided. Was it her? Was it *the Germans*? Reading between their lines was still an art, a gamble.

Stefanie traipsed in, briskly tossing a folder full of loose papers, spilling them onto the conference table in the shape of a fan. The dozen mouths at the table were silent; no one ever wanted to rock the boat. She started the meeting before her bottom even hit the chair, simultaneously scanning her phone for new emails, messages, anything to confirm her elevated status.

"I think we're set with our Christmas planning, so let's talk about January — the time when no one really wants to eat."

Alex was right. Sarah had been keeping a low profile. Her to-do list was shrinking with her relevance, incrementally with the number of work days left. There was no reason to be the first in the office, no reason to miss the last of the afternoon sunlight, no one looking over her shoulder, no one caring enough to chew her out in a meeting.

Hearty soups were on the editorial agenda in January, along with portraits of two German superfood startups. Smoothies and porridge. Glorified baby food. Not that Sarah wouldn't eat it, even pay more for it, but she'd come to accept that, to be her friend, food needed to nourish both her body and her soul. Winter, the coldest, most comfortless part of the year, seemed like the worst time to go on a diet. What was wrong with a no-fail plate of whole wheat noodles and parmesan? It was less like frilly Mozart and more like solid, foundational Bach.

"Lauren, where do we stand with the profiles?" Stefanie leaned over the table to peer past Sarah and look directly at Lauren.

"Both pieces will be in next week. I think they're going to be real highlights." Lauren, still a newcomer, was overly eager to please. "Max is going to deliver some really artistic smoothie photos. You can do some neat stuff with all those colors. And Ellen wants to include graphs on the popularity of porridge over time and in different European countries."

Max and Ellen — Sarah would have contacted them only in a real pinch. Now Lauren would have to deal with sloppy copy and unusable graphs. Sarah doodled a treble clef and staff in her notebook, filling in the first few bars of the melody to "Twinkle, Twinkle, Little Star," turning each quarter note into a tiny cupcake with a hat of frosting.

Yaaawn. The too-long, too-dry discussion on the new content management system, planned for next summer, could have segued into a group nap session, until Stefanie finally ended the meeting abruptly.

"Sorry everyone, but I'm already late for my next meeting." She stood up, wobbling on her heels and typing on her phone as she walked. It was a miracle she found the door.

He was waiting. Sarah's armpits dampened as she rushed downstairs to Bavarian Brew; for old time's sake. Christoph was there with two cappuccinos, a warming kiss, a hand on the small of her back. The barista blushed; she didn't.

"Thanks for this!" She raised her cup in a kind of toast. "The weekly meetings get a lot more boring when you have nothing left to say."

"Talking less means more time to think, doesn't it? I used to spend those meetings brainstorming beats and lyrics for when my DJ career took off again and I'd get to write tracks with a big shot musician like, I don't know, like Die Fantastischen Vier or..." He nodded toward the inside of the coffee cart. Nena. The eternally youthful Nena. "99 Red Balloons," the bubble gum sound, unmistakably eighties, was faintly audible from a small speaker next to the espresso machine.

"Don't laugh, but I always wanted to record something with Nena."

"You just think she's hot."

"Everyone thinks Nena's hot. She's as old as our parents! But German music wouldn't be the same — hell, it wouldn't even *be* without her."

"Time is kind to valuable things, isn't it? Even though we're still too young to know that, right? It always looked to me like you were paying attention at the meetings."

"That's the art. Sometimes I would just pray or, you know, ponder the universe."

"Something we all should do more of. I know, wasting time is not someone else's fault — not even Stefanie's." That name. It was a waste of time to say it on a coffee break, especially with Christoph. She rolled her eyes and zipped up her jacket as a chilly breeze whipped around the stand.

The barista was wearing fingerless gloves and an XXL scarf wrapped four or five times around his neck. He pounded the sapped espresso grounds into a box, overpowering Nena's red balloons as they were mistaken for UFOs and shot down by war-hungry politicians. Christoph pulled the sleeves of his hoodie down to his knuckles, under the sleeves of his leather jacket.

"You want to know what concerns me the most about New York? That the city will be too draining, that it will suck out all my energy and creativity. It's supposed to be a haven of freedom and new ideas, but few things are everything they're made out to be." He ate the miniature biscotti on his saucer with the spoon in one bite, undipped, still crunchy.

She put a gloved hand over his fingers and pulled them briefly to her lips. "It is a really exhausting place. The noise, the dirt, the straight-faced people — it all takes energy. But it's what you make of it. I wasn't there long enough the first time to make it *my* city, but I know there's a lot more to discover."

"Then it's a good thing you'll have a second chance." He put down his spoon, clink-clinking on the saucer. "Is there anything that scares you about New York?"

She scooped up the last of the milk foam in his cup with her spoon and said, "Not anymore. You make me feel safe."

NOVEMBER 25

"Herr Steinmann is feeling poorly today, Frau Johnson." The receptionist looked up from her desk, over red-rimmed reading glasses. Large orange flowers bulged over her bosom and rippled in smaller waves over the folds around her middle. "He's in his room. It would be best if you kept your visit short." It was not a suggestion.

A man in white escorted Sarah to room 626 and left quickly. She walked in alone. It would have seemed larger inside if it weren't for the curtain; two walls for him, two for another ebbing soul. The walls were painted peach like her grandmother's rouge, a tone picked up in the generically abstract pictures on the walls: swishes and circles on fade-away backgrounds, hung in thin, teal frames.

She found him lying in a bed folded at sixty degrees with a remote control in his hand and a blanket pulled up to his waist. He was wearing a plaid button-down shirt and brown cardigan; bulky earphones were stretched over his head. His eyes were closed, and his index finger was tapping lightly on his lap; a cord connected his head to the phone on the nightstand.

A minute passed, then another. Sarah pulled up the chair and waited until he opened his eyes.

"Mozart." He finally said hoarsely. "*La Clemenza di Tito*. One of his last works. Grace is a beautiful thing. Even an old man like me, especially me — we could all use a little grace sometimes, don't you think?"

In Mozart's Italian-language opera, the Roman emperor pardons his would-be assassin, who is jealously in love with the future empress. Love, holiness, and sin are often a hair's breadth apart.

"Antonio Salieri was supposed to be commissioned to write the opera, you know, but he turned down the opportunity." He was speaking slowly, deliberately, as if to overcome his own mumbling. "Salieri was the most respected Italian opera composer in Vienna at the time. I suppose we'll never know whose would've been better."

"Salieri. He didn't poison Mozart in the end, did he? Isn't Mozart's death still a mystery?" A rumor, her music history instructor had said, just a storyteller's exaggeration.

"Death is always a mystery, is it not?"

She tugged at her earlobe, toying with her earring. Even dressed in his own clothes, lying in a bed tore at his dignity, undermined the vast collection of days he held within his frail frame. He was not the first human to have worked, loved, lost, then ceased to be. He was one of millions, billions, trillions. Death, the most natural of human experiences, is inherently inhuman.

He pulled off the headphones and held them with quivering hands in his lap. Gerda's left eye was brutally separated from her childish face, marred by the frame's haphazard split, sitting on the nightstand next to a glass of sparkling water. There was no empty coffee cup, stained with the residue of passing pleasure. Gerda's youthfulness was alien among the odor of last days, the scent of many more days than she was given.

"It is dark again, like when we first met to play Mozart. All of the seasons have passed. But you have more light now. The dark season is a good time to go to the light." Drawn eggshell curtains cast the room in gray. His eyes were trained at the floor between Sarah and his bed.

Another bout of delirium? Constantin wasn't here to help carry him to bed; he and his nonsense were already in it.

"This is one of my favorite seasons, because I love Thanksgiving." It was a feeble attempt to reel him in from the light and dark. His half-coherent words reeked of endings, so she kept talking.

"Thanksgiving is on Thursday and everybody at home is traveling and baking and cooking this week. My dad has a secret recipe for his turkey stuffing. It's worth going all the way there for it. My mom makes the best apple pie in the world, and I don't even like apple pie — except for hers." Hunger is the first symptom of homesickness.

"*Apfelstrudel*. A nice woman in a white suit brought me *Apfelstrudel* today. But no coffee, dammit. The doctor said my blood pressure..." *Ghack, khack!* Explosive coughs, in bursts, shook his torso; one fist at his mouth, he was unable to take the water glass she held out to him.

Cherry, raspberry, another day, another place, it would have been a melting popsicle or a sloshed Cabernet on his hand, not the intimate fluid that was never intended to leave the body. The man in white walked in, frowning, not terribly rushed, with a tray of basic medical tools in his hand: stethoscope, blood pressure monitor, pain medication.

"It's probably best if you go." He didn't sound particularly concerned.

She stepped out quietly, as if she had never been there; his coughs resonated in the hall. The wall was painted in the same shade of peach, but only the lower half; the upper portion was a stark hospital white. What else did he want to say? How silly to have gotten sidetracked on stuffing and pie.

DECEMBER 5

The *Glühwein* would have been too sweet if it weren't for the extra shot of rum. Sarah's cheeks glowed; her temples buzzed. She'd left her gloves on; Christmas market mugs were always sticky. The heavy air was finally releasing its weight, birthing a million crystals, each unique but equally able to defy gravity until it found the perfect landing pad: a wool hat, a warm nose, a bare branch, the cold asphalt.

"I got the next round." Lauren collected the four porcelain mugs. "We can't stand here empty-handed now, can we? We'll catch a fucking cold!"

Like moths to a bulb, Lauren joined the pilgrimage to the inviting light inside the rustic Alpine hut for mulled wine. She'd suggested they meet one last time before Sarah morphed from coworker into acquaintance. "Not that we can't go for drinks after that," Lauren had wagged her finger, "but you never know where you might end up."

Her new boyfriend, Sven, a fitness trainer with arrestingly tropical green eyes, hung on her hand like jewelry. Sarah's hand rested on Christoph's tail bone. They were speaking English because Lauren started off that way. It made Sarah self-conscious; she wasn't a tourist.

Sven switched to German. "Shit weather, isn't it? Did Lauren tell you we're escaping to Cape Verde over Christmas? It's supposed to be warm down there on the equator — and cheap as hell. We got a little condo on Sal for ten days. No breakfast or nothing, but if we don't find anything to eat on the island, we'll just catch our own fish. What are you two doing?"

"My family is pretty small, just my parents and my aunt, but we always make pierogis on Christmas Eve," offered Christoph. "We're not even Polish! It became a tradition after a family trip to Wrocław a long time ago." He used the Polish, not the German name for the Silesian city, once part of the German Empire, then Nazi Germany, then post-war Poland.

"Cape Verde sounds amazing. I heard there's great kitesurfing there, if you're into that." Speaking German, Sarah's voice deepened, her mouth grew squarer. Language, like music, is also physical and not just aural.

Lauren returned before Sarah had to answer the question. Christmas? She and Christoph hadn't talked about it; gray, empty January loomed over red and green December.

Christoph squeezed Sarah's gloved hand. Lauren distributed the mugs, sloshing a few drops. "That line isn't for lame asses! You gotta have sharp elbows." Too loudly, embarrassingly loudly, a decibel never employed by locals. Young British men passed, weaving like a herd of sheep, peeking over the crowd to pin down their next watering hole. A group of older German couples followed, mugs in hand, making under-their-breath utterances about how much more charming the Christmas market used to be, their tongues stained with disappointment.

"You're right about the kitesurfing." Sven brightened. English again, making their mouths higher, rounder, with back-tongue Ls and mid-tongue Rs. "If Lauren lets me, I'm hoping to get in the water every day." He touched a playful elbow to her rib.

"I told you, you can kitesurf as long as you teach me how." She planted a tipsy kiss on his five-o'clock shadow. The ocean, the salt, the equatorial sun — they seemed like a Hollywood figment, real but not real. Sarah imagined the sand on her dry, cracking toes.

Their mugs were empty, the handles syrupy. Christoph returned them and collected the deposit he'd paid with the first round. Lauren and Sven, his hand under her coat, hers fingering his neck below his beanie, seemed intent to split off, so the couples went their separate ways.

"I just realized we haven't eaten anything." Christoph checked his wrist; it was nearly eight. The snowflakes had merged their molecules, sacrificing themselves to become ordinary sleet. "And *Glühwein* doesn't count as dinner."

"That's why I feel like I'm on roller skates the whole time." Sarah grabbed his arm with both hands; he anchored her, gripped the back of her hand with his, then lurched away from the crowd and into the dark entryway of a shuttered boutique. Their lips found each other's as their breaths materialized, mingling together in the air. They held each other tightly, as if the chill, the crowd might push them apart.

"Do you want to come to my parents' place for Christmas?" He caressed her face while he asked.

She caught her breath, grounding both feet on an icy patch in the dark doorway. "Yeah. Yes, I would."

"I don't know if you like pierogis, but we think they're pretty special."

"I think you're pretty special, Christoph."

"Like *in a relationship* kind of special?"

"Yeah... like *we* kind of special."

And just like that, everything had changed, but nothing was really different. The excitement of starting a relationship lies in unspoken promises: to ask, to answer, to try, to let. Every voyage is risky, but this one was worth it — and she was no longer navigating alone. They continued walking arm in arm, agreeing to stop at the first sign of something edible. He hadn't asked her again about New York City; he knew it was a question that wouldn't be forgotten. Would they decide to share an apartment or just the occasional night? Would they trade off taking care of the trash, getting the mail and stocking the kitchen with more than frozen vegetables and wine? Those were questions that could wait. For now, *New York, the second movement* was starting to feel like something that would make her happy.

December 9

Cinnamon, nutmeg and disinfectant filled Sarah's nostrils as she heard a buzzing harpsichord, raw Baroque violins, and the shuffle-shuffle-clop of a cane in the hall. It was Bach, the first section of the Christmas Oratorio, BWV 248: the birth.

Wie soll ich dich empfangen
Und wie begegn' ich dir [5]

The work was an expansive, six-part masterpiece, joyful and reflective. Baroque music was complex — sedimented like the earth, at times even chromatic — but painfully honest.

"Frau Johnson." The woman behind the desk put down her pen and took off her reading glasses. She looked at Sarah with a mixture of discomfort, empathy and surprise. "I thought maybe you'd heard."

An uncertain pause. Four measures of Bach, a boy soprano singing recitative. Pure and fleeting; just months until his voice would change.

"Herr Steinmann passed away a few days ago."

It wasn't shock that pierced Sarah; it was the sudden differentness of everything.

The apartment, his home for decades, was now a pile of stuff that would become someone else's problem; Mondays no longer marked by Mozart; the picture album with Benjamin's photo an artifact. The Bechstein, driverless.

---

[5] How should I receive you, and how should I meet you?

"I'm very sorry." She was sincere, if rather awkward. She should know how to do condolences.

"When did it happen?" He must have been alone for the final exhalation, the ensuing stillness. Was it Benjamin, Hannelore or Gerda that he thought of in the seconds beforehand — or the paid people who would take his corpse away?

"It was last week. It must have been Thursday evening around 8:00. I was told he passed quietly without a great deal of pain." She moved a short stack of papers from one side of her desk to the other. Thursday evening. Sarah had been giddy with *Glühwein* and the exhileration of her unwritten beginning with Christoph.

"He left you this." She handed her a white envelope. "If you hadn't come back, I'd have passed it on to Herr Steinmann's daughter when she arrives later this week to collect his things."

Wrinkled around a small object, it bore Sarah's name in wobbly script. She unbuttoned her coat and slid her chapped index finger through the seal. Three drops of blood oozed onto the envelope: a paper cut, how clumsy. She licked her finger and tasted iron.

Inside, she found a short note, a one-dollar bill, and a silver key with the letters CB inside an oval on the handle.

Dear Sarah,

Enclosed you will find a one-dollar bill that Benjamin gave me in 1946. I now pass it on to you for the privilege of being your orchestra.

The key fits the lid of my Bechstein. I have amended my will. If you are reading this, then it now belongs to you. My lawyer will work out the details. I know that you will appreciate it more than anyone else. Indeed, I would be pleased if it landed in your home country one day.

Like Benjamin did a lifetime ago, you brightened my last year indescribably and I will forever be indebted to you for that. Music may bring you joy or rob you of it, but I hope that you experience it as liberation rather than chains. May it never hold you back from what is truly important.

Yours,

Otto Steinmann

The script was old-fashioned and had been penned with a shaky hand. Below the signature was the name of his attorney and a telephone number. She looked up at the receptionist (who sat there entirely unaware, without a trace of curiosity), then back at the letter.

Sarah opened her mouth, but there was nothing to say. Not there, not then. The chorus sang, celebrating mutedly, from the small speaker on the counter.

Er ist auf Erden kommen arm
dass er unser sich erbarm
und in dem Himmel mache reich
und seinen lieben Engeln gleich[6]

She returned the bill, key and letter to the envelope, placed it carefully in her bag, buttoned her coat, adjusted her scarf, thanked the woman, and stepped out into the dark. Streetlights were forming murky puddles on the path. The music silenced as the heavy wooden door closed behind her. A chill made Sarah's nose run; her legs were numb, but not from the cold.

A good hour is what she would need to walk all the way home. The oratorio would be over by then, all six parts, the Feast of Epiphany long digested.

They'd been swept away, fall's burnt leaves, or absorbed into the patches of perpetually damp earth; the sidewalks were clear. It was just after five, still early. Families were coming together after work and school. Bulbs glowed in inhabited rooms, curtains were undrawn, lives shared.

In one home, a mother was helping two children with homework at the kitchen table, surrounded by stacks of binders, books, the square-framed backpacks younger German pupils tended to carry. In another, an elderly man was reading a book in an armchair, a glass of red wine on the table next to him, a woman on the couch with a laptop. In the next, two middle-aged men were preparing dinner, interrupting their slicing and stirring to wrap their arms around each other.

Sarah pulled her hat down over her ears, reached for Herr Steinmann's letter and reread it while she walked, glancing up between sentences. Could he have known more about Benjamin than he'd let on? She had waited too long to tell him, unwilling to shatter his adoration. Professor West would be coming in January; his portrait of his father would forever be unamended.

---

[6] He has come to earth in poverty so that he may have mercy on us and make us rich in heaven and like his beloved angels.

She urgently needed to hear Christoph's voice; he was working late to meet a deadline. He hadn't hurried her, but she wanted to get off the fence and give him an answer. Then she'd worry about how to get the Bechstein to New York. She could pay the shipping expense by selling the Schimmel.

At the next house, a piano. She stopped in front of the small front yard to listen. Mozart's Minuet in D major; she'd played it, on an empty stomach, at her first recital. The simple, stand-alone work was slow enough for young pianists, but wealthy with chromatic harmonies beyond Mozart's time. Suddenly she heard the notes doubled, though not perfectly aligned, like a letter traced twice with the same pen. Twenty fingers at work, at play.

At the floor-length window, the curtain was drawn; a crack at the bottom revealed the four front legs of two side-by-side grands. Child-sized feet in pink socks dangled. A boxy house shoe, the teacher's, was hovering above the sostenuto pedal of the other piano. She heard a botched trill, a long pause, then a fresh start, this time alone, cleaner but less brilliant.

Sarah strained her ears for the delicious dissonance until it resolved suddenly, unspectacularly, after just three minutes. She took her gloves out of her pockets, put them on, and kept walking.

ACKNOWLEDGEMENTS

Each book is built on one author's vision, but with the hands of many. It has been a tremendous pleasure working with Blackwater Press, particularly my editor, Elizabeth Ford, who brought her multifaceted expertise and enthusiasm to this book. I would like to thank my earliest readers, including Cristina, Stuart, Tina, Jody, Jean, and Jeanie, for molding this book and helping me find my voice. I would especially like to acknowledge and thank David Imrie from noveledit.net for his invaluable development edit and for going above and beyond to shape my manuscript and encourage and guide me in the process. A huge thank you to my mom, Jane Bowen, for faithfully enduring more versions than anyone should have to. And finally, to my husband Dominic Mueser, thank you for always believing in me and in this project, for your unconditional love and support, and for taking the kids to the park countless times so I could squeeze in another hour of work. I love you!

Quoted material is taken from William Shakespeare's plays, *Hamlet*, *As You Like It*, *A Midsummer Night's Dream*, *Twelfth Night*; Heinrich Heine's poem "Ich grolle nicht" as set to music by Robert Schumann in his song cycle, Dichterliebe; an excerpt from the first leaflet published by Munich resistance group The White Rose in 1942; Johann Wolfgang Goethe's poem "Das Veilchen" as set to music by Wolfgang Amadeus Mozart; an excerpt from Mozart's opera *The Magic Flute*, libretto by Emanuel Schikaneder; an excerpt from J.S. Bach's *Christmas Oratorio* BWV 248.